Francis Hitchman

Richard F. Burton

Vol. I

Francis Hitchman

Richard F. Burton
Vol. I

ISBN/EAN: 9783337216382

Printed in Europe, USA, Canada, Australia, Japan

Cover: Foto ©Raphael Reischuk / pixelio.de

More available books at **www.hansebooks.com**

RICHARD F. BURTON,

K.C.M.G.:

HIS EARLY, PRIVATE AND PUBLIC LIFE

WITH

AN ACCOUNT OF HIS TRAVELS AND EXPLORATIONS.

BY

FRANCIS HITCHMAN,

AUTHOR OF 'THE PUBLIC LIFE OF THE EARL OF BEACONSFIELD,
ETC., ETC.

IN TWO VOLUMES.—Vol. I.

Toto passim vagus errat in orbe.
Ovid. Met. xiv. 680.

LONDON:

SAMPSON LOW, MARSTON, SEARLE & RIVINGTON,
St. Dunstan's House,
FETTER LANE, FLEET STREET, E.C.,
1887.

LONDON :

PRINTED BY WILLIAM CLOWES AND SONS, LIMITED,

STAMFORD STREET AND CHARING CROSS.

TO

FLORENCE BLAIR,

OF FINCHCOCKS PARK, STAPLEHURST,

THESE VOLUMES ARE

𝔇𝔢𝔡𝔦𝔠𝔞𝔱𝔢𝔡

BY THE AUTHOR,

IN MEMORY OF MUCH KINDNESS AND MANY
TOKENS OF GOOD-WILL.

PREFACE.

IN the preface to the last volume of the *Tatler*, Steele says, speaking of Addison's contributions :—"I fared like a distressed prince, who calls in a powerful neighbour to his aid. I was undone by my auxiliary. When I had once called him in, I could not subsist without dependence upon him." To compare small things with great, this is precisely my own case. Like Sir Richard Steele, "I am undone by my auxiliary." It had been a plan of mine for many years to tell the story of the adventurous and romantic life of Richard Burton and the idea had been encouraged by Lady Burton from the outset. When, however, I set fairly to work, I found that the materials for such a biography as I wished to write were in many particulars exceedingly imperfect. In my extremity I applied to Lady Burton, who, with a generous kindness, for which I cannot be too grateful, searched through her husband's voluminous collections of letters, diaries and notes, and from them compiled the two lengthy chapters which deal with Sir Richard Burton's life to the time of his leaving India, and extracted from his private papers that other and, as I think, deeply interesting chapter (the fifth in these volumes) which relates his experiences "with Beatson's Horse."

In addition to this Lady Burton has done me the honour to afford an immense amount of information especially upon those matters which came within her personal cognizance. The Damascus chapter, for example, would have been but a bare and meagre record but for her help, and many things have been added through her kindness which have, I hope, turned what once threatened to be a mere compilation into a genuine contribution to contemporary history.

My own part in these volumes has thus become a comparatively humble one, but when I mention that the writings of Burton, the *doyen* and pioneer of African travel fill about eighty more or less bulky volumes, that I have found it necessary to read attentively about twice as many more, including the works of Livingstone, Grant, Speke, Baker, and the prince of African travel, Stanley ; and that I have on my table somewhere about two hundred letters all bearing more or less on the subject of this book, I hope I may be allowed to claim the credit, as Carlyle did on a somewhat similar occasion, of having turned out "an honest piece of journey-work."

FRANCIS HITCHMAN.

FINCHLEY,
September, 1887.

CONTENTS TO VOL. I.

CHAPTER I.

EARLY DAYS.

CHAPTER II.

OXFORD AND INDIA.

CHAPTER III.

AN ENGLISH HAJI.

CHAPTER VI.

ZANZIBAR—A TRIAL TRIP.

CHAPTER VII.

TO LAKE TANGANYIKA.

LIST OF ILLUSTRATIONS.

VOLUME I.

RICHARD F. BURTON:

A BIOGRAPHY.

———◆◇◆———

CHAPTER I.

EARLY DAYS.

AUTOBIOGRAPHERS generally begin too late. Elderly gentlemen of eminence sit down to compose memories, describe with fond minuteness, babyhood, child-hood, and boyhood, and drop the pen before reaching adolescence. Physiologists say that a man's body changes

B

totally every seven years. However that may be (Burton
says), I am certain that the moral man does, and I cannot
imagine anything more trying than for a man to meet
himself as he was. Conceive his entering a room, and
finding a collection of himself at the several decades. First,
the puling squalling baby, one year old, then the pert
unpleasant schoolboy of ten, the collegian of twenty, who,
like Lothair, knows everything and has nothing to learn.
The *homme fait* of thirty in the full warmth and hey-day
of life ; the reasonable man of forty, who first recognizes
his ignorance and knows his own mind ; of fifty, with white
teeth turned dark, and dark hair turned white, whose experience is mostly disappointment, with regrets for lost time
and vanished opportunities. Sixty, when the man begins
to die, and mourns for his past youth ; seventy, when he
ought to prepare for his long journey, and never does.
And at all these ages he is seven different beings, not one
of which he would wish to be again.

First, I would make one or two notes on Richard Burton's
genealogy :—

Richard Burton's grandfather was the Rev. Edward
Burton, Rector of Tuam in Galway (who with his brother,
Bishop Burton, of Killala, were the first of this branch to
settle in Ireland). They were two of the Burtons of Barker
Hill, near Shap, Westmoreland, who own a common ancestor with the Burtons of Yorkshire, of Carlow, of North-
amptonshire, of Lincolnshire and Shropshire.

The Burtons of Shap derive themselves from the
Burtons of Longnor, like Lord Conyngham and Sir
Charles Burton of Pollacton, and the two above named
were the collateral descendants of Francis Pierpoint Burton,
first Marquis of Conyngham, who gave up the name of
Burton. The notable man of the family was Sir Edward
Burton, a desperate Yorkist, who was made a Knight-
Banneret by Edward IV., after the second battle of St.

Albans, and who added to his arms the Cross and four
Roses.

The Bishop of Killala's son was Admiral James Ryder
Burton, who entered the Navy in 1806. He served in the
West Indies, and off the North Coast of Spain, when in an
attack on the town of Castro, July 1812, he received a
gun-shot wound in the left side, from which the ball was
never extracted. From 1813 to 1816, he served in the
Mediterranean and Adriatic, and was present at the bombardment of Algiers, when he volunteered to command one
of the gunboats for destroying the shipping inside the
Mole. His last appointment was in May 1820, to the
command of the *Cornelian* brig, in which he proceeded,
early in 1824, to Algiers, where, in company with the
Naiad frigate, he fell in with an Algerine corvette, the
Tripoli, of 18 guns and 100 men, which after a close and
gallant action under the batteries of the place, he boarded
and carried. This irascible veteran at his death was in
receipt of a pension for wounds. He was Rear-Admiral
in 1853, Vice-Admiral in 1858, and Admiral in 1863. He
married in 1822, Anna Maria, daughter of the 13th Lord
Dunsany; she died in 1850, leaving one son, Francis
Augustus Plunkett Burton, Colonel of the Coldstream
Guards. He married the great heiress, Sarah Drax, and
died in 1865, leaving one daughter, Erulí, who married
her cousin John Plunkett, the future Lord Dunsany.

Writing of his father, Richard Burton says, " My father,
Joseph Netterville Burton, was a Lieut.-Colonel in the
36th Regiment, and was son of the Rev. Edward Burton,
Rector of Tuam, in Galway. He must have been born in
the latter quarter of the eighteenth century, but he had
always a superstition about mentioning his birthday, which
gave rise to a family joke that he was born in Leap Year.

Although of very mixed blood, he was more of a Roman
in appearance than anything else. Of moderate height,

with dark hair, sallow skin, high nose, and piercing black eyes, he was considered a very handsome man, especially in uniform, and attracted attention even in the street. Even when past fifty he was considered the best looking man at the Baths of Lucca." As handsome men generally do, he married a plain woman, and Burton says " just like Provy," the children favoured (as the saying is) the mother.

In mind Colonel Burton was a thoroughbred Irishman. When he received a commission in the Army it was on condition of so many of his tenants accompanying him. Not a few of the younger sort volunteered to enlist, but when they joined the regiment and found that the "young master" was all right, they at once levanted. The only service that he saw was in Sicily, under Sir John Moore, afterwards of Corunna, and there he fell in love with Italy. He was a bit of a duellist, and shot one brother officer twice, nursing him tenderly each time afterwards.

When peace was concluded, he came to England and visited Ireland. As that did not suit him he returned to his regiment in England. Then took place his marriage, which was favoured by his mother-in-law, and opposed by his father-in-law. The latter being a sharp old man of business, tied up every farthing of his daughter's property (£30,000) and it was well that he did so. The gallant officer, like too many of his cloth, developed a decided taste for speculation. He was a highly moral man, who would have hated the idea of *rouge et noir*, but he gambled on the Stock Exchange, and when railways came out he bought shares. Happily he could not touch his wife's property, or it would speedily have melted away. Yet it was one of his grievances to the end of his life that he could not use his wife's money to make a gigantic fortune. He was utterly reckless, where others would be extra prudent ; during his wedding tour he passed through Windermere, and would not call upon an aunt who was

settled near the lakes, for fear that she might think he
expected her property. She heard of it, and left every
farthing to some more dutiful nephew. He never went to
Ireland, after his marriage, but received occasional visits
from his numerous brothers and sisters.

The eldest of the family was the Rev. Edmund Burton,
who had succeeded to the living. He wasted every
farthing of his property, and at last had the sense to
migrate to Canada, where he built a little Burtonville. In
his younger days he intended to marry a girl who preferred another man. When she was a widow with three
children, and he a widower with six children, they married,
and the result was eventually a total of about a score,
Such families do better than is supposed. The elder
children are old enough to assist the younger ones, and
they seem bound to hang together. Colonel Burton's
sisters, especially Mrs. Matthews, used to visit him when in
England, and as it was known that he had married an
heiress, they all clung to him apparently for themselves
and their children. They managed to get hold of all the
Irish land that fell to his share, and after his death they
were incessant in their claims upon his children.

Richard Burton's mother was Martha Baker, one of
three sisters, co-heiresses, and was the second daughter.
The third daughter married Robert Bagshaw, Esq., M.P.
for Harwich, and died without issue. The eldest, Sarah,
married Francis Burton, the youngest brother of Colonel
Burton. He had an especial ambition to enter the church,
but circumstances compelled him to become military
surgeon in the 66th Regiment.

Richard Francis Burton, was born at 9.30. P.M. on the 19th
of March (Feast of St. Joseph in the Calendar), 1821, at Barham House, Herts, and was baptized at the Parish Church.
His birth took place in the same year, but the day before
the grand event of George the Fourth visiting the opera

the first time after the Coronation, March 20th. He was
the eldest of three children.

The second was Maria Catharine Eliza, who married
Henry Stisted, afterwards General Sir Henry Stisted, a very
distinguished officer, who died leaving only two daughters,
one of whom, Georgina Martha, survives. Thirdly, Edward
Joseph Netterville, late Captain in the 37th Regiment,
unmarried.

The first thing Richard remembers, and it is always
interesting to record a child's first memories, was his
being brought down after dinner at Barham House to
eat white currants, seated upon the knee of a tall man with
yellow hair and blue eyes, but whether the memory is
composed of a miniature of his grandfather, and whether
the white frock and blue sash with bows come from a
miniature of himself, and not from life, he could never
make up his mind.

Barham House was a country place bought by Burton's
grandfather, Richard Baker, who determined to make him
his heir, because he had blue eyes and red hair, an unusual
thing in the Burton family. Those eyes grew up dark and
the hair also, which seems to justify the following remarks
by Alfred Bate Richards in a pamphlet printed for private
circulation. They are as follows :

Richard Burton's talents for mixing with and assimilating natives
of all countries, but especially Oriental characters, and of becoming
as one of themselves without any one doubting or suspecting his
origin ; his perfect knowledge of their languages, manners, customs,
habits, and religion ; and last, but not least, his being gifted by nature
with an Arab head and face, favoured this his first great enterprise.
One can learn from that versatile poet-traveller, the excellent Théophile
Gautier, why Richard Burton is an Arab in appearance ; and account
for that incurable restlessness that is unable to wrest from fortune a
spot on earth wherein to repose when weary of wandering like the
Desert sands.

"There is a reason," says Gautier, who had studied the Andalusian
and the Moor, "for that fantasy of nature which causes an Arab to be
born in Paris, or a Greek in Auvergne ; the mysterious voice of blood

which is silent for generations, or only utters a confused murmur, speaks at rare intervals a more intelligible language. In the general confusion race claims its own, and some forgotten ancestor asserts his rights. Who knows what alien drops are mingled with our blood ? The great migrations from the tablelands of India, the descents of the Northern races, the Roman and Arab invasions, have all left their marks. Instincts which seem *bizarre* spring from these confused recollections, these hints of a distant country. The vague desire of this primitive Fatherland moves such minds as retain the more vivid memories of the past. Hence the wild unrest that wakens in certain spirits the need of flight, such as the cranes and the swallows feel when kept in bondage—the impulses that make a man leave his luxurious life to bury himself in the Steppes, the Desert, the Pampas, the Sáhara. He goes to seek his brothers. It would be easy to point out the intellectual Fatherland of our greatest minds. Lamartine, De Musset, and De Vigny, are English ; Delacroix is an Anglo-Indian ; Victor Hugo a Spaniard ; Ingres belongs to the Italy of Florence and Rome."

Burton's mother had a wild half-brother, Richard Baker, jun., a barrister-at-law, who refused a judgeship in Australia, and died a soap boiler. To him she was madly attached, and delayed the signing of the will as much as possible to the prejudice of her own babe. His grandfather Baker drove in his carriage to see Messrs. Dendy, his lawyers, with the object of signing the will, and dropped dead on getting out of the carriage of ossification of the heart, and the document being unsigned, the property was divided. It would now be worth half a million of money.

When Richard was sent out to India as a cadet in 1842, he ran down to see the old house for the last time, and started off in a sailing-ship round the Cape for Bombay in a frame of mind to lead any forlorn hope, wherever it might be. Warren Hastings, Governor-General of India, under similar circumstances threw himself under a tree and formed the fine resolution to come back and buy the old place, but *he* belonged to the eighteenth century. The nineteenth is far more cosmopolitan. Richard always acted upon the saying, *Omne solum forti patria*, or, as he translated it, " For every region is a strong man's home."

Meantime his father had been obliged to go on half-pay by the Duke of Wellington for having refused to appear as a witness against Queen Caroline. He had been Town-Major at Genoa when she lived there, and her kindness to the officers had greatly prepossessed them in her favour, so when ordered by the War Office to turn Judas, he flatly refused. A great loss to himself, as Lord William Bentinck, Governor-General of India, was about to take him as aide-de-camp ; and to his family, as he lost all connection with the army, and lived entirely abroad, and eventually coming back, died, with his wife, at Bath in 1857. However, he behaved like a gentleman, and none of his family ever murmured at the step, though one of his sons began life as an East-Indian cadet, and the other in a marching regiment, whilst their cousins were in the guards and the rifles and other crack corps of the army.

The family went abroad when Richard Burton was a few months old and settled at Tours, the charming capital of Touraine, which then contained some two hundred English families (now reduced to a score or so), attracted by the beauty of the place, the healthy climate, the economy of living, the facilities of education, and the friendly feeling of the French inhabitants, who, despite Waterloo, associated freely with the strangers.

They had a chaplain, the Rev. Mr. Way (whose son afterwards entered the Indian Army ; Richard met him in India, and he died young). Their schoolmaster was Mr. Clough, who bolted from his debts, and then Mr. Gilchrist, who, like the Rev. Edward Irving, Carlyle's friend (whom the butcher once asked if he couldn't assist him), caned his pupils to the utmost. The celebrated Dr. Brettoneau took charge of the invalids. They had their duellist, the Honourable Martin Hawke, their hounds that hunted the forest of Amboise, and a select colony of Irishmen, Messrs. Hume and others, who added immensely to the fun and frolic of the place.

At that period a host of these little colonies were scattered over the Continent nearest England—in fact an oasis of Anglo-Saxondom in a desert of continentalism, somewhat like the society of English country towns as it was in 1800, not as it is now, where "company" is confined to the parson, dentist, surgeon, general practitioner, the bankers, and the lawyers. And in those days it had this advantage, that there were no snobs, and one seldom noticed the *aigre discorde*, the *maladie chronique des ménages bourgéoises.* Knowing nothing of "vulgar respectability," the difference of the foreign colonies was that the *weight* of English respectability appeared to be taken off them, though their lives were respectable and respected. The Mrs. Gamps and Mrs. Grundys were not so rampant. The English of these little groups were intensely patriotic, and cared comparatively little for party politics. They stuck to their own Church because it was their Church, and they knew as much about the Catholics at their very door as the average Englishman does of the Hindu. Moreover, they honestly called themselves Protestants in those days, and the French, Catholics ; there was no quibble about "our being Anglo-Catholics and the others Roman Catholics." They subscribed liberally to the Church, and did not disdain to act as churchwardens. They kept a sharp look-out upon the parson, and one of your modern High Church Protestants, or Puseyites or Ritualists would have got the sack after the first sermon. They were intensely national. Any Englishman in those days who refused to fight a duel with a Frenchman was sent to Coventry and bullied out of the place. English girls who flirted with foreigners were looked upon very much as white women who permit the addresses of a nigger are looked upon by those English who have lived in black countries. White women who do these things lose caste.

Beauséjour, the château taken by the family, was

inhabited by the Maréchale de Menon in 1778, and
eventually became the property of her *homme d'affaires*,
Monsieur Froguet. The dear old place stands on the right
bank of the Loire, half way up the heights that bound the
stream, commanding a splendid view, and fronted by a
French garden and vineyards now uprooted. In 1875,
Richard Burton paid it a last visit, and found a friend from
Brazil, a Madame Izarié, widow of his friend the French
Consul of Bahia, who had come to die in the house of her
sister, Madame Froguet.

Tours was in those days, 1820–30, the most mediæval
city in France. The western half of the city, divided from
the eastern by the Rue Royale, contained a number of old
turreted houses of freestone, which might have belonged
to the fifteenth century. Here also was the tomb of the
venerable St. Martin, in a crypt where lamps are ever
burning, and where the destroyed Cathedral has not yet
been rebuilt. The eastern city contained the grand
cathedral of St. Garcien, with its domed towers, and the
Archevêché or Archbishop's palace, with beautiful gardens.
Both are still kept in the best order. In forty-five years the
city has grown enormously. The southern suburbs, where
the Mall and Ramparts used to be, have become Boulevarts
Heurteloup and Béranger ; and in Places, such as that
of the Palais de Justice, where cabbage gardens fenced
with palings and thorn hedges, once showed a few pauper
cottages defended by the fortifications, are seen Crescents
and Kiosks for loungers, houses with tall mansard roofs, and
the large railway station that connects Tours with the outer
world. The river, once crossed by a single long stone
bridge, has now two suspension bridges and a railway
bridge ; and the river-holms, formerly strips of sand, are
all grown to double their size, covered with trees and
defended by stone dykes.

Richard remembers passing over the river on foot when

it was frozen, but with the increased population that no longer happens. Still there are vestiges of the old establishments. The Boule d'Or, with its golden ball, and the Pheasant Hotel, both in the Rue Royale, still remain. You still read "Maison Piernadine recommended for *is* elegance, *is* good taste, and *is* new fashions of the first choice." Madame Fisterre, the maker of admirable apple puffs, has disappeared and has left no sign. This was, as may be supposed, one of Richard's first childish visits. The young ones enjoyed themselves very much at the Château de Beauséjour, eating grapes in the gardens, putting their Noah's ark animals under the box hedges, picking snail shells and cowslips in the lanes, playing with the dogs, Juno, Jupiter and Ponto, three black pointers of splendid breed, much admired by the Duke of Cumberland when he afterwards saw them in Richmond Park. Charlotte Ling, the old nurse, daughter of the lodge-keeper at Barham House, could not stand the absence of beef and beer and the presence of kickshaws and dandelion salad, and after their aunt Georgina Baker had paid them a visit, she returned with her to old England. A favourite amusement of the children was swarming up the tails of their father's horses, three in number, and one—a horse of Mecklenburg breed—was as tame as an Arab. The first story his aunt used to tell of Richard was of his lying on his back in a broiling sun and exclaiming, "How I love a bright, burning sun!" (Nature speaking in early years.) Occasional drawbacks were violent storms of thunder and lightning, when the children were hustled out of their little cots under the roof, and taken to the drawing-room, lest the lightning should strike them, and the daily necessity of learning the alphabet, and so forth, multiplication table, and their prayers. Richard was intended for that wretched being the infant phenomenon, and he began Latin at three and Greek at four. Things are better now.

The father used to go out wild boar hunting in the
Forêt d'Amboise, in the Château of which Abd-el-Kadir
was imprisoned by the French Government, from 1847 to
1852, when he was set free by Napoleon III. at the
entreaties of Lord Londonderry. ("It is said that his
Majesty entered his prison in person and set him free.
Abd-el-Kadir at Damascus," adds Burton, "afterwards
expressed his obligations to the English and warmly
welcomed any English face. On one occasion I took a
near relation of Lord Londonderry's to see him, and he
was quite overcome.") Colonel Burton was periodically
brought home hurt by running against a tree. Sport was
so much in vogue then as to come between the parson
and his sermon.

This pleasant life came to a close one day. The
children consisted of three, Richard six, Edward three,
and Maria. One morning saw the hateful school-books
fastened with a little strap, and the two boys and the
little bundle conveyed in a carriage to the town, where
they were introduced into a room with a number of English
and French lads, who were sitting opposite hacked and
inkspotted desks, looking as demure as they could, though
every now and then they broke out into wicked grins and
nudges. The lame Irish schoolmaster (Clough) smiled most
graciously at them as long as their father was in the room,
but was not half so pleasant when they were left alone.
They wondered what they were doing in that *galère*, especially as they were sent there day after day. Soon they
learned the dread truth that they were at school at the
ripe ages of six and three. Presently it was found that the
house was at an inconvenient distance from school, and
the family transferred itself to the Rue de l'Archevêché, a
comfortable house in the north-eastern corner of what is still
the best street in the town (Rue Royale being mostly
commercial). It is close to the Place and the Archbishop's

palace, which delighted them, with small deer feeding about the dwarf lawn.

Presently Mr. Clough ran away, leaving his sister to follow as best she could, and the children were transferred to the care of Mr. John Gilchrist, a Scotch pedagogue of the old brutal school, who took an especial delight in caning the boys, especially with a rattan, across the palm of the hand ; but the children were not long in discovering a remedy by splitting the end of the cane and inserting a bit of hair.

They took lessons in drawing, dancing, French, and music, in which each child showed its individuality. Maria loved all four ; Edward took to French and music, and hated dancing ; Richard took to French and drawing, . and disliked music and dancing. The two boys took by nature to the study of arms as soon as they could walk, at first with popguns and spring pistols, and tin and wooden sabres. Richard often declares that he can remember, at five years old, longing to kill the porter because he laughed at their *sabres de bois* and *pistolets de paille.*

He was a boy of three ideas, as he afterwards called it. Usually if a child is forbidden to eat the sugar or lap up the cream, he either simply obeys or does the contrary, but Dick used to place himself before the sugar and the cream, and carefully ask himself the question. " Have you the pluck not to touch them ? " When he had thoroughly convinced himself he had the courage, he instantly rewarded resolution by emptying one or both. Moreover, like most boys of strong imagination and lively feeling, he was a resolute and unblushing liar, and used to ridicule the idea of his honour being in any way attached to telling the truth. He never could understand what moral turpitude there could be in a lie, unless it was told for fear of the consequences of telling the truth. That feeling continued for many a year, and at last, as very often happens, it

ran into quite the other extreme—a disagreeable habit
of scrupulously telling the truth, whether it were timely
or not.

School was mostly manned by English boys, sprinkled
with French, and the mixture of the two formed an ungodly
article. The Italian proverb,

> " Un Inglese Italianato
> È un diavolo incarnato,"

may be applied with quite as much truth to English
boys brought up in France. Lads, for home-life, must
be educated in a particular groove, first the preparatory
school, then Eton and Oxford, with an occasional excursion
to France, Italy and Germany to learn languages not of
Stratford atte Bowe, and to find out that England is not the
whole world.

Burton has often said that he never met any of his Tours
school-fellows save one—Blayden E. Hawke—who became
a commander in the Navy and died in 1877. Thus the
children became perfect devilets and played every kind
of trick despite the rattan. Fighting the French gutter-
boys with sticks and stones, fists and snowballs was a
favourite amusement, and many a donkey lad went home
with ensanguined nose, whilst occasionally the Britishers got
the worst of it from some big brother. The next favourite
game was playing truant, passing the day in utter happiness, fancying themselves Robinson Crusoes and wandering
about the strip of wood (long since doomed to fuel) at the
top of the Tranchée.

The father and mother went much into the society of
the place, which was gay and pleasant; and the children
were left to the servants. They beat all their *bonnes*,
generally by running at their petticoats and upsetting
them. There was one particular case when a new nurse
arrived, a huge Norman girl who at first imposed upon this

turbulent nursery by her breadth of shoulder and the
general vigour of her presence. One unlucky day they
walked to the Faubourg at the south-east of the town, the
only part of old Tours now remaining. The old women
sat spinning and knitting at their cottage doors and
remarked loud enough for the children to hear, "*Ah ça ! ces
petits gamins ! Voilà une honnête bonne qui ne laissera
pas faire des farces !*" Whereupon Eufrosine became as
proud as a peacock and insisted upon a stricter discipline
than they had been used to. That first walk ended badly.
A jerk of the arm on her part brought on a general attack
from the brood ; the poor *bonne* measured her length
upon the ground and they jumped upon her. The party
returned ; she with red eyes, torn cap and downcast looks,
and the children hooting and jeering loudly and calling the
old women *Les Mères Pomponnes*, who screamed predic-
tions that they would come to the guillotine.*

Talking of the guillotine, the schoolmaster unwisely
allowed the boys by way of a school treat, to see the
execution of a woman who killed her small family by
poisoning, on condition they should look away when the

---

* Colonel and Mrs. Burton had not much idea of managing their
children : it was like the old tale of the hen who hatched ducklings.
By way of a wholesome and moral lesson of self-command and self-
denial, Mrs. Burton took them past Madame Fisterre's windows and
bade them look at all the good things there, during which they fixed
their ardent affections upon a tray of apple puffs. Then she said,
"Now, my dears, let us go away ; it is so good for little children to
restrain themselves." Upon this the three devilets turned flashing
eyes and burning cheeks upon their moralizing mother, broke the
windows with their fists, clawed out the tray of apple puffs and bolted,
leaving poor Mrs. Burton, a sadder and a wiser woman, to pay the
damage of her lawless brood's proceedings. The same thing used to
be done to me, but I, being a Catholic, was so brought up to denials
and penances and having to give up everything, that it used to—well
as the saying is—"roll like water off a duck's back," and I never
thought twice of it. In short, I was never disappointed, because when
I was asked what I should like, I knew what was coming.—*Isabel
Burton.*

knife descended, but of course that was the time (with such
an injunction) when every small neck was craned and eyes
strained to look and the result was that the whole school
played at guillotine for a week—happily without serious
accident.

The residence at Tours was interrupted by occasional
trips, summering in other places, especially at St. Malo.
The seaport then thoroughly deserved the slighting notice
to which it was subjected by Captain Marryat, and the
house in the Faubourg was long remembered from its tall
avenue of old yew-trees, which afforded abundant bird's-
nesting. At Dieppe the gallops on the sand were very
much enjoyed, for the young ones were put on horseback as soon as they could straddle. Many a fall was of
course the result, and not a few broken heads, whilst the
rival French boys were painfully impressed by the dignity
of spurs and horse-whips.

At times relations came over to visit them, especially
Grandmamma Baker. Grandmamma Baker was a very
peculiar character. She had been very handsome in her
youth and still retained signs of beauty in age. When her
family came to grief in money matters, she, like some of
the ruined *ancienne noblesse* of France, put her Scotch
gentillesse (she was a MacGregor) into her pocket and
bravely started a dress-making establishment. In later
life she used to boast that she had made the wedding-dress
of her cousin the Duchess of Gordon. Her energy and
good management enabled her to make a fine fortune, after
which she gave up her beloved establishment and became
once more a MacGregor.

Her arrival was a signal of presents, and used to be
greeted with tremendous shouts of delight; but the end of
a week always brought on a quarrel. The mother was
rather thin and delicate, but the grandmother, a thorough
old MacGregor of the Helen or the Rob Roy type, was as

quick to resent an affront as any of her clan. Her miniature shows that she retained her good looks to the last.
When her step-son Richard Baker, jun., inherited his
money (£80,000) he went to Paris, and fell into the hands
of the celebrated Baron de Thierry. This French friend
persuaded him to embark in the pleasant little speculation
of building a bazaar. By the time the walls began to grow
above ground the Englishman had finished £60,000, and
seeing that a million would hardly complete the work he
sold off his four greys and fled Paris post-haste in a post-
chaise. The Baron Thierry followed him to London and,
bold as brass, presented himself as an injured creditor at
Grandmamma's pretty little house in Park Lane. The old
lady replied by summoning her servants and having him
literally kicked downstairs in true Highland fashion. That
Baron's end is well known in history. He made himself
King of one of the Cannibal Islands in the South Sea and
ended by being eaten by his ungrateful subjects.

Grandmamma Baker was determined to learn French,
and accordingly secured a professor. The children's great
delight was to ambuscade themselves and to listen with joy
to the lessons.

" What is the sun ? "
" *Le Soleil, Madame.*"
" *La Solelle.*"
" *Non Madame, Le Soleil.*"
" *Oh pooh ! La Solelle.*"

After about six repetitions of the same, roars of laughter
issued from the curtains, the children, of course, speaking
French like English, upon which the old lady would jump
up and catch hold of the nearest delinquent and minister
condign punishment. She had a peculiar knack of starting
the offender, compelling him to describe a circle of which
she was the centre, whilst holding with the left hand, she
administered smacks and cuffs with the right ; but as every

mode of attack has its proper defence, it was soon found
that the proper corrective was to throw oneself on one's
back and give vigorous kicks with both legs. It need
hardly be said that Grandmamma predicted that Jack
Ketch would make acquaintance with the younger scions of
her race and that she never arrived at speaking French like
a Parisian.

Grandmamma Burton was also peculiar in her ways. To
this lady attaches a very singular and a very romantic story:—

With regard to Louis XIV. there are one or two curious and
interesting legends in the Burton family, well authenticated, but
wanting one link, which would make Richard Burton great-great-
great-grandson of Louis XIV. of France, by a morganatic marriage ;
and another which would entitle him to an English baronetcy, dating
from 1622.

One of the documents in the family is entitled, " A Pedigree of the
Young family, showing their descent from Louis XIV. of France," and
which runs as follows :—

Louis XIV. of France took the beautiful Countess of Montmorency
from her husband and shut him up in a fortress. After the death of
(her husband) the Constable de Montmorency, Louis *married* the
Countess. She had a son called Louis le Jeune, who was " brought
over to Ireland by Lady Primrose," a very remarkable personage,
and a strong ally of the Jacobites. Her maiden name was Drelincourt, and the baby was named Drelincourt, after his godfather and
guardian, Dean Drelincourt (of Armagh), who was the father of Lady
Primrose. He grew up, was educated at Armagh, and was known as
Drelincourt Young. He married a Drelincourt, and became the
father of Hercules Drelincourt Young, and also of Miss (Sarah) Young,
who married the Rev. John Campbell, LL.D., Vicar-General of Tuam
(ob. 1772). Sarah Young's brother, the above-mentioned Hercules
Young, had a son George, a merchant in Dublin, who had some
French deeds and various documents, which proved his right to
property in France.

The above-named Dr. John Campbell, by his marriage with Miss
Sarah Young (rightly Lejeune, for they had changed the name from
French to English), had a daughter, Maria Margaretta Campbell, who
was Richard Burton's grandmother. The same Dr. John Campbell
was a member of the Argyll family, and a first cousin of the " three
beautiful Gunnings," and was Richard Burton's great-grandfather.

These papers (for there are other documents) affect a host of families
in Ireland—the Campbells, Nettervilles, Droughts, Graves, Burtons,
Plunketts, Trimlestons, and many more.

In 1875, *Notes and Queries* was full of this question, and the various documents, but it has never been settled.

The genealogy, if proved, would run thus :—

Louis XIV.

Son, Louis le Jeune (known as Louis Drelincourt Young), by Countess Montmorency ; protected and assisted by Lady Primrose (see Earl of Rosebery), daughter of Drelincourt, Dean of Armagh.

Daughter, Sarah Young; married to Rev. John Campbell, LL.D., Vicar-General of Tuam, Galway.

Daughter, Maria Margaretta Campbell; married to the Rev. Edward Burton, Rector of Tuam, Galway.

Son, Lieutenant-Colonel Joseph Netterville Burton, 36th Regiment.

Son, Richard Burton, whose biography we are now relating.

Anent the Baronetcy, the wife of Richard Burton received, in 1875, two very tantalizing anonymous letters, which she published in *Notes and Queries*, but which she has never been able to turn to account, through the writer declining to come forward, *even secretly*.

One ran thus :—

" MADAM,—There is an old baronetcy in the Burton family to which you belong, dating from the reign of Edward III.—I rather believe *now in abeyance*—which it was thought Admiral Ryder Burton would have taken up, and which after his death can be taken up by your branch of the family. All particulars you will find by searching the Herald's Office ; but I am positive my information is correct.— From one who read your letter in *N. and Q.*"

[N.B.—It was very'ignorant to speak of Baronetcies in the time of Edward III., but Mrs. Burton did not feel justified in changing a word of the letter.]—*A. B. Richards.*

She shortly after received and published the second anonymous letter ; but, though she made several appeals to the writer in *Notes and Queries*, no answer was obtained, and Admiral Ryder Burton eventually died.

" MADAM,—I cannot help thinking that if you were to have the records of the Burton family searched carefully at Shap, in West-moreland, you would be able to fill up the link wanting in your husband's descent, from 1712 to 1750, or thereabouts. As I am *quite positive* of a baronetcy *being in abeyance* in the Burton family, and that *an old one*, it would be worth your while getting all the information you can from Shap and Tuam. The Rev. Edward Burton, Dean of Killala and Rector of Tuam, whose niece he married—viz., a Miss Ryder, of the Earl of Harrowby's family, by whom he had no children. His second wife, a Miss Judge, was a descendant of the Otways, of Castle Otway, and connected with many leading families in Ireland. Admiral James Ryder Burton could, if he *would*, supply you with

information respecting the missing link in your husband's descent.
I have always heard that *de Burton* was the proper family name, and I
saw lately that a *de Burton* now lives in Lincolnshire.
" Hoping, madam, that you will be able to establish your claim to
the baronetcy,

"I remain, yours truly,
"A READER OF *N. and Q.*"

"P.S.—I rather think also, and advise your ascertaining the *fact*,
that the estate of Barker Hill, Shap, Westmoreland, by the law of
entail, will devolve, at the death of Admiral Ryder Burton, on your
husband, Captain Richard Burton."

From the Royal College of Heralds, however, the following information was forwarded to Mrs. Richard Burton :—
There *was* a baronetcy in the family of Burton. The first was Sir
Thomas Burton, Knight, of Stokestone, Leicestershire ; created
July 22nd, 1622, a baronet, by King James I. Sir Charles was the last
baronet. He appears to have been in great distress—a prisoner for
debt, 1712. He is supposed to have died without issue, when the title
became extinct—at least nobody has claimed it since. If your husband
can prove his descent from a younger son of any of the baronets, he
would have a right to the title. The few years must be filled up
between 1712 and the birth of your husband's grandfather, which was
about 1750 ; and you must prove that the Rev. Edward Burton,
Rector of Tuam, in Galway, your husband's grandfather (who came
from Shap, in Westmoreland, with his brother, Bishop Burton, of
Tuam), was descended from any of the sons of any of the baronets
named."

From such romantic combinations sprang Richard Francis
Burton, in whose veins English, Scottish, Irish and French
blood thus curiously commingle. Whether there may not
be also a tinge of Arab, or perhaps of Gypsy blood in
Burton's race is a point which is perhaps open to question.
For the latter suspicion an excuse may be found in the
incurable restlessness which has beset him since his infancy,
a restlessness which has effectually prevented him from ever
settling long in any one place, and in the singular idio-
syncrasy which his friends have often remarked — the
peculiarity of his eyes. "When it (the eye) looks at you,"
says one who knows him well, "it looks through you, and
then glazing over, seems to see something behind you.

Richard Burton is the only man (not a Gypsy) with that
peculiarity, and he shares with them the same horror of
a corpse, death-bed scenes, and grave-yards, though caring
little for his own life." When to this remarkable fact be
added the scarcely less interesting detail that "Burton"
is one of the half-dozen distinctively Romany names, it
is evident that the suspicion of Sir Richard Burton having
a drop of Gypsy blood in his descent—crossed and com-
mingled though it be with an English, Scottish, French and
Irish strain—is not altogether unreasonable.

Grandmamma Burton's portrait shows the regular Bourbon traits, the pear-shaped face and head culminating in
Louis Philippe. Although the wife of a country clergyman, she never seems to have attained the meekness
popularly associated with that peaceful calling. The same
story is told of her as was told of the Edgeworth family.
On one occasion during the absence of her husband the
house at Tuam was broken into by thieves—probably
some of her petted tenantry. She lit a candle, went
upstairs to fetch some gunpowder, loaded her pistols and
ran down to the hall, when the robbers decamped. She
asked the raw Irish servant girl who accompanied her what
had become of the light, and the answer was that it was
standing in the barrel of "black salt" upstairs. Whereupon
Grandmamma Burton had the pluck to walk up to the
garret and expose herself to the risk of being blown to
smithereens.

When Colonel Burton returned from service in Sicily at
the end of the war, he found the estate in a terrible
condition, and obtained his mother's leave to take the
matter in hand. He invited all the tenants to dinner
and when speech-time came on, after being duly blarneyed
by all present, he made a little address dwelling with some
vigour upon the necessity of being for the future more
regular with the "rint." Faces fell, and the only result was

that when the rent came to be collected he was fired at so frequently that, not wishing to lead the life of the "Galway Woodcock," he gave up the game and allowed matters to take their own course.

Another frequent visitor, popularly known as "Aunt G.," was Georgina Baker—the youngest of the three sisters—who was then in the heyday of youth and high spirits. An extremely handsome girl, with blue eyes and dark hair and fine tall figure, she was the life of the house as long as her visits lasted. Her share of the property being £30,000, she had of course a number of offers from Englishmen as well as foreigners. On the latter she soon learned to look shy, having heard that one of her rejected suitors had exclaimed to his friend *Quelle dommage avec cette petite ferme à vendre*, the wished-for farm adjoining his property happening then to be in the market. Heiresses are not always fortunate, and she went on refusing suitor after suitor till ripe middle age, when she married Robert Bagshaw, M.P. for Harwich.

She had wanted to adopt Richard, intending to accompany him to Oxford, and leave him her property, but the project had no stay in it. At the time she was at Tours, Aunt Georgina had a kind of "fad" that she would marry one of her brothers-in-law—Burton's brothers. The eldest sister, Sarah, had married Dr. Burton, elder brother of Colonel Burton, who, sorely against his wish, which pointed to the Church, had been compelled by the failure of the "rint" to become an Army surgeon.

At last it became apparent that Tours was no longer a place for children who were approaching the ticklish time of teens. The Anglo-French boys were remarkable young ruffians who at ten years of age cocked their hats and loved the ladies. Instead of fighting and fagging, they broke the fine old coloured glass church windows, purloined their father's guns to shoot at the monuments in the churchyards, and even the shops and bazaars were not safe from their impudent raids. The ringleader was a certain Aleck G——m, the son of a Scotchman of good family, who was afterwards connected with, or the leading spirit of a transaction which gave a tablet and an inscription to Printing House Square. Aleck was very handsome, and his two sisters were as good-looking as himself. He died sadly enough in a hospital in Paris.

Political matters too began to look queer. The Revolution which hurled Charles X. from the throne produced no outrages in quiet Tours, beyond large gatherings of the people with an immense amount of noise especially of *Vive la Chatte* (for *la Charte*), the good *commères* turning round and asking one another whom the Cat might be that the populace wished so long a life. But when Casimir Perier had passed through the town and "the three Glorious Days of July" had excited the multitude, things began to look black, and cries of *à bas les Anglais* were not uncommon. An Englishman was threatened with prison because the horse he was driving accidentally knocked down an old woman, and a French officer of the line, who was fond of associating with English girls, was grossly insulted and killed in a dastardly duel by a pastrycook.

At last, after long deliberation, the family resolved to leave Tours. Travelling in those days, especially for a large family, was a severe infliction. The old travelling carriages which had grown shabby in the coach-house had to be taken out and furbished up, and all the queer receptacles, Imperial, boot, sword-case, and plate-chest to be stuffed with miscellaneous luggage. After the usual sale by auction, Colonel Burton took his departure, perhaps mostly regretted by a little knot of Italian exiles, whom he liked on account of his young years spent in Sicily, and whose society not improbably suggested his ultimate return to Italy.

Then began the journey along the interminable avenues
of the old French roads lined with parallel rows of poplars
which met at a vanishing point of the far distance.*
Mighty dull work it was whilst the French postilion in
his Seven League boots jogged along with his horses at
the rate of five miles an hour, never dreaming of increasing the rate till he approached some horridly paved
town, when he cracked his whip like a succession of
pistol shots to the awe and delight of all the *sabots.*
Very slow hours they were, especially as the night wore
on, and the road gleaming white between its dark edges
looked of endless length. And when at last the inn was
reached it proved very unlike the hotel of the present
day. A hard bargain had to be driven with a rapacious
landlady who, if you objected to her charges, openly roared
at you with arms akimbo, that if you were not rich enough
to travel you ought to stay at home. Then the beds had
to be inspected, the damp sheets to be aired, and the
warming pans to be ordered, and as dinner had always to
be prepared after arrival, it was not unusual to sit hungry
for a couple of hours.

The fatigues of the journey seriously affected Mrs.
Burton's health, and she lost no time in falling seriously ill
at Chartres. Then Grandmamma Baker was sent for to act
Garde-malade and to awe the children (who were wild with
delight at escaping school and masters) with the weight of
her sturdy Scotch arm. The family passed through Paris,
where the signs of fighting, bullets in the walls and burnt
houses, had not been wholly obliterated, and were fortunate
enough to escape the cholera which then for the first time
attacked Europe in its very worst form. Grandmamma
Baker was very nearly as bad, for she almost poisoned her
beloved grandchildren by stuffing their noses and mouths

---

* Richard found exactly the same thing when travelling through
Lower Canada in 1860.

full of the strongest camphor whenever they happened to pass through a town.

The cold plunge into English life was broken by loitering on the sands of Dieppe. A wonderful old ramshackle place it was in those days, holding a kind of intermediate place between the dulness of Calais and the liveliness of "Boolone" as the denizens called it. It wanted the fine hôtels and the Établissement which grew up under the Second Empire, but there was during summer a pleasant natural kind of life, living almost exclusively upon the sands and dipping in the water, galloping about on little ponies, watching the queer costumes of the bathers, and discussing the new-comers. Though railways were not dreamt of, many Parisians used to affect the place, and part of the French nature seems to be to rush into the sea as soon as it can be seen.

Landing in England was dolorous. Grandmamma Baker inflated her nostrils ; and, delighted at escaping from those Crapauds and their Kickshaws; quoted with effusion her favourite Cowper, "England, with all thy faults, I love thee still." The children scoffed. The air of Brighton, full of smoke and blacks, appeared to them unfit for breathing. The cold grey seas made them shudder. In the town everything appeared to them so small, so prim, so mean, the little one-familied houses contrasting in such a melancholy way with the big buildings of Tours and Paris. They revolted against the coarse and half-cooked food, and accustomed to the excellent Bordeaux of France, they found port, sherry, and beer like strong medicine. The bread all crumb and no crust, appeared to be half baked, and milk meant chalk and water. The large joints of meat made them think of Robinson Crusoe, and the vegetables *cuites à l'eau*, especially the potatoes, which had never heard of a *maître d'hôtel*, suggested the roots of primitive man.

Moreover the national temper, fierce and surly, was a
curious contrast to the light-hearted French of middle
France. The little children punched one another's heads
on the sands ; the boys punched one another's heads in the
streets, and in those days a stand-up fight between men
was not uncommon. Even the women punched their children, and the whole of lower-class society seemed to be
governed by the fist. No wonder that the Continental
lady cautioned her son, when about to travel, against
ridicule in France and the *canaille* in England.

Colonel Burton had determined to send his boys to Eton
to prepare for Oxford and Cambridge. In the meantime
some blundering friend had recommended him a preparatory
school. This was kept by the Rev. Charles Delafosse, who
rejoiced in the title of Chaplain to the Duke of Cumberland.
Accordingly the family went to Richmond, the only
excitement of the journey being the rage of the post-boys
when the two lads on the box furtively poked their
horses with long sticks. After sundry attempts at housing
themselves in the tiny doll-rooms in the stuffy village,
they at last found a house—so called by courtesy—in
Maid of Honour's Row, between the river and the Green ;
a box with a strip of garden fronting it which a sparrow
could hop across in thirty seconds. Opening upon the
same green stood that horror of horrors, the school or the
" Establishment " as it would *now* be called. It consisted of
a large block of buildings, detached, lying between the
Green and the Old Town, which has long been converted
into dwelling houses. In those days it had a kind of paling
forming a long parallelogram which enclosed some fine
old elm-trees. One side was occupied by the house
and the other by the schoolroom. In the upper stories
of the former were the dormitories with their small white
beds, giving the idea of the Lilliput Hospital ; a kind of
outhouse attached to the dwelling was the place where

the boys fed at two long tables stretching the whole length
of the room. The only decorations of the palings were
names cut all over their inner surfaces and rectangular nails
at the top acting *chevaux de frise.* The school-room was
the usual scene of hacked and well-used benches and stained
desks—everything looking as mean and uncomfortable
as possible.

This was the kind of Dotheboys Hall, to which in those
days gentlemen were contented to send their sons, paying
£100 a year, besides "perquisites" (plunder): on the
Continent the same treatment would be had for £20.
The Rev. Charles was a bluff and portly man with dark
hair and short whiskers, whose aquiline nose took a prodigious deal of snuff. He was not over active with the
rod, but he was no more fit to be a schoolmaster than
the Grand Cham of Tartary. He was, however, rather a
favourite with the boys, and it was shrewdly whispered that
at times he returned from dining abroad half seas over.
His thin-lipped wife took charge of the *ménage*, looked severely after the provisions, and swayed with an iron sceptre
the maid-servants who had charge of the smaller boys.

The ushers were the usual consequential lot of those days.
There was the handsome and dressy usher, a general
favourite with the fair ; the shabby and mild usher, despised
by even the smallest boy; and the unfortunate French usher,
whose life was a fair foretaste of Purgatory. Instead of
learning anything at this school, the two Burtons lost much
of what they knew, especially French.

Their principal acquisitions were a certain facility of
using their fists and a general development of ruffianism.
Richard was in one perpetual season of fights. At one time
he had thirty-two "affairs of honour" to settle, the place of
meeting being the schoolroom, with the elder boys sitting
in judgment. On the first occasion he received a blow in
the eye which he thought most unfair, and having got his

opponent down he proceeded to hammer his head against the ground, using his ears by way of handles. His indignation knew no bounds when he was pulled off by the bystanders and told to let his enemy stand up again. "Stand up?" he cried, "after all the trouble I've had to get the fellow down." At last the fighting went on to such an extent that he was beaten as thin as a shotten herring, and the very servant-maids when washing him on a Saturday night used to say:—"Drat the child! what has he been doing? He's all black and blue!" Edward fought just as hard, but was younger and more peaceable.

The parents very unwisely determined to correct all personal vanity in their offspring by always dwelling upon their ugliness. Richard's nose was called "cocked" and was a perpetual plague to him. He was assured that the only decent feature in his face was his teeth. Maria, on account of her fresh complexion, was called "Blousabella"; and even Edward, whose features were perfect and whom Frenchmen used to stop and stare at in the street and call *le Petit Napoléon,* was told to nauseousness that "Handsome is that handsome does." In later life the children were dressed in a marvellous fashion, and pieces of yellow nankin would be bought to dress the whole family like three sticks of barley sugar. Such was the discipline of the day, and nothing could be more ill-judged than to inflict an amount of torment upon sensitive children which certainly was not intended, but which had the very worst effect.

Maria describes Richard as being a thin, dark little boy with small features and large black eyes, and as being extremely proud, sensitive, shy, nervous, melancholy, and affectionate in disposition. Such is the effect of a boys' school after a few months' trial, when the boys learn to despise mothers and sisters and to affect the rough as much as possible, and this is not only in England but everywhere when the boy first escapes from petticoat government. He

does not know what to do to show his manliness. There
is no stronger argument in favour of mixed schools of
boys and girls brought up together till a certain age.
If the children quarrelled and turned up their noses at
the food in English hotels, what must have been their
surprise at the food of an English school? Breakfast at
9 A.M. consisted of blue milk and water in chipped and
broken handled mugs of the same colour. The boys were
allowed tea from home, but it was a perpetual battle to get
a single drink of it. The substantials were a wedge of
bread with a glazing of butter, and epicures used to collect
the glazing to one end of the slice in order to convert
it into a final *bonne bouche.* The dinner at 1 o'clock began
with "stick-jaw" (pudding) and ended with meat, as at all
second-rate schools. The latter was as badly cooked as
possible—black outside and blue within, gristly and sinewy.
The vegetables were potatoes which might serve as grape-
shot and the hateful carrot. Supper was a repetition of
breakfast, and at an age when boys were making bone and
muscle they went hungry to bed. Occasionally the pocket-
money and tips were clubbed, and a room would go in for a
midnight feed of a quartern loaf, ham, polonies and saveloys,
with a quantity of beer and wine, which generally led to half
a dozen fights. Saturday was a day to be feared on account
of its peculiar pie, which contained all the waifs and strays
of the week. On the Sunday there was an attempt at
plum pudding of a peculiarly pale and leaden hue as if it
had been unjustly defrauded of its due allowance of plums ;
and this dull routine lasted throughout the scholastic year.
School hours were from 7 to 9 and 10 to 1 and 3 to 5
without other change save at the approach of the holidays
when a general outburst of singing, locally called "challenging," took place.

Very few were the schoolfellows whom Richard met in
after life. The exceptions are Guildford Onslow, the

Claimant's friend. Tuckey Baines, as he was called on account of his exploits on Saturday's pie, went into the Bombay Army and was as disagreeable and ill-tempered then as when he was at school. He was locally celebrated for hanging the wrong Mohammed, after which he was much improved in meekness, and for his cure for Sindi litigiousness, by making complainant and defendant flog each other in turn. The only school-boy who did anything worthy of mention was Bobby Delafosse, who was appointed to the 26th Regiment N. I., and who showed immense pluck and died fighting bravely in the Indian Mutiny. Richard met him in Bombay shortly before he went off to the North-West Provinces, but his remembrances of the school were so painful that he could not bear to recognize him. In fact, that part of his life upon which most boys dwell with the greatest pleasure and concerning which most autobiographers tell the longest stories —school and college—was ever a night-mare to him. It was like the "blacking shop" of Charles Dickens.

Before the year concluded an epidemic of measles broke out in the school : several of the pupils died, and it was found necessary to disperse the survivors. The boys without being hard-hearted were delighted to get home. Already they had made one abortive attempt to run away, and had been brought back condignly by boatmen and bargees in hopes of half-a-crown for the service rendered. They worked successfully on the fears of Aunt G., assisted by Richard's cadaverous appearance, and it was resolved to remove them from school, to their infinite joy.

Colonel Burton had also become thoroughly sick of Maid of Honour Row and Richmond Green. He was sighing for shooting and boar hunting in the French forests, and he felt that he had done quite enough for the education of the boys which was turning out so badly. He resolved to bring them up abroad, and picked up the necessary

assistance for educating his children by tutor and governess. Miss Ruxton, a stout, red-faced English girl, was
thoroughly up in the "three R's," and was intended to
direct Maria's education. Mr. Du Pré, an undergraduate
of Exeter College, Oxford, and son of the old Rector
of Berkhampstead, wanted to see life on the Continent,
and was not unwilling to see it with a sufficient salary.
He was an awkward looking John Bull article, with a
narrow forehead, eyes close together, and thick lips, which
secured him a perpetual course of caricaturing. He used
to hit out hard whenever he found the caricatures, but
only added bitterness to them. Before he had been in the
family a week Richard had obliged him with a sketch of
his tomb and the following inscription :—

> " Stand passenger ! hang down thy head and weep,
> A young man from Exeter here doth sleep.
> If any one ask who that young man be,
> 'Tis the devil's dear friend and companion—Du Pré "

—which was merely an echo of Shakespeare and John à
Combe, but it showed a fine sense of independence.

Richard caught the measles at the school, and was nursed
by Grandmamma Baker in Park Street : it was the only
infantile malady that he ever had. The whooping-cough
only attacked him on his return from Harar, when staying
with his friend, Dr. Steinhäuser, at Aden in 1853. As
soon as he was well enough to travel, the family embarked
at the Tower Wharf for Boulogne. The boys scandalised
every one on board. They shrieked, they whooped, they
danced for joy. They shook their fists at the white cliffs,
and loudly hoped they would never see them again. They
hurrahed for France, and hooted for England, until the
sailor who was hoisting the Jack looked upon them as a
pair of little monsters.

In their delight at getting away from school and the
stuffy little island, they had no idea of the disadvantage

which the new kind of life would inflict on their future
careers. A man who brings up his family abroad, and
who lives there for years, must expect to lose all the
friends who could be useful to him when he wishes to start
them in life. The conditions of society in England are so
complicated and so artificial, that those who would make
their way in the world, especially in public careers, must
be broken to it from the earliest day. The future soldiers
and statesmen must be prepared by Eton and Oxford
or Cambridge. The more English they are, even to the
cut of their hair, the better. In consequence of being
brought up abroad, the boys never thoroughly understood
English society, nor did society ever understand them.
And lastly, it is a real advantage to belong to some parish.
It is a great thing when you have won a battle, or have
explored Central Africa, to be welcomed home by some
little corner of the Great World which takes a pride in
your exploits, because they reflect honour upon itself. In
the contrary condition you are a waif and stray—you are
a blaze of light without a focus.

No man ever gets on in the world, or rises to the head of
affairs, unless he is a representative of his nation. Taking
the marking characters of the last few years—Palmerston,
Thiers, Cavour, and Bismarck—what were they but simply
the types of their various nationalites? In point of intel-
lect Bismarck was a strong man ; Cavour a magnificent
genius ; Thiers second-rate ; Palmerston third-rate. Their
success in life was solely owing to their representing the
failings as well as the merits of their several nationalities.
Thiers, for instance, was the most thorough-bred *épicier*
possible, and yet look at his success : and his death was
mourned even in England, though he was the bitterest
enemy that England ever had. His Chauvinism did more
than the Crimean War to abolish the *prestige* of England.

Mr. Du Pré, the tutor, and Miss Ruxton, the governess,

had their work cut out for them. They attempted to
commence with a strict discipline. For instance, the family
passing through Paris lodged at the Hôtel Windsor, and
they determined to walk the youngsters out school fashion.
The consequence was that when the walk extended to the
Boulevards, the young ones, on agreement, suddenly ran
away. They were home long before the unfortunate
strangers could find their way, and reported that the
unfortunate tutor and governess had been run over by an
omnibus. There was immense excitement till the supposed victims walked in tremendously tired, having wandered over half Paris, not being able to find their way.
A scene followed, but the adversaries respected each other
more after that day.

The difficulty was now where to colonize. One of the
peculiarities of the little English colonies was the unwilling-
ness of their denizens to return to them when once they
had left them. Colonel Burton had been very happy
at Tours, and yet he religiously avoided it. He passed
through Orleans—a horrid hole with as many smells as
Cologne—and tried to find a suitable country house near
it, but in vain. Everything seemed to smell of goose and
gutter.

Thence he drifted on to Blois, in those days a kind
of home of the British stranger, and there he thought
proper to call a halt. At last a house was found on the
high ground beyond the city, which like Tours lies mainly
on the left bank of the river and where most of the English
colonists dwelt. There is no necessity for dwelling upon this
little bit of England in France. It was very like Tours,
and when one describes one colony, one describes them all.
The notables were Sir Joseph Leeds, Colonel Burnes, and a
sister of Sir Stamford Raffles, who lived in the next-door
villa, if such a term may be applied to a country house in
France in 1831. The only differences from Tours were

that there was no celebrated physician, no pack of hounds, and no parson, consequently service on Sundays had to be done at home by the tutor, and the evening was distinguished by one of Blair's sermons. This was read out by the children, each taking a turn. The discourse was from one of the three old volumes which appeared, Richard said, to have a soporific effect upon the audience. Soft music was gradually heard proceeding from the nasal organs of father and mother, tutor and governess, and thus the children, preserving the same tone of voice, entered into a conversation and discussed matters until the time came to a close.

At Blois the young ones were now entering upon their teens; their education was now beginning in real earnest. Poor Miss Ruxton soon found her task absolutely impossible and threw up the service. A school-room was instituted where time was wasted upon Latin and Greek for six or seven hours a day. Besides which there was a French master—one of those little obsolete old men who called themselves *Professeurs-ès-lettres*, and the great triumph of his life was that he had read Herodotus in the original. The dancing-master was a large and pompous oldster—of course an *ancien militaire*—whose kit and whose capers were by contrast peculiarly ridiculous, and who quoted at least once every visit, "Oh Richard! Oh mon Roi!" He taught, besides country dances, square and round, the *Minuet de la Cour*, the *Gavotte de Vestris*, and a *Danse Chinoise*, which consisted mainly in turning up thumbs and toes.

The only favourite amongst all these professors was the fencing master, also an old soldier, who had lost the thumb of his right hand in the wars, which of course made him a *gauché* in loose fencing. The boys gave themselves up with ardour to this study, and passed most of their leisure hours in exchanging thrusts. They soon learned not to neglect the mask: Master Richard passed his foil down Master Edward's throat and nearly destroyed his uvula.

The amusements consisted chiefly of dancing at evening parties, the boys choosing the tallest girls, especially a very lofty Miss Donovan. A little fishing was to be had, Colonel Burton being a great amateur. There were long daily walks, swimming in summer, and brass cannons bought in the shops were loaded to bursting. The swimming was very easily taught. In the present day boys and girls go to school and learn it like dancing. In Burton's case M. Du Pré supported his pupils by a hand under the stomach, taught them how to move their arms and legs, and to lie upon their breasts, after which he withdrew his hand and left them to float as they best could.

This life lasted for a year, till all were thoroughly tired of it. Colonel Burton and his wife were imperceptibly lapsing [into the category of professed invalids, as people do who have no other business in life except to be sick. This was a class exceptionally common in the little unoccupied English colonies that studded the country. It was a far robuster institution than the Parisian invalid whose object in life was to appear *maladif et souffrant.* The British *malade* consumed a considerable quantity of butcher's meat, but although he always saw death in the pot he had not the moral courage to refuse what disagreed with him. He tried every kind of drug and nostrum, known and unknown, and answered every advertisement whether it agreed with his complaint or not. His *table de nuit* was covered with bottles and gallipots ; he dosed himself three or four times a day for the change of climate, and insensibly acquired a horror of driving out or passing the evening away from home. He had a kind of rivalry with other invalids, and nothing offended him more than to tell him that he was in strong health, and that if he had been a hard-worked professional man in England, he would have been

D 2

ill once a year instead of once a month. Homœopathy was
a great boon to him, and so was hydropathy, so was the
Grape Cure, the Cold Water Cure, and all the humbugs
invented by non-professionals.

Colonel Burton and his wife suffered from asthma, an
honest and respectable kind of complaint, which if left
to itself allows you, like gout, to last till your 80th year;
but which treated systematically and with the aid of the
doctor is apt to wear you out. Grandmamma Baker,
who came over to Blois, compared them in homely
Scotch fashion to two buckets in a well, and she was
very wroth with Colonel Burton when, remembering the
days of his youth, he began to hug the idea of returning
to Italy and seeing the sun. The general conclusion
of her philippics—" You'll kill your wife, Sir!" was not
likely to change his resolve. She even insinuated that
in the olden day there had been a Sicilian young woman
who received the Englishman's pay and so distributed it
as to keep off claims. There was a battle-royal, and
Grandmamma Baker was sent off to her beloved England,
whose faults she still loved.

The old yellow chariot was brought out of the dusty
coach-house and furbished up, and after farewell dinners
and parties all round, the family turned their backs on
Blois. The journey was long, being broken by sundry
attacks of asthma, and the posting and style of travel
were full of the usual discomforts. In crossing over
the Tarare a drunken postilion nearly threw one of the
carriages over the precipice, and in shooting the Pont de
St. Esprit the steamer almost came to grief under one of the
arches. They stayed a short time in Lyons ; in those days
a perfect den of thieves. From Avignon Richard and his
tutor were driven to the Fountain of Vaucluse, the charming blue well in the stony mountain, and the memories
of Petrarch and Laura were long retained. The driver

insisted on a full gallop, and the protests of No. 3, an unfortunate Englishman, who declared every quarter of an hour that he was the father of a large family, were utterly disregarded. The first view of Provence was something entirely new, and the escape from the long flat fields and poplar avenues of Central France was hailed with delight. Everything, even the most squalid villages, appeared to fall into a picture. It was something like a sun that beat upon the rocks. The olive-trees, laden with purple fruit, were a delight after the apples and the pears, and the contrast between the brown rock and the blue Mediterranean was a new and a charming sensation.

At Marseilles they embarked for Leghorn, which was then in Italy very much what Lyons was in France—it was the headquarters of petty larceny and brigandage. Indeed it was reported that a society existed whose members were pledged to stab their fellow-creatures whenever they could do it with safety; and it was brought to light by the remorse of a son who had killed his father by mistake. The Grand Duke of Tuscany, with his meek benevolence, was averse from shedding blood, and the worst that these wretches expected was to be dressed in the red or the yellow of the Galeotti, to sweep the streets, and to bully the passengers for bakhshish. Another unpleasant develop-ment was the quantity of vermin: even the washer-woman's head appeared to be walking off her shoulders. Still there was a touch of Italian art about the place; in the days before politics and polemics had made Italian art, with the sole exception of sculpture, the basest thing on the Continent: the rooms were large, high, and airy; the frescoes on the ceiling were good, and the pictures had not been sold to Englishmen, and replaced by badly-coloured daubs and cheap prints of the illustrated paper type.

After a few days, finding Leghorn utterly unfit to inhabit Colonel Burton determined to transfer himself to

Pisa. There after the usual delay he found a lodging on the wrong side of the Arno—that is to say, the side which does not catch the winter sun—in a huge block of buildings opposite the then highest bridge. Dante's "Vituperio delle Gente" was then the dullest abode known to man except perhaps his sepulchre. The climate was detestable—Iceland on the non-sunny, Madeira on the sunny side of the river— but the doctors thought it good enough for their patients. Consequently it was the hospital of a few sick Britishers who had been much better left at home, instead of being sent to die of discomfort in Tuscany. The monotony of the place was something preternatural. The Italians had their own amusements : the principal was the Opera—a perfect den of impurity, where you were choked by the effluvia of the *Pastrane*, or brigands' cloaks, which descended from father to son through many generations. The singing, instrumenta- tion, and acting, were equally vile, but the Pisani had not the critical ferocity of the Livornesi, who used to visit the smallest defect with *torni in iscena, bestia.*

The other form of amusement was the Conversazione. Here you entered at about six o'clock, and found an enormous room with a dwarf sofa, and an avenue of two lines of chairs projecting from it perpendicularly. You were expected to walk through the latter, which was occupied by the younger women, to the former, upon which sat the dowagers, and after the three *saluts d'usage*, and the compliments of the season, you backed out by the way you came in, and passed the evening leaning over the back of the chair of the fair dame whose *cavaliere servente* you were supposed to be. The refreshments were an occasional glass of cold water ; in luxurious houses there were water-ices and sugared wafers. They complain that we English are not happy in society without eating, and most men will confess to preferring a good beef-steak to cold water and water-ices. There was no bad feeling between the Italians and the English; they simply ignored one another.

Nothing could be shadier than the English colony at Pisa. As they left England, the farther they went, the more wretched they became till they reached the climax at Naples. They had no club as at Tours, and they met to read their *Galignani* at a grocer's shop on the Lung' Arno. They had their parson and their doctor and their tea-caddies, but the inhospitable nature of the country—and certainly Italy is the least given to the savage virtue—seemed to have affected the strangers. Equally unknown were the dinner-parties of Tours and the "hops" of Blois. No one shot and no one fished. A madman used to plunge through the ice in the Lung' Arno in mid-winter, but most of them contented themselves with promenading the Quai, and basking in the wintry sun till they returned to their stuffy rooms.

A good many of them were half-pay officers; others were Jamaica planters and men who had made their fortunes in trade, while the rest were nondescripts whom nobody knew. At times some frightful scandal broke out in consequence of the discovery of some gentleman who left his country for his country's good.

The discomforts of Pisa were considerable. The only fire-place in those days was a kind of brazier put in the middle of the room. The servants were perfect savages who had to be taught the very elements of service, and often at the end of the third day a great rough peasant would take leave, saying, *Non mi basta l'anima.* Colonel Burton started a fearful equipage in the shape of a four-wheel trap, buying for the same a hammer-headed brute of a horse which at once obtained the name of Dobbin. Dobbin was a perfect demon-steed and caused incalculable misery. As every person was supposed to steal his oats one of the boys was sent down to superintend his break-fast, dinner, and supper. On journeys it ·was the same, and the lads would have been delighted to see Dobbin hanged, drawn, and quartered. They tried riding him in private; but the brute used to plant his forelegs, and kick up and down like a rocking-horse. The trap was another source of intense misery. The wheels were always supposed to want greasing, and as the natives would steal the grease, it was necessary that one of the boys should superintend the operation. No greater mistake can be made than that of setting boys to do servant's work with the idea of making them useful.

The work of education went on nimbly, if not merrily. To former masters was added an Italian master, who was at once dubbed " Signor No!" on account of the energy of his negations. The French master unfortunately discovered that his three pupils had poetic talents. The consequence was that they were set to write versified descriptions, which they hated worse than 'Telemachus' and the 'Spectator.' A new horror appeared in the shape of the violin master. Edward took kindly to the infliction, worked very hard, and became an amateur almost equal to a professional. He was offered fair pay as member of an orchestra in Italy, and kept his music up after joining the army, till the "calls" of the mess made it such a nuisance, that he gave it up. Richard always hated his fiddle, and, after six months, managed to bring the study to an untimely end. His professor was a thing like Paganini—length without breadth, nerves without flesh, hung on wires, and all hair and no brain, except for fiddling. The creature, tormented to madness by a number of false notes made on purpose, addressed his pupil in his grandiloquent Tuscan manner, *Gli altri scolari sono bestie, ma voi siete un' arcibestia.* Richard, highly offended by the "*arci,*" instantly broke his violin upon his master's head, and, curiously enough, Colonel Burton made the discovery that his eldest son had no talent for music.

Amongst other English at Pisa, the family met with some Irish cousins. Their name had been Conyngham, but they had, for a fortune, very sensibly added " Jones " to it, and very foolishly were ashamed of it ever afterwards. There was a boy whose face looked as if cut badly out of a half-boiled potato, dotted with freckles so as to resemble a goose's egg ; and then there was a very pretty girl, who afterwards became Mrs. Seaton. The mother was an exceedingly handsome woman of the Spanish type, and it was grand to see her administering correction to " bouldness." They seemed principally to travel in Italy for the purpose of wearing out old clothes, and afterwards delighted in telling how many churches and palaces they had "done " in Rome *per diem*. Altogether the Conyngham-Joneses were as fair specimens of Northern barbarians invading the South as have been since the days of Brennus.

The summer of 1832 was passed at Sienna, where a large, rambling old house was found inside the walls. The venerable town, whose hospitality was confined to an inscription over the City Gate, was perhaps one of the dullest places under Heaven. No country in the world shows less hospitality, even amongst Italians themselves, than Italy, and in the case of strangers they have perhaps many reasons to justify that churlishness.

Almost all the English at Sienna were fugitives from justice, social or criminal. One man had walked off with his friend's wife, another with his purse. There was only one old English lady in the place who was knowable, and that was a Mrs. Russell, who afterwards killed herself with mineral waters. She lived in a pretty little quinta outside the town, where moonlight nights were delightful, and where the nightingales were louder than usual.

Beyond this amusement the children had little to do, except at intervals to peep at the game of " Pallone," to study very hard, and to hide from the world their hateful

suits of nankin. The weary summer drew to a close : the
long-surviving chariot was brought out, and, with Dobbin and
the " cruelty van," made ready for the march. " Travelling
vetturino " was not without its charms ; it much resembled
marching in India during the slow, old days. It is true
you seldom covered more than five miles an hour, and
up hill three, while the harness was perpetually breaking, and at times a horse fell lame. But you saw the
country thoroughly ; the *vetturino* knew the name of every
house, and you went slowly enough to impress everything
upon your memory. The living, again, was none of the best,
and seemed to consist mostly of omelettes and pigeons.
The pigeons, it was said, used to desert the dovecotes
whenever they saw an English travelling-carriage approaching, and the omelettes showed more of human hair in
them than eggs usually produce. The bread and wine,
however, were good, and adulteration was then unknown.
The lodging was on a par with the food, and insect
powder not being invented or known, the nights were
often restless. Still, taking all in all, it is to be doubted
whether we are more comfortable in the Grand Hotel in
these days, when every hotel is grand, when all mutton is
pré salé, when all beer is bitter, and when all sherry is dry.

The journey was short, and the family took a house on
the north side of the Arno, near to the Boboli Gardens,
Florence. The City of Flowers has always had a reputation beyond what it deserved. Though " too fair to be
looked upon, save on holidays," it has discomforts of its
own. The cold, especially during the Tramontana blowing
from the Apennines, is that of Scotland. The heat during
the dog-days, when the stone pavement seems to be fit
for baking, reminds one of Cairo during a Khamsín, and
the rains are at times as heavy and persistent as in Central
Africa.

The Italians and the English, even in those days, despite all the efforts of the amiable Grand Duke, did not mix well. The Anglo-Florentine flock certainly contained some very black sheep. They were always divided into cliques, and they were perpetually grumbling. The parson led a terrible life. One of the churchwardens was sure to be some bilious old Indian, and a common character was a half-pay Indian officer who "had given laws," as he said, "to millions," who supported himself by gambling, and who induced all his cronies to drink hard, the whispered excuse being that he had shot a man in a duel somewhere. The old ladies were very scandalous. There were perpetual little troubles, such as a rich and aged widow being robbed and deserted by her young Italian *sposo;* and resident old gentlemen when worsted at cards used to quarrel and call one another liars. Amongst the number was a certain old Dr. Harding, who had a large family. His son was sent into the army, and was badly wounded under Sir Charles Napier at Sind. He lived to be Major-General Francis Pim Harding, C.B., and died in 1875. Another remarkable family was that old Colonel de Courcey. He had some charming daughters, and his son John was last met by Richard when he was in the Turkish Contingent.

Still Florence was always Florence. The climate, when it was fine, was magnificent. The views were grand, and the most charming excursions lay within a few hours' walk or drive. The English were well—perhaps too well— treated by the local Government, and the opportunities of studying Art were first-rate. Those wonderful Loggie and the Pitti Palace contained more high art than is to be found in all London, Paris, Berlin and Vienna put together, and the young ones soon managed to become walking catalogues.

A heavy storm, however, presently broke the serenity of the domestic atmosphere. At Sienna the boys had been allowed to begin regular shooting with an old single-

barrelled Manton, a hard hitter, which had been changed
from flint to percussion.   The parents, however, made a
grand mistake about these shooting excursions, especially
the mother, who, frightened lest anything should occur,
used to get up quarrels, to have an excuse to forbid
them by way of punishment.   This was soon found out,
and resented accordingly.   The boys practised gunnery
in secret every moment they could, and presently gave
their tutor a specimen of their proficiency.   He had
been instituting odious comparisons between Edward's
length and that of his gun, and went so far as to say that
for sixpence he would allow a shot at fifty yards.   On this
being accepted, with the firm determination of peppering
him, he thought it better to substitute his hat, and he got
away just in time to see it riddled like a sieve.   The boys
then began to despise shooting with small shot.   They
hoarded the weekly franc which each received, borrowed
the sister's savings—the poor girl was never allowed to
keep it for a day—and invested in what was then known
as "a case of pistols."   Colonel Burton saw the turn that
matters were taking, and ordered the "saw-handles" to be
ignominiously returned to the shop.   The shock was too
severe to the *pundonor* of the two Don Quixotes, who
instantly resolved to leave the house, and retired to Pistoja,
where Richard cast about for something to do, whilst
Edward engaged himself in the orchestra.   This dream of
liberty was crushed by a descent of the police, who insisted
on their returning home on the pain of being put in gaol.

   It was now resolved to pass the Holy Week at Rome,
and the journey went on as usual.   The only events of the
journey were the breaking down of Dobbin's "cruelty van"
in a village near Perugia, where the tutor and the boys were
left behind to look after repairs.   They long remembered
the peculiar evening which they passed there.   The head
ostler informed them that there was an opera, and that he

was the *primo violino.* They went to the big barn that formed the theatre, where a kind of Passion Play was being performed, with lengthy intervals of music, in which all the mysteries of religion were submitted to the eyes of the Faithful. The only disenchanting detail was that, on a certain occasion a dove not being procurable, its place was supplied by a turkey-cock, and the awful gobbling of the ill-behaved wretch caused much more merriment than was decorous.

The children, who had already examined Volterra with great interest, were delighted with the old Etruscan city of Perugia, and were allowed a couple of hours' leave to visit Pietro Aretino's tomb; they loitered by Lake Thrasymene, and, after a slow but most interesting drive, they reached the Eternal City, and, like all the world, were immensely impressed by the entrance at the Porta del Popolo. Colonel Burton secured apartments in the Piazza di Spagna, which was then, as it is now, the capital of English Rome. Everything in it was English, the librarian, the grocer, and all the other little shops; and mighty little it has changed during half a century. When Richard saw it in 1873, the only points of difference he observed were the presence of Americans, and the long gilded advertisements of the photographers. The sleepy atmosphere was the same, and the same was the drowsy old fountain.

At Rome sight-seeing was carried on with peculiar ardour. With Mrs. Starke under the arm—for Murray and Baedeker were not invented in those days—the young ones went from Vatican to Capitol, from Church to Palazzo, from ruin to ruin. They managed to get introductions to the best studios, and made acquaintance with all the shops which contained the richest collections of coins, of cameos, of model temples in *rosso antico* and *giallo antico*, and of all the treasures of Roman art, ancient and modern. They passed their days in running about the town, and, whenever they found an opportunity, they made excursions into the country, even ascending Mount Soracte.

In those days Rome was not as it is now. It was the ghost of the Imperial City, the mere shadow of the Mistress of the World. The great Forum was a level expanse of ground, out of which the half-buried ruins rose. The Coliseum had not changed for a century. The Palatine Hill never dreamt of excavation. The greater part of the space within the old walls that represent the ancient city was a waste—what would in Africa be called "bush"—and it was believed that turning up the ground caused fatal fevers. It had no pretensions to be a Capital. It wanted fortifications, and the walls could be breached with six pounders. The Tiber was not regulated, and periodically flooded the lower town. The Ghetto was a disgrace; nothing could be fouler than the Trastevere and the Leonine city, with the exception of St. Peter, and the Vatican was a piggery.

At Rome there was then very little society, and the principal amusements were conversazioni, where the only conspicuous object was some toothless Cardinal, sitting in red, enthroned upon a sofa. Good old Gregory XVI. did not dislike foreigners, and was even intimate with a certain number of heretics, but that could not disperse the sleepy atmosphere of the place, whilst the highest classes of society were what the satirical French duchesse called *une noblesse de Sacrement*—and yet it was the season of the year.

Then, as now, the wondering world pressed to Rome to see the ceremonies of Holy Week, to hear the music of the Sistine Chapel, to assist at the annual conversion of a Jew at St. John of Lateran,* to walk gaping about at the interior of St. Peter's, and to enjoy the magnificent illuminations, which were so generally spoiled by a high wind and a flood of rain.

* *Vide* Browning's poem, ' Holy Cross Day.'—ED.

ROME IN 1832.

Nothing could be more curious than the contrast between the sons of the Holy City and the barbarians from
the North and the Far West. When the Pope stood in the
balcony delivering his benediction, *urbi et orbi*, the Anglo-
Catholics seemed to be overwhelmed with awe, whilst the
Romans delivered themselves of small jokes, very audible
withal, upon the demeanour of the *Vecchierello*. Inside
the Cathedral the crowd used to be of the most pushing
kind, and young priests attempted to scale one's shoulders :
Protestant ladies consumed furtive sandwiches, and here
and there an aged sight-seer was thrown down and severely
trampled upon. In fact, there was a perfect opposition
between the occasion of the ceremony and the way it was
carried out.

It was necessary to leave Rome in time to reach Naples
before the hot season began, and retire into summer quarters.
In those days the crossing of the Pontine Marshes was
considered not a little dangerous. Heavy breakfasts were
eaten to avoid the possible effect of malaria upon an
empty stomach, and the condemned pistols were ostenta-
tiously loaded to terrify the banditti, who were mostly the
servants and hangers-on of the foul little inns.

At Terracina the family found an Englishman temporarily under arrest. This was Mr. St. John, who had just
shot in a duel Count Controfiani. The history of the latter
was not a little curious. He was a red-haired Neapolitan,
plain in appearance and awkward in manner, but touchy
and sensitive in the extreme. His friends and acquaintances
chose to make a butt of him, little fancying how things
were going to end. One day he took leave of them all,
saying he was going to travel for some years. He disguised himself with a wig and lived in the suburbs prac-
tising pistol shooting, foil, and broadsword. When satisfied with his own progress he reappeared suddenly in
society, and was received with a shout of ironical welcome,

Ecco il nostro bel Controfiani. He slapped the face of
the ringleader, and in the duel which followed cut him almost
to pieces. After two or three affairs of this kind his reputation was thoroughly made even in a city where duelling
was so common as at Naples. At last, by some mischance,
he met St. John at Rome and the two became intimate.
They used to practise pistol-shooting together, and popular
report declared that both concealed their skill. At last a
quarrel arose about some "young person," and Controfiani
was compelled to fight at the pleasure of a member of the
royal family of Naples, of whose suite he was. The duel
was to be *à la barrière*, first shot at twenty-five paces, and
leave to advance twelve after standing the fire. The delay
was so great that the seconds began to show signs of impatience, when St. John levelled his pistol and hit his adversary in the flank above the hip. Controfiani had the courage
to plug his wound with the forefinger of his left hand, and
the folly to attempt advancing. Mortally stricken as he
was, the movement shook him ; his hand was unsteady ;
his bullet whizzed past St. John's head, and he was dead
a few hours after.

The family halted a short while at Capua, then a quiet
little country town, equally thoughtless of the honours of
the past and the fierce scenes that awaited it in the future.
Many years afterwards Richard and his friend Blakeley, of
the Gun, offered the Government of King Francis to go
out and rifle the cannon which were to defend them against
Garibaldi and his banditti, but the offer came too late. It
would have been curious had a couple of Englishmen, by
shooting Garibaldi, managed to baffle the plans which
Lord Palmerston had laid with so much astuteness, *finesse*,
and perseverance.

At Naples a house was found upon the Chiaja, and after
trying it for a fortnight, and finding it perfectly satisfactory,
and agreeing to take it for the next season, the family went

over to Sorrento. This, in those days, was one of the most pleasant *villeggiature* in Italy. The three little villages that studded the long tongue of rock and fertile soil were separated from one another by tracts of orchard and olive-ground, instead of being huddled together as they are now. The people preserved all their rural simplicity, baited buffalo-calves in the main square, and had sarcastic songs and sayings to enrage one another. The villas, scattered about the villages, were large, rambling old shells of houses, and Aunt G. could not open her eyes sufficiently wide when she saw what an Italian villa really was.

The bathing was delightful. Breakneck paths led down the rocks to little sheltered bays, with the yellowest of sands and the bluest of waters and old smugglers' caves, which gave the coolest shelter after long dips in the tepid seas. There was an immense variety of excursions. At the root of the tongue arose the mountain of St. Angelo, where the the snow-harvest, lasting during the summer, was one per-petual merry-making. There were boating trips to Ischia and to Procida, to romantic Capri, with its blue grotto and purple figs ; to decayed Salerno, the splendid ruin ; and to the temples of Paestum, more splendid still. Amongst other amusements at Sorrento the boys indulged them-selves with creeping over the Natural Arch, simply because the Italians said " *Ma ; non è possibile, signorini.*" It was a dangerous proceeding, as the crumbling stone was ready at any moment to give way. The shooting was excellent. During the quail season tall poles and immense nets formed *chevaux de frise* on the hill-tops, but the boys went to windward and shot the birds before they were trapped by the nets in the usual ignoble way. In fact, nothing could be more pleasant than Sorrento in its old and uncivilized days.

There was naturally little variety in amusements. The few English families lived in scattered villas. Old Mrs.

Starke, "Queen of Sorrento," as she loved to be called, and author of the Guide Book, was the local lion and she was sketched and caricatured in every possible way, in her old Meg Merrilies cloak. Game to the last, she died on the road travelling. An Englishman named Sparkes threw himself into one of the jagged volcanic ravines that seam the tongue of Sorrento ; but there is hardly a place in Italy, high or low, where some Englishman has not suicided himself. A painter, a Mr. I——, brought over an introduction, and was very tipsy before dinner was half over :— the Marsala wine shipped by Iggulden & Co. would have floored a Polyphemus. The want of excitement out of doors produced a correspondent increase of it inside. The boys were getting too old to be manageable, and Mr. Du Pré taking high grounds on one occasion very nearly received a knife thrust.

Colonel Burton being a man of active mind, with nothing in the world to do, began to be unpleasantly chemical. He bought Parks' Catechism ; filled the house with abominations of all kinds, made a hideous substance that he called soap, and prepared a quantity of abominations that he termed citric acid for which he spoiled thousands of lemons.

When this fit passed over it was succeeded by one of chess and the whole family were bitten by it. Every spare hour, especially in the evening, was given to check, and Richard soon learned to play first one and then two games with his eyes blindfolded. He had the sense to give it up completely, but while the fit lasted his days were full of Philidor, and he dreamed of gambits all night.

Amongst other classical fads the boys determined to imitate Anacreon and Horace. They crowned themselves with myrtle and roses, chose the prettiest part of the garden and caroused upon the best wine they could afford, out of cups, disdaining to use glasses. Colonel Burton aware of this proceeding kindly gave them three bottles of sherry upon the principle that the grocer opens to the young shop boy his drawers of figs and raisins. But they easily guessed the meaning of the kind present and contented themselves with drinking each half a bottle a day as long as it lasted, and then asked for more to the great disgust of the donor. They also diligently practised pistol shooting and delighted in cock-fighting at which the tutor duly attended. Of course the birds were fought without steel, but it was a fine game breed, probably introduced by the Spaniards, and it not a little resembles the Derby game-cock which has spread itself to South America.

The dull life was interrupted by a visit from Aunt G. She brought with her a Miss Morgan who had been governess to the three sisters and still remained their friend. She was a woman of good family in Cornwall but was compelled by loss of fortune to take service.

Miss Morgan was very proud of her nephew, the Rev. Morgan Cowie,* who was Senior Wrangler at Cambridge. He had had the advantage of studying mathematics in Belgium, where in those days the entering examination of a College was almost as severe as the passing examination of an English University.

She was also very well read, and she did not a little good in the house. She was the only one who ever spoke to the children as if they were reasonable beings instead of scolding and thrashing with the usual parental brutality of those days. That unwise saying of the wise man, " Spare the rod and spoil the child " has probably done more harm to the junior world than any other axiom of the same size, and it is only of late years that people have begun to spoil the rod and spare the child. So Miss Morgan could do with the juniors what all the rest of the house completely failed in doing. The only thing that was puzzling about

* The present Dean of Exeter.—ED.

her was that she did not play at chess. Aunt G. waxed
warm in defence of her friend, and assured the scoffers that
"Morgan, with her fine mind, would easily learn to beat
the whole party." "Fine mind!" said the scoffers, "why
we could easily give her a Queen."

Naples after Sorrento was a Paris. In those days it was
an exceedingly pleasant city, famous as it always has been
for some of the best cooks in Italy. The houses were good
and the servants and provisions were moderate. The Court
was exceedingly gay, and Colonel Burton found a cousin
there—old Colonel Burke—who was so intimate with the
King (afterwards known as "old Bomba") as to be admitted
to his bedroom. There was also another Irish cousin, a
certain Mrs. Phayre, who for many years had acted duenna
to the Misses Smith, Penelope and Gertrude. Penelope had
already distinguished herself by mounting wild horses in
the Bois de Boulogne, which ran away with her and shook
her magnificent hair loose. She became a favourite at the
Court of Naples and amused the dull royalties with her
wild Irish tricks. It is said that on one occasion she came
up with a lift instead of the expected *vol-au-vent* or pudding.
She ended by marrying the Prince of Capua greatly to the
delight of the king who found an opportunity of getting
rid of his brother and putting an end to certain scandals.
It was said that the amiable young Prince once shot an old
man whom he found gathering sticks in his grounds, and
that on another occasion he was soundly thrashed by a
party of English grooms whom he had insulted in his cups.
The happy pair had just run away and concluded the
"Triple Alliance" as it was called,* when the Burton family
settled in Naples and found Mrs. Phayre and Gertrude
Smith, the other sister, in an uncomfortable state, banished

---

* That is to say that by way of making sure, the contracting parties
were married in Catholic and Protestant churches and civilly before
the Syndic.—ED.

by the Court and harassed by the police. All their letters were stopped at the Post Office, and they had had no news from home for months. Colonel Burton saw them carefully off to England, where Gertrude, who had a very plain face and a very handsome figure, presently married the rich old Lord Dinorben. Poor Miss Morgan also suffered considerably at Naples from the stoppage of all her letters, she being supposed at least to be a sister of Lady Morgan ("the wild Irish Girl") whose writings at that time had considerably offended the Italian Courts.

Naples contained a Colony presided over by the Hon. Mrs. Temple, Lady Eleanor Butler, Lady Strachan, and Berkeley Craven. The good-natured Minister was the Hon. John Temple, Lord Palmerston's brother, who cared nothing for a man's catechism and condition provided he kept decently clear of scandal. The Secretary of Legation was a Mr. Kennedy who married a Miss Briggs and died early: these were great friends of the family. Society was easy, if somewhat mixed, and the rule of the old king if despotic was not intolerable.

On the other hand, the Consul, Captain Galway, R.N., was anything but pleasant. He was in a perpetual state of "rile" because his Consular Service prevented his being received at Court. Moreover he heard (possibly correctly) that Mrs. Phayre and her two *protégées* were trying to put Colonel Burton in his place. He was also much troubled by his family, and one of them (the parson) especially worried him. This gentleman having neglected to provide for a young Galway whose mamma he had omitted to marry, the maternal parent took up a position outside the church and as the congregation streamed out cried in a loud voice pointing to the Curate: "This is the father of my child!"

Another element of confusion at Naples was poor Charley Saville, Lord Mexborough's son, who had quar-

relled himself out of the Persian Legation. He was a
good hand with his sword, always ready to fight and
equally ready to write.

There was a charming family of the name of Oldham.
The father, when an English officer serving in Sicily, had
married one of the beauties of the island, a woman of high
family and graceful as a Spaniard. The children followed
suit. The girls were beautiful and the two sons were
upwards of six feet in height and as handsome men as
could well be seen. One (in the 2nd Queen's) was tortured to death by the Kaffirs when his cowardly soldiers
ran away and left him wounded. The other after serving
in the 86th in India was killed in the Light Cavalry charge
at Balaklava. The families became great friends and
Richard met them both in India.

Naples was a great place for excursions. To the north
you had Ischia and the Solfatara—a miniature bit of
Vulcanism somewhat like the Geysir ground in Iceland—
where ignoramuses thought themselves in the midst of
untold volcanic grandeur.

Nothing could be more snobbish than the visit to the
Grotto del Cane where a wretched dog was kept for the
purpose of being suffocated half-a-dozen times a day.
There one of the boys determined to act dog and was
pulled out only just in time to prevent his being thoroughly
asphyxiated.

The Baths of Nero are almost equal to an average
Turkish Hammam but nothing more. To the south the
excursions were far more interesting. Beyond Hercu-
laneum, dark and dingy, lay Pompeii, in those days very
different from the tame Crystal Palace affair it is now.
You engaged a cicerone as you best could, for you had
nothing to pay because there were no gates. You picked
up what you liked in the shape of bits of mosaic, and
if you were a swell, a house or a street was opened up in

your honour. And overhanging Pompeii stood Vesuvius, which was considered prime fun. The walk up the ash-cone amongst a lot of serious old men dragged up by *lazzaroni* and old women carried up in baskets upon *lazzaroni*'s backs was funny enough, but the descent was glorious. What took twenty minutes to go up took four minutes to go down. Imagine a dust-bin magnified by 10,000 and tilted up at an angle of 35°. In the descent you plunged to the knees; you could not manage to fall unless you hit a stone and, arrived at the bottom, you could only feel incredulous that it was possible to run at such a rate. The boys caused no end of trouble, and Richard was found privily attempting to climb down the crater because he had heard that an Englishman had been let down in a basket. Many of these ascents were made : on one occasion during an eruption when the lava flowed down to the sea and the Neapolitans with long pincers were snatching pieces out of it to stamp and sell, the boys to the horror of all around jumped on the top of the blackening fire-stream, burnt their boots and vilely abused all those who would not join them.

At Naples more was added to the work of education. Carracioli the celebrated marine painter was engaged to teach oil painting, but he was a funny fellow, and the hours which should have been spent in exhausting palettes passed in pencil caricaturing of every possible friend and acquaintance.

The celebrated Cavalli was the fencing master, and in those days the Neapolitan school which has now almost died out was in its last bloom. It was a thoroughly business-like affair and rejected all the elegancies of the French school, and whenever there was a duel between a Neapolitan and a Frenchman the former was sure to win. The boys worked at it heart and soul and generally managed to give four hours a day to it. Richard determined even at that time to produce a combination between the Neapolitan and French school so as to supplement the defects of the one by the merits of the other. A life of very hard work did not allow him any leisure to carry out his plan, but the man of real perseverance stores up his resolve and waits for any number of years till he sees the time to carry it out. The plan was made in 1836 and was completed in 1880 (41 years).

Colonel Burton spared no pains or expense in educating his children. He had entered the army at a very early age. Volunteers were called for in Ireland, and those who brought a certain number into the field received commissions gratis. The old Madam Burton's tenants' sons volunteered by the dozen. They formed a very fair company to accompany the young master to the wars, and when the young master got his commission they all, with the exception of one or two, levanted, bolted, and deserted. Thus Colonel Burton found himself an officer at seventeen when he ought to have been at school, and recognising the deficiencies of his own education he was determined that his children should complain of nothing of the kind. He was equally determined that none of them should enter the army, the consequence being that both the sons became soldiers and the only daughter married a soldier.

Some evil spirit whispered that the best thing for the two boys would be to send them to Oxford in order that they might rise by literature—an idea which they both thoroughly detested. Moreover, in order to crush their pride, they were told that they should enter "Oxford College" as "Sizars—poor gentlemen who are supported by the alms of others." The feelings of those threatened may be imagined. They determined to enlist or to go before the mast or to turn Turks, Banditti or Pirates rather than undergo such an indignity.

Parthenope was very beautiful, but so true is English

blood that the most memorable part of it was "Pickwick" who happened to make his way there at the time of the sojourn of this family. They read with delight the description of the English home ; they passed their nights as well as their days in devouring the book ; even Ettore Fiera-mosca and the other triumphs of Massimo d'Azeglio were mere outsiders compared with it. But how different the effect of the two books !—Pickwick the good humoured caricature of a boy, "full of liquoring up " and good spirits, and the Disfida di Barletta one of the foundation stones of Italian independence.

At last the house on the Chiaja was given up and the family took another inside the city for a short time. Colonel Burton was getting tired of Naples and thinking of starting northwards. The change was afflicting : the loss of the view of the Bay was a misfortune ; and the only amusement was prospecting the streets where the most extraordinary scenes took place. It was impossible to forget the absurd Englishman as he stood eating a squirting orange, sur-rounded by a string of gutter boys : the dexterity of the pick-pockets too gave scenes as amusing as a theatre. It was related of one of the Coryphæi that he had betted with a friend that he would take the handkerchief of a Britisher, who in turn had betted that no man in Naples could pick his pocket. A pal walked up to the latter as he was promenading the streets, flower in buttonhole, solemnly spat on his cravat and ran away. The principal, with thorough Italian politeness, walked up to the outraged foreigner, drew his pocket-handkerchief and proceeded to remove the offence, exhorting the outraged man to keep the fugitive in sight, and, in far less time than it takes to tell, transferred the handkerchief to his own pocket and set out in pursuit of the thief. The lazzaroni too were a per-petual amusement. The boys learned to eat macaroni like them and so far mastered their dialect that they could exchange chaff by the hour. In 1869 Richard found them all at Monte Video and Buenos Ayres, dressed in *cacciatore* and swearing *M'naccia l'anima tua.* They were impressed with the conviction that he was himself a lazzarone in luck. The shady side of the picture was the cholera ; it caused a fearful amount of destruction, and the newspapers owned to 1300 cases a day, which meant, say 2300. The much-abused King " Bomba " behaved like a gentleman. The people declared that the cholera was poison, and doubtless many made use of the opportunity to get rid of husbands and wives and other inconvenient relations ; but when the mob proceeded to murder the doctors and to gather in the Market Square with drawn knives, declaring that the Government had poisoned the provisions, the King drove himself up in a phaeton and jumped out of it entirely alone ; told the mob to put up their ridiculous weapons and to show him where the poisoned provisions were, and seating himself upon a bench ate as much as his stomach would contain. The *lazzaroni* were not proof against this heroism and *viva'd* and cheered him to his heart's content.

The boys had seen too much of cholera to be afraid of it. They had passed through it in France ; it had followed them to Sienna and Rome, so that at Naples it only excited their curiosity. They persuaded the Italian man-servant to assist them in a grand escapade. He procured them the necessary dress, and when the dead-cart passed through the streets in the stillness of night they went the rounds with it as some of the *croque-morts*. The visits to the pauper houses where the corpses lay in the rooms were anything but pleasant, and less still the final disposal of the bodies. Outside Naples was a long plain pierced with pits like the Silos or underground granaries of Algeria and North Africa. They were lined with stone, and the mouths, closed with one big slab, were just large enough to allow a corpse to squeeze through. Into these flesh-pots were thrown the unfortunate bodies of the poor after being stripped of the rags which served as their winding-sheets. Black and rigid they were shot down the apertures like so much rubbish into the festering heap below, and the decay caused a kind of lambent blue flame about the sides of the pit which lit up a mass of human corruption—a scene worthy to be described by Dante.

The family left Naples in the spring of 1836. The usual mountain of baggage was packed in the enormous boxes of the period, and the Custom House officers never even opened them, relying as they said upon the word of an Englishman that they contained nothing contraband. How different from the " Italia Unita," where even the dressing bag is rummaged to find a few cigars or an ounce of coffee.

In 1881, a distinguished officer, and a gentleman allied to Royalty, wrote as follows :—

" You threw some doubts on the efficiency of the Italian post, and I believe you.

" I do not think I was ever so glad to get home. Malta looks so clean after the filth of Naples. I think Italy, the Italians, their manners, customs and institutions, more damnable every time I see them, and feel sure you will meet with less annoyance during your travels on the Gold Coast than I met with coming through Italy. Trains, crowded, unpunctual ; starvation, filth, incivility, and extortion at every step, and were it not that there is much of interest to see, I doubt if any one would care to visit the country a second time.

" Here is an account of a purchase made to transfer to Rome. A small table was packed in a little case, and firmly nailed down. At the station they refused to let it go in the luggage van unless it was corded, lest it might be opened *en route.* The officials offered to cord it for bakhshish, which was paid, but the cord was not put on.

They cut open his leather bag, and tried to open his portmanteau, but when he called this fact to the notice of the Station Master at Rome, he simply turned on his heel and declined to answer.

"At Naples they opened the little case, because furniture was subject to octroi, and, on leaving, the case was again inspected, lest it might contain a picture, then not allowed to leave the country.

"It is no longer the classical Italy of Landor, nor the mountain Italy of Leigh Hunt, nor the ideal Italy of the Brownings, nor the spiritualized Italy of George Eliot, nor the everyday Italy of Charles Lever. It is a brand new, noisy, vulgar, quarrelsome and contentious Italy. Do not suppose, however, that this is the National Italy, nor the good Society, nor the Government. It is the new self-made little official, the little Jack-in-office with his halo of red tape, who we hope will be licked into shape by his superiors as soon as they have time to attend to it, and before they lose all their good foreign visitors."

The voyage was full of discomforts. Mrs. Burton after a campaign of two or three years had been persuaded to part with her French maid, Eulalie, an old and attached servant, who made their hours bitter and their faces yellow. The steamer of the day was by no means a floating palace, especially the English coasting steamers which infested the Mediterranean. The machinery was noisy and offensive, the cabins were dogholes with a pestiferous atmosphere, and the food consisted of greasy butter, bread which might be called dough, eggs with a perfume, rusty bacon, milkless tea and coffee that might be mistaken for each other, waxy potatoes, graveolent greens *cuites à l'eau*, stickjaw pudding, and cannibal hunches of meat charred without and blue within. The only advantage was that the vessels were manned by English crews, and in those days the British sailor was not a tailor and showed his value when danger was greatest.

They steamed northwards in the good old way, puffing
and panting, pitching and rolling, and in due time made
Marseilles. The town of the Cannebière was far from being
the splendid city that it is now ; but it could always boast
one great advantage—that of being in Provence. Richard
ever had a particular propensity for this bit of Africa in
Europe, and for years his good friend Dr. Steinhäuser and
he had indulged in visions of a country cottage, where they
could pass their days in hammocks, and their nights in bed
and never admit books or papers, pens or ink, letters or
telegrams. This retreat was intended to be a rest for
middle age in order to prepare for senility and second
childhood. But the fair vision passed into the limbo of
things imagined ; it was in fact the vision of two hard-
working and over-worked men.

But, however agreeable Provence was, this change from
Italians to Frenchmen was not pleasant. The subjects of
Louis Philippe, the Citizen King, were rancorous against
Englishmen, and whenever a fellow wanted a row he had
only to cry out :—" These are the miserables who poisoned
Napoleon at St. Helena." This pleasant little scene occurred
on board a coasting steamer between Marseilles and Cette,
when remonstrance was made with the cheating steward
backed by the rascally captain. Cette was beginning to be
notorious for the imitation wines, due to the ingenuity of
M. Guizot, brother of the *austère intrigant*. He could turn
out any wine from the cheapest Marsala to the choicest
Madeiran Bual ; but he did his counterfeiting honestly, as
a little G was always branded on the bottom of the cork.
And Cette gave a good lesson about ordering wine at hotels.
The sensible traveller when in a strange place always calls
for the carte and chooses the lowest priced : he knows by
sad experience, by cramps and acidity of stomach, that the
dearest wines are often worse than the cheapest, and at
best that they are the same with different labels. The

proprietor of the hotel at Cette had charged his *dame de comptoir* with robbing the till. She could not deny it, but she replied with a *tu quoque*, "If I robbed him, I only returned tit-for-tat; he has been robbing the public for the last quarter of a century. Only the other day he bought a *Botte* of *ordinaire* and *escamoté'd* it into sixteen kinds of *vins fins*." The landlord thought it better to drop the *procès*. From Cette the travellers journeyed in hired carriages (as Dobbin and the carriages had been sold at Naples) to Toulouse. The parents periodically fell ill with asthma, and the young ones availed themselves of the opportunity of wandering far and wide over the country. They delighted in these journeys, for though the tutor was there the books were in the boxes. They stayed at Toulouse for a week, and Richard was so charmed with the student life that he asked his father's leave to join them; but Colonel Burton was always determined on the fellowship at Oxford. Richard's own remembrances of Toulouse are finding the mistress of the hotel correcting her teeth with the forks of the *table d'hôte* and being placed opposite the model Englishman of Alexandre Dumas and Eugène Sue.

In due time the family reached Pau—the capital of the Basses-Pyrénées and the old Béarnais. The little town on the Gave de Pau was no summer place : the heats are intense, and all who can, rush off to the Pyrenees which are in sight and distant only forty miles. The family followed suit and went off to Bagnères de Bigorre, where they hired a nice house in the main square. There were few foreigners in that "Spa." It was at that time a thoroughly French watering place, periodically invaded by a mob of Parisians of both sexes, the men dressed in fancy costumes intended to be "truly rural," and capped with Basque bonnets white or red. The women were more wonderful still, especially when on horseback—somehow

PAU IN THE PYRENEES.

or other the Française never dons a riding habit without some solecism. Picnics were the order of the day and they were organised on a large scale, looking more like a squadron of irregular cavalry going out for exercise than a party of pleasure. The boys obtained permission to accompany one of these caravans to the Brêche de Roland, a nick in the mountain-top clearly visible from the plain, supposed to have been cut by the good sword "Joyeuse."

Here they were mightily tempted to accept the offer made to them by a merry party of contrabandists who were smuggling to and fro chocolate, tobacco and aguardiente.

Nothing could be jollier than such a life. They travelled *au clair de la lune*, armed to the teeth ; when they arrived at the hotels the mules were unloaded and turned out to pasture, the guitar—played *à la Figaro*—began to tinkle, and all the young women, like "The Buffalo Girls," came out to dance. Wine and spirits flowed freely, the greatest good humour prevailed, and the festivities were broken only sometimes by "knifing" or "shyuting."

The boys also visited Tarbes, which even in those days was beginning to acquire a reputation for "Le Shport;" it presently became one of the centres of racing and hunting in France, for which the excellent climate and the fine rolling country admirably adapted it. It was no wonder that the young French horse beat the English at the same age: in the Basque Pyrénées a colt two years old is as well-grown as a Newmarket weed at two and a half.

When the great heat was over the family returned to Pau, where they found a good house over the arcade on the Place.

Pau boasts of being the birthplace of Henri IV., Gaston de Foix, and Bernadotte. Strangers go through the usual routine of visiting the castle—called after the Protestant-

Catholic King, Henri IV.—of driving to Ortez, where
Marshal Soult fought unjustifiably the last action of the
Peninsula War, and of driving about the flat moorlike
Landes, which not a little resemble those about Bordeaux.

The society at Pau was an improvement upon that of
Naples. The most interesting person was Captain (R.N.)
Lord William Paget, who was living with his mother-in-law,
(Baroness de Rothenberg), wife and children, and enjoying
himself as usual. Though ever impecunious, he was the best
of boon companions and a man generally loved. But he
could also make himself feared ; and, as the phrase is,
he "would stand no nonsense." He once had a little affair
with a man, and as he was going to the meeting-place he
said to his second, "What is the fellow's pet pursuit ?"
"Well," answered the second, "I don't know—but—let me
see—oh ! ah ! I remember—a capital hand at waltzing."
"Waltzing, eh ?" said Lord William, and in due time hit him
accurately on the hip bone, and spoiled his waltzing for
many a long month. Years and years after when both
were middle aged men, Richard met his son—whom he
remembered straddling across a diminutive donkey—at
Shepheard's Hotel, Cairo—General "Billy" Paget. He also
had entered the Indian Army, and among other things he
had distinguished himself by getting the better in an official
correspondence of General John Jacob, the most obstinate
and rancorous of men. "Billy" had come out to Egypt with
the intention of returning to India, but the Red Sea looked
so swelteringly hot and its shores so disgustingly barren,
that he wrote to Aden to recall his baggage, which had been
sent forward ; then and there retired from the service,
married a charming woman, and gave his old friend a very
excellent dinner in London.

There were also some nice L'Estranges—one of the
daughters a very handsome woman ; some pretty Foxes and
old Captain Sheridan, with two good-looking daughters,

also the Ruxtons, whom Richard afterwards met at the baths
of Lucca. Certain elderly maidens of the name of Shannon
lived in a house almost overhanging the Gave de Pau :
upon this subject O'Connell the " Big Beggarman " produced
a *bon mot*, which is however not fit for print. The town was
then a kind of invalid colony for consumptives, although the
native proverb about its climate is, that it has eight months
winter and four of the inferno. Dr. Diaforus acts upon the
very intelligible system of self-interest : he does not wish
his patients to die upon his hands, and consequently sends
them to die abroad. In the latter days of the last century he
sent his moribunds to Lisbon and to Montpellier, where the
vent de bise is as terrible as a bleak east wind is in Harwich.
Then he packed them off to Pisa, where the tropics and
Norway meet, and to damp, muggy, reeking Madeira, where
patients have lived a quarter of a century with half a
lung, but where their sound companions and nurses suffer
from every description of evils which attend " liver."
Then they found out that the arid heat of Tenerife allowed
invalids to be out even after sunset, and lastly they discovered that the dry, cold air of Colorado and of Iceland,
charged with ozone as it is, offers the best chance of a
complete cure. Richard has proposed to utilize the regions
around the beautiful Dead Sea, about 1300 feet below the
level of the Mediterranean, where oxygen accumulates, and
where, run as hard as you like, you can never be out of
breath. This will be the great consumption hospital of
the future.

At Pau the education went on merrily. Richard was
provided with a French master of mathematics, whose greasy
hair swept the collar of a *redingote* ever buttoned up to the
chin. He was a type of his order : he introduced mathematics everywhere : he was a red republican of the reddest
type, hating wealth and rank : he held that the *bon Dieu*
was not proven, because he could not express Him by

a mathematical formula, and he called his fellow-men *bon Dieusistes.* The boys, now grown to lads, began to seriously prepare for thrashing their tutor, and diligently took lessons in boxing from the Irish groom of a Captain Hutchinson, R.N. Whenever they could escape from study they passed their hours in the barracks, fencing with the soldiers, and delighting every *piou-piou* (recruit) by their powers of consuming the country spirit (white and unadulterated cognac). They also took seriously to smoking, although, as usual with beginners in those days, they suffered in the flesh : in the later generation, you find young children—even girls—who, although their parents have never smoked, can finish off a cigarette without the slightest inconvenience even for the first time. Smoking and drinking led them, as they usually do, into trouble.

What the young ones learned best at Pau was the Béarnais dialect, a charmingly *naïve* mixture of French, Spanish and Provençal, and containing a number of peasant songs exceedingly pretty. The country folk were delighted when addressed in their own lingo, and Richard found that it considerably assisted him in learning Provençal, the language of *Le Gay Saber.* He also found it useful in the most out-of-the-way corners of the world, even at Rio de Janeiro ; nothing goes home to the heart of man so much as to speak to him in his own *patois :* even a Lancashire lad can scarcely resist the language of Tummus and Meary.

At length the wheezy, windy, rainy, foggy, sleety, snowy winter passed away, and the approach of the warm four months warned strangers to betake themselves to the hills. This time the chosen place was Argélès. In those days it was a little village composed mainly of one street, not unlike a mining Arrayal in Brazil, or a negro village on the banks of the Gaboon. But the scenery around it was beautiful. It lay upon a brawling stream, and the contrast

of the horizontal meadow-land with the backing of almost
vertical hills and peaks thoroughly satisfied the eye. There
had been cruel weather in the cold time and a sad accident
had just happened. A discharged soldier had rested at the
village in mid-winter when the snow lay deep and the
wolves were out: the villagers strongly dissuaded him
from trying to reach his father's house in the hills, but he
was armed with his *briquet*, the little curved sword then
carried by the French infantry soldier, and laughed all
caution to scorn. It was towards night-fall ; he had hardly
walked a mile before a pack came down upon him raging
and raving with hunger. He set his back against a tree
and defended himself manfully, killing several wolves and
escaped whilst they were being devoured by their companions ; but he sheathed his sword without taking the
precaution to wipe it, and when he was attacked again it
was frozen to the scabbard. The wolves paid dearly for
their meal, for the enraged villagers organized a battue and
killed about a score of them as an expiatory sacrifice for
the poor soldier.

The two brothers, abetted by their tutor, had fallen into
the detestable practice of keeping their hands in by shooting
swifts and swallows, of which barbarity they were afterwards heartily ashamed. Their first lesson was from the
peasants. On one occasion when they shot a harmless bird
that fell among the reapers, the latter charged them in a
body, and being armed with scythes and sickles, caused a
precipitate retreat. In those days the swallow seemed to
be a kind of holy bird in the Béarnais, somewhat like the
pigeons of Mecca and Venice. One can only remember
that this was the case with the old Assyrians (Aramæans)
who called the swift or devilling, the " Destiny " or foretelling
bird, because it heralded the spring.

There was a small society at Argélès consisting chiefly
of English and Spaniards. The latter were mostly refugees

driven away from home by political changes : none of them
were overburdened with money, and of course all looked for
cheap quarters. They seemed to live chiefly upon chocolate,
which they made in their own way in tiny cups, so thick
and gruelly that sponge cakes stood upright in it, and they
smoked cigarettes with maize-leaf for paper, as only a
Spaniard can. The little cylinder hangs down as if it were
glued to the smoker's lip : he goes on talking and laughing
and then by some curious movement of the muscles, developed in no other race, he raises the weed to the horizontal and
puffs out a cloud of smoke. These exiles passed their spare
time in playing the guitar and singing party songs, being
very much disgusted when asked to indulge the company
with Riego el Cid. There was a marriage at Argélès when
a Scotch maiden of mature age married M. le Maire : an
old French *mousquetaire*, a man of birth and courtly
manners, he was the delight of the young ones, but his
plaisanteries are utterly unfit for record. There was also a
Baron de Meydell, with his wife and her sister, and two
very handsome daughters, the eldest engaged to a rich
young planter in the Isle of Bourbon. The two lads
fell desperately in love with them, and the old father, who
had served in the Hessian brigade in the English army,
only roared with laughter when he saw and heard their
polissonneries : he liked them both and delighted in
nothing more than to see them working upon each other
with foil and sabre. The parting of the lovers was very sad,
and three of them at least shed tears : the eldest girl was
beyond such childishness.

As the mountain fogs began to roll down upon the valley,
Colonel Burton found that his chest required a warmer
climate. This time the family travelled down the Grand
Canal du Midi in a big public barge which resembled a
Dutch Trekschuyt. At first, passing through the locks was
a perpetual excitement, but this soon palled. The Le-

stranges were also on board, and the French part of the company was not particularly pleasant. They were mostly tourists returning home, mixed with a fair proportion of Commis-voyageurs, a class that corresponds with, but does not resemble, our Commercial Travellers. The French species seem to have but two objects in social life ; first to glorify himself, and secondly to glorify Paris : M. Victor Hugo having carried the latter mania to the very verge of madness, and left to his countrymen an example as bad as could be. The peculiarity of the Commis-voyageur in those days was the queer, thin varnish of politeness which he thought it due to himself to assume. He would help himself at break-fast or dinner to the leg, wing and part of the breast, and pass the dish to his neighbour, when it contained only a neck and a drumstick, with a pleased smile and a ready bow, anxiously asking, *Madame, veut-elle de la volaille ?* He was frightfully unprogressive : he wished to let sleeping dogs lie : he hated to move quiet things. It almost gave him an indigestion to speak of railways : he found the diligence and the canal-boat quite fast enough for his purpose ; and in this to a certain extent he represented the Genius of the *Nation.* With the excellent example of the Grand-Canal du Midi before them, the French allowed half a century to pass before they even realized the fact that their rivers give them most admirable opportunities for inland navigation, and that by energy in spending money they could lay out a water line from Marseilles to Paris, and down from Paris to the Mediterranean. In these days of piercing isthmuses they seem hardly to have thought of a Canal that would save the time and expense of running round Spain and Portugal when it would be so easy to cut the neck which connects their country with the Peninsula.

The rest of the journey was as eventless as usual. The family took the steamer at Marseilles, ran down to Leghorn and drove up to Pisa. There they found a house on the south side of the Lung' Arno belonging to a widow of the name of Pini. It was a dull and melancholy place enough, but it had the advantage of a large garden that grew chiefly cabbages. This move was something like a return home ; a number of old acquaintances were met and a few new ones were made. The studies were carried on with unremitting attention. Richard kept up drawing, painting and classics, and it was happy for him that he did ; he thus has been able to make his own drawings and to illustrate his own books. It is only in this way that a correct idea of unfamiliar scenes can be given : travellers who bring home a few scrawls and put them into the hands of a professional illustrator have the pleasure of seeing the illustrated paper style applied to the scenery and people of Central Africa and Central Asia. And even when the drawings are carefully done by the traveller-artist it is hard to persuade the professional to preserve their peculiarities. For instance, a sketch from Hyderabad, the inland capital of Sind, showed a number of straight, mast-like poles, which induced the English artist to write out and ask if there ought not to be yards and sails. In sending a sketch home of a Pilgrim in his proper costume, the portable Korán worn under the left arm narrowly escaped becoming a revolver. On the chocolate-coloured cover of a work on Zanzibar stands a negro in gold, straddling like the Colossus of Rhodes, instead of being propped crane-like upon one leg, supporting himself with his spear, and applying (African fashion) the sole of the other foot to the perpendicular calf.

Music did not get on so well. The brothers and sister had good speaking voices, but they sang with a *voce di gola* —a throaty tone which was terrible to hear. It is only in England that people sing without voices : this may do very well when chirping a comic song or half speaking a ballad, but in nothing higher. Richard had begun singing with all his might at Pau in the Pyrenees, and he kept it up at

Pisa, where Signor Romani, Mario's old master, rather
encouraged him instead of peremptorily bidding him hold
his tongue. He wasted time and money, and presently
found out his mistake and threw up music altogether. At
stray times he took up the flageolet and other simple instruments, as though he had a kind of instinctive feeling how
useful music would be to him in later life, and he never
ceased to regret that he had not practised sufficiently to be
able to write down an aria at hearing. Had he been able to
do so he might have collected over 2000 motives from
Europe, Asia, Africa and America, and have produced a
musical note-book which would have been useful to a
Boito or a Verdi.

The youths had now put away childish things, that is
to say they no longer broke the windows across the river
with slings, or engaged in free fights with their coevals.
But the climate of Italy tends to precocity so, as the Vicar
of Wakefield has it, "they cocked their hats and they loved
the ladies," and their poor father was once appalled by
strange heads being put out of windows in an unaccustomed
street with the words, *Oh! S'or Riccardo! Oh! S'or
Odoardo!* Madame Pini, the landlady, had three children.
Sandro, the son, was a tall gawky youth, who wore a
cacciatora, or Italian shooting jacket of cotton leather, not
unlike the English made loose with the tails cut off. The
two daughters were extremely handsome girls in very
different styles. Signorina Caterina, the elder, was tall, slim
and dark with the palest possible complexion and regular
features. Signorina Antonia, the younger, could not boast
of the same classical lines, but the light brown hair and the
pink and white complexion made one forgive and forget
every irregularity. Consequently Richard fell in love with
the elder and Edward with the younger. Proposals of
marriage were made and accepted. The girls had heard
that in her younger days Mamma owned half-a-dozen strings

to her bow, and they were perfectly ready to follow parental
example. But a serious obstacle occurred from the difficulty
of getting the ceremony performed. As in England there
was a popular, if mistaken idea, that a man might put a
rope round his wife's neck, take her to the market and
sell her like a quadruped, so there was, and perhaps there is
still, in Italy, a legend that any affianced couple standing up
together in front of the congregation at the time of the
Elevation during Mass, and declaring themselves man and
wife, are very much married. Many inquiries were made
about the procedure, and at one time it was seriously
intended ; but the result of questioning was "that *promessi
sposi* so acting are at once imprisoned and punished by
being kept in separate cells." It became evident therefore
that the game was not worth the candle. This is like a
Scotch marriage, with a difference. The Italian is binding
in religion, the Scotch in law ; the former is legally invalid ;
and the latter has no religious sanction.

The winter at Pisa ended very badly. The hard studies
of the classics during the day occasionally concluded with
a carousal at night. On one hapless occasion a bottle òf
Jamaica rum happened to fall into the wrong hands. The
revellers rose at midnight, boiled water, procured sugar and
lemons and sat down to a streaming soup-tureen full of punch.
Possibly it was followed by a second, but the result was
that the youngsters sallied out into the streets determined
upon what is called a spree. Knockers did not exist, nor did
Charleys confine themselves to their sentry boxes, and it was
vain to ring the bells when every one was sound asleep.
Evidently the choice of amusements was limited, and mostly
confined to hustling inoffensive passers-by. But as one of
those feats had been performed and cries for assistance had
been raised, up came the watch at the double, and the " Mo-
hawks " had nothing to do but to make tracks. Richard's
legs were the longest and he escaped. Edward was seized

and ignobly led off, despite his fists and heels, to the local *violon* or guard-house. One may imagine Colonel Burton's disgust next morning when he was courteously informed by the prison authorities that a *giovanotto* bearing his name had been lodged during the night at the public expense. The father went off in a state of the stoniest severity to the guard-house, and found the graceless one treating his companions in misfortune, thieves and ruffians of every kind, to the contents of a pocket flask with which he had provided himself in case of need.

This was the last straw. Colonel Burton determined to transfer his headquarters to the Baths of Lucca and then to prepare for breaking up his family: the adieux of Caterina and Antonia were heart-rending and it was agreed to correspond every week. The journey occupied but a short time and a house was soon found in the upper village. In those days the Lucchese Baths were the only place in Italy that could boast of a tolerably cool summer climate, and a few of the comforts of life. Sorrento, Montenero (near Leghorn), and the hills about Rome were frequented by very few ; they came under the category of "cheap and nasty." Hence the Bagni collected what was considered to be the most distinguished society: it had its parson from Pisa even in the days before the travelling Continental clergyman was known, and this one migrated every year to the hills like the flight of swallows or the beggars who desert the hot plains and the stifling climate of the lowlands. There was generally at least one English doctor who practised by the kindly tolerance of the *then* Italian Govern-ment. The Duke of Lucca at times attended the balls. He was married, but his gallant presence and knightly manner committed terrible ravages in the hearts of susceptible English maidens and matrons. The Queen in ordinary was a Mrs. Colonel Stisted, as she called herself—who as "Miss Clotilda Clotworthy Crawley" was so rudely treated by the

"Wild Irish Girl," Lady Morgan. Richard also settled an old score with her in "Sind ; or, the Unhappy Valley."

"She indeed had left her mark in literature, not by her maudlin volume, 'The By-ways of Italy,' but by her abuse of her fellow-creatures. She was 'the sea-goddess, with tin ringlets and venerable limbs,' of the irrepressible Mrs. Trollope. She also gave Lever one of the characters which he etched in with his most corrosive acid."

In one season the baths collected Lady Blessington, Count d'Orsay, the charming Lady Walpole, Mrs. Elizabeth Barrett-Browning, the poetess, whose tight sacque of black silk gave the youngsters a series of caricatures. There, too, was old Lady Osborne, full of Greek and Latin, who married her daughter to Captain Bernal, afterwards Bernal Osborne. Amongst the number was Mrs. Young, whose daughter became Madame Manteucci, wife of the celebrated scientist and electrician of Tuscany : she managed, curious to say, to hold her own in her new position. Finally, Richard remembers Miss Gabriell, daughter of old General Gabriell, commonly called the "Archangel Gabriell." She afterwards made a noise in the musical world as "Virginia Gabriell," composed beautiful ballads, published many pieces, married, and died in St. George's Hospital (August 7, 1877), from the effects of a carriage accident. She showed her *savoir faire* at the earliest age. At a ball given to the Prince all appeared in their finest dresses and richest jewellery : Miss Virginia was in white, with a single necklace of pink coral. They danced till daylight, and when the sun rose Miss Artful was like a rose amongst the faded dahlias and sunflowers. Another remarkable young person was Miss Helen Croly, a girl of the order "dashing," whose hair was the brightest auburn, and complexion the purest white and red. Her father was the Rev. George Croly, D.D. (afterwards Rector of St. Stephen's, Walbrook), an Irish "Fraserian," whose Jewish novel 'Salathiel' made a small noise in the world. But either he or his wife disliked children, so Miss Helen had been turned over to the charge of aunts. These were two elderly maiden ladies whose "agnosticism" was of the severest description. "Sister, what is that noise?" "The howling of hymns, sister." "The beastly creatures!" was the reply when the faint and distant harmony across hill and dale reached her most irreverent ears. Richard met these two "young persons" in later life, and it is enough to say that all three had terribly changed.

Amongst the remarkable people here were the Desanges family, who had a phenomenon in the house. A voice seemed to come out of it of the very richest volume, and every one thought it was a woman's. It really belonged to Master Louis, who afterwards made for himself so great a name for battle scenes—the Desanges' Crimean Gallery —and also for portraits. The voice did not recover itself thoroughly after breaking, but sufficient remained for admirable comic songs, and no man who ever heard *Le Lor Maire* and *Vilikins et sa Dinah,* came away without aching sides. There was also a learned widow of the name of Graves, whose husband had been a connection of Colonel Burton's ; and her daughter, who prided herself upon the breadth of her forehead and general intellectuality, ended by marrying the celebrated historian Von Ranke. Intellectual Englishwomen used to expect a kind of literary paradise when they espoused German professors. They were to share their labours, assist in their discoveries, and generally to wear a kind of reflected halo or gloria as the moon receives its light from the sun. But they were perfectly shocked when they were ordered to the kitchen, and addressed perhaps with *Donnerwetter Sacrament,* if the dinner was not properly cooked.

There was a very nice fellow of the name of Ward, who had just married a Miss Stisted, one of the nieces of the Queen of the Baths, with whom all at the baths were in love.

The little colonies, like the Baths of Lucca, began to decline about 1850 and came to their nadir about 1870. The gambling in stocks and shares lost England an immense sum of money, and the mishaps were most felt by that well-to-do part of the public that has a fixed income, and no chance of increasing it. The squandering of some £500,000,000 sterling rendered England too expensive for a large class, and presently drove it abroad; and it gained numbers in 1881, when the Irish Land Act, soon to be followed by a corresponding English Land Bill, exiled a multitude of landowners. So the small English centres, which had dwindled to the lowest expression, gradually grew and grew and became stronger than they had ever been.

It was evident that the Burton family was ripe for a break up. Colonel Burton was an Irishman, perfectly happy as long as he was the only man in the house, but the presence of younger men irritated him. His temper became permanently soured. He could no longer use the rod, but he could make himself very unpleasant with his tongue. " *Senti come me li rimangia quei poveri ragazzi !* " " Hear how he's chawing up those poor boys ! " said the old Pisan ladiesmaid. And the youths were not pleasant inmates of a household. They were in the *Sturm und Drang* of the teens. They had thoroughly mastered their tutor ; they threw their books out of window if he attempted to give a lesson in Greek or Latin, and they applied themselves with ardour to Pigault le Brun, Paul de Kock, the *Promessi Sposi*, and the *Fiametta* of Aristo. Instead of taking country walks they *jodelled* all about the hill-sides under the directions of a Swiss scamp. They shot pistols in every direction, and whenever a stray fencing-master passed they persuaded him to give them a few hours of "point." They made experiments of everything imaginable, including swallowing and smoking opium.

The break-up which took place about the middle of the

summer was comparatively tame. Italians marvelled at the Spartan nature of the British mother, who, after the habits of fifteen years, can so easily part with her children at the cost of a lachrymose last embrace, and watering her prandial beefsteak with tears. Amongst Italian families nothing is more common than for all the brothers and sisters to swear that they will not marry if they are to be separated from one another; and even now, in these subversive and pro-gressive days, what a curious contrast is the Italian and the English household. Let me sketch one of the latter, a family belonging to the old nobility, once lords of the land, and now simple proprietors of a poor estate. In a large garden, and a larger orchard of vines and olives, stands a solid antique house, as roomy as a barrack, but without the slightest pretension of comfort or luxury.

The old countess, a widow, has the whole of her progeny around her, two or three stalwart sons married, and the others partially so, and a daughter who has not yet found a a husband.

The servants are aged family retainers ; they consider themselves part and parcel of the household, they are on the most familiar terms with the family, although they would resent with the direst indignation the slightest liberty on the part of outsiders. Their day is one of extreme simplicity, and some might even deem it mono-tonous. Each individual leaves his bed at the hour he or she pleases, and finds coffee, milk, and small rolls in the dining-room.

Smoking and dawdling pass the hours until about mid-day, when a *dejeuner à la fourchette*, or rather a small dinner, leads very naturally up to a siesta. In the after-noon there is a little walking or driving, and even shooting in the case of the most energetic. There is a supper after nightfall, and, after that, dominoes or cards, or music, or conversazione, keep them awake for half the night. The

even tenor of their way is broken only by a festival or a
ball in the nearest town, or some pseudo-scientific congress
in a city not wholly out of reach ; and so things go on from
year to year, and all are happy, because they look to
nothing else.

The journey began in the summer of 1840. Mrs. Burton
and her daughter were left at the Baths of Lucca, and
Colonel Burton with Mr. Du Pré and the two sons set out
for Switzerland. They again travelled *Vetturino*, and the
lads cast longing eyes at the country which they were
destined not to see again for ten years. How melancholy
they felt when on their way to the chill and dolorous
North. At Schintznach, Richard was left in charge of
Mr. Du Pré, while the father and the younger son set
out for England direct. These Hapsburgian baths in the
Aargau had been chosen because the abominable sulphur
water, as odorous as that of Harrowgate, was held as
sovereign in skin complaints, and Richard was suffering
from exanthemata—an eruption brought on by a sudden
check of perspiration. These trifles are very hard to cure,
and they often embitter a man's life. The village consisted of a single establishment, in which all nationalities
met : amongst them was an unfortunate Frenchman, who
had been attacked at Calcutta with what appeared to be
a leprous taint. He had tried half-a-dozen places to no
purpose, and he had determined to blow his brains out
if Schintznach failed him. The only advantage of the
place was its being within easy distance of Schaffhausen
and the Falls of the Rhine.

CHAPTER II.

OXFORD AND INDIA.

Return to England—The brothers separated—Oxford—Effects of a foreign education — Boyish pranks — Fencing — College life and amusements—Newman and Pusey—Arabic—London again—Oxford companions—Study—A family meeting—The Continent once more —The Rhine—Wiesbaden—Students' duels—Back in Oxford—An escapade—Richard is sent down—Obtains a commission in the H.E.I.C.'s service—Sails for India—Life on board the *John Knox* —Bombay life—The Services—A Military day—Baroda—Sport— Joining the regiment — Sepoys — Indian politics — Passing in Hindustani—The voyage down—Gujerati—Transferred to Sind— Karáchi—Napier and Outram—Freemasonry—Joins Captain Walter Scott—Goa—Return to Sind—New studies—Weakened sight— Passed over for Promotion—Natural disgust—Return to England by long sea route—Studying fencing—Awarded the *Brevet de Pointe*— Publishes system of bayonet exercise—Official wrath—A grateful country—How to accept a slight—Sir John Holker's sixpence— Negotiations with the Royal Geographical Society.

WHEN the six weeks' cure was over, Richard was hurried by his guardian across France and Southern England to the rendezvous. The grandmother and the two aunts finding Great Cumberland Street too hot, had taken country quarters at Hampstead. Grandmamma Baker received the lads with something like disappointment. She would have been better contented had they been six feet high, bony as Highland cattle, with freckled faces and cheek-bones like horns. Miss Georgina Baker embraced and kissed her nephews with effusion: she had not been long parted from them. Mrs. Burton, the other aunt, had never seen them for ten years and of course could not recognise them. They found two very nice little girl cousins who assisted them to pass the time, but the old dislike to their

surroundings returned with redoubled violence. Everything
appeared to them so small, so mean and so ugly : the
faces of the women were the only exception to the general
rule of hideousness. The houses were so unlike houses and
so like Nuremberg toys magnified, and the little bits of
garden were mere slices, as if they had been sold by the
inch. The outsides looked so prim, so priggish, so utterly
inartistic, and the interiors were cut up into such wretched
little rooms, more like ships' cabins than what were called
stands in Italy. The drawing-rooms were crowded with
miserable little tables that made it dangerous to pass from
one side to the other, and these tables were heaped with
nick-nacks that served for neither use nor show. Lastly
there was a desperate neatness and cleanness about everything that made the lads remember the old story of the
Stoic who spat in the face of the house-master because it
was the most untidy place he could find.

Then came a second parting. Edward was to be placed
under the charge of the Rev. Mr. Havergal, Rector of some
country parish. Later on he wrote to say that Richard
must not correspond with his brother, as he had turned his
name into a peculiar form of ridicule. He was musical and
delighted in organ playing, but Edward seemed to consider
the whole affair a bore, and was only too happy when he
could escape from the harmonious parsonage. In the meantime Richard had been tried and found wanting. One of
Colonel Burton's sisters, Mrs. General d'Aguilar, as she
called herself, had returned from India, after an uninter-
rupted residence of a score of years, with a large supply of
children of both sexes. She had settled herself temporarily
at Cambridge to superintend the education of her eldest
son, John Burton d'Aguilar, who was intended for the Church
and who afterwards became a Chaplain on the Bengal
Establishment. Amongst her many acquaintances was a
certain Professor Scholefield, a well-known Grecian. Colonel

Burton had rather suspected that very little had been done
in the way of classical study during the last two years. The
Professor put Richard through his paces in Virgil and
Horace, and found him lamentably deficient: he did not
even know who Iris was! Worse still, it was found out that
the said youth who spoke French and Italian like a native
and had a considerable smattering of Béarnais, Spanish and
Provençal barely knew the Lord's Prayer and broke down
in the Apostles' Creed—a terrible revelation.

As it was long vacation at Oxford and Richard could not
take rooms at once in Trinity College, where his name had
been put down, it was necessary to place him somewhere
out of mischief. At the intervention of a friend, a certain
Dr. Greenhill agreed to lodge and coach him until the
opening of term. The said Doctor had just married a relation of Dr. Arnold of Rugby, and he had taken his bride to
Paris in order to show her the world, and to indulge himself
in a little dissecting. Meanwhile, Richard was placed
pro tem. with another medical man, Dr. Ogle, in whose house
he enjoyed himself greatly. The father was a genial man
and he had nice sons and pretty daughters. As soon as
Dr. Greenhill returned to his house in High Street, Oxford,
however, Richard was taken up there by his father and
consigned to his new tutor. Mr. Du Pré vanished and was
never seen again.

The first sight of Oxford struck Richard with a sense
of appal. " O Domus antiqua et religiosa," cried Queen
Elizabeth in 1564, standing opposite Pembroke College,
which changed its style in 1875. He could not imagine
how such fine, massive and picturesque old buildings as
the Colleges could be mixed up with the mean little buildings that clustered round them, looking as if they were
built of cardboard. In after days he remembered the
feeling when looking at the Temple of the Sun in Palmyra,
surrounded by Arab huts, like swallows' nests perched

upon a palace wall. And everything except the Colleges
looked so mean. The good old Mitre was, if not the only,
at least the principal inn of the place, and it had the
outward and visible presence of an ancient hostelry. The
River with the classical name of Isis was a mere moat,
and its affluent the Cherwell was a ditch. The country
around, especially just after Switzerland, looked flat and
monotonous in the extreme. The skies were a brown-grey,
and to an Italian nose the smell of the coal smoke was a
perpetual abomination. Queer beings walked the streets
dressed in aprons that hung behind from their shoulders,
and caps consisting of a square, like that of a Lancer's
helmet planted upon a semi-oval to contain the head.
These queer creatures were carefully shaven, except perhaps a diminutive mutton cutlet on each side of their
faces, and the more serious sort were invariably dressed
in vestibus nigris aut subfuscis. Moreover an indescrib-
able appearance of donnishness, or incipient donnishness
pervaded the whole lot: the juniors looked like school
boys who aspired to be schoolmasters, and the seniors as
if their aspirations had been realized.

At last term opened, and Richard transferred himself from
Dr. Greenhill to Trinity College,* and in the Michaelmas
term of 1840 he went into residence. He asked after the
famous Grove of Trinity, where Charles I. used to walk
when tired of Christ Church Meadows, and which the wits

---

* Here his University career began, and readers must be prepared
not to hear the recital of a college course of the goody-goody boy of
yesterday, nor yet that of the precocious and vicious youth of to-day.
It is that of a lad of the old school, full of animal spirits and manly
notions, a lively sense of fun, reckless of the consequences of playing
tricks, but without a vestige of vice in the lower and meaner forms—
a lad in short who wanted to be a gentleman and man of the world
in his teens, and who from his foreign travel had seen more of life
than most boys brought up with the silver spoon at home. I give
his account as nearly as possible in his own words, as I have copied
it from his private notes and reminiscences.—I. B.

called Daphne. It had long been felled and the ground was covered with buildings. His quarters were a pair of dog-holes, called rooms, overlooking the garden of the Master of Balliol. His reception in College was not pleasant. He had grown an incipient moustache, which all the advice of Drs. Ogle and Greenhill failed to make him remove, and he declined to be a shaveling until formal orders were issued by the authorities of the College. He had already formed strong ideas upon the " shaven age of England," as the period when, with some brilliant exceptions—as Marlborough, Wellington, and Nelson—her history was at the meanest. As he passed through the gate of the College, a couple of brother undergraduates met him, and one of them laughed in his face. Accustomed to Continental decorum, he handed him his card, and at once called him out. But the College lad, called by courtesy an Oxford " man," had possibly read of duels, but had probably never touched a weapon—sword or pistol— and his astonishment at the invitation knew no bounds. Explanations succeeded, and Richard went his way sadly —he thought that he had fallen amongst *épiciers*. The College porter had kindly warned him against tricks played by the older hands upon " fresh young gentlemen," and strongly advised him to " sport his oak "—in other words, to bar and lock his outer door. With dignity deeply hurt, Richard left the entrance wide open, and thrust a poker into the fire, determined to give all intruders the warmest possible reception. This was part and parcel of that unhappy education abroad. The English public school-boy learns first to " take," and then to " give." He begins by being tossed in a blanket, and ends by tossing others. Those were days when practical jokes were in full force. Happily they are now extinct. Every greenhorn, coming to college or joining a regiment was liable to the roughest possible treatment, and it was only by submitting with the utmost good humour that he won the affection of his comrades, and was looked upon as a gentleman. But the practice also had its darker phase. It ruined many a prospect, and it lost many a life. The most amusing specimen that Richard ever saw was that of a charming youngster who died soon after joining his Sepoy Regiment. The oldsters had tried to drink him under the table at mess, and had notably failed. About midnight, when he was enjoying his first sleep, he suddenly awoke, and found a ring of spectral figures dancing round between his bed and the tent-walls. After a minute's reflection he jumped up, seized a sheet, and joined the dancers, saying, "If this is the fashion, I suppose I must do it also." The jokers baffled a second time, could do nothing but knock him down and run away.

The example of the "larky" Marquis of Waterford seemed to authorise all kinds of fantastic tricks. The legend was still fresh that he had painted the door of the Dean of Christ Church red, because this formidable dignitary had objected to his wearing "pink" in the "High." Another and far less excusable prank, was his sending all the accoucheurs in the town to the house of a middle-aged maiden lady, whose father—a Don—had offended him. In the Colleges men did not fly at such high game, but they cruelly worried everything in the shape of a freshman. One unfortunate youth—a fellow who had brought with him a dozen of home-made wine, elder or cowslip—was made shockingly "tight" by brandy being mixed with his port, and was put to bed with all his bottles disposed on different parts of his person. Another, of æsthetic tastes, prided himself upon his china, and found it next morning all shivered in pieces about his bed. A third, with carrotty whiskers, had them daubed with mustard also while in a state of insensibility, and next morning had to allow them to fall beneath the barber's hands. Richard caused himself

to be let down by a rope into the garden of the Master of
Balliol, where he plucked up some of the choicest flowers,
by the roots, and planted in their stead great, staring mari-
golds : — the study of the old gentleman's countenance
when he saw them the next morning was a joy for ever.
Another prank was to shoot with an air-cane—an article
strictly forbidden in College—at a brand-new watering-
pot, upon which the venerable Master greatly prided
himself ; and the way in which the water spirted over his
reverend gaiters afforded an ineffable delight to the knot
of mischievous undergraduates who were prospecting him
from behind. Richard, however, had always considerable
respect for the sturdy common sense of old Dr. Jenkins,
and made a kind of *amende* to him in "Vikram and the
Vampire," where he is the only Pandit who objected to the
Tiger being resurrectioned. But the real use of the air-
cane was to shoot the unhappy rooks over the heads of the
dons as they played at bowls. The grave and reverend
signors would take up the body and gravely debate what
had caused the sudden death, when a warm stream of blood
trickling into their shirts explained it only too clearly.
No undergraduate in College could safely read his classics
out loud after 10 P.M., or his "oak" was broken with dumb
bells, and the dirty oil-lamp that half-lit the stairs was
thrown over him and his books. Richard made amends
to a certain extent, for his mischief, by putting his fellow-
collegians to bed, and he has often said that his Welsh
men-friends were those who gave him the most trouble.

The Oxford day, considered with relation to the acquisition of knowledge, was a farce pure and simple. It began
in the morning with Chapel, during which time most men
got up their Logic. They then breakfasted, either in their
rooms or in large parties, where they consumed an immense
quantity of ham, bacon, eggs, mutton-chops, and indigestible muffins, and hereupon attended a couple of lectures—

time completely thrown away. They were now free
for the day, and every man passed his time as he best
pleased. Richard could not afford to keep horses, and
always hated the idea of riding hired hacks: his only
amusements, therefore, were walking, rowing, and the
School of Arms. The walks, somehow or other, always
ended at Bagley Wood, where a pretty gypsy girl, Selina,
dressed in silks and satins, sat in state to receive
the shillings and the homage of the undergraduates. He
worked hard under a coach at sculling and rowing;
he was one of the oars in the College. Torpid and he
and a friend challenged the river in a pair-oar, but, un‥
fortunately, both were rusticated before the race came
off. Richard's friend in misfortune belonged to a distinguished ecclesiastical family. Returning from Australia, he landed at Mauritius without a farthing: most
strangers under the circumstances would have gone to the
Governor, told their names, and obtained a passage to
England. But the man in question had far too strong an
individuality to take so common-place a step. He wrote
home to his family for money, and meanwhile took off his
coat, tucked up his sleeves, and worked like a coolie on the
wharf. When the cheque for his passage was sent, he
invited his brother-coolies to a spread of turtle, cham-
pagne, and all the luxuries of the season, at the swell hotel
of the place, and left amid the blessings of Shem, and the
curses of Japhet. Another of Richard's college companions
—the son of a bishop by the bye—made a cavalry regiment
too hot to hold him, and took his passage to the Cape of
Good Hope in an emigrant ship. On the third day he
brought out a portable roulette-table, which the Captain
sternly ordered off the deck. But the ship was a slow
sailer; she fell in with calms about the Line, and official
rigour was relaxed. First one began to play, and then
another, until the ship became a perfect "Hell." After a

hundred narrow escapes, and all manner of risks by fire and water, and the fists and clubs of enraged losers, the distinguished youth landed at Cape Town with about £5000 in his pocket.

The great solace of Richard's life was the fencing room. When he first entered Oxford the only *Salle d'armes* was kept by Angelo, the grandson of the gallant Italian mentioned by Edgeworth, but who knew about as much of fencing as a French collegian after six months' practice. He was a priggish old person, too, celebrated for walking up to his pupils and for whispering stagily after a salute with the foil :—" This, sir, is not so much a School of Arms as a School of Politeness." Presently a rival appeared in the person of Archibald Maclaren, who soon managed to make his mark : he established an excellent saloon, and he gradually superseded all the wretched gymnastic yards which lay some half-a-mile out of the city. He was determined to make his way. He went over to Paris, where he could work with the best masters, published his Systems of Fencing and Gymnastics, and he actually wrote a little book of poetry, which he called, " Songs of the Sword." Richard and he became great friends. The only question that ever arose between them was touching the advisability or non-advisability of eating sweet buns and drinking strong ale at the same time.

At the fencing rooms Richard made an acquaintance which afterwards ripened into friendship with poor Alfred Bate Richards. He was upwards of six feet high, broad in proportion and very muscular. Richard found it unadvisable to box with him, but could easily master him with foil and broadsword. He was one of the first who would take the trouble to learn. Mostly Englishmen who go to a fencing school clamour after six weeks' lessons to be allowed to fence loose, and very loose fencing it is and is always fated to be. In the same way almost before they can fix their colours they want to paint *tableaux de genre*, and to play *bravura* pieces when they barely know their scales. On the Continent men work for months and even years before they think themselves even within sight of their journey's end. Richard and A. B. Richards often met in after life and became intimates. The erratic career of the latter is well known, and he died at a comparatively early age editor of the *Morning Advertiser*; he had raised the tone of the Licensed Victuallers' organ to such a position in the rank of journalism that even Lord Beaconsfield congratulated him upon it. Richards was furious to see the neglect of his old fellow-collegian; and he always stood up bravely for him both with word and pen.

The hour for "Hall," that is to say for the College dinner, was 5 P.M., and the scene was calculated to astonish a youngster brought up on the Continent. The only respectable part of the scene was the place itself, not a bad imitation of some old convent refectory. The details were mean in the extreme and made Richard long for the commonest *table d'hôte*. Along the bottom of the hall raised upon a dwarf dais ran the high table intended for the use of Fellows and Fellow Commoners: the other tables ran along the sides. Wine was forbidden, malt liquor being the only drink, and the food certainly suited the heavy strong beer and ale brewed in the College. It consisted chiefly of hunches of meat cooked after the Homeric or Central African fashion and very filling at the price. The vegetables were as usual plain boiled without the slightest aid to digestion: in fact the stomach had to do all its own hard labour, whereas a good French or Italian cook does half the work for it in his saucepans. This cannibal meal was succeeded by stodgy pudding and concluded with some form of cheese, Cheshire or Double Gloucester, pain-

fully suggestive of beeswax. And this was called dinner!*
Very soon Richard's foreign stomach began to revolt at
such treatment, but he soon found out a place in the town,
where, when he could escape Hall, he could make something of a meal.

The *morale* of the scene offended all his prepossessions.
The " Fellow Commoners " were simply men who by paying
double what the Commoners paid secured double privileges.
This distinction of castes is something odious, except in the
case of a man of a certain age who would not like to be
placed in the society of lads. But worse still was the
" Gold Tuft " who walked the streets with a silk gown and
a gorgeous tassel on his College cap : these were " noblemen," the offensive English equivalent for men of title.
Generosus nascitur, nobilis fit. The grandfathers of these
noblemen may have been pitmen or grocers, but the
simple fact of having titles entitled them to most absurd
distinctions. For instance, with a smattering of letters
sufficient to enable a Commoner to sqeeze through an
ordinary examination, Gold Tuft took a first class, and
it was even asserted that many took their degrees by
merely sending up their books. They were allowed to
live in London as much as they liked and to condescend
to College at the rare times they pleased. Some Heads of
Houses would not stoop to this degradation, especially
Dean Gaisford, of Christ Church, who compelled Lord
W—— to leave it and betake himself to Trinity ; but the
place, with notable exceptions, was a hot-bed of toadyism
and flunkeyism. When Mr., now Sir Robert Peel, first
appeared in the High Street, man, woman and child stood to
look at him, because he was the son of the Prime Minister.

After dinner it was the custom to go to wine. These
desserts were another abomination. The table was spread

* Yet the college cooks were great swells. They were paid as much
as an average clergyman, and put most of their sons into the Church.

with a vast variety of fruits and sweetmeats, supplied at the very highest prices, and often on tick, by the Oxford tradesmen—model sharks.   Some men got their wines from London ; others bought them in the town.   Claret was then hardly known, and Port, Sherry and Madeira, all of the "strong military-ditto" type, were the only drinks. These "wines" were given in turn by the undergraduates, and the meal upon meal would have injured the digestion of a young ostrich.   At last about this time some unknown fellow, whose name deserves to be immortalized, drew out a cigar and insisted upon smoking it, despite the disgust and uproar that the novelty created.   However, the fashion made its way and the effects were admirable.   The cigar and afterwards the pipe soon abolished the cloying dessert, and reduced the consumption of the loaded wines to a minimum.

But the English have been very peculiar about smoking. In the days of Queen Anne it was so universal that jury-men who could not agree were locked up without meat, drink or *tobacco*.   During the Continental wars it became "un-English" to smoke, and consequently men and even women took snuff, and for years it was considered as disgraceful to smoke a cigar out of doors as to have one's boots blacked, or to eat an orange at Hyde Park Corner. "Good Gracious! You don't mean to say that you smoke in the streets?" said an East Indian Director in after years when he met Richard in Pall Mall with a cigar in his mouth. Admiral Henry Murray, too, vainly endeavoured to break through the prohibition by leading a little squad of smoking friends through Kensington Gardens.   Polite ladies turned away their faces, and unpolite ladies muttered something about "snobs."   At last the Duke of Argyll spread his plaid under a tree in Hyde Park, lighted a cutty pipe and beckoned his friends to join him.   Within a month every one in London had a cigar in his mouth.   A pretty lesson to inculcate respect for popular prejudice.

After the dessert was finished not a few men called for cognac, whiskey and gin, and made merry for the rest of the evening. But what else was there for them to do? Unlike a foreign university the theatre was discouraged. It was the meanest possible little house ; decent actors were ashamed to show themselves in it, and an actress of the calibre of Mrs. Nesbitt appeared only once in four years. Opera, of course, there was none, and if there had been not one in a thousand would have understood the language and not one in a hundred would have appreciated the music. Occasionally there was a concert given by some wandering artists with the special permission of the College authorities, and a dreary two hours' work it was. Balls were unknown, whereby the marriageable demoiselles of Oxford lost many an uncommonly good chance. A mesmeric lecturer occasionally came down and caused some fun. He called for subjects, and amongst the half-dozen that presented themselves was one young gentleman who had far more sense of humour than discretion. When thrown into a deep slumber he arose with his eyes apparently fast closed, and passing into the circle of astonished spectators began to distribute kisses right and left. Some of these salutations fell upon the sacred cheeks of the daughters of Heads of Houses and the tableau may be imagined.

This dull monotonous life was varied in Richard's case by an occasional dinner with families whose acquaintance he had made. At Dr. Greenhill's he once met at dinner Dr. (now Cardinal) Newman and Dr. Arnold. He expected great things from their conversation, but it was mostly confined to discussing the size of the Apostles in the Cathedral of St. Peter at Rome, and both these eminent men showed a very dim recollection of the subject. Richard took a great fancy for Dr. Newman, and used to listen to his sermons when he would never give half an hour to any other preacher. The great divine was then Vicar of

St. Mary's, and used to preach there, and at times the University Sermon. There was a stamp and seal upon him—a solemn music and sweetness in his tone and manner which made him singularly attractive. Yet there was no change of inflexion in his voice : action he had none ; his sermons were always read and his eyes were ever upon his book ; his figure was lean and stooping ; and the *tout ensemble* was anything but dignified or commanding. The delivery, however, suited the matter of his speech, and the combination suggested complete candour and honesty : he said only what he believed, and he induced others to believe with him. On the other hand, Dr. Pusey's University Sermons used to last for an hour and a half, were filled with Latin and Greek, dealt with abstruse subjects, and were delivered in the dullest possible way. To Richard they seemed a veritable nightmare.

At Dr. Greenhill's, too, he met Don Pascual de Gayangos, the Spanish Arabist. Already wearying of Greek and Latin, Richard had attacked Arabic, and soon was well on in Erpenius' Grammar, but there was no one to teach him, so he began to teach himself, and to write the Arabic letters from left to right, *i.e.* the wrong way. Señor Gayangos, who was visiting Oxford, when witnessing this burst out laughing and showed him how to copy the alphabet. In those days learning Arabic at Oxford was not easy. There was a Regius Professor, but he had other occupations than to profess. If any unhappy undergraduate went up to him and wanted to learn, he was assured that it was the duty of a professor to teach a class and not an individual. All this was presently changed, but not before it was high time.

The Sundays used generally to be passed in outings. It was a pleasure to get away from Oxford and to breathe an air which was not half smoke. Another disagreeable of the dull town was the continuous noise of bells : you could not make sure of five minutes without one giving tongue, and in no part of the world is there a place where there is such a perpetual tinkle of metal. The madding jingle seems to have been the survival of two centuries ago. In 1698 Paul Heutzner wrote : " The English are vastly fond of great noises that fill the ear, such as firing of cannon, drums, and the ringing of bells, so that it is common for a number of them that have got a glass in their heads, to go up into some belfry and ring the bells for hours together, for the sake of exercise." A favourite Sunday trip was to Abingdon, which, by the wisdom of the Dons, was in those days the railway station for Oxford. Like most men of conservative tendencies who disliked to move quiet things, who cultivated the *status quo* because they could hardly be better off and might be much worse off, and who feared nothing more than innovations because they might force on inquiry into the disposal of revenue, and other delicate monetary matters, they had fought against the line with such good-will that they had kept it nearly ten miles distant from the town. Their conduct was by no means exceptional.* Thousands did the same. For instance, Lord John Scott determined to prevent the surveyors passing through his estate, engaged a company of Nottingham " lambs," and literally strewed the floors of the porter's lodge with broken surveying instruments.

The Rev. Thomas Short was at that time doing Sunday duty at Abingdon. He was not distinguished for ability as a College tutor, but he was a gentlemanly and kindhearted man ; and careful not to be too sharp-eyed when he met undergraduates at his village. They generally

---

* Nor was it without the amplest justification. Brunel, who utterly ruined the beautiful South Devon and Cornish coast, was notoriously anxious to run the main-line of the Great Western close to Oxford and to erect there his engine shops and factories.—ED.

drove out in tandems, which the absurd regulations of the place kept in fashion by forbidding them ; no one would have driven them had they not possessed the merits of stolen fruit. Richard, having carefully practised upon Dobbin in his earlier days, used thoroughly to enjoy driving. In later years he met with his old tutor, the Rev. Thomas Short, who lived to a great age, and died universally respected and regretted by all who knew him.

At last the lagging autumnal term passed away, and Richard went up to his grandmother and aunts in Great Cumberland Street. "It was not lively," he remarks ; "a houseful of women rarely is." He was in a very promiscuous style of society. The Rev. Mr. Hutchins, the clergyman under whom they "sat" in the neighbouring Quebec Chapel, introduced him to the eccentric Duke of Brunswick, who used to laugh consumedly at Richard's sallies of high spirits. Lady Dinorben, with whom Mrs. Phayre still lived, gave him an occasional invitation. Their near neighbours were old General Sutherland, of the Madras Army, whose son Aleck, Richard afterwards met in the Neilgherry Hills. Mr. Lawyer Dendy was still alive, and one of his sons shortly after followed Richard to India as a Bombay civilian. Another pleasant acquaintance was Mrs. White, wife of the Colonel of the 3rd Dragoons, whose three stalwart sons were preparing for India, and gave Richard the first idea of going there. A man who dances and who dresses decently, and who is tolerably well introduced, rarely lacks invitations to balls in London, and so he found some occupation for his evenings. But he sadly wanted a club, and in those days the institution was not as common as it is now. At odd times he went to the theatres, and amused himself with the humours of the "Little Pic" and the old Cocoa Nut Tree. But hazard is a terrible game : it takes a man years to learn it well, and by that time he has lost all the luck with which he began. Richard always disliked private play, although he played a tolerable hand at whist, écarté, and piquet, but he found it almost as unpleasant to win from his friends as to lose to them. On the other hand, he was unusually lucky at public tables. He went upon a principle, not on a theory, which has ruined so many men : he noted, as a rule, that players are brave enough when they lose, whereas they begin to fear when they win. His plan, therefore, was to keep a certain sum in his pocket, and resolve never to exceed it : if he lost it he stopped, one of the advantages of public over private playing, but he did not lay down any limits to winning when he was in luck. He boldly went ahead, and stopped only when he found fortune turning the other way.

The grandmother's house was hardly pleasant to a devoted smoker. Richard was put out on the leads leading from the staircase whenever he wanted a weed. So he took lodgings in Maddox Street, and there became as it were a man upon town. His brother Edward joined him, and they had, as the Yankees say, " a high old time." It appeared only too short, and presently came on the spring (Lent) term. When Richard returned to his frowsy rooms in Trinity College, where he had not found many friendships, the big school had made a name for " fastness " amongst the last generation of undergraduates, and now a reaction had set in. The lads had laughed at him at his first lecture because he pronounced Latin like the Italians. The only men of his own College whom he met in after-life were unknown to him. One was Father Coleridge, S. J., and the other E. A. Freeman, the historian. He had a few friends at Exeter, including Richards, and at Brazenose, which was as famous as Bonn or Heidelberg for drinking heavy beer and ale, especially on Shrove Tuesday, when certain verses, chaffingly called the Carmen Seculare, used to be sung. But he delighted in Oriel, which, both

as regarded fellows and undergraduates was certainly the
nicest College of his day. There he spent the chief part
of his time with Wilberforce, Foster, and a little knot,
amongst whom was Tom Hughes ("Tom Brown"). They
boxed regularly, and took lessons from Goodman, ex-
pugilist and pedestrian, and actual tailor, who came down
to Oxford at times. They had great fun with Burke, the
fighting man, who on one occasion honoured Oxford with
his presence. The "deaf 'un," as he was called, had a face
that had been hammered into the consistency of sole-
leather, and one evening, after being too copiously treated,
he sat down in a heavy arm-chair, and cried out :—"Now,
lads, half-a-crown a hit!" They all tried their fists upon
his countenance, and hurt only their own knuckles.

Balliol (it was chiefly supplied from Rugby) then held
her head uncommonly high. As all know, Dr. Arnold had
made the fortune of Rugby and caused it to be recognized
amongst public schools. During his early government the
Rugbæans had sent a cricket challenge to Eton, and the
Etonians had replied that "they would be most happy to
send their scouts." But as scholarship at Eton seemed to
decline, so it rose at Rugby ; and at Oxford, scholarship
means £ s. d. At Balliol Richard made acquaintance
with a few men who afterwards made a noise in
the world, all belonging to a generation, academically
speaking, older than his own. Coleridge, now Lord Chief
Justice, was still lingering there, but had taken his
Bachelor's degree. Ward, of Balliol, who like Coleridge's
brother became a Catholic, was chiefly remarkable for his
minute knowledge of the circulating library novels of the
Laura Matilda School. He suffered from insomnia and
before he could sleep he was obliged to get through a
dozen volumes of a night. Lake of Balliol, then a
young Don, afterwards turned out a complete man of the
world, and there is no need to speak of Jowett who had

just passed his B.A. and was destined to be Master of Balliol.

Oxford between 1840 and 1842 was entering upon great changes. The old style of fellow—a kind of survival of the Benedictine monks—was rapidly becoming extinct and only one or two remained ; men who had lived surrounded by their books on vertical stands, were capable of asking you "if cats let loose in wood, would turn to tigers," and tried to keep pace with the age by reading up the *Times* of eight years past. But a great reform was still wanted. The popular idea of Oxford was that the classic groves of Isis were hotbeds of classical scholasticism whilst Cambridge succeeded better in mathematics, but Richard soon found that a man might learn more Greek and Latin in one year at Bonn or Heidelberg than in three at Oxford. The College teaching, for which one was obliged to pay, was of the most worthless description. Two hours a day were regularly wasted, and those who read for honours were obliged to choose and to pay for a private "coach." Amongst the said coaches were some *drôles* who taught in very peculiar ways, by rhymes not always of the most delicate description. The worst of such teaching was that it had no order and no system. Its philology was ridiculous and it did nothing to work the reasoning powers. Learning foreign languages as a child learns its own tongue is mostly a work of pure memory which requires after childhood every artificial assistance possible. Richard's system of learning a language in two months was entirely his own invention and thoroughly suited himself. He bought a simple grammar and vocabulary, marked out the forms and words which he knew to be absolutely necessary and learnt them by heart by carrying them in his pocket and looking over them at spare moments during the day. He never worked more than a quarter of an hour at a time, for after that the brain lost its freshness. After learning

some three hundred words, easily done in a week, he
stumbled through some easy book (one of the Gospels is
the most come-at-able) and underlined every word that he
wished to recollect in order to read over his pencillings at
least once a day. Having finished his volume he completely worked up the grammar, minutiæ and all, and then
chose some other book whose subject most interested him.
The neck of the language was now broken and 'progress
was rapid. If he came across a new sound, like the Arabic
Ghayn he trained his tongue to it by repeating it so many
thousand times a day ; and when he read he invariably read
out loud so that the ear might assist the memory. He
was delighted with the most difficult characters, Chinese
and Arabic, because he felt that they impressed themselves more strongly upon the eye than the eternal Roman
letters. This, by the way, made him resolutely stand aloof
from the hundred schemes for transliterating Eastern
languages such as Arabic, Sanscrit, Hebrew and Syriac
into Latin letters. And whenever he conversed with
anybody in a language that he was learning he took the
trouble to repeat the words inaudibly after him and so
to learn the trick of pronunciation and emphasis.

The changes which followed 1840 made an important
difference in the value of Fellowships. They were harder
to get and harder to keep. They were no longer what
the parlous and supercilious youth described them :—" an
admirable provision for the indigent members of the
middle classes." The old half-monk disappeared or rather
he grew his moustaches and passed his vacations *sur le
Continong*. But something still remains to be done. It is
a scandal to meet abroad in diplomacy and other pro-
fessions a gentleman belonging to the class of *bene nati,
bene vesti et modice docti* of All Souls, drawing their pay
moreover for doing nothing. The richest University in the
world is too poor to afford the host of professors still

required and it is a disgrace that an English University, whose very name means the acquisition of universal knowledge, should not be able to teach Cornish, Gaelic, Welsh and Irish, the original languages of the Islands. Again, the endowment of research, a *sine quâ non*, is simply delayed because money is not forthcoming. A little sensible economy would remedy all this and make Oxford what she ought to be, a seat of learning—not as the old fellows of Christ Church defined, a place to make "rather ignorant gentlemen."*

During the term Richard formally gave up his intention of reading for a first class. *Aut primus aut nullus*, was ever his motto, and though many "second-class" men have turned out better than "firsts" he did not care to begin life with a failure. He soon ascertained the fact, that those who may rely upon first classes are bred to the career from their childhood as horses and dogs are trained. They must not waste time and memory upon foreign tongues ; they must not dissipate the powers of the brain upon anything like general education ; they may know the —isms, but they must be utterly ignorant of the —ologies, while above all things they must not indulge themselves with learning what is popularly called "the world." They must confine themselves to one straight line as college curriculum, and even then they can never be certain of success ; at the very moment of gaining the prize, health may break down and compel them to give up work. Richard surprised Dr. Greenhill by his powers of memory when he learned "Adams's Antiquities" by heart ; but the doctor, who had not taken a class himself, threw cold water on his pupil's ambition, perhaps the best thing he

* The competition fellowships at Oxford were started in 1854 ; they were expected to change the whole condition of things ; but they left everything in the same old groove. Oxford is still, not a University, but a congeries of colleges, or rather, of high schools.

could do, and frankly told him that though he *could* take
a first class he could by no means answer that he *would*.
The fellows of Trinity were pleasant, gentlemanly men,
but Richard by no means wished to become one of their
number.   His father had set his heart upon both sons
being provided for by the Universities : very often, however,
when fathers propose, sons dispose.

Richard's disgust at the idea of University honours was
perhaps not diminished by his trying for two scholarships
and failing to get either.   He, however, attributed his non-
success at University College (where he was beaten by a
man who turned a chorus of Æschylus into doggrel verses)
chiefly to his having stirred the bile of his examiners by
pronouncing his Latin vowels in the Italian way.   At
times, too, the Devil palpably entered into him, and made
him speak Greek Romaically by accent and not by quantity, even as they did, and still do, at Athens.   He had
learned this much from one of the Rodokanakis—Greek
merchants at Marseilles.

The history of the English pronunciation of Latin is
curious.   In Chaucer it was after the Italian fashion; in
Spenser the English appears, and the change begins to
make itself felt under the successors of Elizabeth.   It was
certainly encouraged by the leaders of education in order
to emphasize the breach with Rome ; so clearly was this
the case, that for at least a century the two pronuncia-
tions were distinguished as " Protestant " and "Catholic"
Latin.   The effect was, that after learning Greek and Latin
for twenty years a lad could hardly speak a sentence,
because he had never been taught to converse in the
absurdly-called " dead languages," and if he did speak, not
a soul but an Englishman could understand him.   The
English pronunciation of Latin vowels happens to be the
very worst in the world, because we have an O and an A
which belong peculiarly to English, and which destroy all

the charm of those grand sounding assonants. Years after Richard was laughed at, at Oxford, public opinion took a turn, and the Continental pronunciation of Latin was adopted in many of the best schools. He was anxious to see them drop their absurd mispronunciation of Greek, but all the authorities whom he consulted on the subject declared to him that schoolmasters had quite enough to do with learning Italianized Latin and could not be expected to trouble themselves with learning Athenianized Greek. He had another most Quixotic idea, which was truly breaking one's head against a windmill. He wanted the public to pronounce Yob for Job, Yericho for Jericho, Yakoob for Jacob, Hierusalem for Jerusalem. The writers of the Anglican version must certainly have intended this, and it is inconceivable how the English public dropped the cognate German pronunciation of J and took to that of France and Italy.

At last the dreary term passed away, and a happy family meeting was promised. Colonel Burton brought his wife and daughter ·from Pisa to Wiesbaden and the boys, as they were still called, were invited over to spend the long vacation. They were also to escort Mrs. D'Aguilar, who, with two of her daughters, was determined to see the Rhine. One of the girls, Emily, died soon : the other, Eliza, married a clergyman named Pope, and her son, Lieutenant Pope of the 24th Queen's, died gallantly at Isandula : though surrounded by numbers, he kept firing his revolver and wounding his enemies till he received a mortal wound in the breast from an assegai. This was on the 22nd January, 1879. In the end of 1875 he came to Folkestone to take leave of his cousin Richard, who liked him much.

In those days (1841) travellers took steamer from London Bridge, dropped quietly down the Thames, and gaining varied information about the places on both sides of it dined as usual on a boiled leg of mutton and caper sauce or roast ribs of beef with horse-radish; slept as best they could in those boxes called berths, and if there was not too much head-wind awoke in the Scheldt the next morning. The little party passed a day at Antwerp, which looked beautiful from the river: the Cathedral tower, the tall roofs, and tapering spires of the churches around it, made a matchless group. They visited the fortifications which had lately done such good work, and they had an indigestion of Rubens, who appeared gross and fleshy after the Italian school. Mrs. D'Aguilar was dreadfully scandalized at suddenly coming into a room and finding her two nephews at romps with a pretty little *soubrette*, whose short petticoats enabled her to deliver the sharpest possible kicks, while she employed her hands in vigorously defending her jolly red cheeks. The poor lady threw up her hands and her eyes when she came upon this little scene, but she was even more shocked when she found that her escort had passed Sunday evening in the theatre.

From Antwerp they travelled to Bruges; examined the belfry, listened to the carillon (chimes), and then went on to Cologne. A marvellously picturesque old place it was with its combination of old churches, crumbling walls, gabled houses, and the narrowest and worst paved streets they had ever seen. The old Cathedral in those days was not finished and threatened never to be finished: still there was the grand solitary tower, with the mystical-looking crane on the top and a regular garden growing out of the chinks and crannies of the stone-work. Coleridge's saying about Cologne was emphatically true in those days, and all travellers had recourse to Jean Marie Farina *Gegenüber*. What a change there is now, with that hideous Gothic railway-bridge and its sham battlements, and loop-holes to defend nothing; with its hideous cast-iron turret over the centre of the church, where the old architect had intended a

light stone lantern-tower; with the ridiculous terrace surrounding the building, and with the frightful finials wherewith the modern German architects have disfigured the
grand old building. At Cologne they took the steamer and
ran up the Rhine—a far more sensible proceeding than that
of these days when tourists take the railway, and consequently can see only one side of the river. The river-craft
was comfortable, the meals were plentiful, the *Bisporter*
was a sound and unadulterated wine, and married remarkably well with Knaster tobacco, smoked in long pipes with
painted china bowls. The crowd, too, was good-tempered,
and seemed to enjoy its holiday. Bonn, somehow or other,
always manages to show at least one very pretty girl with
porcelain-blue eyes and gingerbread-coloured hair. Then
came the "castled crag of Drachenfels" and the charming
Siebengebirge, which in those days were not spoiled by
factory chimneys. They landed at Frankfort, and thence
drove over to the old Fontes Mattiáce, called in modern
days Wiesbaden.

It has been said that to enjoy the Rhine one must go to
it from England, not the other way from Switzerland, and
travellers' opinions are very much divided about it, some
considering it extremely grand and others simply pretty.
Richard was curious to see what the effect upon him would
be after visiting the four quarters of the globe, so in May
1876 he dropped down the river from Bâle to the mouth.
The southern and northern two-thirds he found utterly
uninteresting, but the middle length was as charming as
ever, and, in fact, he enjoyed the beautiful and romantic
river more than when he had seen it as a boy. The
section beginning at Bingen he found delightful, although
Bishop Hatto's tower had become a cockneyfied affair, and
the castles, banks, and islands, were disagreeably suggestive of Richmond Hill. But the Drachenfels, Nonnens-
worth, and Rolandseck, were admirably picturesque, and

he quite felt the truth of the saying that this is one of the Paradises of Germany At Düsseldorf the river becomes old and ugly, and so continues till Rotterdam. Wiesbaden, in those days intensely " German and ordinary," as Horace Walpole says—was a kind of Teutonic Margate, with a *chic* of its own. In the age before railways this was the case with all these baths, where people went either to play, or to get rid of what the Germans call *eine sehr schöne corpulenz*—a corporation acquired by stuffing with greasy food during nine or ten months of the year. It was impossible to mistake princely Baden-Baden, and its glorious Black Forest, for invalid Kissengen or for Homburg, which combined mineral waters with gambling on the largest scale. Wiesbaden was so far interesting that it showed the pure and unadulterated summer life of middle-class Germany. Here you saw daily the grave blue-green German eye, the food of three kinds, salt, sour, and greasy. You are surprised at the frequency of the name Johann—if Johann, it was a servant; Johannes, a professor; Schani, a swell; Jean, a kind of *fréluquet;* Hans, a peasant; and Hansl, a village idiot. Albrecht, with flat occiput and bat-like ears, long, straight hair and cap, with unclean hands, a huge signet ring on his forefinger, and a pipe rivalling a Turkish *chibouque* in size, took his regular seat on one of the wooden benches of the promenade, with his Frau Mutter knitting stockings on one side, and Fräulein Gretchen knitting mittens on the other. This kind of thing would continue perhaps for ten seasons, but on the eleventh you met Albrecht *aux petits soins* with Mütze as his bride, and Gretchen being waited upon by her bridegroom Fritz, and thus everything went on as before. Amongst the women the Kaffee-Gesellschaft flourished, where coffee and scandal took the place of scandal and tea—the beverage irreverently called chatter-water. The lady of the house invites one or two friends to come and bring their work, and drink a cup of coffee. Before the hour arrives the invitation may number twenty. They dress in afternoon promenade toilette which was very unadorned at Wiesbaden, and they drop in one by one. Much kissing and shaking of hands, and then each one pulls out knitting and various pieces of work which are mutually admired, and patterns borrowed, and then they fall to talking over children, servants, toilettes, domestic economy, and the reputations of such of their friends as are not there. This goes on for hours, only interrupted by the servant wheeling in a table covered with cakes, sweetmeats, jam and coffee. In the evening there was a dance at the Kursaal, admirable waltzing, and sometimes quadrilles with steps. Here the bald old Englishman, who in France would collect around him all the ancient ladies in the room to see him dance, was little noticed. The hearty and homely Germans danced even when they had grey hair.

The family had found a comfortable house at Wiesbaden, and the German servants received the "boys" with exclamations of *Ach! die schöne schwarze Kinder!* They paid occasional furtive visits to the Kursaal, and lost a few sovereigns like men. But their chief amusement was the fencing-rooms. Here they found a new style of play with the Schläger, a straight pointless blade with razor-like edges. It was a favourite student's weapon, used to settle all their affairs of honour, and they used it with the silly hanging guard. Some of them gave half an hour every day to working at the post, a wooden pillar in the middle of the room, bound with vertical ribbons of iron. When they were tired of Wiesbaden, the boys amused themselves with wandering about the country. They visited the nearer watering-places, the first being Schwalbach (the swallows' brook), where the rusty waters turned their hair red. They then went off to Schlangenbad (the snakes' bath),

whose Kalydor made the Frenchman fall in love with
himself. These waters had such a reputation that one lady
(of course she was called a Russian princess) used to have
a supply sent across half Europe for daily use. In those
days there were not many English in such out-of-the-way
places, and the greater number were Oxford and Cambridge men. They were learning German, and made the
most extraordinary mistakes. Amongst other people they
found here the daughters of Archbishop Whately, who
were very nice girls. The Burtons returned to Wiesbaden,
and thence to picturesque Heidelberg, where they found a
little colony of English, and all fraternized at once. The
boys wanted to enter one of the so-called " Brigades,"
and chose the Nassau, which was the fightingest of all.
An Irish student, who also was one of the champions of
the corps, and who had distinguished himself by slitting
more than one nose, called upon them, and over sundry
schoppes of beer declared that they could not be admitted
without putting in an appearance at the Hirschgasse.
This was a little pot-house at the other side of the river,
with a large upper room, where " monomachies " were
fought. The appearance of the combatants was very ridiculous. They had thick felt caps over their heads, whose
vizors defended their eyes : their necks were swathed in
enormous cravats ; the arms were both padded, and so
were the bodies from the waist downwards. There was
nothing to hit but the face and the chest : that, however
did not prevent disagreeable accidents. Sometimes too
heavy a cut went into the lungs, and at other times took
effect upon either eye : but the grand thing was to walk
off with the tip of one's adversary's nose by a dexterous .
snick from the hanging guard. Two " nose stories " may
here find a place. One is of a duel between a handsome man and an ugly one : Beauty had a lovely nose,
and Beast so managed that presently it was found upon

the floor, where Beauty made a rush for it, but Beast stamped it out of all shape. The other is of a doctor who attended a student's duel, and when the pet cut was given, and a nose was lost, the doctor flew at it, picked it up, popped it in his mouth to keep it warm, whipped out his instruments, needle and thread, and so skilfully stitched on the nose and strapped it with plaster that the edges united, and in a few weeks the feature was as handsome and useful as ever. There was very little retreating in those affairs, for the lines were chalked upon the ground. The seconds stood by also armed with swords, and protected the principals, to see that there was nothing like a *sauhieb* (foul cut). A medical student was always present, and when a cut went home, the affair was stopped to sew it up ; sometimes, however, the artery shrank, and the patient was marked with a cross, as it was necessary to open his cheek above and below, in order to tie it.

The boys did not see the fun of this kind of thing, and when their Irish friend told them what the ordeal was, they said that they were perfectly ready to turn out with foils or rapiers, but that they could not stand the paddings. Duels with the broadsword, and without protection, were never fought except upon desperate occasions. Their friend promised to report it to the brigade, and the result was that some time afterwards they were introduced to a student who said that he knew a little fencing and should like to try a bout with them. They smelt a rat, as the phrase is, and showed him only half what they could do. But apparently that was enough. Their conditions were not accepted, and they were not admitted into the Nassau brigade.

At Heidelberg Richard informed his father that Oxford life did not in any way suit him. He pleaded for permission to go into the army, or, failing that, to emigrate to Canada or Australia. Colonel Burton was inexorable ;

he was always thinking of that Fellowship. Edward, too, was deadly tired of Dr. Havergal, and swore that he would rather be a private soldier than a "Fellow of Cambridge." However, he was sent *nolens volens* to the University on the Cam, and there he very speedily came to grief. It was remarked of him before the end of his first term that he was never seen at chapel. His tutor sent for him and permitted himself strong language on this delinquency: "My dear sir," was the reply, "no party of pleasure ever gets me out of bed before ten o'clock, and do you *really* think I am going to be in chapel at eight?" "Are you jesting, or is that your mature decision?" asked the tutor. "My very ripest resolve," said Edward, and consequently he was obliged to leave the College without delay.

When the visit was over and Michaelmas term was beginning, Richard left Germany and steamed down the Rhine. Everything that he saw made him less likely to be pleased at the end of his journey. He had, however, no choice. He arrived in London and found his grandmother and aunts still at the sea-side in a house over the cliffs at Ramsgate. Ramsgate he rather liked. There were some pleasant London girls there—the Ladies P——t —and the place had a kind of distant resemblance to Boulogne. The raffles at the libraries made it a caricature of a German Bath. He wandered about the country, visited Margate, where the tone of society was perfectly marvellous, and he rambled over the small adjacent bathing-places like Broadstairs and Herne Bay. This brought on the time when he was obliged to return to Oxford : he went there with no good will, and as his father had refused to withdraw him from the University, he resolved to withdraw himself.

Of his course of action the less said the better. Dark reports of revels and merry-makings were spread : everywhere whispers were heard concerning parodies on vener-

OXFORD AND INDIA. 109

able subjects ; squibs appeared in the local papers—in those days an unpardonable offence—caricatures of Heads of Houses were handed about, and certain improvisations were passed from mouth to mouth. Richard had a curious power of improvising any number of rhymes without the slightest forethought, but the power, such as it was, was perfectly useless to him, as it was accompanied with occasional moments of nervousness when he despaired without the smallest reason whatever of finding the easiest rhyme. Probably the professional Italian who declaims a poem or a tragedy labours under the perfect conviction that nothing in the world can stop him : and then it is so much easier to rhyme in Italian than in English. So Richard's efforts were mostly confined to epigrams and epitaphs at soirées and supper-parties, and you may be sure that these brilliant efforts did him no good.

This was the beginning of the end. His object was to be rusticated, not to be expelled : the former may happen in consequence of the smallest irregularity, whilst the latter implies ungentlemanly conduct. He cast about in all directions for the safest line, when fortune put the clue into his hands. A celebrated steeple-chaser, Oliver the Irishman, came down to Oxford, and Richard was determined to see him ride. The collegiate authorities with questionable wisdom forbade all to be present at the races, and especially at what they called "the disgraceful scenes of race ordinaries." Moreover, to make matters sure, they ordered all the undergraduates to be present at the lecture at the hour when the race was to be run. A number of high-spirited youngsters of the different colleges swore that they would not stand this nonsense, that it was infringing the liberty of the subject, and that it was treating them like little boys, which they did not deserve. Here doubtless, they were right. But well foreseeing what would be the result, they acted upon the common saying, "In for

a penny, in for a pound." So the tandems were ordered
to wait behind Worcester College, and, when they should
have been attending a musty lecture in the tutor's room,
they were flicking across the country at the rate of
twelve miles an hour. The steeple-chasing was a delight,
and Oliver was very amusing at the race ordinary, although
he did not express much admiration for the riding of what
he called the "Oxford lads."

Next morning there was eating of humble pie. The
various culprits were summoned to the Green Room, and
made conscious of the enormity of their offence. Richard
secured the respect of the little knot by arguing the point
with the College dignitaries. He boldly asserted that there
was no moral turpitude in being present at a race: he
vindicated the honour and dignity of collegiate men by
asserting that they should not be treated as children: he
even dropped the general axiom that "Trust begets trust,"
and "they who trust us elevate us." Now this was too
much of a good thing—to commit a crime, and declare it a
virtuous action. Consequently, when all were rusticated,
he was singled out from the οἱ πολλοί by an especial
recommendation not to return to Oxford. Stung by a
sense of injustice, he declared at once that he would leave
the College, and expressed a vicious hope "that the caution-
money deposited by his father would be honestly returned
to him." This was the climax. There was a general rise of
dignitaries, as if a violent expulsion from the room was
intended. Richard made them his lowest and most courtly
bow, Austrian fashion, which, bringing the heels together,
bends the body nearly double, wished them all happiness
in the future, and retired from the scene. He did not see
Oxford again until 1850, when the Prodigal Son returned
to Alma Mater with a half-resolution to finish his terms,
and take his B.A. But the idea came too late: he had
given himself up to Oriental studies, and he had begun to

write books. Yet he never neglected during his occasional visits home to call at his old College, have a chat with the reverend and venerable Thomas Short, and to breakfast and dine with the Dons who had been Bachelors or undergraduates at the time of his departure.

The way in which he left Oxford was characteristic. One of his rusticated friends—Anderson of Oriel—had proposed that they should leave with a splurge—"go up from the land with a soar." There was now no need for the furtive tandem behind Worcester College : it was driven boldly up to the College doors. Richard's bag and baggage were stowed away in it, and, with a cantering leader and a high-trotting horse in the shafts, carefully driven over the beds of the best flowers, they started for the High Street and the Queen's highway to London, Richard energetically performing upon a yard of tin, waving adieux to his friends, and kissing his hand to the pretty shop-girls. He thoroughly felt the truth of the sentiment—

"I leave thee Oxford, and I loathe thee well,
Thy saint, thy sinner, scholar, prig and swell."

Arrived in London, he was received by the feminine family with some little astonishment, for they already knew enough of "terms" to be aware that the last was unfinished. Richard thoroughly satisfied all the exigencies of the position by declaring that he had been allowed an extra vacation for taking a double first class with the very highest honours. A grand dinner party was given, quite the reverse of the fatted calf. Unfortunately amongst the guests was the Rev. M. Phillipps,* a great friend of Richard's, who grinned at him, and indiscreetiy ejaculated, " Rusticated, eh ? " The aunts said nothing at the time, but they made

* The brother of Major-General Sir B. T. Phillipps, who served long and well in the Bengal Army, was rather a noted figure as a young old man in London, and died in Paris in 1880.

inquiries, the result of which was a tableau on which we will draw the curtain.

These are wild oats with a witness, but most men sow them, and it is better they should be sown in early youth. Youth is like new wine, that must be allowed to ferment freely, or it will never become clear, strong, and well flavoured. Nothing more melancholy than to see a man suddenly emancipated from family rule and playing tricks when the heyday is past.

Richard was asked what he intended to do, and he replied simply that he wished to go into the army, but he preferred the Indian service, as it would show him more of the world. There was no great difficulty in getting a commission. The Directors were bound not to sell them, but every now and then they would give a nomination to a friend, and the friend did not throw away his chance. Richard's conviction is that the commission cost £500. It was arranged that he should sail in the spring, and meanwhile he determined to have a jolly time. He made a number of new acquaintances, including old Mr. Varley, the artist, of whom he was very fond ; this eccentric genius had just published a book,* which he called 'Zodiacal Physiognomy,' in order to prove that every man resembled, after a fashion, the sign under which he was born. Readers will remember that in the old Zodiacs all the figures were either human or bestial. Mr. Varley was a great student of occult sciences, and perhaps his favourite was astrology. It is curious how little London people know of what goes on in the next house : a book on alchemy was lately printed, and the curious fact came out that at least a hundred people in town were in search of the philosopher's stone. Mr. Varley drew out his young friend's horoscope, and prognosticated that he was to become a great astrologer,

* Which was to have been published in many parts, but never went beyond the first.—ED.

but the prophecy came to nothing, for although Richard had read Cornelius Agrippa, and others of the same school at Oxford, he found Zadkiel quite sufficient for him. Amongst the people he met was the Rev. Robert, popularly called " Satan," Montgomery, who had come up on a preaching campaign. He had written a quantity of verse, which was very much admired by his feminine devotees, and which was savagely mangled by critical Macaulay in the 'Edinburgh.' He was an effective figure in the pulpit —a pale face, and tolerably straight features, very black hair, a white hand with a large diamond, and a very white pocket-handkerchief. He had a marvellous extent of what is commonly called the " gift of the gab," and would speak for an hour without a moment's hesitation ; but there was something solid below all this froth, and he had carefully read up all the good old theological works. The women, (including the aunts,) went literally mad : they crowded the little Quebec Chapel ; they mobbed him as he came in and went out, and they overwhelmed him with slippers, chest-protectors, and portable articles to administer the Sacrament. His reign was short. He married, came up to London, took a chapel, subsided into the average popular preacher, and in 1855 died. Amongst others that Richard met was a certain Robert Bagshaw from Calcutta, who was destined afterwards to marry his aunt, Georgina Baker. Richard managed to offend him mortally. He was boasting of a new dress coat, when the Oxonian delicately raised the tail and said, " You don't mean to say you call this thing a coat ? "

With all this wasting of time, Richard kept his eyes steadily fixed on the main chance. He gave up boxing at Owen Swift's, and fencing at Angelo's, and spent all his spare hours in learning Hindustani with old Duncan Forbes, a curious specimen of a shrewd Scotchman. He had spent a year or so in Bombay, and upon the strength of it he was perfect master of all Oriental languages, and he had two passions : one was for smoking a huge meerschaum stuffed with the strongest possible tobacco, the other was for chess, concerning which he published some then interesting and novel studies. Perhaps his third passion was not quite so harmless—it was simply for not washing. He spoke all his Eastern languages with the broadest possible Lowland accent, and he cared much more for telling anecdotes than for teaching. He published a number of books, and he certainly had not the *suaviter in modo :* he attacked Eastwick, the Orientalist, in the most ferocious style. However, he laid a fair foundation, and Richard's slight studies of Arabic secured him the old man's regard.

Presently the day came when Richard was to be sworn in at the India House. In those times the old building stood in Leadenhall Street, which gave Thackeray an opportunity of attacking it as "the Hall of Lead." A wonderfully dull and smoky old place it was, with its large and gorgeous porter outside, and the gloomy and stuffy old rooms inside, an atmosphere which had actually produced the Essays of 'Elia.' At that period, however, it kept up a certain amount of respect for itself. If an officer received the gift of a sword, he was conducted by the portly porter to the general meeting of the Directors, and duly addressed and complimented in form ; but, as times waxed harder, the poor twenty-four kings of Leadenhall Street declined from Princes into mere Shaykhs. They actually sent a sword of honour to one of their officers by a street messenger, and the donee returned it, saying he could not understand the manner of the gift. And so the Court went on gradually declining and falling, till at last the old House was abandoned and let for offices : the shadowy Directors flitted to the West End into a brand new India House, which soon brought on their euthanasia.

Richard was much scandalised by the sight of his future

comrades and brother officers. The Afghan disaster was still fresh in public memory : the aunts had been patriotic enough to burst into tears when they heard of it ; and certainly it was an affecting picture—the idea of a single Englishman, Dr. Brydone, riding into Jellalabad, the only man out of thirteen thousand. Poor General Elphinstone had been Colonel Burton's best man at his marriage, and was as little fitted for such field service as Job was at his worst. Alexander Burns was the only headpiece in the whole number : he had shown the moral courage to report how critical the position was, but he had not the moral courage to insist upon his advice being taken, and, that failing, to return to his regiment as a captain. MacNaghten was a mere Indian civilian : like too many of them, he had fallen into the dodging ways of the natives, and he distinctly deserved his death. The words used by Akbar Khan, when he shot him, were *Shumá mulk-e-má mí giríd?* " So you are the fellow who has come to take our country ? "

But the result of the " massacre " was a demand for soldiers and officers, especially Anglo-Indians. Some forty medical students were sent out, and they naturally got the name of "the Forty Thieves." The excess of demand explained the curious appearance of the embryo cadets when they met to be sworn in at the India House : they looked like raw country lads, mostly dressed in home-made clothes, with hair cut by the village barber, village boots and no gloves. Richard and his friend, Colonel White's son, who was entering the service on the same day, looked at each other in blank dismay : they had fallen amongst young Yahoos, and they looked forward with terror to such society. Richard was originally intended for Bengal, but, as has been seen, he had relations there, and he was not going to subject himself to surveillance by his uncle by marriage, an old General of Invalids. Moreover, one of his D'Aguilar cousins was married to a Judge in Calcutta, and as he was determined to have as much liberty as possible he chose Bombay. He was always of opinion that a man proves his value by doing what he likes: there is no merit in so doing when you have a fair fortune and an independent position, but for a man bound by professional ties, and too often lacking means to carry out his wishes, it was a prime success to choose his own line, and stick to it.

The next thing to do was to obtain an outfit. This was another great abuse of those days. As the friends of the Directors made money by the cadets' commissions, so the friends of the friend made money by sending them to particular houses. The unfortunate youths, or rather their parents, were, in fact, plundered by every one who touched them. The outfit, which was considered *de rigueur*, was absurdly profuse, including as it did dozens upon dozens of white jackets and trousers, fit only to breed rheumatism, and such things as nigger-head and pigtail tobacco, to give away in presents to the sailors. Even the publishers arranged that their dictionaries and grammars of Hindustani should be forced upon these unhappy youths, and their boxes were crammed with Wellington's Dispatches, Mill's ponderous ' History of India,' the Army Regulations, and whatever else the booksellers and the outfitters chose to agree upon. The result was absolutely ridiculous. As a rule, the bullock-trunks were opened during the voyage, the kit was displayed, and on " fast " ships it was put down as a stake at cards. Stories were told of sharp hands landing in India after winning half-a-dozen outfits, which literally glutted the market. The guns, pistols, swords, and saddlery were of the most expensive and useless description, and were all to be bought much better at a quarter the price in any Indian port. On an average the voyage lasted four months; two or three changes of suits only were necessary; the rest of the outfit (£100) was simply so much plunder to the shopkeeper. One unusual article was ordered by Richard—a wig from Winter in Oxford Street. Early in life he had found the advantage of shaving the head, enabling him to keep it cool when it was normally in the other condition. An old Joe Miller was told in Bombay about a Scotch doctor famous for selling hog-maned ponies to new-comers. He also shaved his head, and, being in medical attendance upon the cadets, he took the opportunity of pocketing his wig, and persuading them that a shaven head was the official costume. He accompanied them on their first official visit, and, as they were taking off their caps, he whipped on his wig, and presented to the astonished Commanding Officer half-a-dozen utterly bald pates, which looked as if they belonged to so many lunatics.

The next thing was to choose a ship, and the aunts were directed by their friend of the Commission to the *John Knox* (Captain Richard B. Cleland), Sailing Barque, belonging to Messrs. Guy and Co. Richard was to embark at Greenwich. The family went with him ; he was duly wept over, and dropped down the river with the scantiest regret for leaving Europe on June 18, 1842. His only companion was a bull terrier of the Oxford breed, more bull than terrier : its box-head and pink face had been scarred all over during a succession of dog-fights and mixed tussles with rats : it was beautifully built in the body, and the tail was as thin as a little finger, showing all the vertebræ. The breed seems to have almost become extinct, but Richard found it at Oxford when he went there again in 1850. The little jewel bore a fine litter of pups, and died at Gujarát, with every sign of old age, half-blind eyes and staggering limbs. The pups grew up magnificently. One, which rejoiced in the name of Bachhun,—the young 'un,—received the best of educations : he was entered on mice, rats, and gilahris or native squirrels, which bite and scratch like cats, and he became so thoroughly game that he would sally out alone in the morning and kill a jackal single-handed. He was the pride of the regiment and came as usual to a bad end. On one of his journeys dressed as a native, his master had to leave him behind in charge of his friend Dr. Arnott, surgeon of the regiment. Dr. Arnott also when absent entrusted him to the care of a brother medico, who had strict opinions on the subject of drugs. This wretch actually allowed the gallant little dog to die of some easy disease because he could not give him a dose of medicine belonging to the Company.

Richard's public life now begins. His fellow passengers were Ensign Boileau of the 22nd Regiment, Ensign Thompson of the Company's service, and Mr. Richmond, going out to a commercial house in Bombay.* There was an equal number of the other sex—a lady calling herself Mrs. Lewis, and three sturdy wives of serjeants. Fortunately, there were also three native servants who spoke Hindustani.

The voyage opened by a straight run down the Channel and a June-weather passage along the coast of Europe and Africa. There were delays in the Doldrums and calms near the Line : Neptune came on board as usual but there was very little fun, the numbers being too small. At such times troubles are apt to break out on board. The captain, Richard Cleland, was one of the best seamen that ever commanded a ship, yet his career had been unlucky : as Vasco da Gama said to Don Manoel, " those who are unfortunate at sea should avoid the affairs of the

---

*   GENERAL ORDER OF THE COMMANDER-IN-CHIEF.

" To rank from date of sailing from Gravesend of the ship by which they proceeded in the following order, viz :—

Charles Thompson, per barque ' John Knox,' June 18, 1842.

Richard Francis Burton, per barque ' John Knox,' June 18, 1842.

The latter appointed to the 14th Regiment, Bombay N. I., Sept. 24, 1842 ; transferred to the 18th Regiment, Bombay N. I., Oct. 25, 1842.

Date of arrival in Bombay, Oct. 28, 1842.

No. 106."

sea." He had already lost one ship, which was simply ill-fortune, for no seaman could be more sober and more attentive to his duty. He managed, however, to have a row on board, and called upon the cadets to load their pistols and accompany him to the fo'castle, where he was about to make a mutineer prisoner. These were very disagreeable things to interfere with, and the Supreme Court of Bombay always did its best to hang an officer if a seaman was shot on these occasions—one man in particular had a narrow escape.

The discipline on the ship was none of the best. Captain Cleland had begun early, and determined to establish a reputation, invited Richard to put on the gloves with him. The result was that the tall, lanky Scotchman, who was in particularly bad training, got knocked into a cocked hat. Then arose the usual troubles among the passengers. Normally on such voyages all begin by talking together, and end by talking to themselves. Of course there were love passages, and these only made matters worse. The chief mate, a great hulking fellow, who ought to have hit like Tom Spring, but whose mutton fist would not dent a pat of butter, was solemnly knocked down on quarter deck for putting in his oar. Then followed a sham duel, the combatants being brought up at midnight, and the pistols being loaded with balls of blackened cork instead of bullets. During the day there were bathings outside the ship over a sail, to keep out the sharks, and shooting flying fish, and the massacring unhappy birds. Richard, however, utilised his time by making the three native servants who were on board talk with him, and by reading Hindustani stories from old Shakespear's text-book. He made a final attempt to keep up musical notation, and used the flageolet to the despair of all on board. The chief part of his time was passed in working at Hindustani, reading all the Eastern books on board, in gymnastics, and in teaching his brother youngsters the sword. There was also an immense waste of gunpowder, for were not all those young gentlemen going to be Commanders-in-Chief?

The good ship *John Knox* ran past the Cape in the dead of winter, and a magnificent scene it was. Waves measuring miles in length came up from the South Pole, in lines as regular as those of soldiers marching across a dead plain. Over them floated the sheep-like albatrosses, which the cadets soon tired of shooting, especially when they found it was almost impossible to stuff the birds. The little stormy petrels were respected, but the Cape pigeons were drawn on board in numbers with a hook and a bit of bait. Nothing could be brighter than the skies and seas, and the experience of what is called a "White gale" gave universal satisfaction. It came down without any warning, except ploughing up the waters, and had not Captain Cleland been on deck and let go his gear, most of the muslin would have been on the broad bosom of the Atlantic. There was little interest in sailing up the Eastern coast of South Africa. They saw neither the shore-lands nor Madagascar, but struck north-east for the Western coast of India. The usual tricks were played upon new-comers. They had been made to see the Line by a thread stretched over a spy-glass, and now they were told to "smell India" after a little oil of cloves had been rubbed upon the bulwarks. When the winds fell, the cadets amused them-selves with boarding the pattymars, and other native craft, and went ferreting all about the cabins and holes, to the great disgust of the owners. They gaped at the snakes which they saw swimming about, and were delighted when the *John Knox* one fine night lumbered on her way through nets and fishing-stakes, whose owners set up a noise like a gigantic frog-concert. Next morning (October 28) as the Government Pilot came on board, excited questions were put to him: "What was doing in

Afghanistan ?" "What of the war ?" At his answer all hopes fell to zero. Lord Ellenborough had succeeded Lord Auckland ; the avenging army had returned through the Khaybar Pass ; the campaign was finished ; Ghuznee had fallen ; the prisoners had been given up ; Pollock, Sale, and Pratt, had been perfectly successful. No chance of becoming Commanders-in-Chief within the year.

Richard never expected to see another Afghan war, and yet he did so before middle age was well over.

> " Thy towers, Bombay ! gleam bright they say,
> Against the dark blue sea,"

absurdly sings the poet. It was no picture like this they saw on the morning of October the 28th, when their long voyage ended. The bay, so celebrated, appeared anything but beautiful : it was a great splay thing, too long for its height, and it had not one of the beautiful perpendiculars that distinguish Parthenope. The high background is almost always hidden by the reek that rises during the day, and the sun seems to burn all the colour out of the land-scape ; the rains had just ceased, yet the sky seemed never clear, and the water wanted washing. After this preliminary glance, the companions shook hands, and, not without something of soreness of heart, separated, after having lived together for nearly five months. Richard went to the British Hotel in the Fort, then kept by an Englishman named Blackwell, who delegated all his duty to a Parsee, and never troubled himself about his guests. A Tontine Hotel had been proposed, but there is a long interval between sayings and doings in India.

When Richard landed at Bombay (Oct. 28th, 1842), "Mombadevi" town was a marvellous contrast with the "Queen of Western India," as she thrones it in 1887 : no city in Europe, except perhaps Vienna, can show such a difference. The old Portuguese port-village, temp. Caroli

Secundi, with its silly fortifications and useless esplanade, its narrow alleys and squares like *places d'armes*, had not developed itself into "Sassoon Town," as we may call the older, and "Frere Town," the modern moiety.

Under the patriarchal rule of the Court of Directors to the Hon. East India Company, a form .of torpidity much resembling the paternal government of good Emperor Franz, no arrangements were made for the reception of the queer animals called "Cadets." They landed and fell into the knowing hands of some rascal ; they lodged at a Parsee tavern, the "British Hotel," all uncleanness, and at the highest prices, they had a touch of "seasoning sickness ;" and came under the charge of " Paddy Ryan," Fort Surgeon and general favourite. They were duly drafted into the sanitary bungalows, thatched hovels facing Back Bay, whence ever arose a pestilent whiff of roast Hindu, and which opened the eyes of those who had read about the " luxuries of the East." Life was confined to a solitary ride at dawn and dusk, a dull monotonous day, and a night in some place of dissipation—to put it mildly— such as the Bhendi Bazar, whose attractions consisted of dark young persons in gaudy dress, mock jewels and hair japanned with cocoa-nut oil ; and whose especial diversions were an occasional "row"—a barbarous manner of "town and gown." But a few days of residence taught Richard that India, at least Western India, offered only two specialties for the Britisher ; first Shikár or sport, and secondly, opportunities of studying the people and their languages. These were practically unlimited ; he found that it took him seven years of hard study before he could walk into a Bazar, distinguish the several castes, and know something of their manners and customs, religion and superstitions. He at once engaged a venerable Parsee, Dosabhái Sohrabji ; a mobed, or priest, as the white cap and coat showed, who had coached many a generation of griffs, and under such guidance dived deep into the 'Ethics of Mind' (Akhlak-i-Hindi) and other such text-books.

This was the year after the Heir Apparent was born; when Pollock and Sale revenged the destruction of some 13,000 men by the Afghans; when the Chinese war broke out; when Lord Ellenborough succeeded awkward Lord Auckland; and when Major-General Sir Charles J. Napier, commanding at Poonah, was appointed to Sind (August 25th, 1842), and when his subsequent unfriend Brevet Major James Outram was on furlough to England. Lastly, and curious to say, most important of all to him was the fact, that Ensign Burton was ranked and posted in the G. G. O. of October 15th, 1842, to the 18th Regiment Bombay N. I.

The first sight of a "Sepoy" nearly threw him off his balance. A picturesque article in turban and flowing clothes, he was a pure figure of fun in his European cap and whiskers, with his waspish waist, his legs parting from his person below the breast, his back, arms, and legs in comparative tights, and his delicate feet in ammunition shoes. There was a total want of the "fitness of things" in this ultra-European dress upon an ultra-Asiatic person; and, as the Sepoy mutiny afterwards proved, the mental contrast was even more grotesque than the corporeal. Richard's first impulse was to re-embark, to fly the country; but a reference to Forbes' bank proved that finance forbade. Nor was he less surprised by the boasting of his brother officers. The Sepoys had thrashed the French in India, and else-where; they were the flower of the British Army and so forth—fine specimens of the *esprit de corps* run mad and destined miserably to change tone after 1857. Meanwhile this loud brag covered an ugly truth: officers of the Indian Army held Her Majesty's commission, but Company's officers were looked upon by the Queen's troops as mere auxiliaries, locals without general rank, as it were black policemen. Moreover the rules of the service did not allow them to rise above a certain rank — what a contrast to the French private who carries a marshal's batôn in his knapsack !

Captain Cleveland introduced Richard to his sister, the wife of a field-officer, and she to sundry of her friends whose tone somewhat surprised him. There and then a reference was made to the "immortal soul," and he was overwhelmed with oral treatises upon what was expected from a Christian in a heathen land : also these ladies "talked shop," at least so it appeared to him, like non-commissioned officers. After Shikár and the Linguistics, the only popular pursuit in India is (or rather *was*) "Society." But indigestible dinners are not pleasant in a Turkish bath, dancing is at a discount in a region of eternal dog-days : picnics are unpleasant on the "palm-tasselled strand of glowing Ind," where scorpions and cobras come uninvited : horse-racing, like Cicero's "mercatura," to be honoured, must be on a large scale : the mess-tiffin is an abomination ruinous to digestion and health ; the billiard-table may pass an hour or so pleasantly enough, but it becomes a monotonous bore and waste of time, and the evening band or meet at "Scandal Point" is also open to the charge of a deadly dulness. Visits became visitations, because that tyrant Madam Etiquette commanded them about noon, despite risk of sunstroke ; and "the ladies" insisted upon them without remorse of conscience. Needless to say that in those days the "Gym Khanah" was unknown, and that the Indian world ignored lawn-tennis, or even croquet.

The worst of colonial life was that in 1842 there were very few white faces in Bombay, and every man, woman, and child knew his or her neighbour's affairs as well as their own. It was, in fact, a garrison, not a colony ; and people lived in a kind of huge barracks. Essentially a middle-class society, like that of a small country-town in England, it was suddenly raised to the top of the tree, and lost its head accordingly. Men whose parents were small tradesmen in England, or bailiffs in Scotland, found themselves ruling districts and commanding regiments, driving in carriages, and owning more pounds a month than their parents had pounds a year. Those who had interest, especially in Leadenhall Street, monopolised the best appointments, and gathered in clans at the Presidency, as head-quarters were called. They formed the usual ring—a magic circle into which no intruder was admitted save by the *peine forte et dure* of intermarriage. Caste is so powerful in India that it even affects Mlenchha or outcast races. The children were hideously brought up, and, under the age of five, used language that would make a coal-porter's hair stand on end. The parents, of course, separated into cliques, and at that time Bombay was ruled by two queens, who in subaltern circles went by the names of "old Mother Plausible" and "old Mother Damnable."

To give a taste of Mother Damnable's quality :—Richard had been waltzing with a girl who, after too much exertion, declared herself fainting. He led her into what would, at home, be called the cloak-room, fetched her a glass of water, and was putting it to her lips, when the old lady stood at the door. "Oh, dear! I never intended to interrupt you!" she said ; made a low bow, and went out of the room positively delighted. Mother Plausible's style was being intensely respectable. She was terribly exercised about a son at Addiscombe, and carefully consulted every new cadet about his proficiency in learning. "But does he prefer the Classics ? " she asked a wild Irishman. "I don't know that he does," was the answer. "Or mathematics ? " the same result. "Or modern languages ? "—"Well, no."— "Then, what does he do ? "—"Faix," said the informant, scratching his head, "he's a mighty purty hand at football ! "

Another point in Bombay Society at once struck him; and

he afterwards found it flourishing in the Colonies and most highly developed in the United States. At home men and women lived under an incubus, a perfect system of social despotism, which is intended to make amends for an unnatural political equality amongst classes born radically unequal. Abroad, the weight is taken off their shoulders, and the result of its removal is a peculiar rankness of growth. The pious become fanatically one idea'd, pharisaic, unchristian, monomaniacal: he knew one officer who climbed a tree every morning and cried out " Dunyá chhor-do ; Jesus Christ pakro ! "—Shun the world and cleave to Jesus. The unpious run to the other extreme, believe nothing, sneer at the " holies," and look upon the mere Agnostic as a " slow coach." Eccentricity develops itself Bedlamwards. One of his friends had a mediæval mania, and swore " By my halidom ! " Another had an image of Ganpati over his door which he never passed without the prayer, " Shri Ganeshaya namahá—I bow to auspicious Janus." A third of whom he heard had studied Aristotle in Arabic, and when shown the Novum Organon asked indignantly who the fellow might be who talked such stuff. And in matters of honesty the social idea was somewhat large : to sell a spavined horse to a friend was considered a good joke, and to pass off plated ware for real silver was looked upon only as a trifle too smart. The press faithfully reflected on these *nuances* with a little extra violence and virulence. By-the-bye he does not forget making the acquaintance of a typical Scot, Dr. Buist, afterwards Sir Charles Napier's " blatant *beast* of the Bombay Times." He wrote much (so badly that only one clerk could read it) and washed little, and as age advanced he married a young wife.

The Governor of Bombay at this time was Colonel Sir George Arthur, Bart., K.C.H., who figured in ' Jack Hinton the Guardsman.' He was supposed to be connected with the Royal Family through George IV., and had some curious ideas about his visitors "backing" from the "Presence." The Commander-in-Chief was old Sir Thomas MacMahon, popularly called "Tommy." He was one of the old soldiers that had served under the Duke of Wellington, who certainly had the merit of looking after his friends as well as his enemies, but "Tommy" was unfortunately utterly unfit for any command beyond that of a brigade. It would be impossible to tell one tithe of the stories current about him. One of his pet abominations was a certain Lieutenant Pilfold, of the 2nd Queen's, whose commanding officer, Major Brough, was perpetually court-martialling. Pilfold belonged to that order of soldiers who are popularly called "lawyers," and invariably argued himself out of every difficulty. He was first court-martialled in 1840, then in 1841 and 1844, when, after being nearly cashiered, he changed into a regiment serving in Australia and died. He had revenged himself on the Commander-in-Chief by declaring that "as hares go mad in March, so Major-Generals go mad in May," the date when "Tommy" confirmed the proceedings of a court-martial, which were quashed at home.

The Bombay Marine, or as the officers preferred to call it, the Indian Navy, had come to grief: Their excellent Superintendent, Admiral Sir Charles Malcolm, was a devoted geographer, in fact he was the man (one of many?) who provoked the saying, "capable of speaking evil even of the Equator." Under his rule, when there was peace at sea the officers were allowed ample leave to travel and explore in the most dangerous countries, and they did excellent service. But Sir Charles was succeeded by a certain Captain Oliver, R.N., a sailor of the Commodore Trunnion type, and a martinet of the first water. He made his officers stick to their monotonous and wearisome duties in the Persian Gulf and other places popularly said to be separated from the fiery place of punishment only by a sheet of brown paper. He was as vindictive as he was one-idea'd, and the service will never forget the way in which he broke the heart of an unfortunate Lieut. Bird.

After a month or so at Bombay, chiefly spent in mugging up " Hindustani," and in providing himself with the necessaries of life, servants, headed by Salvador Soares, a handsome Goanese ; a horse in the shape of a dun-coloured Katiawár nag, also a dog, a tent, and so forth, Richard received his marching orders, and set out to "join." The simple way of travelling in those days, before steam and rail, was by palanquin or pattimár. Richard has described the latter article in "Goa," and I may add that it had its advantages. True, it was a "slow coach," creeping on seventy or eighty miles a day, and on some days almost stationary : it had few comforts and no luxuries : he began by actually missing "pudding," and has often smiled at the remembrance of his stomach's comical disappointment. *En revanche*, the study of the little world within, was most valuable to the young Anglo-Indian ; and the slow devious course allowed landing at places rarely visited by Europeans. During his repeated trips he saw Diu, once so famous in Portuguese story ; holy Dwarká, guarded outside by sharks and filled with fierce and fanatic mercenaries, and a dozen less interesting spots. The end of this trip was Tankaria Bunder, a small landing in the Bay of Cambay, a most primitive *locale*, to be called a port, where a mud-bank adapted for a mooring-stake was about the only convenience. It showed him, however, a fine specimen of the Ghorá or bore, known to our Severn and other rivers, an exaggerated high tide when the water comes rushing up the shallows like a charge of cavalry. Native carts were also to be procured at Tankaria Bunder for the three days' short march to Baroda, and a mattress spread below made the rude article comfortable enough for young limbs and strong nerves.

Guzarát, the classical Gujaráshtra, or Land of the Gujar clan, which renamed the Syrastrena Regio of Arrian, surprised Richard by its tranquil beauty and its vast natural wealth. Green as a card-table, flat as a prairie, it grew a marvellous growth of trees, which stunted our English oak and elm trees,—

> "to ancient song unknown
> The noble sons of potent heat and flood "—

a succession of fields breaking the glades, of townlets and villages, walled by luxuriant barriers of caustic milk-bush (euphorbia), and all teeming with sights, sounds, and smells peculiarly Indian. The sharp bark of Hanuman the monkey, and the bray of the Shankh or conch-shell, near the bowery Pagodas were surprising to the ear, and not less to the nose was the blue vapour which settled over the hamlets morning and evening, a semi-transparent veil, mostly the result of "gobar," smoke from " cow-chips." Many a time for miles off shore Richard has noted a faint spicy odour, as if there were curry in the air, which about the abodes of man seems to be crossed with an aroma of drugs as though proceeding from an apothecary's store. Wondrous peaceful and quiet lay those little Indian villages, outlaid by glorious banyan and pipal trees, topes or clumps of giant figs which rain a most grateful shade and sometimes provided by the piety of some long departed chief, with a tank of cut stone and a Baurá, or draw well of fine masonry and large dimensions. But what "exercised" not a little of his "griffin" thought was to note the unpleasant difference between the villages under English rule and those belonging to " His Highness the Gaekwar," or cow-keeper; the penury of the former, and the prosperity of the latter. Mr. Boyd, the then Resident at the local court, soon enlightened him upon the evils of our unelastic rule of " smart collectors," who cannot and dare not make any allowance for deficient rain-fall or

injured crops, and it is better to have something to lose
and to lose it, even to the extent of "being ousted of one's
possessions and disseized of one's freehold," with the
likely hope of gaining it again, than to own nothing worth
plundering.

The end of the march introduced him to his corps, the
18th Regiment Bombay Native Infantry, whose head-
quarters were in Gujarat, one wing being stationed at
"Mhow" on the Bengal frontier. The officer commanding, Captain James, called upon him at the Traveller's
Bungalow, the rudimentary inn which must satisfy the
stranger in India, suggesting the while such sad contrasts,
and bore him off to his bungalow, formally presented him at
mess—then reduced to four members besides himself and
the Assistant-Surgeon Arnott—and put him in the way of
lodging himself. The regimental dining-room with its large
cool alcoves and punkha (swing-fan), its clean napery and
bright silver, its servants each standing behind his master's
chair, and the cheroots and hookahs which appeared with
the disappearance of the table cloth, was a pleasant surprise, the first sight of comfortable home-life he had seen
since landing at Bombay. Not so the "Subaltern's bungalow," which gave the idea of a dog-hole at which British
Ponto would turn up his civilized nose. The business
of the day was mainly goose-step, studying the drill-book
and listening to such equivocal words of command as
"Tandelees" (stand at ease), and "Fiz bagnet" (fix
bayonets). Long practice with the sword, which he had
begun at the age of twelve, sometimes taking three lessons
a day, soon eased his difficulties and led to the study of
native swordsmanship, whose grotesqueness and buffoonery
can be rivalled only by its inefficiency.* The wrestling,

---

* Those curious upon the subject should consult his 'Book of the
Sword,' vol. i. p. 163. Remember, young swordsman, these people
never give point, nor can they parry it!

however, was another matter, not a few natives in his company had at first the advantage of him ; and this induced a trial of Indian training, which consisted mainly of washing down balls of " Gur " (unrefined sugar) with bowls of hot milk hotly spiced. The result was that in a week he was blind with bile. Another set of lessons suggested by common-sense, was instruction by a Chábuk-sawár, or native jockey. All nations seem to despise one another's riding, and none seem to know how much they have to learn. The Indian style has the merit of holding the horse well in hand, making him bound off at a touch of the heel, stopping him dead at a hand gallop, and wheeling him round as on a pivot. The Hindu will canter over a figure of 8, gradually diminishing the dimensions till the animal leans over at an angle of 45°, and throwing himself over the off-side and hanging by the heel to the earth will pick up sword or pistol from the ground. Our lumbering chargers brought our troops to notable grief more than once in the great Sikh war. And, as Richard was somewhat nervous about snakes, he took lessons of a "charmer," and could soon handle them with coolness.

The military day was then passed in India as follows :— Men woke early, for the sun in India keeps decent hours, not like the Greater Light in England, which in summer seems to rise shortly after midnight, and in winter shortly before noon. The first proceeding was a wash in cold water and a cup of tea. After that the horse was brought round, and carried the rider to the dull drill-ground. Work usually began as soon as it was light and lasted till shortly after sunrise. In the Bengal Presidency the officers used to wash their teeth at 3 A.M., and scarcely ever saw the face of the sun ; consequently the Qui-hyes (Bengalis) died off like sheep, upon a march, when much exposure was necessary. In India the sun demands a little respect : it is not wise for instance to wade through cold water with its rays beating upon the upper part of the body, but it is always advisable to accustom oneself to sunshine. After the parade was over the officers generally met at what was called a coffee-shop, where one of the number lodged. Chhoti-hazri or little breakfast consisted of tea or *café au lait*, biscuit, bread-and-butter and fruit. The heavy work of the day being then done, each proceeded to amuse himself as he best could, some to play at billiards, others sought a few hours for sport.

The Shikár all about Baroda was excellent. In the thick jungle to the east of the city, tigers were to be bagged, and native friends would always lend their elephants for a day's work. In the broad plains to the north, large antelopes called the Nilghae browsed about like cows and were almost as easy to shoot—consequently no one shot them. It was different with the splendid black buck, shy and wary animals always brought home in triumph. Cheetahs or hunting leopards were also to be had for the asking. As for birds they were in countless numbers, from the huge adjutant crane, the heron (*Grus Antigone*) vulgarly called Sáras, which dies if its mate be shot, and the peacock, which there, as in most parts of India, is a sacred bird, to the partridge which no one eats because it feeds on the road, the wild duck which gives excellent shooting, and the snipe equal to any in England. During the early rains quails were to be flushed in the compounds or yards attached to the bungalows. In fact in those days sensible men who went out to India took one of two lines; they either shot or they studied languages.

Baroda was not a great place for pig-sticking. The old grey boars abounded, but the country was too much cut up by deep and perpendicular nullahs, which were death to horse and man. Richard invested in an aged grey Arab, which followed the game like a bloodhound with distended nostrils, and ears viciously laid back : he began (as was the cruel custom of the day), by spearing Pariah dogs for practice, and his first successes brought him a well-merited accident. Not knowing that the least touch of the sharp leaf-like spear-head is sufficient to kill, he made a mighty thrust with his strong male bamboo shaft, which was carried under the arm Bombay fashion, instead of overhand as in Bengal. The point passed right through the poor brute, and deep into the ground ; when the strong elastic spear raised the rider bodily out of the saddle and flung him over the horse's head. It was a good lesson for teaching how to take " first blood." The great centres for pig-sticking were in the Deccan, and in Sind : the latter, however, offered too much danger, for riding through tamarisk bushes is very much like charging a series of well-staked fishing nets. Baroda, however, abounded in wild beasts. The jackals swarmed round the bungalows every night, and a hyena once crossed the parade ground in full day. One of the captains (Partridge) cut it down with his regimental sword and imprudently dismounted to secure it : the result was a bite in the arm which he had reason long to remember.

There was no such thing as society in Baroda. The Station was commanded by an old brigadier named Gibbons, who had no wife, but a native family. He was far too infirm to mount a horse ; he never "received ; " he ignored dinners, either at home or abroad, and he lived as most old general officers did in those days. But he managed to get into a tremendous row, and was removed from his command for a reason highly suggestive of one of the farcical " Nabob " comedies of the last century. The 18th Bombay Native Infantry was brigaded with the 4th Regiment *alias* Rifles, under the command of Major C. Crawley. These Sepoys in their dingy green uniform, which seemed to reflect itself upon their chocolate coloured cheeks, looked even worse than those dressed in red. There was also a company of what were called

Golandáz, a sort of regular Native Artillery, commanded by a Lieutenant Aked. Gunners are everywhere a peculiar race, quite as peculiar as sailors: in India they have the great merit of extreme attachment to their weapons, which after a fashion they adore as weapons of destruction. "One could hit a partridge with a gun like this!" said a pink-faced youngster to a grisly old cannonier. "A partridge?" cried the veteran, "*This* does not kill partridges, it smashes armies, it slaughters cities, and it would bring down Shiva himself!" In Baroda city the Gaikwar had two guns to which regular adoration was offered : they were of massive gold, built around steel tubes, and each was worth about £10,000. Yet the company of Native Artillery was utterly absurd in European eyes. Nothing is more beautiful than the Gujarat bullocks, with their noble horns, and pure white coats ; Europe has seen them in the Cascine of Tuscany. But it was truly absurd to see these magnificent animals dragging a gun into position at a shambling and dislocated trot. Satirical subalterns used to speak of "the cow batteries:" in these days, of course all are horsed. Literature was at a discount, although one youth in the Bombay Rifles was addicted to rhyme, and circulated a lay which began as follows:—

> " 'Tis merry, 'tis merry, in the long jungle grass,
> When the Jánwars around you fly,
> To think of the slaughter that you will commit
> On the beasts that go passing by."

Hospitalities used to be exchanged between the corps on certain ceremonious occasions, but a mess dinner was the extent of sociality. As in all small societies there were little tiffs, likings and dislikings. But the age of duelling had passed away, especially after a fatal affair of Col. Fawcett of the 55th Regt. and his brother-in-law, Mr. Monro. A most pernicious practice common in those days was that of eating tiffin, — in other words a full luncheon at 2 o'clock—following the normal breakfast or Pakki Hazri at 9. Tiffin was generally composed of heating meats, and the never-failing curry, washed down with heavy bottled beer, followed by two or three Manilla cheroots, and possibly a siesta. Nothing could be more anti-hygienic than this: it is precisely the course of proceeding by which the liver of the Strasbourg goose is prepared for *pâté de foie gras*. The amount of oxygen present in the air of India is not sufficient to burn up all this carbon, and hence the dingy complexions and the dull, dark hair which distinguishes veteran Anglo-Indians on their return home. Richard contented himself with his biscuit and a glass of port, something being required to feed the brain after the hard study of many hours.

The French in India order these things much better. They keep up their national habits, except that they rise very early ; take a very light meal chiefly consisting of *café noir*, and eat a heavy breakfast at 11. Between that and dinner which follows sunset they rarely touch anything, and the consequence is that they return with livers comparatively sound. But Anglo-Indian hours of meals have been modelled upon those of England, and English hours are laid down by the exigencies of "business." Hence the Briton, nationally speaking, breakfasts at 9. As he rises late and has little appetite at that hour, he begins the work of the day upon such a slender basis as tea, bread and butter, an egg or a frizzle of bacon. It was very different in the age of Queen Elizabeth, and certainly the beefsteaks and beer produced a stronger race ; but in those times all rose early, and lived much in the open air.

During the fine weather there was generally something to do on the parade ground shortly before sunset, after which the idlers mounted their nags and took a lazy ride. The day ended at mess, which was also characteristically Indian. A long table in the mess bungalow was decorated

with the regimental plate, and surmounted by creaking
punkahs that resembled horizontally slung boards with a
fringe along the lower part. A native concealed behind
the wall, set those unpleasant articles in motion, generally
holding the rope between his toes. At the top of the
hall sat the Mess President; at the bottom the Vice,
and their duty was to keep order, and especially to
prevent shop-talking. The officers, dressed like so many
caterpillars in white shell jackets, white waistcoats, and
white overalls, were a marvellous contrast to the gorgeous
Moslem Khidmatgars, who stood behind them with crossed
arms, turbans the size of tea tables, and gaudy waist shawls
in proportion. The dinner consisted of soup, a joint of roast
mutton at one end, and boiled mutton, or boiled fowls at
the other, with vegetables in the side dishes. Beef was
never seen because the cow was worshipped at Baroda, nor
was roast or boiled pork known at native messes, where
the manners and customs of the unclean Bazar-pig were
familiar to all, and where there were ugly stories about the
insults to which his remains were exposed on the part of
the Mohammedan scullions. At times, however, a ham
made its appearance disguised under the name of Wiláyati
bakri—*Anglicè* Europe mutton.

The substantial part of the dinner always concluded with
curry accompanied by dried fish, Bombay ducks and Pápri or
assafœtida cake. Anglo-Indians appreciate curry too much
to allow it, as in England, to precede other dishes and rob
them of all their flavour. After this came puddings and tarts,
which very few men touched, as they disagreed with beer and
with cheese which was a universal favourite. Coffee, curious
to say, was unknown ; ice was rare, except at the Presidency,
and tinned vegetables, like peas and asparagus, had only
lately been invented. After cheese all lit their cigars, which
in those days were invariably Manillas : they cost only
twenty rupees a thousand, so few were driven to the economy

of the abominable Trichinopoly smoked in Madras. Havanas were never seen: pipes were as little known, and only the oldsters had an extensive article with a stand two feet high and a pipe twenty feet long, in which they smoked an article called Guraku. This was a mixture of tobacco with plenteous conserve of roses and a dozen different kinds of spices, that gave out a very peculiar perfume. The Hookah was, however, then going out of fashion and presently died the death: it is now as rarely seen in Anglo-India as the long chibouque at Constantinople. On festive occasions there was a Nach, which most men pronounced Nautch. The scene has been often described in its picturesque aspect; but it had its dark side, and nothing could be more ignoble than this, two or three debauched and drunken musicians squealing and scraping the most horrible music, and the *figurantes* with thin simiad faces dressed in magnificent brocades and performing in the most grotesque way. The scene gave one a shiver. Yet not a few of the old officers who had been brought up to this kind of thing enjoyed it as much as the Russians of the same epoch delighted in the Gypsy *soirées* of Moscow where they ruined themselves with Madeira and Veuve Cliquot.

The mess dinner sometimes concluded with a game of whist, but the wing of a Native corps had not officers enough to make it interesting. After a *quantum sufficit* of cheroots and spirits-and-water, the mess broke up and the members strolled home, immensely enjoying the clear moonlight which looked as if frost were lying on the emerald green of Gujarat. It was very different during the rains which here, as in most parts of the Western Lowlands of India, were torrential—sometimes lasting seven days and seven nights without an hour's interruption. The country was mostly under water, and those who went to mess had to protect themselves with waterproofs, and if they

wished to save their horses from the dangerous disease
called Barsáti, to walk messwards and home, with bare legs
and feet.

There was little variety in such days. At times they rode
to Baroda City which seemed like a mansion to which
the cantonment acted porter's lodge. " Good water " (the
Sanskritists translate it) was a walled capital lying on the
north bank of the Visvamitra River and containing some
150,000 souls, mostly hostile, who eyed us with hateful
eyes, and who seemed to have taught even their animals to
abhor us. The town was a mélange of low huts and tall
houses grotesquely painted, with a shabby palace and a
chauk or Bazar where four streets met. At times H. M.
the Gaikwar would show the regiment what blacks called
sport, a fight between two elephants with cut tusks or a
caged tiger and a buffalo, the last being generally the
winner, or a wrangle between two fierce stallions which bit
like camels. The cock-fighting, however, was of a superior
kind, the animals being of first-class blood and so well
trained that they never hesitated to attack a stranger.
An occasional picnic, for sport, not society, was a most
pleasant break. The native prince would always lend
his cheetahs, or hunting-leopards, or his elephants; the
jungles inland of the city swarmed with game from a snipe
to a tiger, and the broad plains to the north were herds of
antelope and the glorious black buck. About twenty-eight
miles due east rose high above the sea of verdure the
picturesque hill known as Pávangarh, the fort of Eolus, and
the centre of an old civilisation ; tanks and Jain temples
were scattered about it, and the ruins of Champanir
cumbered the base. In a more progressive society, this
place, 2500 feet high and cooler by 18° or 20° (F.), would
have become a kind of sanitarium, but men apparently
could not agree. When the Baroda races came round,
some of the officers following the lead of a mal-content

in consequence of some fancied slight, used openly to ride out of cantonment: and Brigadier Gibbons, the commander, did nothing for society, he was presently obliged to quit the service for flogging the Kitwal or native Bazar-Master with an offending leg of mutton. But the crowning excitement of the season was the report of Sir Charles Napier's battle of Miani (Feb. 21),[followed by the affair of Dubba (March 25), "the tail of the Afghan war." The account seemed to act as an electric shock upon the English frame, followed by a deep depression and a sense of mortal injury at the hands of Fate in keeping us out of the fray.

This even tenor of existence was varied by only two things. The first was the annual review, when old General Morse came from Ahmedabad to inspect the corps—a ceremony for which preparations had been going on for a couple of months. These old officers were greatly derided by the juniors, chiefly because their brains seemed to have melted away. They had forgotten almost everything except drill, which they had learned in their youth. This venerable veteran prided himself in particular upon his Hindustani and suffered accordingly. "How would you say, 'Tell a plain story,' General?"—"Maydan-ki-bát bolo!"—which means "speak a word of a level country."

The other great event was the annual race meeting. Even here, however, there was a division of the small society. The races were encouraged by the Company's President, Mr. Boyd, and by Major Henry Corsellis, who had come up with his wife to take command of the regiment. They were discouraged on the other hand by Major Crawley of the 4th Rifles, who invariably had a picnic during the race week. The reason, however, was not "principle," but some quarrel about an old bet. Richard was one of the winners at the Welter Stakes, having beaten an experienced rider, Lieutenant Raikes.

The state of things at Baroda was not satisfactory. The French govern their colonies too much ; the English too little. The latter, instead of taking their stand as the Masters and declaring

"Sic volo, sic jubeo, sit pro ratione voluntas,"

seemed, in Baroda at least, to rule on sufferance. They were thoroughly the masters of the position and could have deposed the Gaikwar or destroyed the town in a week. But the rule of the Court Directors was not a rule of honour. The officers in cantonments, distant only half an hour's ride from the palace, were actually obliged to hire Rámosis or Paggis to protect their lives and properties. These men were simply professed thieves, who took blackmail to prevent their friends and relations from plundering. In the quarters on the borders of the camp a couple of these scoundrels were necessary : in two bungalows officers had been cut down, and one of them in which Richard lived showed sabre cuts on the door lintel. Officers were constantly robbed, and even murdered when travelling about the district, and the universally expressed wish was that some Director's son might come to grief and put an end to such miserable state of misrule. Now these things could have been put a stop to by a single dispatch of the Court of Directors to the Resident at Baroda : they had only to make the Gaikwar and the native authorities answerable for the lives and property of their employés. A single hanging and a few heavy fines would have settled the business at once and for ever ; but I repeat, the rule of the Court of Directors was not a rule of honour, and already the childish doctrine was being preached that "Prestige is Humbug." The officers marvelled at the proceedings of their rulers, and marvelled without understanding things, because they little knew what was going on at home. Here, Mr. Richard Cobden, one of the most single-minded of men, whose main strength was that he embodied most of the weaknesses and all the prejudices of the British middle-class public, was watching the affairs of India with a jealous and unfriendly eye. As a military and despotic government, an acquisition of impolitic violence and fraud and as the seat of unsafe finance, India appeared to him utterly destitute of any advantage either to the natives or to their foreign masters. He looked upon the East India Company in Asia as simply a monopoly, not merely against foreigners but against their own countrymen. He openly asserted that England had attempted an impossibility in giving to herself the task of governing one hundred million of Asiatics. He declared, as if he had been taken into supernatural confidence, that God and His visible natural laws have opposed unspeakable obstacles to the success of such a scheme. His opinion as a professional reformer was that Hindustan must be ruled by those who live on that side of the globe, and that its people will prefer to be ruled badly by its own colour, kith and kin, than subject itself to the humiliation of being better governed by a succession of transient intruders from the Antipodes. He declared that ultimately, of course, Nature (of which he knew nothing) will assert the supremacy of her laws, and the white skins will withdraw to their own latitudes, leaving the Hindus to the enjoyment of the climate for which their dingy hides are suited. All this was the regular Free Trade bosh, and the Great Bagman would doubtless have been thunderstruck had he heard the shouts of Homeric laughter with which his mean-spirited utterances were received by every white in British India. There was not a subaltern in the 18th Bombay, N.I., who did not consider himself perfectly capable of governing a million Hindus, and such a conviction realizes itself

> " By the sword we won the land,
> And by the sword we'll hold it still."

For each subaltern felt (if he could not put the feeling

into words) that India had been won, despite England, by the energy and bravery of men like himself. Every history tells one so in a way that all can understand. The Company began as mere traders, and presently they obtained the right of raising guards to defend themselves ; the guards naturally led to the acquisition of territory, and that territory increased till its three centres, Bengal, Madras, Bombay, became foci of kingdoms. The native princes were startled and frightened : they attacked their energetic neighbours with little success, and the islanders became more intrusive than before. Next they began to elect Governors and Governors-General. Whenever a new man was sent out from England the natives, after the fashion of their kind, thought that they saw their opportunity, and losing their fear of the old Governor declared war against the new one. The latter assembled an army and duly reported the fact home. It took from eight to nine months before the document was received and considered. The general tone of the reply was a fierce diatribe against "territorial aggrandisement," but in the meantime a great battle or two had been fought, a province had been conquered and duly plundered, and a large slice of territory had been added to Anglo-Indian rule. This is the way in which the British Empire in the East rose and grew, and probably it was the least objectionable way. For when the Company came to power it began to juggle Native Princes out of their territory, to deny the right of adoption, and to perpetrate all kinds of injustice.* A fair example was the case of the Rajah of Satara, and the same proceedings in Oude led to the celebrated mutiny in 1857 and nearly wrecked British dominion in India.

As soon as Richard had passed his drill, he was placed

---

* It is interesting to note in this place how completely Sir Richard Burton's personal observation justifies the line of policy with respect to India consistently advocated by Lord Beaconsfield.—ED.

in charge of a company and proceeded to teach what he had just learned. He greatly encouraged his men in sword-exercise, and used to get the best players to his quarters for a good long bout every day. The usual practice in India is with a kind of single stick, ribboned with list-cloth up to the top and a small shield in the left hand: this style of work appears to have been borrowed from the sword dance of some civilized people like the Bactrian Greeks. The swordsman begins with " renowning it," vapouring with his blade and showing all the curious fantastie that distinguishes a Spanish *Espada*. Then with the fiercest countenance he begins to spring in the air, to jump from side to side, to crouch and to rush forwards and backwards with all the action of an excited baboon. He never thinks of giving point ; throughout India the thrust is confined to the dagger. The cuts as a rule were only two—one at the shoulder and the other in the vernacular, called "Kalam," at the lower legs. Nothing was easier than to guard these cuts, and to administer a thrust that would have been fatal with steel. Richard gave a prize every month to the best swordsman, wrestler and athlete, generally some gaudy turban. But although he did his best, he could never teach them to use a foil.

These proceedings excited not a little wonderment amongst his brother subs., but much more when the new Ensign sent for a Chabuk Sawar, or native jockey, and began to learn the Indian system of riding and training the horse. As a rule this was absurdly neglected in India. Men mostly rode half-broken Arabs and many an annual review showed the pleasant spectacle of a commanding officer being run away with in one direction and the second-in-command in another. When it came to meetings in the field the Englishman was at a terrible disadvantage. An ugly story is told of a *rencontre* between an Indian and an English cavalry officer who had been offended by the

remarks of the former. They charged sword in hand in the
presence of their regiments, but were equally skilful in
parrying attack. Presently, however, the Englishman found
himself in a fix, the Eastern with his sharp light blade having
cut the horse's reins without hurting either horse or man
—a favourite native *ruse*. Upon this the Englishman
drew his pistol and disloyally shot the Indian, who, in his
lingering illness, which ended fatally, declared that he never
meant to hurt the English officer, but only to prove his own
words, that he was not his equal in swordsmanship and
horsemanship. The English officer deeply regretted the
event, and it was hushed up, but such acts are never quite
buried : to prevent a repetition of the difficulty, light
chains were afterwards adopted to accompany the leather
bridle. A similar manslaughter took place during one of
the Sind campaigns. An officer, who shall be nameless,
attacked a Baluch Chief, who being mounted upon a tired
mare made no attempt to fly. The Englishman, who had
some reputation as a swordsman, repeatedly bore down
upon him making a succession of cuts which his opponent
received upon his blade and shield. At last, being unable
to win fairly, the Englishman, who in after life rose high in
command, drew his pistol and shot the Baluch. Curious
to say, he was not court-martialled.

At length, in April, 1843, Richard obtained two months'
leave of absence to the Presidency for the purpose of
passing an examination in Hindustani. He made the
march from Baroda to Tankaria Bunder and there found a
Pattimár for Bombay. The sail southward, despite the
extraordinary heat of the season, was perfectly charming.
The north-east monsoon, about drawing to its end, alternated with the salt sea-breeze and the spicy land-breeze—
the former justly called " the Doctor." The sky was deep
blue, unflecked by a single cloud, and the sea bluer still,
hardly crisped by the wind. There was perfect calm

inside and outside the vessel—no posts and no parades. The living was simple enough, consisting chiefly of rice, curry, and "chapatties," or scones of unleavened bread, with the never-failing tea and tobacco. Tea in India is better than in England, although of inferior quality, because it has a shorter sea voyage : the native servants, however, have a peculiar way of brewing it, and those who have once drunk a " sneaker," or double-sized cup full of Indian tea, will never forget the flavour of tea-tannin.

Despite landing almost every evening, the voyage down the coast occupied only six or seven days. This time the traveller hired a tent with the aid of the old Parsi " General," and pitched it in the strangers' lines, which extended southwards from the Sanitarium along the shore of Back Bay and were not, as now, huddled up into a little space on the other side of the road. With the assistance of old Dosábhai Sohrabji, he worked up the last minutiæ of the language, and on May 5th appeared in the Town Hall, where the examinations were held. These were not without a certain amount of difficulty. The candidate was expected to make a written translation, to translate *vivâ voce* from a native book, to read a written letter often vilely scrawled, and to converse with the Munshí, Mohammed Ibrahim Makbá, who also wrote a book, for which see Quaritch. The candidate was fortunate in his examiner. Captain Pope, who formerly held that position, had been made Assistant Commissary-General, and could no longer indulge in his pet propensity for " plucking " youngsters The committee was composed of Major-General Vans Kennedy and three or four nobodies. The former was an Orientalist after a fashion, and knew a great deal of books, but much more of Indian manners and customs : in fact he lived in native society and was as usual grossly imposed upon. Whenever a servant wanted leave he always begged permission to place a Badli or substitute to do his work, and when No. 1 returned No. 2 remained : consequently the old man was eaten up by native drones. He existed amongst his books in a tumble-down bungalow amidst a tattered compound which was never repaired, and he had a slight knowledge of Sanscrit and Arabic with an abundant acquaintance with Hindustani and Persian and general Oriental literature.   The one grievance of his life was his treatment by Sir John afterwards Lord Keane.   This western barbarian went out to India when advanced in years and imbued with a fine contempt for "the-twenty-years-in-the-country-and-speaks-the-language-man."   He could not understand what was the use of having officers who did nothing but facilitate the study of Orientalism, and he speedily sent off Colonel Vans Kennedy to rejoin his regiment. The latter was deeply in debt, as usual under his circumstances : his creditors tolerated him at the Presidency, where they could lay ready claws upon his pay, but before he could march up country he was obliged to sell for a mere nothing his valuable library of books and manuscripts which had occupied him a lifetime in collecting. He was a curious spectacle, suggesting only a skeleton dressed in a worn-out uniform, and he spoke all his languages with a fine, broad Lowland accent, which is perhaps, Orientally speaking, the best.   The examining munshi, Mohammed "Muckba," was not friendly to Richard, because he had been coached by a rival, old Dosábhai, yet he could not prevent his distancing a field of eleven. Next him came Ensign Robert Gordon, of the 4th Bombay Rifles, and Ensign H. Higginson, of the 78th Highlanders.   The latter brought to the Examination Hall one of the finest Irish brogues ever heard there : he had been humble enough before he passed, but having once got through he was ready to back his knowledge against the world. This "exam." was no great feat on Richard's part, as he had begun Arabic at Oxford and worked at Hindustani in

London and on board ship, and had studied for twelve hours a day at Baroda. Before he quitted the Presidency he had an unpleasantness with a certain Dr. Bird, a pseudo-Orientalist, who, after the fashion of the day, used the brains of Munshí and Pandit to make his own reputation. Richard revenged himself by lampooning him when, at the ripe age of forty-five, he was about to take to himself a spare young rib. The lines began,

> " A small grey Bird goes out to woo,
> Primed with Persian ditties new ;
> To the gardens straight he flew,
> Where he knew Miss Rosebud grew."

The two afterwards met in London and were very good friends. Dr. Bird only regretted that he had wasted his time on native languages instead of studying his own pro-fession : he practised medicine for a short time in town, and there died. He passed on May 5, and on May 12 he had laid in a full supply of Gujerati books and set out by the old road to rejoin.

The " Monsoon," * as it is most incorrectly termed, com-pletely changes the tenor of Anglo-Indian life. It is ushered in by a display of "insect youth," which would have astonished Egypt in the days of the plagues, "flying bugs," and so forth ; at mess every tumbler was pro-tected by a silver lid. And when the downfall begins it suggests that the fountains of the great deep had been opened up—Richard has seen tropical rains in many a region near the line, but never anything that rivals Guja-rát. Without exaggeration, the steady discharge of water-buckets lasted literally on one occasion through seven

---

* The word is a Portuguese corruption of "mausim," in Arabic " a season," and for *per excellentiam* "the sailing season," whence it was transferred to the dry season, when the north-eastern trade-winds blow upon the Indian Ocean. But popular use transferred the name to the south-western, or rainy winds, which last from June to September.

days and nights without intermission ; and to reach mess
the officers had to send on clothes, to wear a single waterproof, and to gallop through water above, around, and
below, at full speed. This third of the year was a terribly
dull and suicidal time, worse even than the "gloomy month
of November." It amply accounted for the card-table
surface, and the glorious tree-clump of Gujarát,

> "The mighty growth of sun and torrent-rains."

On June 26th, 1843, "Ensign Burton" appeared in orders
as " Regimental Interpreter," which added a few rupees—
some 30 a month—to his income. Working at least twelve
hours a day, and doing nothing but work, he found himself
ready in later August for a second trip to the Presidency,
and obtained leave from September 10 to October 30
(afterwards made to include November 10), for proceeding
to Bombay, and being examined in the " Guzerattee language." This time he resolved to try another route, and
despite all warnings against abominable roads, to ride
down coast *viâ* Baroch and Surat : however, he had not
been deceived ; the deep and rich black soil, which is so
good for the growth of cotton, makes a mud truly terrible
to travellers. Baroch, the Hindu Brighu-Kshetra, or Field
of Brighu, son of Brahma, is generally made the modern
successor of Ptolemy and Arrian's " Barygaza," but there
are no classic remains to support the identification, nor
indeed did any one upon the spot seem to care a fig about
the matter. A truly Hindu town of some 12,000 souls on
the bank of the Nerbudda, it boasted only of one sight,
the Kabir-bar, which the English translated " Big Banyan,"
and which meant " Banyan-tree of (the famous, ascetic and
poet, Dás) Kabir." Richard remembers only one of his
lines—

> "Máyá mare na man mare, mar mar gayá sarir."
> ("Illusion dies ; dies not the mind, though body die and die.")

Máyá (illusion) being sensuous matter, and the old Fakir

expresses the idea of the modern Hylozoist *—"all things are thinks." The old tree is hardly worth a visit, although it may have sheltered 5000 horsemen and inspired Milton, for whom see the guide-books.

Surat (Surasthra = good region), for a long time the "Gate of Meccah" where pilgrims embarked instead of at Bombay, shows nothing of its olden splendour. This was the nucleus of British power on the western coast of India in the seventeenth century, and as early as May, 1609, Capt. Hawkins of the *Hector* obtained permission at Agra here to found a factory for his half-piratical countrymen who are briefly described by "molossis suis ferociores." They soon managed to turn out the Portuguese, and they left a graveyard which is not devoid of semi-barbaric interest ; Tom Coryate of the crudities is, however, absent from it. At Surat the traveller met Lieut. Manson, B.A. ; he was going down to "go up" in Maráthi, and they agreed to take a pattimár together. The cruise down the foul Tapti river— all Indian, like West African streams, seem to be made of dirty water—showed them the abandoned site of the Dutch Garden and French Factory, Vaux's Tomb, and Domus Island. They escaped an "elephanta storm," one of those pleasant September visitations, which denote the break up of "the Monsoon," and which not unfrequently bestrew the whole coast of western India with wreckage. This time he found lodgings in the town barracks, Bombay, and passed an examination in the town-hall, before General Vans Kennedy, with the normal success, being placed first. The process also consisted of reading from print (two books) and handwriting, generally some "native letter," of conversing and of writing an address or some paper of the kind.

Returning Barodawards, whence his regiment was transferred to his immense satisfaction to Sind, Richard

---

* See 'Humanism versus Theism, or Solipsism (Egoism) = Atheism. Letters by Robert Lewins, M.D.

assisted in the farewell revelling, dinners and nautches or native dances, the most melancholy form in which Terpsichore ever manifested herself. Then came the pleasant sound :

> "Don't you hear the General say,
> 'Strike your tents, and march away?'"

By far the most agreeable and wholesome part of regimental life in India is the march ; the hours are reasonable, the work not too severe, and the results in appetite and sleep are admirable. At Bombay the regiment encamped on the esplanade, and on January 1, 1844, embarked for Karáchi on board the H. I. E. Co.'s steamer *Semiramis*, whose uneventful cruise is told in ' Scinde ; or, the Unhappy Valley,' chapter I. " The Shippe of Helle."

Yet not wholly uneventful to Richard. On board the *Semiramis* was a certain Captain Walter Scott, Bombay Engineers, who had lately been transferred from commanding in Candeish to the Superintendence of the Sind canals, a department newly organised by the old Conqueror of " Young Egypt," and their chance meeting influenced his career for the next six years. Scott was then in the prime of life, a fine and sympathetic figure, reminding every one of his uncle, the Magician of the North *en beau*, a very handsome likeness with Kaiser-blue eyes and golden-hued beard and straight features that expressed good temper and good character. Another point of resemblance to Sir Walter was his knack in telling anecdotes ; he unconsciously as it were reserved a northern burr for the humorous parts and a half a lisp for the pathetic passages, and right well he told them, although when he put pen to paper nothing could be more bald or disjointed than his style, a peculiarity which Richard at first attributed to his perpetual practice of smoking over his pages. The best of company, and most acceptable to women, he lived and died a bachelor.

The most open-handed and open-hearted of men, he had all the qualities which the vulgar Scotchman has not: he neglected every form of caution and canniness; he thought nothing of "getting on in the world," and he ignored in the ignoble sense the dictum that blood is thicker than water. With short intervals Richard was one of his assistants till 1849; they never had a diverging thought, much less an unpleasant word, and when he died at Berlin in 1875, Richard felt his loss as that of a near relation.

Karáchi, which our Subaltern has twice described in two books,* was in 1844 a mere stretch of a cantonment and nothing if not military; the garrison consisting of some 5000 men of all arms, European and native; in fact, was then swarming with troops.

The 78th Highlanders were cantoned there and were presently joined by the 86th or "County Down Boys." Both consumed a vast quantity of liquor, but in diametrically opposite ways. The "Kilts," when they felt "unco' fou," toddled quietly to bed and slept off the debauch. The "Brogues" quarrelled and fought, made themselves generally disagreeable, and passed the night in the Guard House. There were Horse Artillery, and Foot Artillery, and the former when in uniform turned out in such gorgeous gingerbread gold coats that they gave a new point to the old sneer about "buying a man at your price, and selling him at his own," and there were native regiments enough to justify Brigade parades on the very largest scale.

The discomfort of camp life in this Sahara which represented the Libyan Desert, after Gujarát, the Nile Valley, was excessive; the dust-storms were atrocious, and the brackish water produced the most unpleasant symptoms. Parades of all kinds, regimental and brigade, were the rule, and Sir Charles Napier was rarely absent from anything

* 'Scinde; or, the Unhappy Valley,' two vols., Bentley, 1851; and 'Sind Revisited,' Bentley, 1877.

on a large scale. The seniors abhorred the barren desolate
spot, with all its inglorious perils of fever, spleen, dysentery, and congestion of the brain ; the juniors grumbled in
sympathy, and the Staff officers, ordered up to rejoin the
corps—it was on field service—complained bitterly of
having to quit their comfortable appointments in more
favoured lands without even a campaign in prospect.

Richard now attacked with renewed vigour the Gujarati
language, spoken throughout the country and by the
Parsees of Bombay and elsewhere. His teacher was a
Nagar Brahman, named Him Chand : meanwhile he took
elementary lessons in Sanscrit from the Regimental Pandit.
Every Sepoy corps in those days kept one of these men,
who was a kind of priest as well as a schoolmaster, reading
out prayers and superintending the nice conduct of festivals
with all their complicated observances. Besides these
men the Government also supplied schoolmasters, and the
consequence was that a large percentage of young Sepoys
could read and write. Richard once won a bet from his
brother-in-law, Stisted, by proving that more men in the
18th Bombay Native Infantry than in the 78th Queen's
could read and write. In the latter, indeed, they occasionally had recruits who could not speak English, but only
Gaelic.

Under his two teachers Richard soon became as well
acquainted as a stranger can with the practice of Hinduism.
He carefully read up Ward, Moor, and the publications of
the Asiatic Society, questioning his teachers, and com-
mitting to writing page after page of notes. His knowledge, indeed, not a little surprised his friend, Dr. H. G.
Carter, who was Secretary to the Asiatic Society at Bombay;
and his Hindi teacher officially allowed him to wear the
Brahminical Janéo or thread of the twice-born.

The conqueror of Sind was a noted and remarkable figure
at that time and there is still a semi-heroic ring about the

name. In appearance he was ultra-Jewish, a wondrous contrast to his grand brother Sir William. His country-men called him "Fagin," after Dickens, and his subjects "Shaytan-ká bhái," Satan's brother, from his masterful spirit and reckless energy. There is an idealised portrait of him in Mr. W. H. Bruce's "Life" (London : Murray, 85), but we much prefer the caricature by Lieut. Beresford, printed in Lady Burton's volume " A. E. I." yet there was nothing mean in the Conqueror's diminutive form, the hawk's eye and eagle's beak and powerful chin would redeem any face from the ordinary.

Sir Charles during his long years of Peninsular and European services cultivated the habit of jotting down all events in his diary, with a naïveté, a vivacity, and a fulness which echoed his spirit, and which, with advancing years, degenerated into intemperance of language and extrava-gance of statement. He was hard, as were most men in those days, upon the Great Company. He termed the " Twenty-four kings of Leadenhall Street " " ephemeral sovereigns :" he quoted Lord Wellesley about the " igno-minious tyrants of the east," and he said that every rupee " bore a stain of blood, which, wash it as you may, would not out." Hence, when the prize-money came in, the local wag wrote :—

> " Who, when he lived on shillings swore
> Rupees were stained with Indian gore,
> And ' widows' tears ' for motto bore,
>   But Charley?
>
> " And yet, who in the last five years
> So round a sum of that coin clears,
> In spite of ' gore ' and ' widows' tears,'
>   As Charley? "

In his 60th year he was appointed to the command of Poonah (December 20, 1841), and he was so lacking in the goods of this world, that a Bombay house refused to advance him £500. He began at once to study Hindu-

stani, but it was too late ; the lesson induced irresistible
drowsiness, and the Munshi was too polite to awake the
aged scholar, who always said that he would give 10,000
rupees to be able to address the Sepoys. On September 3,
1842, he set off to assume his new command in Upper and
Lower Sind, and he at once saw his opportunity. Major
Outram had blackened the faces of the Amirs but he
wanted to keep the work of conquest for himself, and he
did not relish this being done by another. He however
assisted Sir Charles Napier, and it was not till his return to
England in 1843 that he ranged himself on the side of
the Directors, whose hatred of the Conqueror grew with
his success ; and two factions, Outramites and Napierites,
directed the little world of Western India.

The battles of Miani and Dubba were much criticised by
military experts, who found that the " butcher's bill " did
not justify the magnificent periods of Sir Wm. Napier.
This noble old soldier's ' Conquest of Scinde ' was a work
of fantasy. The story was admirably told, the picture was
perfect, but the details were so incorrect that it became the
subject of endless "chaff" even in Government House,
Karáchí. The corrective was an official report by Major
(afterwards General) Waddington, Bo. Eng., which gave
the shady rather than the sunlit side of the picture.
And there is a third still to be written. Neither of our
authorities tells us, nor can we expect a fuller document to
do so, how the Mulatto, who had charge of the Amir's
guns, had been persuaded to fire high, and how the Talpŭr
traitor, who commanded the cavalry, openly drew off his
men and showed the shameless example of flight. When
the day shall come to publish details concerning disburse-
ments of " Secret Service Money in India," the public will
learn strange things. Meanwhile those of us who have
lived long enough to see how history is written, can regard
it as but little better than a poor rómance.

However exaggerated, little Miani taught the world one lesson which should not be forgotten, the sole plan to win a fight from barbarians, be they Baloches, Kafirs, or Burmese. It is simplicity itself, a sharp cannonade to shake the enemy, an advance in line or echelon by the ground demons, and a rush and dash of cavalry to expedite the runaways. And presently the victory led to organising the "Land Transport Corps" and the "Baggage Corps," two prime wants of the Indian army. Here Sir Charles Napier's skill as an inventor evolved order out of disorder and efficiency from the most cumbrous of abuses. The pacification of the new province was marvellously brought about by the enlightened despotism of the Conqueror: Outram had predicted ten years of guerilla warfare before peace could be restored. Sir Charles made it safer than any part of India within a year, and in 1844, when travelling down the canals, Richard was loudly blessed by the peasants, who cried out, "These men are indeed worthy to govern us, as they work for our good."

But Sir Charles Napier began India somewhat too late in life, and had to pay the penalty. His mistakes were manifold, and some of them miserable. When preparing for the "Trukkee Campaign," he proposed to content himself with a *numéro cent* tent—for a commander-in-chief! When marching upon Multan, his idea was to quarter the Sepoys in the villages, which could have been destroyed at once; and it was some time before his staff dared put it in this light. From over-deference to English opinion, he liberated all the African slaves in Sind, and turned them out to starve: it would have been wiser to "free the womb" and forbid importation. He never could understand the "Badli system;" when a rich native buys a poor man to be hanged for him who committed the crime; and he terribly scandalised Capt. Young, the civilian Judge-Advocate General by hanging the wrong man. Finding that the offended husband in Sind was justified by public opinion for cutting down his wife, he sent the unfortunate to the gallows, and the result was a peculiar condition of society. On one occasion the Anonymas of Hyderabad sent him a deputation to complain that the married women were "taking the bread out of their mouths."

Sir Charles was a favourite amongst the juniors, in fact amongst all who did not thwart or oppose him. He delighted in Rabelaisian *bon-mot* and the *conte grivois*, as was the wont of field-officers in his days; his comment upon a newspaper's " peace and plenty at Karáchi," was long quoted. He liked men who spoke out their mind ; if an applicant for appointment answered his question, " What do you want ? " by " An adjutancy, sir " (or something specific), the chances were that he obtained it. On the other hand, " Anything you please, Sir Charles," was sure to meet with a contemptuous dismissal. He liked strong measures. Once when Richard was returning from canal-surveying he sent for him and asked him if it was true that the higher classes of landowners, who monopolise the fiefs about the heads of the canals, neglected to clear out the tails, and allowed government ground and the peasants' fields to lie barren for want of water.* Richard answered that he was rightly informed ; and he said, " What would be the best plan in such cases ? " " Simply to confiscate the whole or part of such estate ! " " You don't mince matters," was his only comment. He hated " I don't know," and was pleased with a young engineer, who, when asked about the number of bricks in a newly-built bridge, replied " One hundred and twenty-seven thousand and ten, Sir Charles." And he had a grim appreciation of joke, even at his own expense. He once ordered a large review for the benefit of certain chiefs, and his own interpreter being absent, summoned an officer who was judged capable of the task, and said to him,

* ' Scinde,' vol. i. p. 252.

" Lieutenant Such-and-Such, be pleased to inform these gentlemen that I propose to form the men in line, then to break into echelon by the right, and to form square on the centre battalion," etc., etc. The young officer turned to the chiefs and said, "Listen you folk (*tum log*), the great man says there will be a fine bit of fun" (*bara tamáshá*). After which he touched his cap to the chief. " Have you explained all I said, sir?" asked the latter; and the other replied, "Everything, sir." "A most comprehensive language must be that Hindostani," was Sir Charles Napier's comment, as he rode away with his nose in the air.

After a month of discomfort at Karáchi, rendered more uncomfortable by the compulsory joining of six unfortunate staff-officers who lost their snug appointments in India, they were moved to Gharra, "out of the frying-pan into the fire," a melancholy hole some forty miles by road north of headquarters, and within hearing of the evening gun. Richard has already described its horrors.* Their predecessors had not built barracks or bungalows, and they found only a parallelogram of rock and sand, girt by a tall, dense hedge of bright green " milk bush," and surrounded by a flat of stone and gravel, near a filthy village, whose timorous inhabitants shunned us as walking pestilences. This, with an occasional temperature of 125° F., was to be their "home" for some months. As Richard had no money wherewith to build, he was compelled to endure a hot season in a single-poled tent pitched outside the milk-bush hedge ; and often, to escape suffocation, he was obliged to cover his table with a wet cloth, and to pass the hot hours under it. However, energy was not wanting, and the regimental Pandit proved a good schoolmaster. Richard threw aside Sindhi for Maráthi ; and in October, '44, he was able to pass his third examination at the Presidency, coming off first of half-a-

* ' Scinde,' vol. i. p. 89.

dozen. About this time Southern Bombay was agitated by a small mutiny in Sáwantwádi, and the papers contained a long service correspondence about Colonels Outram and Wallace, the capture of Sámanghar and Lieut. Brassey's descent on Shivadrug, the Elephant Rock. Richard at once laid in a store of Persian books and began seriously to work at that richest and most charming of Eastern languages.

On return to Karáchi, Richard found himself, by the favour of his friend Scott, gazetted as one of his "assistants in the Sind Survey," with especial reference to the Canal department ; his being able to read and translate the valuable Italian works on Hydrodynamics being a point in his favour. A few days taught him the use of compass, theodolite and spirit-level, and on the 10th December, 1844, he was sent with a surveying party and six camels to work at the Fulayli (Phuleli) and its continuation the Guni River. The labour was not small ; after a frosty night, using instruments in the sole of a canal, where the sun-rays seemed to pour as through a funnel, was decidedly trying to the constitution. However, he managed to pull through, and his surveying-books were honoured with official approbation. During the winter he enjoyed some sport, especially hawking, and collected material for ' Falconry in the Valley of the Indus.'* He had begun the noble'art as a boy at Blois, but the poor kestrel upon whom he tried his " 'prentice hand" had soon died, worn out like an Eastern ascetic by the severities of training, especially in the fasting line. Returning northwards he found his corps at Hyderabad,

---

* It was brought out (in 1852) by his friend, John Van Voorst, of Paternoster Row, who, after a long and honourable career, retired at the ripe age of eighty-four to enjoy well-merited rest. He proved himself to be a phœnix amongst publishers. "Half profits are no profits to the author," is the common saying ; however, for the last thirty years I have continually received from him small sums, which represented my gains. Would, that all were as scrupulous !

and passing through deserted Gharra, joined the head-quarters of the survey at Karáchi in April.

Here he made acquaintance with Mirza Ali Akbar, who owed his rank (Khan Bahádur) to his gallant conduct, as Sir Charles Napier's Munshi, at Miani and Dubba, where he did his best to save as many unfortunate Baloch braves as possible. He lived outside the camp in a bungalow which he built for himself, and lodged a friend, Mirzá Dáud, a first-rate Persian scholar. Richard's life became much mixed up with these gentlemen, and his brother officers fell to calling him the "white nigger." He had also invested in a Persian Munshi, Mirza Mohammed Husayn, of Shiraz : poor fellow, after passing through the fires of Sind un-scathed, he returned to die of cholera in his native land. With his assistance Richard opened on the sly three shops at Karáchi,* where cloth, tobaccos, and other small matters were sold exceedingly cheap to those who deserved them, and where he laid in a large stock of native experience, especially regarding such matters as he has treated upon in his 'Terminal Essay' to the 'Thousand Nights and a Night.'† But he soon lost his Munshi friend. Mirza Dáud died of indigestion and Holloway's Pills at Karáchi, and he last saw Mirza Ali Akbar in 1876 at Bombay, where he deceased shortly afterwards. The Mirza had been unjustly and cruelly treated by Bartle Frere, who, in order to please the Court of Directors, systematically persecuted all Sir Charles Napier's friends and favourites, the moment after the old Conqueror set sail from Sind. Despite the high praises of Outram and Napier for the honesty and efficiency of Ali Akbar‡ the new Commissioner brought against the doomed man a number of trumped-up charges proving

---

* 'Falconry,' etc., pp. 100, 101.

† Vol. x. p. 205, *et seqq*.

‡ See in vol. i. p. 53, 'Sind Revisited,' Sir Charles's outspoken opinion.

bribery and corruption, and he managed to effect his dismissal from the service. The unfortunate Mirza in course of time disproved them all; but the only answer to his application for being reinstated was, that what had been done could not now be undone. Richard greatly regretted his loss. He had promised him to write out from his Persian notes a diary of his proceedings during the Conquest of Sind; he was more "behind the curtain" than any man he knew, and the truths he could have told would have been exeedingly valuable.

Karáchi was for India not a dull place in those days. Besides their daily work of plotting and mapping the surveys of the cold season, they organised a "survey mess" in a bungalow belonging to the office "compound." There were six of them—Blagrove, Maclagan, Vanrenen, and afterwards Price and Lambert; and local society pronounced them all mad, although Burton could not see that they were more whimsical than their neighbours. Richard also built a bungalow, which got the title of "The Inquisition," and there buried his favourite gamecock Bhujang (the Dragon), who had won him many a victory—people declared that it was the grave of a small human. He saw much of Mirza Husayn, a brother of Aga Khan Mahallati, a scion of the Isma'iliyyah, or "Old Man of the Mountain," who having fled his country, Persia, after a rebellion, ridiculous even in that land of eternal ridiculous rebellions, turned *condottiere*, and with his troop of 130 ruffians took service with them, and was placed to garrison Jarrak* (Jerruch), when the Baloches came down upon him and killed or wounded about 100 of his troop, after which he passed on to Bombay, and enlightened the Presidency about his having conquered Sind. His brother, Richard's acquaintance, also determined to attack Persia, viâ Makrán, and he managed so well that he found himself travelling to Teheran lashed to a gun-

* 'Scinde,' i. 190.

carriage. The Lodge "Hope" kindly made Richard an "entered apprentice," but he had read Carlile, "the atheistical publisher," and the whole affair appeared to him a gigantic humbug, dating from the days of the Crusades, and as Cardinal Newman expressed it "meaning a goose club.' But he thinks better of it now, as it still serves political purposes in the East, and gives us a point against our French rivals and enemies. As the "Sind Association" was formed, Richard was made honorary secretary, and had no little correspondence with Mr. E. Blyth, then Curator of the Zoological Department, Calcutta. Sir Charles's friends also determined to start a newspaper, in order to answer the enemy in the gate, and to reply to the "base and sordid Bombay faction," headed by the "rampant Buist," with a strong backing of anonymous officials. The *Kurrachee Advertiser* presently appeared in the modest shape of a lithographed sheet on Government foolscap, and through Sir William Napier its most spicy articles had the honour of a reprint in London. Of these the best were "the letters of Omega," by his late friend Rathborne, then collector at Hyderabad; and they described the vices of the Sind Amirs in language the reverse of ambiguous. Richard did not keep copies, nor unfortunately did the clever and genial author. Richard writes :—

'This pleasant, careless life broke up in November, 1845, when I started, with my friend Scott, for a long tour to the north of Sind. We rode by the high road through Gharra and Jarak to Kotri, the station of the Sind Flotilla, and there crossed to Hyderabad, where I found my corps flourishing. After a very jolly week we resumed our way up the right bank of the Indus, and on the extreme western frontier, where we found the Baloch herdsmen in their wildest state. About that time began to prevail the now vulgar reports about the Lost Tribes of Israel (who were never lost), and with the aid of Parkhurst and Lynch,

I dressed up a very pretty grammar and vocabulary which proved to sundry scientists that the lost was found at last. But my mentor (Scott) would not allow the joke to appear in print. On Christmas Day we entered "Sehwán," absurdly styled "Alexander's Camp." Here again the spirit of mischief was too strong for me: I buried a broken and hocussed jar of "Athenæum Sauce," red pottery with black Etruscan figures, right in the way of an ardent amateur antiquary: and the results were comical.

'At Larkháná we made acquaintance with "fighting Fitzgerald," who commanded there; a magnificent figure who could cut a donkey in two; and who, although a man of property, preferred the hardships of India to the pleasures of home. He had, however, a mania for blowing himself up in a little steamer, mainly of his own construction, and after his last accident he was invalided to England, and died within sight of her shores.

At Larkháná the following letter was received :—

"Karachi, Jan. 3, 1846.

'"My dear Scott,—The General says you may allow as many of your assistants as you can spare to join their regiments if going on service, with the understanding that they must resign their appointments, and will not be reappointed, &c.

(Signed) "John Napier."

'This, beyond bazar reports, was our first notice of the great Sikh war which added the Panjáb to Anglo-India. The news made us wild to go; I was mentally certified that, if this opportunity were lost, my lot would be that of a carpet-soldier, fit only to prance up and down my lady's chamber. So, after a visit to Sakhar, Shikarpúr and the neighbourhood, I applied myself with all my might to prepare for the campaign. After sundry small surveyings and levellings about the Indus, I persuaded Scott, greatly against the grain, to send in my resignation, and called upon the local "boss," General James Simpson, who was supposed to be in his dotage, and was qualifying for the Chief Command in the Crimea. •

'My application was refused. Happily, however, suddenly appeared an order from Bengal to the purport that all the Assistant-Surveyors must find sureties. This was enough for me ; I wrote officially, saying that no man would be bail for me, and was told to be off to my regiment. And on February 23 I marched with the 18th from Rohri.

'Needless to repeat the sad story of our disappointment.* It was a model army of 13,000 men, Europeans and natives, and under "old Charley" it would have walked into Multan as into a mutton pie. We had also heard that Náo Mall, the Hindu Commandant under the Sikhs, was wasting his two millions of gold, and we were willing to save him the trouble. Merrily we trudged through Sabzalcote and Khánpúr, and we entered Baháwalpúr, where we found the heart-chilling order to retire and march home. Consequently we returned to Rohri on April 2, and after a few days' halt there, tired and miserable, we made Khayrpur, and after seventeen marches reached the old regimental quarters in Mohammad Khan-ká Tanda on the Phuleli River.†

'But our physical trials and mental disappointments had soured our tempers, and domestic disturbances began. Our colonel was one Henry Corsellis, the son of a Bencoolen civilian, and neither his colour nor his temper were in his favour. The war began about a small matter : I had been making doggerel rhymes on men's names at mess, and knowing something of the colonel's touchiness passed him

* 'Scinde,' ii. p. 258, etc.
† 'Sind Revisited,' i. p. 256, shows how I found my old home in 1876.

over, whereupon he took offence, and seeing that I was
" in for a row," I said, " Very well, colonel, I will write your
epitaph," which was :—

> " Here lieth the body of Colonel Corsellis,
> The rest of the fellow I fancy in Hell is."

Upon which we went at it " hammer and tongs."

' I shall say no more upon the subject ; it is perhaps the
part of my life upon which my mind dwells with the least
satisfaction.   In addition to regimental troubles there were
not a few domestic disagreeables, especially complications
with a young person named Mír Ján.   To make matters
worse, after a dreadful wet night my mud-bungalow came
down upon me, wounding my foot. *   The only pleasant
reminiscences of the time are the days spent in the quarters
of an old native friend † on the banks of the beautiful
Phuleli, seated upon a felt rug spread beneath a shadowy
tamarind tree, with beds of sweet smelling Rayhán (basil)
around, and eyes roving over the broad smooth stream and
the gaily dressed groups gathered at the frequent ferries.
I need hardly say that these visits were paid in native
costume, and so correct was it that I even passed on
camel-back my hostile colonel in the gateway of Fort
Hyderabad without his recognising me.   I had also a host
of good friends, especially Dr. J. F. Steinhäuser, who in
after years, but for an accident, was to have accompanied me
to Lake Tanganyika, and who became my collaborateur in
" The Thousand Nights and a Night."

' The hot season of '46 was unusually sickly, and the white
regiments at Karáchi, notably the 78th Highlanders, suffered
terribly from cholera.   Hyderabad was also threatened, but
escaped better than she deserved.   In early July I went
into "sick quarters," and left my regiment in early
September with a strong case.   At Bombay, my friend

---

* 'Scinde,' i. p. 151.   † 'Falconry,' pp. 103-105.

CATHEDRAL, GOA.

IL BOM JESUS, WHERE ST. FRANCIS XAVIER IS BURIED.

Henry I. Carter assisted me, and enabled me to obtain two years' leave of absence to the Neilgherries.

'My munshi, Mohammed Husayn, had sailed for Persia, and I at once engaged an Arab "coach"; this was one Háji Jauhar, a young Abyssinian who, with his wife of the same breed, spoke a curious Semitic dialect, but was useful in conversational matters. Accompanied by my servants and horse, I engaged the usual Pattimar, the Daryá Prashád (the Joy of the Ocean), and set sail for Goa on February 20th, 1847. A three days' trip landed us in the once splendid capital whose ruins I have described in "Goa and the Blue Mountains" (London: Bentley, 1881). Dr. Pestanha was then Governor-General, Senhor Gomez Secretary to Government, and Major St. Maurice chief aide-de-camp: and all treated me with uncommon kindness. On my second visit to the place, in 1876, every one of my old friends and acquaintances had disappeared, whilst the other surroundings had not changed in the least degree.

'From Goa to Punány was a trip of five days, and from the little Malabar port a terrible dull ride of ten days, halts and excursions included, placed me at Coonoor, on the western edge of the "Blue Mountain." At Ootacamand, the capital of the Sanitarium, I found a friend, Lieut. Dyett, who offered to share with me his quarters. My unhappy "chum" suffered sadly in the Multán campaign, where most of the wounded came to grief, some said owing to the salt in the Silt, which made so many operations fatal: after three amputations his arm was taken out at the socket. I have noticed the humours of "Ooty" in the book before mentioned, and I made myself independent of society by beginning the study of Telugu in addition to Arabic. But the sudden change from dry Sind to the damp cold mountains induced an attack of rheumatic ophthalmia, which began at the end of May, 1847, lasted nearly two years, and would not be shaken off till I had left India in March, 1849. In vain I tried diet and dark rooms, change of place, blisters of all sorts, and the whole contents of the Pharmacopœia : it was a thorn in the flesh which never failed to make itself felt. At intervals I was able to work hard and to visit the adjacent places, such as Kotagherry, the Orange Valley, and St. Catherine's Falls.* Meanwhile I wrote letters to the 'Bombay Times,' studied Telugu and Toda, as well as Persian and Arabic, and worked at the ethnology of Hylobius, the hill-man, whose country showed mysterious remains of civilized life, gold mining included.

'"Ooty" may be a pleasant place, like a water-cure establishment, to an invalid in rude health; but to me nothing could be duller or more disagreeable, and my two years of sick leave was presently reduced to four months. On September 1st, 1847, glad as a partridge-shooter, I rode down the Ghaut, and a dozen days later made Calicut, the old capital of Camoens, "Samorim," the Sámiry Rajah. Here I was kindly received, and sent to visit old Calicut and other sights by Mr. Collector Conolly, whom a Madras civilianship could not defend from Fate. A short time after my departure he was set upon and barbarously murdered in his own verandah by a band of villain Moplahs,† a bastard race got by Arab sires on Hindu dams. He was thus the third of the gallant brothers who came to violent ends.

' This visit gave me a good opportunity of studying on the spot the most remarkable scene of "The Lusiads," and it afterwards served me in good stead. The *Seaforth*, Captain Biggs, carried me to Bombay, after paying visits to Mangalore and Goa, in three days of ugly "Monsoon" weather. On October 15th, I passed in Persian at the town hall, coming out first of some thirty with a compliment from the

---

* 'Goa,' etc., p. 355.   † See Goa, p. 339.

examiners; and this was succeeded by something more substantial in the shape of an "honorarium" of 1000 rupees from the Court of Directors. This bright side of the medal had its reverse. A friend, an Irish medico, volunteered to prescribe for me, and strongly commending frictions of citric ointment, calomel in disguise, round the orbit of the eye, and my perseverance in following his prescription, developed ugly symptoms of mercurialism, which eventually drove me from India.

'My return to Sind was in the s.s. *Dwárká*, the little vessel which in 1853 carried me from Jeddah to Suez, and which in 1862 foundered at the mouth of the Tapti, or Surat River. She belonged to the Steam Navigation Company, Bombay, and she had been brought safely round the Cape by her skipper, a man named Tribe. But "climate" had demoralised him. We set out for Karáchi without even an able seaman who knew the coast, while the captain and his mate were drunk and incapable the whole way. As we were about to enter the dangerous port my fellow-passengers insisted upon my taking command as second officer, and I ordered the *Dwárká's* head to be turned westwards, so that next morning we landed safely.

'My return to the headquarters of the Survey was a misfortune to my colleagues: my eyes forbade regular work, and, the others had to bear my share of the burden. However, there were painless intervals when I found myself able to work at Sindi, under Munshi Nandú, and at Arabic, under Shaykh Háshim, a small half-Bedawi, imported by me from Mascat. Under him also I began the systematic study of practical Moslem divinity; learned about a quarter of the Koran by heart, and became a proficient at prayers. It was always my desire to visit Meccah during the pilgrimage season; written descriptions by hearsay of its rites and ceremonies were common enough in all languages, European as well as native; but none satisfied me: moreover no one seemed practically to know anything about the matter. So to this preparation I devoted all my time and energy, not forgetting a sympathetic study of Sufism, the Gnosticism of Al-Islam, which would raise me high above the rank of a mere Moslem. I conscientiously went through the Chillá or quarantine of fasting and other exercises, which by-the-by proved rather too-exciting to the brain. At times when over-strung I relieved my nerves with a course of Sikh religion and literature; and at last the good old priest solemnly initiated me in presence of the swinging "Granth" or Nának Shah's scriptures. As I had already been duly invested by a strict Hindú with the Janeo or "Brahminical thread," my experience of Eastern faiths became phenomenal.

'There was scant hope of surveying for weak eyes, so I attempted to do my duty by long reports concerning the country and people, addressed to the Bombay Government, and these were duly printed in its "Selections." To the local branch of the Royal Asiatic Society were sent two papers, "Grammar of the Játkí, or Multani Language," and " Remarks on Dr. Dorn's Chrestomathy of the Afghan Tongue." * Without hearing of Professor Pott, the savant of Halle (and deceased only lately), I convinced myself that the Játs of Sind, a race which extends from the Indus mouth to the plains of Tartary, gives a clue to the origin of the Gypsies, as well as the Getæ and Massagetæ (Great Getæ), and this induced me to work with the camelmen who belong to that notorious race, and to bring out a grammar and vocabulary.

'Indeed the more sluggish became my sight the more active became my brain, which could be satisfied only with

* Written with the assistance of a fine old Afghan "Mullah," Ahmad Burhan al-Dín.

twelve to fourteen hours a day of Alchemy, Mnemonics, "Mantik," or Eastern logic, Arabic, Sindi, and Panjábi. The two official exams. in the latter tongues were passed before Captain Stack, the only Englishman in the country who had an inkling of the subject.

'The spring of 1848, that eventful year in Europe, brought in two most exciting items of intelligence. The proclamation of the French Republic reached us on April 8th, and on May 2nd came the news of the murder of Anderson and his companion by Náo Mall of Multani. A campaign was imminent, especially after the defeat of a certain General; and the report was that Sir Charles Napier would return to take command. Scott and a host of my friends were ordered up, and I applied in almost suppliant terms to accompany the force as interpreter. I had passed examinations in six native languages, besides studying two others, Multani included, and yet General Auchmuty's secretary wrote to me that this could not be, as he had chosen for the post "Lieutenant X. Y. Z., who had passed in Hindustani."

'This last misfortune broke my heart. I had been nearly seven years in India working like a horse, volunteering for every bit of service, and qualifying myself for all contingencies. Rheumatic ophthalmia, which had almost left me, when in hopes of marching northward, came on with redoubled force, and no longer had I any hope of curing it except by a change to Europe. Sick, sorry, and almost in tears of rage, I bade adieu to my friends and comrades in Sind on May 13th, 1849. At Bombay there was no difficulty in passing the Medical Board, and at the end of March I embarked at Bombay for a passage round the Cape, as the Austral winter was approaching, in a sixty-year old teak-built craft, the brig *Eliza*, Captain Cory.

'My career in India had been in my eyes a failure, but by no fault of my own : the dwarfish demon called

"Interest" had fought against me, and as usual had won the fight.'

*　　*　　*　　*　　*　　*

There were, however, other matters to occupy Richard's attention at this time. He had always been a good swordsman: he now devoted himself to perfecting his knowledge of the art, and before long was awarded the *Brevet de Pointe.* How many Englishmen, one would like to know have, since the days of the admirable Crichton, been entitled to write themselves *maître d'armes?* That some have so described themselves proves little, save the possession on their parts of an equal share of impudence and mendacity. This mastery of arms was destined to produce its fruit some twenty years later in the form "New System of Sword Exercise," for the present it resulted only in an attempt to reform the art of war as practised in the British infantry. With this view Burton published a "System of Bayonet Exercise," which was printed as a pamphlet by Messrs. Clowes and Sons in 1853. It might have been thought that anything which tended to increase the efficiency of the Service would have been welcomed at the Horse-Guards, but in the pre-Crimean days pipe-clay was paramount and red tape and routine rampant in the military administration of this country. "Dash" and courage were as the small dust of the balance in comparison with such matters as the height of a stock, or the tight fit of a regulation tunic ; and the ideal General was a martinet of the type of Sir George Brown, who, in the midst of the cold of a Crimean winter, insisted on his men shaving themselves up to the regulation two inches of whisker.

It is scarcely surprising, therefore, that the first effect of the publication of this book was an outburst of official wrath. Even the late Colonel Sykes, who was a personal friend of Burton, sent for him officially and reproached him

with having published "a book which would do more harm
than good." All the old Waterloo officers, who swore by
Brown Bess and despised the Minié rifle, proclaimed that
bayonet exercise would make the men "unsteady in the
ranks," and acting upon this hint a severe official "wigging"
was administered to the luckless author. The sequel of
the story is worthy of note. The importance of a system
of bayonet exercise had at that time been recognized
throughout Europe and even in America: England only
refused to consider it, and so our men went to the Crimea
with nothing but their bull-dog courage and weapons which
they hardly knew how to use. When the sanguinary
lessons of that war had driven home upon the authorities
the absolute neccessity for training our men in a proper
way to "the trade of arms," Burton's pamphlet was taken
down from the dusty pigeon hole to which it had been
consigned and a Manual of Bayonet Exercise for use in the
British Army was compiled which was simply Burton's
System with a few modifications which are hardly im-
provements.

Under ordinary circumstances it might have been
thought that a liberal reward would be bestowed upon
the man who had detected the weak point of our military
system and had shown the way to remedy it. Those who
entertain that belief know little of the English official
system. If an inventor or an adapter of the inventions of
other people happen to be in the "ring" he gets very
liberal pay for anything that he does, and may even be
allowed to set up a company of his own to supply the
country with warlike stores at his own price. But if,
unfortunately for himself, he should be simply an officer,
standing upon his own merits, he is likely to fare as Burton
did—to receive, that is to say, a further snub from official-
dom. He did not ask for any pecuniary recompense—
indeed, whatever fault may be found with him by his official

superiors, greed after money is not one of them—but he did hope for a few words of thanks or a compliment from the Commander-in-Chief. Instead he received one day an immense letter from the Treasury with a seal rather larger than a crown piece. Within was no word of thanks, no compliment, no expression of official recognition but a—more or less—gracious permission to draw upon the Treasury for the sum of

ONE SHILLING!

Despite the covert insult conveyed in this bit of official insolence there was a certain humour in the matter which Burton was the first to appreciate. He armed himself therefore with the warrant, and to the intense astonishment of the world of clerkdom, insisted upon being paid his shilling. Such a thing had never been heard of before—the insult was generally found sufficient effectually to deter the person to whom it was offered from ever again presenting himself at the War Office. Burton was made of a different stuff. He insisted on being paid, and after being referred from one room to another for three quarters of an hour at last succeeded. It is lamentable to have to add that having obtained the money he did not fasten it to his watch-chain, as Sir John Holker fastened his sixpence,* "to show that there was at least one coin which he had honestly earned." †

* Sir John Holker, who as his friends knew well was one of the most amiable and humorous of men, was, when Solicitor-General, accosted by two ladies in the public lobby of the House of Commons with a request for some information. Seeing that they were utter strangers he took them round the building, showed them everything of interest, and when they parted accepted the sixpence which they offered him for his trouble. He hung it on his watch-chain with the above expression, and wore it until his lamented and premature death. —*R. I. P.*—Ed.

† Burton gave his shilling to the first hungry beggar he saw on coming out of the War Office.

This is, however, an anticipation. In the spring of the year that witnessed the publication of this pamphlet Burton entered into negotiations with the Royal Geographical Society with the view of undertaking an enterprise such as no Englishman had ever ventured upon before. The details, must, however, be reserved for another chapter.

CHAPTER III.

AN ENGLISH HAJI.

Proposes to explore Arabia in disguise—Is opposed by the authorities — Starts as a Persian " Mirza "—Moslem customs— The
disguise a profound secret—The Dervish—Passport difficulties—
Leaves Alexandria—At Suez—Changes his nationality and becomes
a Pathan—The boy Mohammed—Packing money—Quarrel with
an Albanian—The desert—A moment of danger—Passport troubles
again—The Silk el Zahab—The scene on board—Effects of the
voyage —Yambú —Preparing for the journey —The caravan —A
night journey—El Hamra—" The old man of the mountains "—A bit
of bounce—A review and a brigand attack—El-Medinah and the
blessings—Shaykh Hamid's house—Life in El Medinah—The
Mosque of the Prophet—The sects of El Islam—Moslem theology
—And devotion — The " Fatiyah "—A grand superstition — The
harem at El Medinah—The Persian schism—A change of plan—
Arab quarrels—Goes to Meccah—Departure—Into the desert—
Night travelling—The Simúm—Water—A feast—A murder—The
meeting of the caravans—Assuming the pilgrim garb (El Ihram)—
Disquieting rumours—A robber scare and how to meet it—Meccah
in the distance—The prayers of the faithful—The boy Mohammed
as a host—The water of Zem-zem—The devotions of the Kaabah
—The Black Stone—The pigeons at the Mosque—Muna—Ararat
and its legend—Consecrated sights—" Loosening the Ihram "—A
friendly barber—A visit to the Kaabah—The sacrifice of sheep—
Burton declines—End of the " Great Festival "—Preparing to leave
Muna — The "solemnity of the sermon "—leaving Meccah—A
remarkable tradition— England and El Islam—*Le jeu ne vaut pas
la chandelle*—A rush " down South "—Jeddah—Back again.

THE year 1852 was marked in Burton's life by an expedition which was at once the most daring and the most
successful of the many in which he has been engaged.

Previous practice in North-Western India had afforded him such an insight into the inner life of the Mohammedan races as to make him almost one of themselves, and he now determined to prove his metal by a journey into the heart of Arabia. The seriousness of such an undertaking can hardly be appreciated by the average stay-at-home Englishman. It amounted to his taking his life in his hand for at least six months, going absolutely alone into a curiously unfamiliar country, disguised as a Moslem and liable at any moment, if his disguise were discovered, to a violent and painful death. It meant also, mingling with the strangest and wildest companions, conforming to a thousand unfamiliar manners, and living for many months in the hottest climate in the world upon unaccustomed and often repulsive food. And finally it meant complete and absolute isolation from everything that makes life tolerable, during the whole period of his absence from England. It can hardly be a matter for wonder that Sir James Hogg, as Chairman of the Court of Directors to the then East India Company, should have refused his sanction to the scheme, even though it was supported by such authorities as Sir Roderick Murchison, Colonel Yorke and Dr. Shaw. As some consolation for this refusal, however, the Court of Directors accorded to Burton a furlough of a year " to enable him to pursue his Arabic studies." How those studies were pursued I now proceed to relate.

Following the advice of a brother officer, Burton assumed his Eastern dress and character before leaving London ; and on the evening of the 3rd of April, 1853, a Persian Mirza, accompanied by an interpreter, Captain Henry Grindlay, of the Bengal Cavalry, left London for South- ampton, and embarked on the P. and O. steamer *Bengal.* The voyage, if tedious, was not unprofitable, since the time was spent, as Burton says, 'in falling into the train of Oriental manners'—a business more difficult than is commonly believed. The instance which he gives of the difference is certainly striking. 'Look, for instance,' he says, 'at that Indian Moslem drinking a glass of water. With us the operation is simple enough, but his perform- ance includes no less than five novelties. In the first place he clutches the tumbler as though it were the throat of a foe ; secondly, he ejaculates, " In the name of Allah, the Compassionating, the Compassionate ! " before wetting his lips ; thirdly, he imbibes the contents, swallowing them, not sipping them as he ought to do, and ending with a satisfied grunt ; fourthly, before setting down the cup, he sighs forth, " Praise to Allah ! " of which you will understand the full meaning in the desert ; and, fifthly, he replies, " May Allah make it pleasant to thee ! " in answer to his friends, " Pleasurably and health." Also he is careful to avoid the irreligious notion of drinking the pure element in a standing position, mindful, however, of the three recognised ex- ceptions, the fluid of the holy. well Zemzem, water distributed in charity and that which remains after Wuzu, the lesser ablution.' Brightening up his remembrance of these, and a hundred other and similar customs, he passed his time with such success that on landing at Alexandria he was recognized and blessed as a true Muslim by the native population.

The only person in the secret of Burton's disguise at Alexandria was his friend John Wingfield Larking, at whose villa on the Mahmúdiyah Canal he stayed, though he was lodged not in the house but in an outhouse, the better to blind the inquisitive eyes of servants and visitors. Whilst residing here he obtained the services of a Shaykh, under whose tuition he revived his recollection of the Koran, the usages of the faith generally, and the practice of prayer in particular. His Persian disguise was of great service, inasmuch as the Persians are in the eyes of the Arabs "not good Mohammedans like themselves, but, still, better than nothing." At the same time he ceased to pose as a Mirza, changing his *rôle* for that of a Hakím or doctor, and his title from Mirza, the Persian "Mister," to "Shaykh" Abdullah, fitting name for the part of dervish which he had now to play. Of this part of dervish, Burton says:—

'No character in the Moslem world is so proper for disguise as that of the dervish. It is assumed by all ranks, ages, and creeds; by the nobleman who has been disgraced at court, and by the peasant who is too idle to till the ground; by Dives, who is weary of life, and by Lazarus, who begs his bread from door to door. Further, the dervish is allowed to ignore ceremony and politeness, as one who ceases to appear upon the stage of life; he may pray or not, marry or remain single as he pleases, be respectable in cloth of frieze as in cloth of gold, and no one asks him—the chartered vagabond—Why he comes here? or, Wherefore he goes there? He may wend his way on foot or alone, or ride his Arab mare followed by a dozen servants; he is equally feared without weapons, as swaggering through the streets armed to the teeth.

'The more haughty and offensive he is to the people the more they respect him, a decided advantage to the traveller of choleric temperament. In the hour of imminent danger he has only to become a maniac, and he is safe; a madman in the East, like a notably eccentric character in the West, is allowed to say or do whatever the spirit directs. Add to this character a little knowledge of medicine, a "moderate skill in magic, and a reputation for caring for nothing but study and books," together with capital sufficient to save you from the chance of starving, and you appear in the East to peculiar advantage. The only danger of the "Mystic Path" which leads, or is supposed to lead, to heaven, is, that the dervish's ragged coat not unfrequently covers the cut-throat, and if seized in the society of such a "brother," you may reluctantly become his companion under the stick or upon the stake. For be it known, dervishes are of two orders, the sharai, or those who conform to religion, and the bi-sharai, or luti, whose practices are hinted at by their own tradition that " he we daurna name" once joined them for a week, but at the end of that time left them in dismay, and returned to whence he came.'

The part was not supported without difficulty.* Burton had omitted to provide himself with a passport in England, and it was not without 'much unclean dressing, and an unlimited expenditure of broken English,' backed up by the great influence of his friend Larking with the local authorities, that he at last succeeded in obtaining one from the British consul, setting forth that he was 'an Indo-British subject named Abdullah, by profession a doctor, aged thirty.' To get the passport was easy, compared with the difficulty of getting it *visé*. His disguise was too complete, and dervishes are looked upon with so little respect in Alexandria, that he found himself bandied about from place to place, and from official to official for three entire days before he could get the formality accomplished. That done, however, he provided himself with a few necessaries : a rag containing a tooth-stick, a bit of soap,

* " About this time I met Captain Burton, whose marvellous knowledge of eastern life and languages must alone make him a unique figure, even were he not a brilliant talker and the hero of the daring pilgrimage to Mecca. I met him dining at Turâbi's house, and Turâbi afterwards told me that he was on board the same ship with Captain Burton bound for Alexandria, when the latter was about starting on his great journey. Turâbi was struck with the regularity and earnestness with which a certain poorly-dressed Arab performed his devotions, and watching him rather narrowly suddenly recognised his friend Captain Burton. A burst of laughter followed ; but Burton, seeing his disguise penetrated, merely made a quick sign of silence, and went on with his prayers. Turâbi took the hint, but subsequently they had many a chat in private, and the good little Turk was of service to the Englishman in his initiation as Mussulman."—'Court Life in Egypt,' by A. J. Butler, pp. 55, 56.

and a comb—the last of wood, since bone and tortoise-shell
are not religiously correct—a goat-skin water-bag, a coarse
Persian rug, which besides being couch served as chair,
table and oratory ; a cotton-stuffed chintz-covered pillow, a
blanket and a sheet, a large yellow cotton umbrella, a
dagger, a brass inkstand, and penholder to stick in the
belt, and if last by no means least, 'a mighty rosary,'
which, on occasion,' says Burton, 'might have been converted into a weapon of offence.' This phrase, by the way,
gave immense offence to one of the author's trimestrial
critics, who after two pages of solemn sermonizing on the
wickedness of his conduct generally in disguising himself
at all, solemnly pronounced this particular sentence to be
the crowning proof of his innate depravity. Two saddle-
bags to contain his wardrobe, and a box of pea-green hue,
adorned with flowers, to contain his stock of drugs, completed his equipment.

By the end of May all was ready. 'Not without a
feeling of regret,' he says, 'I left my little room among the
white myrtle blossoms and the rosy oleander flowers with
the almond scent. I kissed with humble ostentation my
good host's hand, in the presence of his servants. I bade
adieu to my patients, who now amounted to about fifty,
shaking hands with all meekly and with religious equality
of attention ; and mounted in a "trap," which looked like a
cross between a wheelbarrow and a dog-cart, drawn by a
kicking, jibbing, and biting mule, I set out for the steamer,
the *Little Asthmatic.*' The journey from Alexandria to
Cairo seems to have been something frightful, lasting as it
did for three days and nights instead of thirty hours, with
nothing to see but muddy water, dusty banks, a sand mist,
a milky sky, and a glaring sun, and nothing to feel but a
breeze like the blast of a furnace, and nothing to interest
or occupy the traveller save the grounding of the steamer,
an event which occurred regularly four or five times

between sunrise and sunset. To make Burton's case the worse, he had in his character of dervish taken a third class or deck passage. The sun burnt through the canvas awning all day, and the night dews were as "raw and thick as a Scotch mist." The cooking was abominable, and the pilgrim dervish could not, of course, eat with the infidel, so that for the whole voyage he was reduced to a diet of bread and garlic, moistened with the muddy water of the canal, drunk from a leathern bucket. As for amusement there was none. The pipe was the only consolation, and when that failed, possibly a certain amount of distraction might be found in telling over the beads of the huge rosary aforesaid. For the rest, the voyage was "deadly dull," and the traveller arrived at Cairo bored to death with it.

Here, however, he found friends. There was no room for him in the native hotels of the best class. It was the pilgrim season, and every place was full, wherefore he was compelled to go to an inn in the Greek quarter, where he succeeded in obtaining "two most comfortless rooms," at the modest rent of 41 piastres a month—about fourpence a day. In that caravanserai a fellow-traveller on the steamer had also found quarters, one Haji Wali, who openly expressed his contempt for the medical profession, and advised Burton "to make bread by honestly teaching languages." The two became fast friends ; dined together ; called on each other frequently, and together "passed the evening in a mosque or some other place of amusement." Together too they smoked hashish, and under his inspiration Burton discarded "the dervish's gown, the large blue pantaloons, the short shirt ; in fact, all connection with Persia and the Persians." More than this he made choice of a new nationality.

'After long deliberation about the choice of nations, I became a "Pathán." Born in India, of Afghan parents,

who had settled in the country; educated at Rangoon, and
sent out to wander, as men of that race frequently are,
from early youth, I was well guarded against the danger
of detection by a fellow-countryman. To support the
character requires a knowledge of Persian, Hindustani, and
Arabic, all of which I knew sufficiently well to pass
muster; any trifling inaccuracy was charged upon my
long residence at Rangoon. This was an important step;
the first question at the shop, on the camel, and in the
mosque, is "What is thy name?" the second, "Whence
comest thou?" This is not generally impertinent, or
intended to be annoying; if, however, you see any evil
intention in the questioner, you may rather roughly ask
him, "What may be his maternal parent's name"—equivalent to enquiring, Anglicè, in what church his mother was
married—and escape your difficulties under cover of the
storm. But this is rarely necessary. I assumed the
polite, pliant manners of an Indian physician, and the
dress of a small efendi, or gentleman, still, however,
representing myself to be a dervish, and frequenting the
places were dervishes congregate.'

Burton—one of whose idiosyncrasies is a fine contempt
for conventionalities of every kind—has views of his own on
the subject of slavery, and does not hesitate to express his
belief that however objectionable it may be in the abstract,
the modified form of that institution which prevails in
Mohammedan countries is a blessing rather than a curse to
those who may be described as its victims. He did not,
however, buy one, though it may be fancied from the
energy of some of his expressions, that he would have had
no particular objection to doing so. Instead, he hired a
man at 80 piastres a month, who being of swarthy skin and
having chubby features readily passed for an Abyssinian
slave. In his company he passed the whole of the ghastly
fast of Ramazan, now observed as strictly as in the first

days of Islam, and studied in Cairo the Moslem faith in its
minutest ramifications. · On the last day of the fast all
gave alms to the poor, and on the day following, the first of
the Eed al-Saghír, or Lesser Festival, he arose before dawn,
performed his ablutions and repaired ·to the mosque to
recite the peculiar prayer of the season and hear the sermon
which bids men be merry and wise. After which 'we ate
and drank heartily, then with pipes and tobacco pouches
in hand we sauntered out to enjoy the contemplation of
smiling faces and street scenery.'

Amongst the preparations for his departure, now rapidly
approaching, Burton engaged another servant, of whom he
gives a characteristic account. 'Among the number of my
acquaintances,' he says, 'was a Meccan boy, Mohammed
ul-Basyúni, and from whom I bought the pilgrim-garb
called *el-Ihram*, and the Kafan or shroud, with which the
Moslem usually starts upon such a journey as mine. He,
being in his way homewards after a visit to Constantinople,
was most anxious to accompany me in the character of a
"companion." But he had travelled too much to suit me ;
he had visited India, he had seen Englishmen, and he had
lived with the " Nawwáb Bálú " of Surat. Moreover, he
showed signs of over-wisdom. He had been a regular
visitor, till I cured one of his friends of an ophthalmia,
after which he gave me his address at Meccah, and was
seen no more. Haji Wali described him and his party to
be *nas jarrár* (extractors), and certainly he had not mis-
judged them. But the sequel will prove how der Mensch
denkt und Gott lenkt, and as the boy Mohammed eventually
did become my companion throughout the pilgrimage, I
will place him before the reader as summarily as possible.

'He is a beardless youth, of about eighteen, chocolate-
brown, with high features, and a broad profile ; his bony
and decided Meccan cast of face is lit up by the peculiar
Egyptian eye, which seems to descend from generation to

generation. His figure is short and squat, with a tendency to be obese, the result of a strong stomach and the power of sleeping at discretion. He can read a little, write his name, and is uncommonly clever at a bargain. Meccah had taught him to speak excellent Arabic, to understand the literary dialect, to be eloquent in abuse, and to be profound at prayer and pilgrimage. Constantinople has given him a taste for Anacreontic singing, and female society of the questionable kind, a love of strong waters— the hypocrite looked positively scandalised when I first suggested the subject—and an off-hand latitudinarian mode of dealing with serious subjects in general. I found him to be the youngest son of a widow, whose doting fondness had moulded his disposition ; he was selfish and affectionate, as spoiled children usually are ; volatile, easily offended and as easily pacified (the Oriental) coveting other men's goods, and profuse of his own (the Arab), with a matchless intrepidity of countenance (the traveller) ; brazen lunged, not more than half brave, exceedingly astute, with an acute sense of honour, especially where his relations were concerned (the individual). I have seen him in a fit of fury because someone cursed his father ; and he and I nearly parted because on one occasion I applied to him an epithet which, etymologically considered, might be exceedingly insulting to a high-minded brother, but which in popular parlance signifies nothing. This *point d'honneur* was the boy Mohammed's strong point.'

Then came the usual troubles. Money had to be obtained and artfully packed and a new passport procured. Our "Pathán" found his old one out of date, and had forgotten or had not known that he required an order from the Foreign Office to obtain the English *visé*, wherefore he was refused by the then English Consul in Cairo, Dr. Walno. After an ineffectual attempt to get himself a Persian passport from the Envoy of the Shah, his Shaykh Mohammed brought him into contact with the chief of the Afghan College at the Azhar Mosque who contrived for a bribe of three dollars and a fee of five piastres to set matters right. What most expedited his departure was a quarrel with one of the Albanian bravoes who are the curse of Egypt—a quarrel which beginning with a violent personal conflict ended in a drinking bout wherein the " Albanian Captain of Irregulars " got shamefully drunk and the Indian doctor lost his Cairene reputation of being " a serious person." Burton tells the story at some length and with a good deal of fun, ending thus :—' " You had better start on your pilgrimage at once," said Haji Wali, meeting me next morning with a goguenard smile. He was right. . . . I wasted but little time in taking leave of my friends, telling them by way of precaution that my destination was Meccah, *viâ* Jeddah, and firmly determining, if possible, to make El-Medinah *viâ* Yambú. " Conceal," says the Arab's proverb, " thy Tenets, thy Treasure, and thy Travelling." '

Off set Burton accordingly. His Indian boy and the heavy baggage had gone before, and he had hired a couple of camels for the march to Suez. He was, he tells us, anxious to see ' how much a four years' life of European effeminacy had impaired his powers of endurance.' He adds—what is perhaps somewhat superfluous—that 'there are few better tests than an eighty-four mile ride in midsummer on a bad wooden saddle, borne by a worse dromedary across the Suez Desert.' The journey was a trial, but it was a trial not without its alleviations.

' We journeyed on till near sunset,' says Burton, ' through the wilderness without *ennui*. It is strange how the mind can be amused by scenery that presents so few objects to occupy it. But in such a country every slight modification of form or colour rivets observation ; the senses are sharpened, and the perceptive faculties, prone to sleep over a confused mass of natural objects, act vigorously when

excited by the capability of embracing each detail. Moreover, desert views are eminently suggestive; they appeal
to the future, not to the past; they arouse because they are
by no means memorial.

'To the solitary wayfarer there is an interest in the
wilderness unknown to Cape seas and Alpine glaciers,
and even to the rolling prairie—the effect of continued
excitement on the mind, stimulating its powers to their
pitch. Above, through a sky terrible in its stainless beauty,
and the splendours of a pitiless blinding glare, the simoon
caresses you like a lion with flaming breath. Around lie
drifted sand-heaps, upon which each puff of wind leaves its
trace in solid waves, frayed rocks, the very skeletons of
mountains, and hard unbroken plains, over which he who
rides is spurred by the idea that the bursting of a water-
skin, or the pricking of a camel's hoof, would be a certain
death of torture; a haggard land infested with wild beasts
and wilder men; a region whose very fountains murmur
the warning words "Drink and away!"

'What can be more exciting? what more sublime?
Man's heart bounds in his breast at the thought of
measuring his puny force with nature's might, and of
emerging triumphant from the trial. This explains the
Arab's proverb, "Voyaging is a Victory."

'In the desert, even more than upon the ocean, there is
present death; hardship is there, and piracies, and ship-
wreck, solitary, not in crowds, where, as the Persians say,
"Death is a Festival;" and this sense of danger, never
absent, invests the scene of travel with an interest not
its own.

'Let the traveller who suspects exaggeration leave the
Suez road for an hour or two, and gallop northwards over
the sands; in the drear silence, the solitude, and the fantastic desolation of the place, he will feel what the Desert
may be. And then the oases, and little lines of fertility—

how soft and how beautiful!—even though the Wady-el-
Ward (the Vale of Flowers) be the name of some stern
flat upon which a handful of wild shrubs blossom while
struggling through a cold season's ephemeral existence.

' In such circumstances the mind is influenced through
the body. Though your mouth glows, and your skin is
parched, yet you feel no languor, the effect of humid heat ;
your lungs are lightened, your sight brightens, your memory
recovers its tone, and your spirits become exuberant.
Your fancy and imagination are powerfully aroused, and
the wildness and sublimity of the scenes around you stir
up all the energies of your soul—whether for exertion,
danger, or strife. Your *morale* improves ; you become
frank and cordial, hospitable and single-minded ; the hypo-
critical politeness and the slavery of civilisation are left
behind you in the city. Your senses are quickened ; they
require no stimulants but air and exercise : in the desert
spirituous liquors excite only disgust.

' There is a keen enjoyment in mere animal existence.
The sharp appetite disposes of the most indigestible food ;
the sand is softer than a bed of down, and the purity
of the air suddenly puts to flight a dire cohort of diseases.
Hence it is that both sexes, and every age, the most
material as well as the most imaginative of minds, the
tamest citizen, the parson, the old maid, the peaceful
student, the spoiled child of civilisation, all feel their hearts
dilate and their pulses beat strong, as they look down from
their dromedaries upon the glorious desert. Where do we
hear of a traveller being disappointed by it ? It is another
illustration of the ancient truth that Nature returns to man,
however unworthily he has treated her. And, believe me,
when once your tastes have conformed to the tranquillity
of such travel, you will suffer real pain in returning to the
turmoil of civilisation. You will anticipate the bustle and
the confusion of artificial life, its luxury and its false

pleasures, with repugnance. Depressed in spirits, you will for a time after your return feel incapable of mental or bodily exertion. The air of cities will suffocate you, and the careworn and cadaverous countenances of citizens will haunt you like a vision of judgment.'

The party was made up at Suez, and the fidelity of his companions having been secured by various "loans" of money—which it was understood were never to be returned—Burton naturally assumed the leadership. All was, however, nearly lost by an imprudence. His new friends had criticised his pistols, looked at his clothes, and overhauled his medicine-chest, when they were staggered by a sextant, and the boy Mohammed, mentioned above, waited only for him to leave the room to declare to the rest that he "was one of the Infidels from India." A council was held to discuss the case, when fortunately for the success of Burton's plans, Umar Efendi, who had that morning looked over a letter of his to Haji Wali containing discussions of several points of high theology, and who had besides had theological discussions with him, was in a position to certify to his perfect orthodoxy. Shaykh· Hamid, who probably looked forward to many dollars in the future to be borrowed and never repaid, supported this view. Mohammed was roundly abused in all the terms of a rich vocabulary, informed that he had no shame, and recommended to fear Allah. Burton suspected the danger, and determining with a sigh to leave his sextant behind, "prayed five times a day for nearly a week."

The party resolved to lose no time in getting on board some ship bound for Yambú on the Arabian coast of the Red Sea, but the usual difficulty arose about passports. Burton's was not in order, though it had been *visé* by the Turkish authorities at Cairo, and there was consequently danger of his being compelled to wait for the Turkish caravan—a fatality which would have deranged

all his plans, and would moreover have deprived him of
the companionship of the men whom he had taken great
pains to conciliate and influence. The difficulty was finally
got over by his taking the boy Mohammed to the British
Consulate with a story of his having been 'a benefactor
to the British nation' in Afghanistan. Mr. Consul West,
who had been told to expect him, received him with great
kindness and having put himself in communication with
the Bey s factotum, succeeded in arranging matters. Then
came the question of passage. The delays—thanks to the
port regulations at Suez—were infinite, and whilst they
lasted the party had to remain in an inn, where 'the
ragged walls were clammy with dirt, the smoky rafters
foul with cobwebs, and the floor, bestrewed with kit in
terrible confusion, was black with cockroaches and flies.'
Other tenants shared the room with these hapless pilgrims
—pigeons, cats, mosquitoes, and the nameless insect-
plagues for which Egypt has been celebrated for countless
generations.

At last the pilgrims were able to get on board their ship,
the *Silk al-Zahab*, or *Golden Wire*. She was a sambuk
(*sambuca*) of about 50 tons, with narrow wedge-like bows, a
clean water-line, a sharp keel and undecked, except upon
the poop, which was high enough to serve as a sail in a gale
of wind. She had two masts 'raking imminently forwards,'
and carried one immense triangular lateen sail. For the
rest 'she had no means of reefing, no compass, no log,
no sounding-lines, not even the suspicion of a chart.'
Within this comfortless craft—a vessel which recalled the
ships depicted in the ancient sculptures of the Pharaohs—
no fewer than ninety-seven unhappy pilgrims with their
baggage were remorselessly packed, while fifteen women
and children were crowded into the cabin. The passengers
were a motley crew—mostly Maghrabis from the Deserts
about Tripoli and Tunis. 'Their manners were rude,'

says Burton, 'and their faces full of fierce contempt or insolent familiarity. A few old men were there, with countenances expressive of intense ferocity; women as savage and full of fight as men ; and handsome boys with shrill voices and hands always upon their daggers. The women were mere bundles of dirty, white rags. The males were clad in burnús, brown or striped woollen cloaks with hoods ; they had neither turban nor tarbush, trusting to their thick curly hair, or to the prodigious hardness of their scalps as a defence against the sun, and there was not a slipper nor a shoe amongst the party.' With such a company, whose ideas of the rights of first-class passengers to precedence were naturally of a somewhat limited order, there were of course considerable difficulties, and the Maghrabis were only kept from the poop after a fierce hand to hand fight, in which the passengers had perforce to look out for themselves. The crew consisted of half-a-dozen Egyptian lads—notoriously neither the strongest nor the bravest of men—and the Rais, or captain, 'was an old fool, who could do nothing but call for the Fatihah, or opening chapter of the Koran, claim Bakhshish at every place where we moored for the night, and spend his leisure hours in the "Caccia del Mediterraneo." '

In such a craft and with such a company the voyage from Suez to Yambú—a distance in a straight line of 600 miles, but protracted by détours to double that space—however interesting it may have been from one point of view, must, from another, have been anything but a foretaste of Paradise. The discomforts were in fact endless, and on some occasions even the hardened Arabs and Africans, who by Burton's account appear capable of enduring almost any extremity of hardship, suffered most severely. For twelve mortal days this purgatory lasted, and then at noon, on the 17th of July, after slowly beating up the creek into Yambú Harbour, the traveller 'sprang into a shore

boat and felt new life, when bidding an eternal adieu to
the vile *Golden Wire.* He had the solitary satisfaction of
knowing that he had done what no Englishman had ever
done before—travelled for nearly a fortnight in a pilgrim
boat, and made himself acquainted in the fullest possible
way with the inner life of Islam. The voyage was not
without its effect upon his health. When he landed at
Yambú, what with the heat of the sun, the heavy night
dews, and the frequent washing of the waves, one of his
feet was so affected that he could hardly place it upon the
ground.

The traveller's duty had to be done, however, and so,
leaning on the shoulder of his " slave," he perambulated
the town. Yambú somewhat agreeably disappointed him.
Being the port of El Medinah, as Jeddah is of Meccah, there
is considerable trade with the interior, and the people are
of a better type than those with whom he had lately been
living. 'There is,' he says, 'an independent bearing
about the Yambú men, strange in the East; they are
proud without insolence, and they look ·manly without
blustering. . . . . The population has a healthy appearance, and fresh from Egypt, I could not help noticing their
freedom from ophthalmic disease. The children too appear
vigorous, nor are they here kept in that state of filth to
which fear of the evil eye devotes them in the Valley of
the Nile.' In the afternoon of the day on which the
party arrived at Yambú arrangements were made for
camels for the journey to El-Medinah, and also for an
escort of irregular cavalry. This last was very necessary,
for the Házimi tribe was " out," and travellers had to fight
every day. The news produced a great effect upon
Burton's party. ' " Sir," said Shayk Nur to me, " we must
wait till all this is over." I told him to hold his tongue, and
sharply reproved the boy Mohammed, upon whose manner
the effect of finding himself suddenly in a fresh country

had wrought a change for the worse. "Why ye were lions at Cairo: and here at Yambú ye are cats—hens!" It was not long, however, before the youth's impudence returned upon him with increased violence.'

Seeing that anything like breaking down Burton's resolution was out of the question, the party sat quietly through the afternoon until the intense heat subsided in some slight degree after sunset, when came dinner in the open air, a body of twenty, master, servants, children and strangers. The dish was a huge cauldron of boiled rice, containing square masses of mutton, the whole covered with clarified butter, round which the party squatted. Coffee, pipes and conversation carried on the evening until 10 P.M., then, says Burton, 'we prayed the Isha or vespers, and spreading our mats upon the terrace we slept in the open.'

The next morning was spent in preparations for the journey and in buying necessaries—amongst others a *shugduf* * or litter, and seven days' provisions for the journey. Arms were polished and loaded, boxes repacked, and changes fitting travellers for the road were made in dress. By the advice of one of the party Burton once more changed his nationality and dressed as an Arab in order to avoid paying the Jizyat—a capitation tax which the settled tribes extort from stranger-travellers. Then, after an early dinner, the camels were loaded with the usual difficulty, and at 3 P.M. all was ready. The start was delayed, however, until 6, from the difficulty of

---

* "Habib was still ill with fever, and had to travel in the Takhtrawàn or Shugduf. A balance was wanted for the other pannier, and as no other could be found I got into it—but I had overtaxed my good-nature—it bumped me and tired me so unmercifully that after half an hour I begged to be let down and made the driver sit in himself. . . . How people travel in it to Meccah and back is a mystery to me." ('Inner Life of Syria,' i. 237.) Lady Burton has explained the mystery a dozen lines earlier : "Captain Burton is certainly made of cast iron."

gathering the members of the caravan, who with true Oriental *insouciance* had scattered themselves all over the town. When at last all had mounted, the brief twilight had almost faded away, but as they passed out from the shadowy streets and through the gates of the town, the moon rose fair and clear, and the sweet air of the desert delightfully contrasted with the close, offensive atmosphere of the town.

Burton's own party consisted of twelve camels travelling head tied to tail, with one outrider, Umar Efendi, whose rank required him to mount a dromedary by himself. There were besides a miscellaneous collection of pilgrims all dressed in the coarsest and meanest of clothing—'the general suit consisting of a shirt torn in divers places, and a bit of rag wrapped round the head. They carried short Chibouks without mouth-pieces, and tobacco pouches of greasy leather.' Besides all these there were two hundred camels carrying grain, attended by the proprietors, and the escort already mentioned, seven irregular Turkish cavalry—men tolerably well mounted, and carrying a perfect armoury of weapons. It might have been thought that such a caravan was safe from the attacks of robbers, but it was not, as was speedily made manifest. On leaving Yambú at seven in the evening the caravan made its way to due east, and marched at a pace so slow that by three in the morning only sixteen miles had been covered. There a halt was called ; the camels were unloaded ; the boxes were piled, and all addressed themselves to slumber. They awoke at 9 A.M. for pipes and breakfast—biscuit, a little rice and a cup of milkless tea. Then came more sleep, and at 2 P.M. dinner. 'Boiled rice, with an abundance of the clarified butter in which Easterns delight, some fragments of kahk, or soft biscuit, stale bread, a handful of stoned and pressed date paste, called Ajwah, formed the *menu.* Our potations began before dinner with a vile-

tasted but wholesome drink called Akit, dried sour milk
dissolved in water ; at the meal we drank the leather-
flavoured element (*i.e.* water from goat-skin), and ended
with a large cupful of scalding tea. Enormous quantities
of liquid were consumed, for the sun seemed to have got
into our throats, and the perspiration trickled as after a
shower of rain.' At three o'clock the caravan got under
way again, and continued on the road for three hours,
when it halted for a short time. As evening came on, and
almost before it was dark, the travellers were alarmed by
the cry of *Harámi* (thieves) from the rear. The camel-men
brandished their huge staves and rushed back vociferating.
They were followed by the horsemen, and the camels in
the van might readily have been driven away had the
thieves but known their evil business a little better. As it
was, the affair was over in a few seconds, with no more
result than the harmless exchange of a few matchlock
bullets. The event caused no inconsiderable excitement,
seeing that it happened in the plain, and was taken
as a hint of what might be expected when the little
caravan was entangled in the hills. In the result these
apprehensions proved by no means unfounded.

On this stage of the journey the travellers did not reach
their destination — Bir Said ; Said's Well — until 8 A.M.
The well they found very different from that pictured
and described by imaginative artists and poets. 'I had
been led to expect at the " well," ' says Burton, 'a pastoral
scene, wild flowers, flocks and flowing waters, so I looked
with a jaundiced eye upon a deep hole full of slightly
brackish water dug in a tamped hollow ; a kind of punch-
bowl with granite walls upon whose grim surface a few
thorns of exceeding hardihood braved the sun for a season.
Not a house was in sight—it was as barren and desolate a
spot as the sun ever viewed in his wide career.' The heat
even at the well was fearful. 'The sun scorched our feet

as we planted our tent,' and so exertion of any kind being
absolutely impossible, the day was passed in 'perspiration
and semi lethargy.'   At 3 P.M. another start was made,
and the caravan moved its perilous way through a
mountainous road until between 10 and 11 at night, when
it reached the first human habitation since leaving Yambú.
This is a long straggling village, called indifferently El-
Hamrá, from the redness of the sands near which it is
built, and El-Wásitah, because it is the half-way station
between Yambú and El-Medinah.

After an hour's search a camping ground was found, and
the usual arrangements were made, but at dawn Burton
was on the alert and busied in examining the position.
He found El-Hamrá to be a collection of stunted houses,
or rather hovels, roofed with palm leaves, built of unbaked
brick or mud, pierced with a few air-holes, and having
sometimes a bit of plank for a shutter.   It is well supplied
with provisions, but like so many Oriental villages it abounds
in ruins.   Mountains are on all sides, so that, as he says,
the traveller finds himself in 'another of those punch-bowls
which the Arabs appear to think choice grounds for settlements.'   There is, however, an excellent reason for the
selection of this site.   'The Fiumara,* hereabouts very
winding, threads the high ground all the way from the
plateau of El-Medinah : during the rainy season it
becomes a raging torrent, carrying westwards to the Red
Sea the drainage of a hundred hills.   Water of good
quality is readily found in it by digging a few feet below the
surface at the re-entering angles where the stream forms the
deepest hollows, and in some places the stony sides give
out bubbling springs.'   All this to the stay-at-home reader

---

* Fiumara, literally " a great river "—more accurately a river, made
great by the agglomeration of many smaller streams.   The word is constantly used by Burton to describe the Arabic " wády " or watercourse
which, a torrent in winter, becomes a road (of a kind) in the dry season.

sounds like one of those "smiling oases" where patriarchal shepherds exercise a generous hospitality, and
practise those virtues which the sentimental philosophers
of the eighteenth century fondly believed must spring up
spontaneously in the bosoms of men who are in daily and
immediate contact with Nature. Of this kind of thing
Burton found no trace. The villagers he more than once
describes as "surly"; they made themselves exceedingly
disagreeable in the matter of the camping ground ; some
of them raised a quarrel with his people, and not one of
the shepherds would let them have a single glass of milk
from their abundant flocks of sheep and goats, even in
exchange for bread or meat.

But the greatest of all discomforts during the day spent
in El-Hamrá was the news that Sa'ed, the robber chief,
and his brother were in the field, and that the march of
the caravan would consequently be delayed for some time.
The whole story of the chief as given by Burton is well
worth transcribing, as illustrating the venerable proverb
which calls upon us to remark " with how little wisdom the
world is governed."

' He is the chief of the Sumaydah and the Mahámid,
two influential sub-families of the Hamidah, the principal
family of the Bani-Harb tribe of Bedawin. He therefore
aspired to rule all the Hamidah, and through them the
Bani-Harb, in which case he would have been, *de facto*,
monarch of the Holy Land. But the Sherif of Meccah,
and Ahmed Pasha, the Turkish Governor of the chief city,
for some political reason degraded him, and raised up a
rival in the person of Shaykh Fahd, another ruffian of a
similar stamp, who calls himself chief of the Bani-Amr,
the third sub-family of the Hamidah family. Hence all
kinds of confusion. Sa'ed's people, who number, it is said,
five thousand, resent, with Arab asperity, the insult offered
to their chief, and beat Fahd's, who do not amount to

O 2

eight hundred. Fahd, supported by the Government, cut
off Sa'ed's supplies. Both are equally wild and reckless,
and nowhere doth the glorious goddess, Liberty, show a
more brazen face than in this Eastern " Inviolate land of
the brave and the free." Both seize the opportunity of
shooting troopers, of plundering travellers, and of closing
the roads. This state of things continued till I. left the
Hejaz, when the Sherif of Meccah proposed, it was said, to
take the field in person against the arch-robber. And, as
will afterwards be seen in these pages, Sa'ed had the
audacity to turn back the Sultan's Mahmal or litter—the
ensign of Imperial power—and to shut the road against its
cortège, because the Pashas of El-Medinah and of the
Damascus caravan would not guarantee his restitution to
his former dignity.

* * * * *

' Sa'ed, the Old Man of the Mountains, was described to
me as a little brown Bedawi ; contemptible in appearance,
but remarkable for courage and ready wit. He has for
treachery a keen scent, which he requires to keep in
exercise. A blood feud with Abd el-Muttalib, the present
Sherif of Meccah, who slew his nephew, and the hostility
of several sultans, has rendered his life eventful. He lost
all his teeth by poison, which would have killed him, had
he not, after swallowing the potion, corrected it by drinking
off a large potful of clarified butter. Since that time he
has lived entirely upon fruits, which he gathers for himself,
and coffee which he prepares with his own hands. In
Sultan Mahmud's time he received from Constantinople
a gorgeous purse, which he was told to open, as it contained something for his private inspection. Suspecting
treachery, he gave it for this purpose to a slave, bidding
him carry it to some distance ; the bearer was shot by a
pistol cunningly fixed, like Rob Roy's, in the folds of the
bag.

'Whether this far-known story be "true or only well found," it is certain that Shaykh Sa'ed now fears the Turks, even when they bring him gifts. The Sultan sends, or is supposed to send him, presents of fine horses, robes of honour and a large quantity of grain. But the Shaykh, trusting to his hills rather than to steeds, sells them ; he gives away the dresses to his slaves, and he distributes the grain among his clansmen. Of his character, men as usual tell two tales ; some praise his charity, and call him the friend of the poor, as certainly he is a foe to the rich. Others, on the contrary, describe him as cruel, cold-blooded, and notably, even among Arabs, revengeful and avaricious. The truth probably lies between these two extremes, but I observed that those of my companions who spoke most highly of the robber chief when at a distance seemed to be in the *sudori freddi* whilst under the shadow of his hills.'

The stay of the caravan in El-Hamrá (the Red Village) was not destined to be prolonged. After mid-day on the 21st of July, when everybody had made up his mind to a long halt, a caravan arrived from Meccah, and a little after 4 P.M. the travellers were able to join it and to go on their way. At sunset there were the usual prayers—said this time with perhaps more than usual unction — and then after supper the way was resumed. An odd incident followed. Soon after sunset there was a sudden halt. A band of Bedawin, who had occupied a gorge, sent forward a " parliamentary " ordering the caravan to stop. They at first demanded money, but at last, hearing that the travellers were " Children of the Holy Cities," they agreed. to let them go on provided that the military—' whom they,' says Burton, 'like Irish peasants, hate and fear' —should return to the place whence they had come. Thereupon this gallant escort, 200 strong and armed to the teeth, turned tail and galloped home again. The

caravan, though deprived of its escort, went on in safety,
some courage having possibly been put into the hearts of its
weaker members by certain words of Burton. When the
fray was impending, his camel man, Mansur, was very
anxious to know why he did not get out of his litter, load
his pistols, and show fight. 'Because,' said Burton loudly,
'in my country when dogs rush at us we thrash them with
sticks.' The danger passed off; the caravan continued its
march, and at four in the morning encamped at Bir Abbar
—a place which in its external aspect resembles El-Hamrá
not a little.

At this "Well of Abbás" Burton was fortunate enough
to witness a review of the Arnaut Irregular Cavalry, who,
after a delay of some twenty-four hours or so started, having
under their escort some three or four caravans. At early
dawn, on July 24th, this huge caravan found itself in a
gorge of evil reputation, known as the Shuab el-Hajj—the
pilgrimage pass. 'Presently from the high precipitous
cliff on our left, thin blue curls of smoke—somehow or
other they caught every eye—rose in the air ; and instantly
afterwards rose the sharp cracks of the hill-men's matchlocks echoed by the rocks on the right. . . . A number of
Bedawin were to be seen swarming like hornets on the
crests of the hills, boys as well as men carrying huge
weapons, and climbing with the agility of cats. They took
up comfortable places on the cut-throat eminence, and
began firing upon us with perfect convenience to themselves.' The affair was one of simple butchery—an ambuscade of the vilest kind. Of course it was perfectly useless
to call upon the Bedawin to come down and fight in the
open. They had scarped the rock, piled up a rough breast-
work of stones, and from behind its shelter they were able
to take "pot shots" at the hapless travellers below. The
Shaykhs were called into council, but of course they could
do nothing. They dismounted from their camels, and

SKETCH OF EL-MEDINAH BY A NATIVE ARTIST.

squatted in council round their pipes, but they 'came to the conclusion that as the robbers would probably turn a deaf ear to their words they had better spare themselves the trouble of speaking.' All that was left for the unfortunate travellers to do was therefore to blaze away as much powder, and veil themselves in as much smoke, as possible. This was done, but the affair cost the lives of twelve men, besides camels and other beasts of burden. No one, however, was captured and carried into the mountains for ransom under pain of death—or, if there were, Burton does not record the fact—the Bedawin apparently preferring to leave that kind of thing to modern Greece.

The caravans had shaken off the "hornets" of the mountain-side. Whether the spoils which had perforce been left upon the slaughtered camels and other beasts of burden slain by the Bedawin in the ill-fated pass, were sufficient to repay the latter for the ammunition they had expended, is perhaps a matter of small consequence, and one which the escaped travellers considered as little as we do. The caravan pushed on, and on the morning of the 25th of July, El-Medinah was in sight. ' Half-an-hour after leaving the " Blessed Valley" we came to a large flight of steps roughly cut in a long black line of scoriaceous basalt.' Over this the caravan passed, then through a lane of dark lava with steep banks on both sides, and then after a few minutes the full view of the Holy City suddenly opened upon the pilgrims who found in all the fair view before them nothing more striking after the desolation through which they had passed than the gardens and orchards about the town. The weary pilgrims, jaded and hungry as they were, sat down to feast their eyes on the spectacle, and to cry out :—

" O Allah! This is the Haram (Sanctuary) of thy Apostle ; make it to us a protection from Hell Fire and a

Refuge from Eternal Punishment! O open the Gates of thy Mercy, and let us pass through them to the Land of Joy!"

And—

" O Allah ! Bless the Last of the Prophets, the Seal of Prophecy, with Blessings in number as the Stars of Heaven, and the Waves of the Sea and the Sands of the Waste! Bless him, O Lord of Might and Majesty, as long as the Corn Field and the Date Grove continue to feed Mankind ! "

And again—

" Live for ever, O Most Excellent of Prophets !—live in the Shadow of Happiness during the Hours of Night and the Times of Day, whilst the Bird of the Tamarisk (the Dove) moaneth like the childless Mother, whilst the West Wind bloweth gently over the Hills of Nejd, and the lightning flasheth bright in the Firmament of El-Hejaz ! "

Burton adds, by the way, with reference to the second of these blessings, a curious and characteristic foot-note. The Arabs he says, in effect, divide mankind into two great classes ; themselves and "Ajam," *i.e.* all who are not Arabs, and he indicates the curious parallelisms already existing elsewhere. ' Similar bi-partitions are the Hindus and Mlenchhas, the Jews and Gentiles, the Greeks and Barbarians, &c.' He might have carried the parallel a good deal further, but he possibly thought with some other people that it is not worth while to work everything out to the *n*th.

After entering El-Medinah Burton took up his abode with the Shaykh Hamid, who received him with great hospitality, expounded to him his duty as one of the Faithful, and made him practically one of his family—for a consideration, of course: for the sons of Ishmael are as keen in their pursuit of the main chance as their elder brothers of the half-blood, the sons of Israel.

' Our life in Shaykh Hamid's house,' says Burton, ' was quiet, but not disagreeable. I never once set eyes upon the face of woman, unless the African slave girls be allowed the title. Even these at first attempted to draw their ragged veils over their sable charms, and would not answer the simplest question ; by degrees they allowed me to see them, and they ventured their voices in reply to me ; still they never threw off a certain appearance of shame. Their voices are strangely soft and delicate, considering the appearance of the organs from which they proceed. Possibly this may be a characteristic of the African races ; it is remarkable amongst the Somali women. I never saw, nor even heard, the youthful mistress of the household, who stayed all day in the upper rooms. The old lady, Hamid's mother, would stand upon the stairs and converse aloud with her son, and, when few people were about the house, with me. She never, however, as afterwards happened to an ancient dame at Mecca, came and sat by my side.

' When lying during mid-day in the gallery, I often saw parties of women mount the stairs to the Gyneaconitis, and sometimes an individual would stand to shake a muffled hand with Hamid, to gossip awhile, and to put some questions concerning absent friends ; but they were most decorously wrapped up, nor did they ever deign to *déroger*, even by exposing an inch of cheek.

' At dawn we arose, washed, prayed, and broke our fast upon a crust of stale bread, before smoking a pipe and drinking a cup of coffee. Then it was time to dress, to mount, and to visit the Haram, or one of the Holy Places outside the city. Returning before the sun became intolerable, we sat together ; and with conversation, Shishas (water-pipes) and Chibouques, coffee, and cold water perfumed with mastich-smoke, we whiled away the time until our "Ariston," a dinner which appeared at the primitive hour of 11 A.M. The meal, here called El-ghadá, was served in the Majlis on a large copper tray, sent from the upper

apartments. Ejaculating "Bismillah"—the Moslem "grace"
—we all sat round it, and dipped equal hands in the dishes
set before us. We had usually unleavened bread, different
kinds of meat and vegetable stews ; and, at the end of
the first course, plain boiled rice eaten with spoons ; then
came the fruits, fresh dates, grapes, and pomegranates.

'After dinner I used invariably to find some excuse—
such as the habit of a "Kaylúlah" (mid-day siesta), or the
being a "Saudáwi," a person of melancholy temperament—
to have a rug spread in the dark passage behind the Majlis ;
and there to lie reading, dozing, smoking or writing, *en
cachette*, in complete *déshabille*, all through the worst part
of the day, from noon to sunset.

'Then came the hour for receiving or paying visits.
We still kept up an intimacy with Umar Effendi and Sa'ed
the Demon, although Salih Skakkar and Amm Jemal,
either disliking our society, or perhaps thinking our sphere
of life too humble for their dignity, did not appear once in
Hamid's house. The evening prayers ensued, either at
home or in the Haram, followed by our Asha or "deipnon,"
another substantial meal like the dinner, but more plentiful,
of bread, meat, vegetables, plain rice and fruits, concluding
with the invariable pipes and coffee.

'To pass our *soirée*, we occasionally dressed in common
clothes, shouldered a Nebút, or quarter-staff, and went to
the *café;* sometimes on festive occasions we indulged in a
Sa'atumah (or Itmiyah), a late supper of sweetmeats, pomegranates, and dried fruits. Usually we sat upon mattresses
spread in the open air upon the ground at the Shaykh's
door ; receiving evening visits, chatting, telling stories, and
making merry, till each, as he felt the approach of the drowsy
god, sank down into his proper place, and fell asleep.'

But our English Haji had not come to El-Medinah
merely to observe the manners of the people, or to watch
the curious street scenes presented by the town which is

the centre of the Moslem world. He had come on a study of the Pilgrimage, and as a pilgrim he had a host of shrines to visit, of ceremonies to perform and of prayers to recite. Wherefore 'having performed the greater ablution, and used the tooth-stick as directed, and dressed in the white clothes which the Apostle loved,' he went forth to visit his tomb, and as his foot was still painful, he was compelled to ride on an ass, greatly to the disgust of the Arabs, who assumed, as a matter of course, that he was a Turk, they themselves considering it a disgrace to mount the humbler animal.

The Masjid el-Nabawi, or Mosque of the Prophet, is one of the two sanctuaries of El-Islam, and in the second of the three most venerable places of worship in the world. 'One prayer in this my mosque is more efficacious than a thousand in other places, save only the Masjid el-Haram' —the Mosque of Abraham, at Meccah. 'It is therefore,' we are further told, 'the visitor's duty, as long as he stays at El-Medinah, to pray there *the five prayers per diem*, to pass the day in it reading the Koran, and the night if possible in watching and devotion.'

'A visit to the Masjid el-Nabawi,' Burton adds, 'and the holy places within it, is technically called "Ziyárat," or Visitation. An essential difference is made between this rite and Hajj, or Pilgrimage. The latter is obligatory by Koranic order upon every Moslem once in his life; the former is only a meritorious action. Tawáf, or circumambulation of the House of Allah at Meccah, must never be performed at the Apostle's tomb. This should not be visited in the Ihram or Pilgrim dress; men should not kiss it, touch it with the hand, or press the bosom against it as at the Ka'abah, or rub the face with dust collected near the Sepulchre; and those who prostrate themselves before it, like certain ignorant Indians, are held to be guilty of deadly sin. On the other hand, to spit upon any part of the Mosque, or to treat it with contempt, is held to be the act of an infidel.'

All this is assuredly precise enough and definite enough, but Burton found that human nature is pretty much the same under one sky as under another, and that the faith of Islam, like Christianity itself, is broken up into a congeries of warring sects. The extremely orthodox hold El-Medinah to be the most sacred of the holy places, because of its possessing the tomb of the prophet; others are uncertain whether they ought not to prefer Meccah, as having been blessed by Abraham; and yet others, the Wahhabis, who may very properly be described as the Protestants of Mohammedanism, deny the efficacy of the intercession of the Prophet at the day of judgment, and holding the reverence paid to his tomb by certain Moslems to be idolatrous, plundered the sacred buildings with sacrilegious violence, and forbade pilgrims to enter El-Medinah. There is, of course, a *juste milieu* which admits nearly everything that is advanced by both sides, and which holds the *Bayt Allah* (House of God) at Meccah to be holier than every part of that city, and at the same time declares El-Medinah to be more venerable than every part of Meccah, and, consequently, all the earth except the Bayt Allah. 'In the meantime,' says Burton, 'the Meccans claim unlimited superiority over the Madani, the Madani over the Meccans.' So much of Moslem theology is perhaps necessary to the proper understanding of the ceremonial through which our English Haji had to pass. His donkey—a wonderfully tattered and torn specimen of much-belauded beast of Oriental regions—bore him to the Gate of Pity, and he entered the place most universally venerated in the Moslem world to find ' the resemblance of a museum of second-rate art, an old curiosity shop, full of ornaments that are not accessories, and decorated with a pauper splendour.' The building itself is about 420 feet in length, and 340 broad; hypaethral in structure, and surrounded by a peristyle with numerous rows of columns like an Italian cloister.

The pilgrim has, however, something to do besides lionizing. His guide leads him to the Bab-el-Salam (Gate of Safety), and inquires markedly if he is religiously pure. 'Then, placing our hands a little below and on the left of the waist, the palm of the right covering the back of the left, in the position of prayer, and beginning with the dexter foot (in this mosque, as in all others, it is proper to enter with the right foot and to retire with the left), we pace slowly forwards down the line called the Muwájihat el-Sharífah, or "the Illustrious Fronting," which, divided off like an aisle, runs parallel with the southern wall of the mosque. On my right-hand walks the Shaykh, who re-cites aloud the following prayer, making me repeat it after him. It is literally rendered, as, indeed, are all the formulæ :—"In the name of Allah and in the faith of Allah's Apostle! O Lord, cause me to enter the Entering of Truth, and cause me to issue forth the Issuing of Truth, and permit me to draw near to Thee, and make me a Sultan victorious!" Then follow blessings upon the Apostle, and afterwards : "O Allah! open to me the door of Thy mercy, and grant me entrance into it, and protect me from Satan the Stoned Devil."'

During this preliminary prayer the pilgrim walks down two-thirds of "the Illustrious Fronting." Passing over mere matters of detail, interesting though they may be, we find him entering the Rauzah, or "Garden," where the ceremonies of the true Visitation begin. Here he is placed with his back to the great stone from which the Muballighs (clerks) recite the Ikámah, or call to divine service, 'with his right shoulder opposite to and about twenty feet distant from the dexter pillar of the Apostle's pulpit. There,' goes on Burton, 'after saying the after-

noon prayer, I performed the usual two bows in honour of
the temple, and at the end of them recited the 109th and
111th chapters of the Koran (a declaration of the Unity of
God) . . . . after which was performed a single Sujdah
(Prostration) of Thanks in gratitude to Allah for making it
my fate to visit so holy a spot.' Then, as usual, came the
clamour for alms, the beggars spreading their napkins on
the ground before the pilgrims and sprinkling them with
coppers to excite generosity.

The Rauzah or Garden itself is, it would seem, a poor
and tawdry building, so decorated as in a conventional
sense to resemble a garden. The pediments are covered
with green tiles, the carpets flowered, and the columns
adorned to the height of a man with gaudy and unnatural
vegetation in arabesque. To make matters worse, 'it is
disfigured by handsome branched candelabras of cut crystal,
the work of a London house.' At night, however, when
the eyes of the pilgrim are dazzled with lamps innumerable,
and huge wax candles, the case is somewhat altered ; but
the whole scene must be viewed with a Moslem bias, and
'until a man is thoroughly imbued with the spirit of the
East, the last place the Rauzah will remind him of is that
which the architect primarily intended it to resemble—a
garden.' After leaving the Garden, the pilgrim is taken on
a fresh perambulation, for the details of which the reader
must be referred to Burton's deeply interesting ' Pilgrimage
to El-Medinah and Meccah,' from which most of the
foregoing extracts have been taken. Here it must be
sufficient to give only the briefest outline.

After marching round the outer courts of the temple,
the pilgrim is brought to the Holy Place, in which are
enshrined the bodies of Mohammed and his successors
Abubekr, Omar, and Fatimah, with a vacant space left for
Isa (Jesus), whom the Mohammedans hold in greater
reverence than do a large proportion of those who call

themselves Christians. Here a prayer is recited, in "awe, fear, and love," calling down upon the Prophet innumerable benedictions, and describing him by almost as many poetical epithets as are given to the Blessed Virgin in her Litany. After all which the pilgrims perform Ziyárat for themselves, and repeat the Fátihah, or "opening," chapter of the Koran. As this chapter has already been mentioned so often, and is likely to be mentioned so many times more, it may be as well to transcribe it in this place. Here, then, is the Moslem confession of faith :—

" In the name of Allah, the Compassionating, the Compassionate !
Praise be to Allah ! who the (three) Worlds made.
The Merciful, the Compassionate.
The King of the Day of Faith.
Thee (alone) do we worship ; and of Thee (alone) do we ask Aid.
Guide us to the path that is straight—
The path of those for whom thy Love is great, not those on whom
    is hate, nor those that deviate.
Amen ! O Lord of Angels, Jinns and Men ! "

After these recitations at the tomb of Mohammed, our Haji was permitted to look through the windows of the chambers enclosing the tombs of Abubekr and Omar, and to commend them to the peace of Allah. Lastly, the guide wrenches the pilgrim from the beggars who encompass him, and allows him to look through the third window and behold the tomb of the Prophet. As this miraculous structure, however, is shaded with curtains half covered with gold embroidery, there is not much to be seen, if we except the *Kaukab el-Durri*, or Constellation of Pearls, concerning which the miracle-mongers have written a good deal, but which Burton thought to resemble 'the round glass stoppers used for the humbler class of decanters.' This judgment, however, he qualifies by saying that he thought the same of the Koh-i-Nur—as a good many other people have probably done.

The pilgrim and his guide now went round the south-eastern corner of the baldaquin and stopped at the *Mahbat Jibrail*—"the Place of the Archangel Gabriel's Descent with the Heavenly Revelations"—said prayers, and then went on to the sixth station, the sepulchre or cenotaph of the lady Fatimah, where a most florid prayer, or rather blessing, is recited. Then turning to the north, the pilgrims recited orisons in honour of Hamzah and of the Martyrs who lie buried at the foot of Mount Ohod; then to the east to bless the blessed of El-Bakia; then to the south with a general prayer for themselves; and this done they returned to the "Apostle's Window," where they recited the following tetrastich and prayer:—

> " O Mustafá ! verily I stand at thy door,
> A man weak and fearful by reason of my sins ;
> If thou aid me not, O, Apostle of Allah !
> I die, for in the world there is none generous as thou art ! "

" Of a truth Allah and his Angels bless the Apostle ! Oh Ye who believe bless Him and salute Him with salutation ! O Allah ! verily I implore Thy Pardon and supplicate Thine Aid in this world as in the next ! O Allah ! O Allah ! abandon us not in this Holy Place to the consequences of our Sins without pardoning them, as to our Griefs without consoling them, or to our fears, O Allah ! without removing them. And blessings and salutations be to Thee, O Prince of Apostles Commissioned (to preach to the world), and laud be to Allah Lord of the (three) Worlds ! "

In another place came another prayer, specially said with reference to Death, and finally the pilgrims returned to the "Garden," where they prayed another "two bow" prayer, ending as they had begun with the worship of the Creator. And after these devotions came the beggars. The "boy Mohammed" had put on an embroidered coat to accompany his master to the shrine, and the result was that the latter was taken for a man of wealth, and all his

address did not extricate him from this motley throng at a
less expenditure than four dollars—nearly a pound sterling.
What was worse he could never afterwards go to the same
place for less than half that sum.

After all these prayers and memorials and blessings, it
is a little disheartening to know that it is not by any means
certain that Mohammed is buried in El-Medinah. Every
Moslem, of course, believes it, but there is no absolute
certainty on the subject. Historians differ ; there was a
tumult on the night when the death of the Prophet was
announced ; and lastly, it is in Burton's opinion impossible
to ' look upon the tale of the blinding light which surrounds
the Prophet's tomb, current for ages past, and still universally believed upon the authority of the attendant eunuchs,
who must know its falsehood, as a priestly gloss intended
to conceal a defect.'

Besides the Great Mosque, there are other places to
which visitations have to be made by the Faithful. Of these
the foremost is Kubá—the first place of public prayer in
El-Islam. A pilgrimage hither is esteemed equal to a
lesser pilgrimage to Meccah in religious efficacy, and more
acceptable to Allah than prostrations at the Bayt al-
Mukaddas (Jerusalem). Wherefore all who make the
visitation to El-Medinah go also to Kubá. Burton went
also, the boy Mohammed procuring him a dromedary on
which he rode through the date gardens around El-Medinah
to the shrine of the miracle of the " kneeling dromedary."
There was nothing particularly interesting in the Mosque
or in the village—which, indeed, is but a ' confused heap
of huts and dwelling houses, chapels, and towers, with trees
between, and foul lanes, heaps of rubbish, and barking
dogs ' — but the pilgrim had to pay pretty smartly for
the pleasure of visiting. The place literally swarms
with beggars, whose first word as pronounced by the
infants in arms is " bakhshish," and whose last from the

blear-eyed *vieillard* on the steps of the Mosque is still
" bakhshish."

Another pilgrimage was to Ohod, a place which owes its
reputation to a cave which sheltered the Apostle when
pursued by his enemies ; to certain springs from which he
drank, and especially to its being the scene of a celebrated
battle. This battle was fought in the third year of the
Hijrah (formerly englished " Hegira "), when Mohammed,
with 700 men encountered 3000 infidels, risked his own
life, and lost his uncle Hamzah, " the Lord of Martyrs."
The spot is further celebrated as being the burial place of
Aaron. It is accordingly one of especial sanctity, and
devout Moslems visit it every Thursday morning, after the
dawn devotions in the Haram, and after going through the
ceremonies return to the Haram for the mid-day worship.
The prayers and the devotions are very similar in their
character to those at the tomb of the Prophet in El-
Medinah, but Burton mentions a curious circumstance
in connection with them. When he went to perform his
part, the Arab custodian drew forth a huge bunch of
quaintly shaped keys which opened the door of the
Mosque with abundant noise of rattling locks and shaking
padlocks. The visitor himself was roughly bidden to
stand aside, the reason assigned being that the Saints
leaving the habitations of clay in which mere mortals
repose until the Day of Judgment, habitually meet within
the walls of the Mosque for spiritual converse. ' What
grand pictures these imaginative Arabs see ! Conceive
the majestic figures of the saints—for the soul amongst
Mohammedans is like the old European spirit, a something
immaterial in the shape of the body—with long grey
beards, earnest faces, and solemn eyes, reposing beneath
the palms, and discussing events now buried in the gloom
of a thousand years.'

Burton's comment on this superstition is worthy of

quotation. 'When in Nottingham,' he says, 'eggs may not be carried after sunset; when Ireland hears Banshees, or apparitional old women with streaming hair and dressed in blue mantles; when Scotland sees a shroud about a person, showing his approaching death; when France has her *loup-garous, revenants,* and *Poules du Vendredi Saint;* as long as the Holy Coat cures devotees at Treves, Madonnas wink at Rimini, San Januarius melts at Naples, and Addolorate and Estatiche make converts to Rome; whilst the Virgin manifests herself to children in the Alps and in France; whilst Germany sends forth Psychography; whilst Europe, the civilised, the enlightened, the sceptical, dotes over clairvoyance and table - turning, and whilst even hard-headed America believes in "mediums," in "snail telegraphs," and "spirit rapping," I must hold the men of El-Medinah to be as wise and their superstition to be as respectable, as that of theirs.' It is of a piece with this characteristic reflection that a little later, finding the "boy Mohammed" exhibiting a certain unpleasant amount of flippancy and disregard for ceremonies—going for example to the Haram "without his Jubbah (gaberdine) and with ungirt loins," in other words in his shirt sleeves—our Haji considered himself bound to interfere. 'Feeling that the youth's moral man was, like his physical, under my charge, and determined to arrest a course of conduct which must have ended in obtaining for me, the master, the reputation of a " son of Belial," I insisted on his joining us in the customary two-bow prayers.'

In the evening Burton went to the Haram at El-Medinah, where he found ample reason for rejoicing that he no longer wore the Persian habit. The Great Caravan, popularly called the Hajj el-Shami or Damascus Pilgrimage, numbering about seven thousand, had arrived on the Sunday, with a new curtain for the Prophet's "Hujrah" (closet); the annual stipends and pensions for the citizens

P 2

212 RICHARD F. BURTON.

of El-Medinah, and many members of its principal families, who had taken advantage of its escort. Amongst the seven thousand pilgrims were some twelve hundred Persians, who are considered anything but orthodox Mohammedans, and who consequently were subjected to any number of taunts and insults by those who could say Shibboleth with the true accent. When on this evening they went to the Mosque, the doorkeepers stopped them with curses, and demanded an admission fee of five piastres—about a shilling—while all other Moslems were allowed to enter free. Perhaps the browbeating which they underwent was good for their soul's health—'they had lost all their Shiráz swagger,' says Burton, 'their mustachios drooped pitiably, their eyes would not look any one in the face, and not a head bore a cap stuck upon it crookedly'—but it was un-questionably unpleasant. Moreover, this browbeating at the door of the Mosque was not the only disagreeable thing the Persians had to endure. Whenever an "Ajami," whatever might be his rank, stood in the way of an Arab or a Turk, he was rudely thrust aside with abuse, muttered loud enough to be heard by all around. All eyes followed them as they went through the ceremonies of Ziyárat, especially as they approached the tombs of Abubekr and Omar—which every man is bound to defile if he can—and the supposed place of Fatimah's burial. Here they stood in parties, after praying before the Prophet's window ; one read from a book a pathetic tale ' The Lady's Life, Sorrows, and Mourning Death,' whilst the others listened to him with breathless attention.

' Sometimes their emotion was too strong to be re-pressed : " Ay, Fatimah ! Ay, Mazlúmah ! Way ! Way ! ---O Fatimah ! O thou wronged one! Alas! Alas!" burst involuntarily from their lips, despite the danger of such exclamations ; tears trickled down their hairy cheeks, and their brawny bosoms heaved with sobs. A

strange sight it was to see rugged fellows, mountaineers
perhaps, or the fierce Ilyát of the plains, sometimes
weeping silently like children, sometimes shrieking like
hysteric girls, and all utterly careless to conceal a grief,
so coarse and grizzly, at the same time so true and real that
I knew not how to behold it. Then the Satanic scowls with
which they passed by, or pretended to pray at the hated
Omar's tomb ! With what curses their hearts are belying
those mouths full of blessings ! How they are internally
canonizing Fayruz, the Persian slave who stabbed Omar
in the Mosque—and praying for his eternal happiness in
the presence of the murdered man ! Sticks and stones,
however, and not unfrequently the knife and the sabre
have taught them the hard lesson of disciplining their
feelings ; and nothing but a furious contraction of the
brow, a roll of the eye, intensely vicious, and a twitching
of the muscles about the region of the mouth, denotes the
wild storm of wrath within. They generally, too, manage
to discharge some part of their passion in words.

"Hail, Omar, thou Hog !"

exclaims some fanatic Madani as he passes by the heretic
—a demand more outraging than requiring a black north
Protestant to bless the Pope.

'" O Allah ! *Hell* him !" meekly responds the Persian,
changing the benediction to a curse, most intelligible to
and delicious in his fellow's ears.'

The visitor who wishes to keep on good terms with the
purely Arab element of El-Medinah does wisely therefore
to shun the Persians, and this Burton did so ostenta-
tiously, that the rumour went abroad that the Shaykh
Abdullah, having slain many of those heretics in mortal
combat, avoided them out of fear lest they might treacherously retaliate upon him. 'I took,' says Burton, 'good
care not to contradict the report.' The myth of his being

a Pathán who had done good service to the English was bearing good fruit.

During the time of his stay in El-Medinah, Burton made a tolerably complete and exhaustive study of the city and its people. As, however, this history is concerned chiefly with his personal career, the reader must be referred to his ' Pilgrimage' for all those matters. Chapters xvii., xviii., xxi., xxiv., xxxi., and the Appendices, contain a perfect mine of information for any encyclopædist who wishes to fill his columns with something a little less jejune and futile than the average article.

Whilst he was thus lingering in El-Medinah events occurred which changed the whole of his plans. When he started under the auspices of the Royal Geographical Society, his intention was to cross the all-but unknown Arabian Peninsula and to map it out, so far as the achievement was possible. The route he proposed to take was either from El-Medinah to Maskat, or diagonally from Meccah to Makallah, on the Indian Ocean. His objects were first, to find out if any market for horses could be opened between Arabia and Central India ; secondly, to obtain some information concerning the great Eastern wilderness marked Ruba' el-Khali (the Empty Abode) in our maps ; thirdly, to determine the hydrography of the Hejaz, its watershed, the slope of the country, and the existence, or non-existence, of perennial streams ; and finally, to make certain ethnographical inquiries concerning the Arab race. Circumstances prevented these excellent intentions from being completely fulfilled. At the first Burton leaned to the Meccah route, and had he carried out his intention he would have had an infinitely more toilsome journey, but he would have opened up an absolutely new region. Certain difficulties which he encountered at Cairo made it necessary for him to proceed *viâ* El-Medinah, and on his arrival there he found the

Arab tribes of the interior quarrelling with prodigious fury. The Hawázim and the Hawámid are usually at daggers drawn, and a very little suffices to kindle a fire between them. The latter clan number not more than about 700 fighting men, while the former have as many as 3000; but what the Hawázim lack in numbers, they make up in courage and ferocity. On the present occasion a Hámidah happened to strike a camel belonging to one of the opposing clan, an insult which was returned with a blow and an evil name. These in their turn were repaid with a pistol-shot; both tribes were called out, and for some days the sound of musketry firing could be heard in the streets of the Holy City, within whose walls might be seen many parties of Bedawin hurrying to the fray, matchlock in hand, or with huge staves on their shoulders. The pilgrims were alarmed, and the peaceable townsfolk—pensioners for the most part of the Porte—heartily cursed both parties to the quarrel, and prayed that they might share the fate of the Kilkenny cats. So far as the immediate neighbourhood of El-Medinah was concerned, the consequences were, perhaps, not very serious. About ten men were killed on each side, and the combatants then withdrew into the desert. But what had happened was quite sufficient to prevent all thought of Burton's crossing to Maskat. An arrangement had, indeed, been made with one Mujrim (the " Sinful "), of the Benu Harb, by which Burton would have slipped out of the house in which he was living, and betaken himself to the desert like a true Bedawi. But when the war broke out Mujrim became uneasy, and finally told him that nobody could leave the city on that side even to get so far as " historic Khaybar "—information which subsequently turned out to be correct.

The disappointment was bitter, but it had its consolation. In the first place the journey of 1500 to 1600 miles across the desert would have occupied at the least ten months, and Burton's leave expired before the end of March ; and in the next, he had been compelled to leave his sextant and all his instruments, save only a pocket compass, at Suez ; so that the results of his journey to geographical science could hardly have been extensive. On the other hand, there was the journey to Meccah, through the wild eastern frontier of the Hejaz, and the prospect of seeing the Ceremonies of that Holy City. After sundry additional Ziyarats (visitations) of famous tombs and mosques, which it is needless to describe at length, each being almost the exact counterparts of the others, Burton set out, therefore, with the Damascus caravan, under the care of a venerable Bedawi, who, at the outset of the negotiations for his passage, nicknamed him Abu Shuwárib— the Father of Moustaches. This, it should be remarked, was done out of no discourtesy. Most men of the Shafei school shave wholly or in part, or at least clip the hair of the upper lip very short. And as Arabs, in view of the paucity of surnames, are apt to give nicknames according to physical peculiarities, so Burton received his. ' In Arabia,' he says, ' you must be " father" of something, and it is better to be father of a feature than father of a cooking-pot or father of a strong smell (" abu zirt "). The journey was one not to be performed without danger. Had our Haji been at Meccah he might have escaped in a few hours to Jeddah, where he would have found an English Vice-Consul, protection from the Turkish authorities and possibly a British cruiser in the harbour. In El-Medinah the case was very different. He was many days distant from all British authority ; he had nothing to rely upon save his own mother wit, and he had before him a desert journey of many days, during which nothing would have been easier than for the local authorities to dispose of him by giving a dollar to a Bedawi.

At nine in the morning of the 31st of August, 1853 (26th Zú 'l-Ka'adah), Burton found himself standing opposite the Egyptian gate of El-Medinah, surrounded by his friends—those friends of a day who cross the phantasmagoria of one's life—*les étoiles qui filent, filent et disparaitrent.* There were affectionate embraces and parting mementoes; the camels were mounted; Burton and the "boy Mohammed" in the litter, and Shaykh Nur in his cot. The train of nine camels wended its way slowly in a direction from north to north-east, gradually changing to eastward. After an hour's travel the caravan halted to turn and take farewell of the Holy City. All the pilgrims dismounted to gaze at the venerable minarets and the green dome which covers the tomb of the Prophet; and then, after an hour's rest, all remounted and pursued their way over the rough and stony path which carries the caravan out of the Medinah basin. The road was something almost too terrible. The air 'was still full of simoom,' but cold draughts occasionally poured down from the hills, making the climate dangerous in the extreme. 'After the long and sultry afternoon beasts of burden began to sink in numbers. The fresh carcasses of asses, ponies and camels dotted the wayside, those that had been allowed to die were abandoned to the foul carrion-birds, the Rakham (vulture) and the yellow Ukab; and all whose throats had been religiously cut were surrounded by groups of Takrúri pilgrims.' These last poor wretches are negroes who hang on to the caravans, and make the obligatory pilgrimage on alms. They carry wooden bowls, which they fill with water by begging. Their only weapon is a small knife, which they bear in a leathern sheath tied above the elbow; their costume an old skull-cap; a couple of strips of leather by way of sandals; and for body clothing either a long shirt of dirty cotton, or more frequently a waist-cloth, and nothing more.

Some had been finely-built men, broad-chested, thin-flanked, and long-limbed, but all were half-starved, and, 'looking at most of them,' says Burton, 'I fancied death depicted in their forms and features.'

The nine camels spoken of above were, of course, only those belonging to the Shaykh Mas'úd ; the caravan itself consisted of some 7000 souls, with their asses, camels, mules and horses. 'There were eight gradations of pilgrims. The lowest hobbled with heavy staves. Then came the riders of asses, camels and mules. Respectable men, especially Arabs, were mounted on dromedaries, and the soldiers had horses. A led animal was saddled for every grandee, ready whenever he might wish to leave his litter. Women, children, and invalids of the poorer classes sat upon a " Haml musattah "—rugs and cloths spread over the two large boxes which form the camel's load. Many occupied Shibriyahs (cots) ; a few Shugdufs (litters), and only the wealthy and noble rode in Takhtrawan (Sedans carried by camels or mules). The morning beams fell brightly upon the glancing arms which surrounded the stripped Mahmal, and upon the scarlet and gilt conveyances of the grandees. Not the least beauty of the spectacle was its wondrous variety of detail : no man was dressed like his neighbour, no camel was caparisoned, no horse was clothed in uniform, as it were. And nothing was stronger than the contrast—a band of half-naked Takruri marching with the Pasha's equipage, and long-capped, bearded Persians conversing with tarbush'd and shaven Turks.'

With this caravan Burton made his journey to Meccah, travelling in the usual uncomfortable Arab fashion, chiefly by night. This night march is, perhaps, the most disagreeable thing ever invented, but the Arabs are inexorable about it. The Prophet has said that they should " Choose early darkness for their wayfarings," and they obey him blindly and implicitly. To a European such a journey is tedious and disappointing in the extreme. It is impossible to "see the country," and the sleep that the wayfarer gets in the daytime is simply an unrefreshing lethargy. And on such a road as that over which Burton was now passing the miseries of the night were intensified. The camels displayed their usual wonderful sagacity, but they had to step from block to block of basalt like mountaineers, and in their perplexity and discontent kept up a continual piteous moaning.

'Here the air was filled with those pillars of sand so graphically described by Abyssinian Bruce. They scudded on the wings of the whirlwind over the plain : huge yellow shafts, with lofty heads, horizontally bent backwards, in the form of clouds ; and on more than one occasion camels were thrown down by them. It required little stretch or fancy to enter into the Arabs' superstition. These sand columns are supposed to be Jinns or Genii of the Waste, which cannot be caught, a notion arising from the fitful movement of the electrical wind-eddy that raises them, and, as they advance, the pious Moslem stretches out his finger, exclaiming, "Iron, O thou ill-omened one ! "

'During the forenoon we were troubled by the Simoom, which, instead of promoting perspiration, chokes up and hardens the skin. The Arabs complain greatly of its violence on this line of road. Here I first remarked the difficulty with which the Bedawin bear thirst. *Yá Latíf,* "O Merciful ! " (Lord), they exclaimed at times ; and yet they behaved like men. I had ordered them to place the water camel in front, so as to exercise due supervision. Shaykh Mas'ud and his son made only an occasional reference to the skins. But his nephew, a short thin, pock-marked lad of eighteen, whose black skin and woolly head suggested the idea of a semi-African and ignoble origin, was always drinking ; except when he climbed the camel's back, and, dozing upon the damp load, forgot his thirst.

In vain we ordered, we taunted, and we abused him : he
would drink, he *would* sleep, but he would *not* work.'

This matter of water was the one great trouble of the
caravan journey, and under the fearful Arabian sky it is
not surprising that it was the source of innumerable quarrels
and difficulties. Burton's own remedy for thirst is characteristic—'to be patient and not to talk. The more you drink,
the more you require to drink—water or strong waters. But
after the first two hours' abstinence you have mastered the
overpowering feeling of thirst, and then to refrain is easy.'
This is as well, seeing that at one of the halts it was found
necessary to send the "boy Mohammed" to certain pits
called after the great Caliph Harun, where after a long
journey he had to part with nine piastres—a fraction over
two shillings—for two skins of water. Later on, Shaykh
Mas'ud had to pay forty piastres, or eight shillings, for the
privilege of watering his camels.

Ninety-nine miles from El-Medinah the traveller enters
the townlet of El-Suwarkiyah, the most northerly possession
of the Sherif of Meccah, on the frontier lands of the Hejaz.
It is a little nest of about a hundred houses built at the
base and on the sides of a basaltic mass which rises out
of a clayey plain. The summit of the rock is converted
into a rude fortalice with a parapet of uncut stone ; the
lower part of the town is protected by a mud wall with the
usual semi-circular towers. Inside is a bazaar where mutton,
wheat, barley, and dates, all of which are grown near the
town, may be bought. The place is essentially Arab. The
fields surrounding the town are divided into little square
plots by earthen ridges and stone walls ; the streets are
very narrow and the houses small ; the palms are fine trees,
and there is an abundance of water though its quality is
not of the best—as Burton frequently found. During the
halt of the caravan he and his party determined to have a
small feast. 'We bought some fresh dates, and we paid a

dollar and a half for a sheep. Hungry travellers consider
"liver and fry" a dish to set before a Shaykh. On this
occasion, however, our enjoyment was marred by the water :
even Soyer's dinners would scarcely charm if washed down
with cups of a certain mineral spring found at Epsom.'

Before many hours were over Burton had an opportunity
of seeing with how wild a race his lot had been cast. In
the course of the day the Simoom, which was blowing
hard, affected the tempers of some of his companions. A
quarrel of the fiercest kind broke out between a Turk who
could not speak Arabic, and an Arab who could speak no
Turkish. The reason for the quarrel was the most trivial
conceivable—whether the pilgrim should or should not add
to the camel's load a few sticks to be used for cooking.
The men screamed with rage, hustled each other, and at
last the Turk struck the Arab a heavy blow. That night
the pilgrim's stomach was ripped open with a dagger, and
in the course of a short time Burton learnt that he had
been left to die in a half-dug grave. This is, he says, the
general practice in the case of the poor and lonely. ' It is
impossible,' he adds, ' to contemplate such a fate without
horror : the torturing thirst of a wound, the burning sun
heating the brain to madness—and worst of all, for they do
not wait till death—the attacks of the jackal, the vulture,
and the raven of the wild.'

On the same night (Monday, the 5th of September), at
the village of El-Sufayná, the Damascus caravan, in which
Burton travelled, encountered that from Baghdad, which
consists of a few Persians and Kurds, and collects the
people of North-Eastern Arabia. It is escorted by the
Agayl tribe, and the fierce hill-men from Jebel Shammar.
The meeting was the signal for fierce quarrelling. Baghdad would not give way to Damascus nor Damascus to
Baghdad. Scarcely were the tents of Burton's caravan
pitched when a dropping fire of musketry and the ominous

tapping of the kettle-drum raised an alarm and called
people from all parts of the camp in haste to know what
was going on. That disturbance passed off apparently
without bloodshed, but at night the Wahhábis came down
and strove to provoke the Damascus men to quarrel. One
of them stood in front of Burton and jeered at his chibouque.
It was impossible to refrain from chastising his insolence
by a polite and smiling offer of the pipe, whereupon he
incontinently drew his dagger, and was restrained from
using it only by the sight of the pistols of Burton and his
companions. These Syrians also proved terribly troublesome companions in other ways. Two nights later in the
course of the march, when the darkness had fallen "like a
pall," one of them had the audacity to untie the halter of
Burton's dromedary and so to throw him adrift—a very
serious matter in a caravan of some twelve or fifteen
thousand souls. Burton would have avenged the insult
with his sword, but his companion for the time being, one
Shaykh Abdullah of Meccah—a gentleman who had been
to Constantinople, and who spoke a little French, Greek,
and Italian—stayed his hand, and got rid of the Syrian
intruder by means of a little very strong language.

Having arrived at El-Zaribah—some forty-seven miles
from Meccah by road, though considerably less in a straight
line—the pilgrims prepared to perform the ceremony of
El-Ihrám or assuming the pilgrim garb. A barber shaved
their hair, trimmed their moustaches between the noonday
and evening prayers. 'Then, having bathed and perfumed
ourselves—the latter is a questionable point—we donned the
attire, which is nothing but two new cotton cloths, each six
feet long by three and a half broad, white, with narrow red
stripes and fringes ; in fact, the costume called *El-Eddeh*
in the baths at Cairo. One of these sheets, technically
termed the *Rida*, is thrown over the back, and, exposing
the arm and shoulder, is knotted at the right side in the

THE IHRAM OR PILGRIM'S GARB.

style *Wishah.* The *Izár* is wrapped round the loins from waist to knee ; and, knotted or tucked in at the middle, supports itself. Our heads were bare, and nothing was allowed upon the instep. It is said that some clans of Arabs still preserve this religious and primitive costume ; it is doubtless the first attire of man, and to this day, in the regions lying west of the Red Sea, it continues to be the common dress of the people.

'After the toilette, we were placed with our faces in the direction of Meccah, and ordered to say aloud, " I vow this Ihram of the Hajj (the pilgrimage) and the Umrah (the little pilgrimage) to Allah Almighty ! " Having thus performed a two-bow prayer, we repeated, without rising from the sitting position, these words, " O Allah ! verily I purpose the Hajj and the Umrah, then enable me to accomplish the two, and accept them both of me, and make both blessed to me ! "

'Followed the *Talbiyat,* or exclaiming

" Here am I ! O Allah ! here am I—
No partner hast thou, here am I !—
Verily the praise and the beneficence are thine, and the kingdom—
No partner hast thou, here am I ! "

'And we were warned to repeat these words as often as possible, until the conclusion of the ceremonies.

'Then Shaykh Abdullah, who acted as director of our consciences, bade us be good pilgrims, avoiding quarrels, immorality, bad language, and light conversation. We must so reverence life that we should avoid killing game, causing an animal to fly, nor even pointing it out for destruction ; nor should we scratch ourselves, save with the open palm, lest vermin be destroyed, or a hair uprooted by the nail. We were to respect the sanctuary by sparing the trees, and not to pluck a single blade of grass. As regards personal considerations, we were to abstain from all oils, perfumes, and unguents ; from washing the head with mallow or lote leaves ; from dyeing, shaving, cutting or vellicating a single pile or hair ; and though we might take advantage of shade, and even form it with upraised hands, we must by no means cover our sconces. For each infraction of these ordinances we must sacrifice a sheep ; and it is commonly said by Moslems that none but the Prophet could be perfect in the intricacies of pilgrimage. Old Ali, the Camel-Shaykh, began with an irregularity : he declared that age prevented his assuming the garb, but that, arrived at Meccah, he would clear himself by an offering.'

The Ihram assumed, the caravan forged forward on its way. Presently came a rumour that the Bedawin had attacked a party of Meccans with stones, which gave rise to no small anxiety ; and this increased from moment to moment after the caravan had entered the " Fiumara " down which they were to travel all night. The scene was right gloomy. Right and left were precipices, and in front rose a rocky barrier round which the stream, down the bed of which the pilgrims were travelling, wound its way after the rare torrential rains. The horrors of the place had their effect on the travellers. The voices of the women and children were hushed into silence, and the loud Lab-bayks of the pilgrims was hushed. Suddenly there was a puff of smoke from the hills, and a high trotting drome-dary in front of Burton rolled over on the sands—shot through the heart—and flung its rider a goodly somersault of some five or six yards. Naturally enough there was terrible confusion ; the women screamed ; the children cried ; the men shouted, every one striving with might and main to get out of the place of death. Nobody seemed to know what to do. The irregular horsemen who formed the escort turned out, as these gentry invariably do, to be perfectly useless, and galloped up and down, each giving orders to the others which no one obeyed. Meanwhile the Pasha in command of the caravan, with Turkish phlegm ordered his carpet to be spread under the rocks on the left and sat down to smoke and to deliberate on what ought to be done. The only people who showed to any advantage were the hated and dreaded heretics, the Wahhábis, who came up 'galloping their camels—

"Torrents less rapid and less rash,"—

with their elf locks tossing in the wind and their flaring matches casting a strange lurid light over their features.' One body took up a position and at once began to fire upon the robbers, while some two or three hundred dismounted and swarmed up the hill under the guidance of the Sherif Zayd—an Arab chieftain of the purest blood and the highest reputation for bravery. He had been urged at El-Zaribah to ride on into Meccah, but he refused—fortunately for the pilgrims—to leave them until they were in safety. Presently the firing was heard far in the rear. The robbers had been beaten back, and personal danger to the pilgrims was now over. Unfortunately the robbers had succeeded in their principal aim—plunder. Many camels and dromedaries had been shot, and their boxes and baggage strewed the shingle. When all was quiet the Utaybah would come back, ransack the baggage, and eat the shot camels. After all, however, their principal ambition was to be able to boast, " We, the Utaybah, on such and such a night, stopped the Sultan's Mahmal one whole hour in the Pass."

On this occasion Burton distinguished himself somewhat curiously, and as he is not one of those who are always the heroes of their own histories, it is worth reproducing here. ' At the beginning of the skirmish,' he says, ' I had primed my pistols and sat with them ready for use. But soon seeing that there was nothing to be done, and wishing to make an impression—nowhere does Bobadil now go down so well as in the East—I called aloud for my supper. Shaykh Nur, exanimate with fear, could not move. The boy Mohammed

ejaculated only an "Oh, sir," and the people around exclaimed in disgust, "By Allah! he eats!" Shaykh Abdullah,
the Meccan, being a man of spirit, was amused by the
spectacle. "Are those Afghan manners, Efendiná?" he
inquired from the Shugduf (litter) behind me. "Yes," I
replied aloud; "in my country we always dine before an
attack of robbers, because those gentry are in the habit of
sending men to bed supperless." The Shaykh laughed, but
those around him looked offended.' At this Burton was
disposed to think that he had made a mistake. In the
result, however, it turned out that he had instinctively
done the wisest thing possible, as will be seen when we
reach his journey from Meccah to Jeddah.

The alarm of robbers was not again raised before the
caravan reached Meccah, and the rest of the march was
broken only by such incidents as the fall of a camel and
a meeting with the Sherif of Meccah, his family and his
attendants. At the time of evening prayer, on the night of
Saturday, 10th of September, 1853, all eyes were strained to
catch a glimpse of the Holy City, and a special prayer for
occasion was added to the usual devotion:—"O Allah!
verily this is Thy Safeguard (*Amín*) and Thy Sanctuary
(*Haram*)! Into it whoso entereth becometh safe (*Amín*)!
So deny (*Harrim*) my Flesh and Blood, my Bones and
Skin to Hell fire! O Allah, save me from Thy wrath on
the Day when Thy Servants shall be raised from the Dead.
I conjure Thee by this, that Thou art Allah, besides whom
there is none, (only Thou) the Compassionating, the Compassionate. And have mercy upon our Lord Mohammed,
and upon the progeny of our Lord Mohammed and upon
his Followers One and All!"

Prayers over, the pilgrims again mounted, the night fell,
and still there were no signs of the Holy City. At last, at
1 A.M., there was a general excitement in the caravan,
and loud cries of "Meccah! Meccah!" from some voices;

" the Sanctuary! Oh the Sanctuary!" from others; then all burst into a loud Labbayk and many wept. Looking out from his Shugduf Burton beheld by the light of the southern stars the dim outline of a large place, a little darker than the surrounding plain. The city was reached by a winding pass, between the two watch towers which command the road from the north, on the morning of Sunday, 11th of September, 1853. The caravan had thus taken ten days and nights to accomplish the 248 miles of desert and mountain which lie between the two Holy Cities of Arabia, and the English pilgrim had seen this much of a country before unknown.

Burton had arranged with the "boy Mohammed" to live in Meccah as his guest—*moyennant* certain pecuniary considerations, of course. The house belonged to his mother, but the "boy" at once assumed all the airs of the courteous host, dropped his boisterous and jaunty demeanour, and became (for a few hours) grave, attentive and ceremonious. The mother received her son with rapture, busied herself with the duties of hospitality with such effect that no sooner were the camels unloaded than a dish of vermicelli, browned and powdered with loaf sugar, was placed before the hungry travellers. Cots were procured from a neighbouring coffee-house, and then came a short rest preparatory to the *Tawáf el-Kudúm,* or "Circumambulation of Arrival" at the Haram, which was to be performed at dawn. ' Scarcely had the first smile of morning beamed upon the rugged head of the Eastern hill when we arose, bathed, and proceeded in our pilgrim garb to the Sanctuary. We entered by the Bab el-Zidáyah or principal northern door, descended two flights of steps, and stood in sight of the Bayt Allah.' After a pause, during which the pilgrim is left to recover from his first emotion of awe and reverence at entering the House of the Lord, the boy Mohammed led his guest

forward through the Bayt Beni Shaybah—" the Gate of the
Sons of the Old Woman," where they raised their hands
and said certain prayers, afterwards drawing their palms
down over their faces. Thence they went to the open space
between the Makam Ibrahim and the Holy well Zemzem,
where more prayers were said ; a cup of water from the
well was then drunk, a gratuity given to the water carriers,
and a large jar of the water bestowed upon pilgrims who
were too poor to pay fees. This well, it should be noted,
is, according to tradition, that from which Hagar drank
when the Father of the Faithful sent her forth into the
desert with his son Ishmael. The water may be sacred,
but it is undeniably nauseous. The Meccans always advise
pilgrims to break their fast with it, but it may be doubted
if they follow their own prescription, seeing that the water
has a tendency to produce diarrhœa and boils. ' I never
saw a stranger,' says Burton, ' drink it without a wry face.
Sale is decidedly correct in his assertion : the flavour is a
salt bitter much resembling an infusion of a teaspoonful of
Epsom salts in a large tumbler of tepid water. Moreover
it is exceedingly " heavy " to the taste. For this reason
Turks and other strangers prefer rain water, collected in
cisterns and sold for five farthings a gugglet. It was a
favourite amusement with me to watch them whilst they
drank the holy water, and to taunt their scant and irreverent potations.' This holy water is bottled and sent to
all the more distant regions of the Mohammedan world, it
being esteemed almost in the same light as the *eau bénite*
of an older faith. Religious men break their Lenten
fast with it, apply it to their eyes to cure imperfect vision,
and strive to swallow a few drops in the hour of death. It
is supposed to be miraculous in its origin, and its consumption is believed to facilitate the study of Arabic, while
everywhere the nauseous draught is considered eminently
meritorious from the religious point of view.

From the well Zemzem the pilgrims advanced towards
the eastern angle of the Ka'abah, in which is inserted the
famous Black Stone, and then standing with upraised
hands they repeated a prayer celebrating the Unity of
Allah. This done, the pilgrims approached the stone as
closely as possible, raised their hands in the first position of
prayer, and uttered various orisons which Burton rehearses
at length, but which after the first half dozen or so have
been read, are apt to pall upon the taste of the general
reader. Then they strove to touch the Holy Stone, but
this was impossible because of the crowd. Under the circumstances they raised their hands to their ears, recited
the various formulæ, blessed the Prophet, and kissed the
finger-tips of the right hand—a practice which, if it be
not absolutely orthodox Moslem, has at least the sanction
of classical antiquity. "Lucian mentions," as Burton
reminds us, "adoration of the Sun by kissing the hand."

'Then commenced .the ceremony of *Tawáf*, or circumambulation, our route being the Matáf—the pavement of
polished granite immediately surrounding the Ka'abah. I
repeated after my Muttawwif, or cicerone, "In the name
of Allah, and Allah is Omnipotent! I purpose to circuit
seven circuits unto Almighty Allah, Glorified and
Exalted!" This is technically called the Niyat (intention)
of Tawáf.'

Into the various devotions at this centre of the Mohammedan world I do not propose to enter in this place.
Truth to tell, they are, except to the student of comparative religion, not a little dull, consisting as they do of
what St. Paul would doubtless have considered "vain
repetitions" at various points of the House of the Lord.
Burton's own adventures are far more interesting. Having
performed his circumambulation he desired to kiss the Holy
Stone—which is neither better nor worse than a hundred
other "holy" articles. By the help of the boy Mohammed,

and of half-a-dozen stalwart Meccans, he cleared a way through the crowd of thin and light-legged pilgrims—Bedawin who had not tasted any food more solid than milk for six months—and forced his way to the stone, the use of which he monopolised for a few minutes, despite the impatient shouts of the dispossessed pilgrims. 'While kissing it, and rubbing hands and forehead upon it,' he says, 'I narrowly observed it, and came away persuaded that it is an ærolite.' Upon this stone Burton adds the further remark: 'It is curious that almost all travellers agree upon one point, namely, that the stone is volcanic. Ali Bey calls it mineralogically a "block of volcanic basalt, whose circumference is sprinkled with little crystals, pointed and straw-like with rhombs of tile-red felspath upon a dark ground like velvet or charcoal, except one of its protuberances which is reddish." Burckhardt thought it was "a lava containing several small extraneous particles of a whitish and of a yellowish substance." '

From the " Black Stone" the pilgrims made their way through the crowd to the place called El-Multazem, where they pressed their stomachs, chests, and right cheeks to the Ka'abah, raising their hands high above their heads, and exclaiming :—

"O Allah! Lord of the Ancient House, free my neck from Hell-fire, and preserve me from every ill deed, and make me contented with that daily Bread which Thou hast given to me, and bless me in all Thou hast granted." Then came the Istighfár, or begging of pardon :—

"I beg pardon of Allah the Most High, who, there is no other God but He, the Living, the Eternal, and unto Him I repent myself."

After these things the pilgrims blessed the Prophet and offered certain private prayers. Other orisons, and the recital of two chapters of the Koran, followed, and then came in due course another nauseous draught from the

well Zemzem, followed by a deluge of two skinfuls of
water, during which the pilgrims prayed :—

" O Allah ! verily I beg of Thee plentiful daily Bread
and profitable Learning, and the Healing of every. disease."

Then followed more prayers in front of the Black Stone,
and so at last the pilgrims, with scorched feet and burning
heads—both extremities having been uncovered since daybreak—were able to leave the Mosque about 10 A.M. The
rest of the day was given to repose, or at least to so much
of it as could be obtained while a host of Syrians and their
friends invaded the house of the "boy Mohammed "'s
mother, where Burton was lodging. In the evening he
returned to the " Navel of the World," in company with
the " boy Mohammed " aforesaid, and Shaykh Nur carrying a lantern and a praying carpet. ' The moon, now
approaching the full,' he says, ' tipped the brow of Abu
Kubays and lit up the spectacle with a more solemn light.
In the midst stood the huge bier-like erection,

> " black as the wings,
> Which some spirit of ill o'er a sepulchre flings,"

except where the moonbeams streaked it like jets of silver
falling upon the darkest marble. It formed the point of
rest for the eye ; the little pagoda-like buildings and
domes around it, with all their gilding and framework
vanished. One object, unique in appearance, stood in
view, the temple of the one Allah, the God of Abraham, of
Ishmael, and of their posterity. Sublime it was, and
expressing by all the eloquence of fancy the grandeur of
the One Idea which vitalized El-Islam, and the strength
and steadfastness of its votaries.'

The passage I have quoted here emphasises somewhat
strikingly the impression which the " strength and steadfastness " of Mohammedanism made upon Burton, as
indeed upon all travellers in Mohammedan countries whose

opinion is worth listening to. One after another they bear
witness to the very remarkable fact that, whilst Christian
missions are, as a rule, a failure amongst the races of what
Burton has so happily christened the " Dark Continent,"
the Mohammedan creed does unquestionably exert a
civilising influence, and does, to a great extent, moralise
the people. The variety of races to which it appeals is
not less remarkable. See what Burton found this night
under the shadow of the Ka'abah.

' The oval pavement around the Ka'abah was crowded
with men, women and children, mostly divided into parties,
which followed a Mutawwif ; some walking staidly, and
others running, whilst many stood in groups, to prayer.
What a scene of contrast! Here stalked the Bedawi
woman in her long black robe like a nun's serge, and
poppy-coloured face veil, pierced to show two fiercely
flashing orbs. There, an Indian woman, with her semi-
Tartar features nakedly hideous, and her thin legs encased
in wrinkled tights, hurried round the fane. Every now
and then a corpse borne upon its wooden shell circuited
the shrine, by means of four bearers, whom other Moslems,
as is the custom, occasionally relieved. A few fair-skinned
Turks lounged about, looking cold and repulsive as their
wont is. In one place a fast Calcutta *Kitmugar* stood, with
turban awry and arms akimbo, contemplating the view
jauntily as those " gentleman's gentlemen " will do. In
another, some poor wretch with arms thrown on high, so
that every part of his person might touch the Ka'abah, was
clinging to the curtain and sobbing as though his heart
would break.'

Another very curious thing, which will appeal to every
student who has used the libraries of the British Museum
or the Guildhall, or who has ever sat under the Lion of
St. Mark at Venice. The courts of the Mosque swarm
with pigeons, which the pilgrims make it a point of faith to

feed. During the day women and children are to be seen sitting in the eastern cloisters with small trays of grain, for each of which they ask a copper coin; and 'religious pilgrims consider it their duty to provide the reverend blue rocks with a plentiful meal.' It would be interesting to know *why* the dove has been considered a sacred or semi-sacred bird for somewhere about six thousand years, and above all why he is held so in Meccah. Burton's explanation, though sufficiently ingenious, is hardly exhaustive. 'The Hindu Pandits,' he says, 'assert that Shiwa and his spouse, under the forms and names of Kapot-Eshwara (pigeon-god) and Kapotési, dwelt at Meccah. The dove was the device of the old Assyrian Empire, because Semiramis was preserved by that bird. The Meccan pigeons, resembling those of Venice, are held sacred, probably in consequence of the wild 'traditions of the Arabs about Noah's dove. Some authors declare that in Mohammed's time, among the idols of the Meccan Pantheon, was a pigeon carved in wood, and above it another, which Ali, mounting upon the Prophet's shoulder, pulled down. This might have been a Hindu, a Guebre, or a Christian symbol. The Moslems connect the pigeon on two occasions with their faith; first when that bird appeared to whisper in Mohammed's ear; and secondly during the flight to El-Medinah. Moreover, in many countries it is called the "proclaimer of Allah," because its movements when cooing resemble prostration.'

The remainder of this eventful night—at least until 2 A.M.—Burton spent in the Mosque, where, amongst other strange sights, he witnessed the spectacle of a negro in a state of what would have been called demoniacal possession in an earlier day. At ten o'clock he found, at last, an opportunity of praying the "two bow" prayer over the grave of Ishmael, and from that time forward he waited in the Holy Place in hope of being able, as he says, to "purloin" a fragment of the venerable veil of the Ka'abah. He was not successful. 'Too many eyes were looking on ;' but he did not leave Meccah without a fragment, for which he was indebted to the "boy Mohammed." At two in the morning he awakened his companions, and 'in the dizziness of slumber they walked with him through the tall, narrow street from the Bab el-Zidayah, to their home in the Shibrayah.'

On the eighth of Zu 'l-Hijjal, the twelfth Arab month, and the first day of the three which form the pilgrimage season proper, the pilgrims set out for Arafát, *viâ* Muna— a place of especial sanctity, distinguished by three standing miracles, which are that : 'The pebbles thrown at the Devil return by angelic agency to whence they came ; during the three days of Drying Meat rapacious beasts and birds cannot prey there ; and lastly, flies do not settle upon the articles of food exposed so abundantly in the bazaars.' The place itself Burton found to be simply a long, narrow, straggling Arab village, with nothing distinctive about it. The chief object of interest was the tomb of Adam in the Mosque El-Khayf. The father of us all, who, in accordance with the usual Arab tradition, was of something more than colossal proportions, lies stretched out beneath a long wall, and has his omphalic region covered by this mosque. After the mid-day prayer the pilgrims passed on to the object of their march, the plain of Arafát—an undertaking not without its perils. 'Arafát,' says Burton, 'is about six hours' very slow journey, or twelve miles on the Taif road, due east of Meccah. We arrived there in a shorter time, but our weary camels, during the last third of the way, frequently threw themselves on the ground. Human beings suffered more. Between the Muna Bazin and Arafát I saw no less than five men fall down and die upon the highway ; exhausted and moribund, they had dragged themselves out to give up the ghost where it departs to instant beatitude. The spectacle showed how easy it is to die in these latitudes ; each man suddenly staggered, fell as if shot, and after a brief convulsion lay as still as marble. The corpses were carefully taken up, and carelessly buried that same evening among the crowds encamped upon the Arafát plain.'

Arafat (the Hill of Recognition) owes its name and honour to a well-known legend—well known in Arabia, that is to say. 'When our first parents forfeited heaven by eating wheat which deprived them of their primeval purity, they were cast down upon earth. The serpent descended at Ispahan, the peacock at Cabul, Satan at Bilbas (others say Semnan and Seistan), Eve upon Arafát, and Adam at Ceylon. The latter, determining to seek his wife, began a journey, to which earth owes its present mottled appearance. Wherever our first father placed his foot— which was large—a town afterwards arose ; between the strides will always be called " country." Wandering for many years, he came to the Mountain of Mercy, where our mother was continually calling upon his name, and their *recognition* gave the place the name of Arafát. Upon its summit Adam, instructed by the archangel Gabriel, erected a *mada'a*, or place of prayer, and between this spot and the Nimrah Mosque the couple abode till death. Others declare that after recognition, the first pair returned to India, whence for forty-four years in succession they visited the sacred place at pilgrimage-time.'

It may be remarked here that the pilgrims on this occasion were by no means Bedawin, but rather citizens of Meccah, who, at this season, make a point of accompanying the stranger pilgrims to the more holy places. Many were not of the best class, some indeed were thieves, some, persons indeed of a baser kind. Shaykh Mas'ud was ineffably disgusted. 'I consoled him with quoting the celebrated song,' says Burton, 'of Maysúnah, the beautiful

Bedawi wife of the Caliph Muáwiyah. Nothing can be more charming in its own Arabic than this little song ; the Bedawin never hears it without screams of joy.

> "O take these purple robes away,
> Give back my cloak of camel's hair,
> And bear me from this tow'ring pile
> To where the Black Tents flap i' the air.
> The camel's colt with falt'ring tread,
> The dog that bays at all but me,
> Delight me more than ambling mules—
> Than every art of minstrelsy ;
> And any cousin, poor but free,
> Might take me, fatted ass, from thee." *

'The old man delighted, clapped my shoulder, and exclaimed, "Verily, O Father of Moustaches, I will show thee the black tents of my tribe this year." '

The second day (9th of Zu 'l-Hijjal) was spent in the inspection of the numerous consecrated sights on the "Mountain of Mercy" and in listening to the "Sermon of the Standing" upon Mount Arafát, and the return journey called El-Nafr or the Flight ; and on the third (10th of Zu 'l-Hijjal), *the* Eed, or Festival Day, the pilgrim went to "the Throwing," the ceremony of Lapidation derived from a tradition which dates back to the days of Abraham. The pilgrims repeat this performance after washing the stones ,"in seven waters" and saying as they cast each stone: "In the name of Allah, and Allah is Almighty (I do this) in hatred of the Devil and to his shame." After which comes the Tahlil and Sana or praise to Allah. In the afternoon of the same day, the victims which give a name to the feast were slaughtered in the Muna Valley, as described in p. 241. Then followed the religious unrobing. The pilgrims went into a barber's booth where they were shaved and had their beards trimmed and nails cut, after

---

* The British reader will be shocked to hear that by the term "fatted ass" the intellectual lady alluded to her royal husband.

which they took off the Ihram or Pilgrim's gear, saying
after the barber, as they did so:

"I purpose loosening my Ihram according to the
practice of the Prophet, whom may Allah bless and
preserve! O Allah, make unto me in every hair, a Light, a
Purity and a generous Reward! In the name of Allah! and
Allah is Almighty!"

'At the conclusion of his labour,' adds Burton, 'the
barber politely addressed to us a "Naiman"—Pleasure to
you! To which we as ceremoniously replied "Allah give
thee pleasure!" We had no clothes with us, but now we
could use our Shúrs or shoulder-cloths to cover our heads,
and slippers to defend our feet from the fiery sun ; and
we could safely twirl our moustaches and stroke our
beards, placid enjoyment of which we had been deprived
by the Laws of Pilgrimage.' Then after resting for an
hour, the pilgrims mounted their asses, still wearing their
primitive attire, and at eleven A.M. started on the return
to Meccah. Shortly after their arrival, the "boy Mohammed" returned home in a state of great excitement,
exclaiming "Rise, Efendi! dress and follow me!" Burton
was to enter the Ka'abah, the Holy of Holies of Islam,
the place which no Englishman has visited before or since
and which it is not likely that any Englishman will ever
enter again. The story of this remarkable visit must be
told in his own words :—

'A crowd had gathered round the Ka'abah, and I had no
wish to stand bare-headed and bare-footed in the mid-day
September sun. At the cry of "open a path for the Haji
who would enter the House," the gazers made way. Two
stout Meccans, who stood below the door, raised me in
their arms, whilst a third drew me from above into the
building. At the entrance, I was accosted by several
officials, dark looking Meccans, of whom the blackest and
plainest was a youth of the Benu Shaybah family, the true

blue blood of El-Hejaz. He held in his hand the huge
silver gilt padlock of the Ka'abah, and presently taking his
seat upon a kind of wooden press in the left corner of the
hall he officially inquired my name, nation, and other
particulars, the replies were satisfactory, and the boy
Mohammed was authoritatively ordered to conduct me
round the building and to recite the prayers. I will not
deny that looking at the windowless walls, the officials at
the door, and a crowd of excited fanatics below,

"And the place death, considering who I was,"

my feelings were of the trapped-rat description, acknow-
ledged by the immortal nephew of his Uncle Perez. This
did not, however, prevent my carefully observing the scene
during our long prayers, and making a rough plan with a
pencil upon my white Ihram.

'Nothing is more simple than the interior of this celebrated
building. The pavement, which is level with the ground,
is composed of slabs of fine and various coloured marbles,
mostly however white, disposed chequerwise. The walls,
as far as they can be seen, are of the same material, but
the pieces are irregularly shaped, and many of them are
engraved with long inscriptions in the Suls and other
modern characters. The upper part of the walls, together
with the ceiling, at which it is considered disrespectful to
look, are covered with handsome red damask, flowered over
with gold, and tucked up about six feet high, so as to be
removed from pilgrims' hands. The flat roof is upheld by
three cross-beams, whose shapes appear under the arras,
they rest upon the eastern and western walls, and are supported in the centre by three columns about twenty inches in
diameter, covered with carved and ornamented aloe wood.

'In the Iraki corner there is a dwarf door, called Bab el-
Tawáb (of Repentance). It leads into a narrow passage
and to the staircase by which the servants ascend to the

roof : it is never opened, except for working purposes. The "Aswad" or "As'ad" corner is occupied by a flat-topped and quadrant-shaped press or safe, in which at times is placed the key of the Ka'abah. Both door and safe are of aloe wood. Between the columns, and about nine feet from the ground, ran bars of a metal which I could not distinguish, and hanging to them were many lamps, said to be of gold.

'Although there were in the Ka'abah but a few attendants engaged in preparing it for the entrance of pilgrims, the windowless stone walls and the choked-up door made it worse than the Piombi of Venice ; perspiration trickled in large drops, and I thought with horror what it must be when filled with a mass of furiously jostling and crushing fanatics. Our devotions consisted of a two-bow prayer, followed by long supplications at the Shamío (west) corner, the Iraki (north) angle, the Yemení (south), and lastly, opposite the southern third of the back wall. These concluded, I returned to the door, where payment is made. The boy Mohammed told me that the total expense would be seven dollars. At the same time he had been indulging aloud in his favourite rhodomontade, boasting of my greatness, and had declared me to be an Indian pilgrim, a race still supposed at Meccah to be made of gold. When seven dollars were tendered, they were rejected with instance. Expecting something of the kind, I had been careful to bring no more than eight. Being pulled and interpellated by half-a-dozen attendants, my course was to look stupid, and to pretend ignorance of the language. Presently the Shaybah youth bethought him of a contrivance. Drawing forth from the press the key of the Ka'abah, he partly bared it of its green silk gold-lettered *étui*, and rubbed a golden knob, quatrefoil-shaped upon my eyes, in order to brighten them. I submitted to the operation with a good grace, and added a dollar, my last, to the former offering.

The Sherif received it with a hopeless glance, and, to my satisfaction, would not put forth his hand to be kissed. Then the attendants began to demand vails. I replied by opening my empty pouch. When let down from the door by the two brawny Meccans, I was expected to pay them, and accordingly appointed to meet them at the boy Mohammed's house ; an arrangement to which they grumblingly assented. When delivered from these troubles, I was congratulated by my sharp companion thus " Wallah, Efendi ! thou hast escaped well ! Some men have left their skins behind."

' All pilgrims do not enter the Ka'abah ; and many refuse to do so for religious reasons. Umar Efendi, for instance, who never missed a pilgrimage, had never seen the interior. Those who tread the hallowed floor are bound, among many other things, never again to walk barefooted, to take up fire with the fingers, or to tell lies. Most really conscientious men cannot afford the luxuries of slippers, tongs and truth.

'Amongst the Hindus, I have met with men who have proceeded upon a pilgrimage to Dwarka, and yet who would not receive the brand of the god, because lying would then be forbidden to them. A confidential servant of a friend in Bombay naïvely declared that he had not been marked as the act would have ruined him. There is a sad truth in what he said : lying to the Oriental is meat and drink, and the roof that shelters him.

'The Ka'abah had been dressed in her new attire when we entered. The covering, however, instead of being secured at the bottom to the metal rings in the basement, was tucked up by ropes from the roof, and depended over each face in two long tongues. It was of a brilliant black, and the Hizám, the zone, or golden band, running round the upper portion of the building, as well as the Burka' (face veil), were of dazzling brightness.

'The origin of this custom must be sought in the ancient practice of typifying the church visible by a virgin or bride.

'After quitting the Ka'abah,' Burton goes on, 'I returned home exhausted'—as well he might be—and then performed a somewhat elaborate toilette, washing himself with henna and warm water to mitigate the pain of the sunscalds on arms, shoulders, and breasts, and donning his gayest raiment in honour of the great festival. His hostess —the Kabirah, mother of the boy Mohammed—was most anxious that he should sacrifice a sheep, in accordance with the usual custom, but as this is only a Sunnat, or "Practice of the Prophet," and as his purse was growing somewhat attenuated, he refrained, and contented himself with watching others. He carefully describes the sacrificial business in the Indiná Basin, which seems curiously out of place in so intellectual a religion as Mohammedanism, and his reports about the danger of breeding cholera by the filth of the punch-bowl have led to some hygienic precautions. The Sherif and his principal dignitaries slaughtered camels ; the Indians contributed to buy a lean ox, and the Bedawin bought a sheep for a dollar and a quarter, or thereabouts. The pilgrims dragged their victims to a smooth rock near the Akabah, above which stands a small open pavilion, whose sides, red with fresh blood, showed that the prince and his attendants had been busy at sacrifice. Others stood before their tents, and directing the victim's face towards the Ka'abah, cut its throat, ejaculating, " Bismillah ! Allahu Akbar !" It is worth while to remark in this place that Burton finds an opportunity of correcting the usually accurate Burckhardt, who makes the Moslem say at this point, " In the name of the most Merciful God "—the fact being that, on this occasion, all allusion to God's mercy is studiously omitted. After the sacrifice, the Takruri disposed of the victims in a fashion

which made the holy place 'to resemble the dirtiest
slaughter-house,' and at night there were fireworks and
the discharge of cannon in front of the Muna Mosque.
'But, during the spectacle, came on a windy storm, whose
lightnings flashing their fire from pole to pole, paled the
rockets ; and whose thunderings, re-echoed by the rocky
hills, dumbed the puny artillery of man. We were disappointed in our hopes of rain. A few huge drops pattered
upon the plain, and sank into its thirsty entrails ; all the
rest was thunder and lightning, dust-clouds, and whirlwind.'

So ended the Great Festival, after which "all was dull."
The night had to be spent in watching the goods of the
pilgrims under the clear, pure moonlight, and after midnight,
the ceremony of Lapidation already described had to be
repeated. On the Thursday, the pilgrims arose before dawn
to visit and pray at the *Majarr el-Kabsh*—the "dragging-
place of the ram." This, it should be understood, is a very
small enclosure erected to commemorate the event recorded
in the twenty-second chapter of Genesis. It is in two
compartments, in each of which the pilgrims made a "two-
bow prayer," after which they went out in hope of seeing
some of the apes which haunt the mountain—El-Hejaz
being, according to Burton, "a wilderness of monkeys."
Failing to see any, they retired to their tents in anticipation of a terrible day. Nor were they disappointed. The
heat was intense, the flies came in swarms, and the blood-
stained earth reeked with noisome vapours. Nothing
moved in the air except kites and vultures ; nothing could
be done from breakfast until nightfall, save lying upon a
mat, smoking, and consuming chilled water. When the
moon arose, a second Lapidation had to be performed, after
which came a stroll amongst the coffee-houses, where business was carried on until midnight. Here a little difficulty
arose. Burton, who had published notes on the Pushtú or
Afghan dialect, could no longer speak it, and so, when

going into the houses of the acquaintance of "the boy Mohammed," he found himself somewhat at a loss. Happily ' the Meccans, in consequence of their extensive intercourse with strangers and habits of travelling, are admirable conversational linguists. They speak Arabic remarkably well,' and Arabic, it may be remarked in passing, is the most distinctively scholarly of living languages—' and with a volubility surpassing the most lively of our continental nations. Persian, Turkish, and Hindustani, are generally known ; and the Mustawwifs, who devote themselves to various races of pilgrims, soon become masters of many languages.' The day closed with an exhibition of dancing Bedawin, which Burton regarded with much amusement. ' The performance is wild in the extreme,' he says, ' resembling rather the hopping of bears than the inspirations of Terpsichore.' The wild men sing also a nonsense verse, to which no meaning whatever can be attached, and a couplet—

> " On the great festival-day at Muna I saw my lord.
> I am a stranger amongst you; therefore pity me ! "

concerning which he says that it ' may have, like the puerilities of certain modern and European poets, an abstruse and mystical meaning, to be discovered when the Arabs learn to write erudite essays upon nursery rhyme '— a flippant remark which serves only to prove that in 1853 Richard Burton had not heard of the "sun myth," and did not know that the tales of ' Mother Hubbard' and ' Jack and the Bean Stalk ' are but variations of it.

On the Friday the camels appeared at dawn, and the pilgrims made all haste to leave Muna. It was time, for ' literally the land stank.' Five or six thousand animals— camels, oxen, goats, and sheep—had been slaughtered in this bowl in the mountains, and as there is no provision for draining away their blood, it is allowed to sink into the soil, and to fester and putrefy under the tropical sun. No

precautions against infection were taken in those days,
and even at Meccah, the headquarters of the faiths of
El-Islam, 'a desolating attack of cholera was preferred
to the impiety of flying in the face of Providence, and the
folly of endeavouring to avert inevitable decrees.' *Nous
avons changé cela.*

The pilgrims hurried back to Meccah for the great
solemnity of the Sermon. 'Descending to the cloisters
below the Bab el-Zidayah,' says Burton, 'I stood wonder-
struck by the scene before me. The vast quadrangle was
crowded with worshippers sitting in long rows, and everywhere facing the central black tower. The showy colours
of their dresses were not to be surpassed by a garden of
the most brilliant flowers, and such diversity of detail
would probably not be seen massed together in any other
building upon earth.

' The women, a dull and sombre-looking group, sat
apart in their peculiar place. The Pasha stood on the
roof of Zemzem, surrounded by guards in Nizam uniform.
Where the principal Olema stationed themselves the crowd
was thicker, and in the more auspicious spots nought was
to be seen but a pavement of heads and shoulders. Nothing
seemed to move but a few dervishes, who, censer in hand,
sidled through the rows, and received the unsolicited alms
of the Faithful.

'Apparently in the midst, and raised above the crowd
by the tall, pointed pulpit, whose gilt spire flamed in the
sun, sat the preacher, an old man with snowy beard. The
style of head-dress called Taylasán covered his turban,
which was white as his robes, and a short staff supported his left hand. Presently he arose, took the staff
in his right hand, pronounced a few inaudible words, and
sat down again on one of the lower steps, whilst a Muezzin
or Crier, at the foot of the pulpit, recited the call to sermon.
Then the old man stood up and began to preach. As

the majestic figure began to exert itself there was a deep silence. Presently a general "Amín" was intoned by the crowd at the conclusion of some long sentence : and at last, towards the end of the sermon, every third or fourth word was followed by the simultaneous rise and fall of thousands of voices. I have seen the religious ceremonies of many lands, but never—nowhere—aught so solemn, so impressive as this.'

After a few more days Burton left Meccah. The heat of the place, walled in as it is by baked rocks on every side, became simply unendurable. The houses are unusually strong and well-built, of brick, granite and sandstone from the neighbouring hills, and might be cool enough if the people had the faintest idea of the art of thermantidote. But they have none, and the consequence was that the house in which Burton lived was an oven. He was fortunate enough to obtain a room in which, for some six hours out of the twenty-four, he could enjoy a little privacy—during which with one eye on the door, be it understood—he could jot down his notes. His visitors were, however, not numerous. ' Sometimes,' he says, ' a patient would interrupt me, but a doctor is far less popular in El-Hejaz than in Egypt. The people being more healthy have less faith in physic : Shaykh Mas'ud and his son had never tasted in their lives aught more medicinal than green dates and camel's milk.' Occasionally the black slave girls came into the room, asking if the pilgrim wanted a pipe or a cup of coffee. They generally retired in a state of delight, attempting vainly to conceal with a corner of a tattered veil a grand display of ivory consequent upon some small and innocent facetiousness. Other callers came ; amongst them the Moslem Abdullah, with whom Burton became exceedingly friendly. His curiosity about the English in India was great, and our Haji gratified it by praising their policy, extolling their "good star," and exalting their even-handed justice—a quality on which, despite their many faults, Englishmen have a right to pride themselves. In the course of the conversation Burton became aware of the singular tradition, commonly believed on the shores of the Mediterranean and in the Red Sea, which perhaps accounts for the ascendency of Christian England in the territories of El-Islam ; the tradition, that is, that the English sent a mission to Mohammed to inquire into his doctrines, but that the envoys arrived too late. Although an abstract of the " Saving Faith " was sent to them, they refused to accept it, but accompanied their refusal with expressions of regard. ' For this reason,' says Burton, 'many Moslems in Barbary and other countries hold the English to be of all " People of the Books " the best inclined towards them.'

For the rest the pilgrim's life in Meccah was uneventful. ' Late in the afternoon I used to rise to perform ablution and repair to the Haram or wander about the bazaars until sunset. After this it was necessary to return home and prepare for supper—dinner it would be called in the West. The meal concluded, I used to sit for a time outside the street-door in great dignity, upon a broken-backed black wood chair, traditionally said to have been left in the house by one of the Princes of Delhi, smoking a shishah, and drinking sundry cups of strong green tea with a slice of lime, a fair substitute for milk. At this hour the scene was as in a theatre, but the words of the actors were of a nature somewhat too fescennine for a respectable public. After nightfall we either returned to the Haram or retired to rest. Our common dormitory was the flat roof of the house ; under each cot stood a water gugglet, and all slept, as must be done in the torrid lands, *on* and not *in* the bed.'

Having done so much, and risked so much, it is a little painful to find Burton saying, as he does, that if he were asked the question, whether the results of such a journey as that which he undertook justify the risk, he must reply in the negative.

The "little Pilgrimage" calls for no special notice, except for the fact that it is performed as a representation of Hagar seeking water for her son Ishmael. In all its principal particulars it resembles the greater Pilgrimage which has already been described, even to the operations of the barber, who, however, has a quite new and very orthodox prayer for this occasion : "O Allah! this my forelock is in thy right hand ; then grant me for every Hair a Light on the Resurrection Day, O Most Merciful of the Merciful ! "

The Moslems' "Holy Week" being over, and their past lives being a *tabula rasa*, the pilgrims, as Burton puts it, ' lost no time in making a new departure "down south " and opening a fresh account.', Burton was one of those who longed to get away, and, accordingly, having hired a couple of camels for thirty-five piastres, he sent on his heavy boxes in advance under the care of Shaykh, now Haji Nur, and betook himself to Jeddah. The journey was uneventful, though the companions of the journey—amongst whom was a courier whose linguistic attainments were as great as those of Burton himself—were not unamusing. At last the English Haji arrived in Jeddah, with precisely tenpence, and that borrowed coin, in his pockets. It was necessary to cash the draft of the Royal Geographical Society upon the British Vice-Consul, Mr. Cole. ' But,' says Burton, with that grim humour which makes his book such delightful reading, ' his dragoman did by no means admire my looks ; in fact, the general voice of the household was against me. After some fruitless messages I sent up a scrawl to Mr. Cole, who decided upon admitting the importunate Afghan.' There was, of course, the usual astonishment, and equally, of course, the usual hospitable welcome. Matters were soon arranged, and, after a day or two spent in inspecting the tomb of our mother Eve, who, according to tradition, lies buried in Jeddah—her grave being of the somewhat unusual length of two hundred paces—and in a few preliminary arrangements, Burton embarked on the 26th of September on the Dwarka, "worn out with fatigue and the fatal fiery heat." Probably no man, living or dead, has ever done so much, seen so many changes, or passed through so tremendous an ordeal as he had done since he stepped into the train at Waterloo Station on the night of April 3, 1853.

As even the learned Orientalists often confuse the three days of the Moslem pilgrimage, misplace the Kurbán or sacrifice, and so forth, it is as well to offer a synopsis of the ecremonies :—

First Day (8th of Zu 'il-Hijjah), called Yaum al-Tarwi-yah = watering day ; march from Meccah, camp and sleep under the Arafát hilloch.

Second Day (9th of do.), termed Yaum Arafát ; perform Wurkúf or standing on Arafát ; hear the sermon which ends about sunset and hurry off (technically known as Al Dafa') to the Muzdalifah village, where the night is passed.

Third Day and *the* day (10th Zu 'il-Hijjah), also called Yaum Nahr = of slaughtering camels, Bakar 'Eed = Ox fête, and by Turks Kurbán Bayrám = Sacrifice fête ; Stone the Devil, shave head, etc., perform Al-Nafr or the Flight (to Meccah), hear the sermon and return to Muna for the Sacrifices.

These three days form the period of the Hajj or Pilgrimage proper. The three following are called the " Days of Flesh-drying," after which the pilgrims begin to disperse.

CHAPTER IV.

EXPLORATION OF HARAR.

AFTER this prolonged pilgrimage to the Holy Places of Islam, Burton returned up the Red Sea to Egypt, and rested there for the remainder of his leave. From Egypt

he returned to Bombay, and the wandering fever being
strong upon him he placed himself in communication with
Lord Elphinstone, the then most amiable Governor of that
Presidency, with the view of obtaining permission to lead
an expedition into Somali Land, which, as every one who
looks up one of Lord Salisbury's famous " large maps " may
see is the extreme East of Africa, and lies opposite the
sun-baked cinder heap which men call Aden, and at which
Eastward-bound steam-ships call for coal. Now Somali
Land was then, and is indeed at the present time, one of
the least-known regions of the globe. It is inhabited by a
race whom it were flattery to call half civilised—a race
which has all the suspiciousness, jealousy, and irritability
of the Arab with the worse qualities of the pure-blooded
negro. No white man had ever penetrated to its capital,
and indeed he who first went to Abyssinia was detained,
after the custom of the " blameless Ethiopian," a prisoner
until his death—a Christian, if not altogether an agreeable, substitute for the Ethiopic custom of sacrificing their
prisoners. For many years there had been a desire on the
part of the East India Company that this region should be
explored. Aden is not the most wholly satisfactory port
of call which could have been selected ; first, because it is
little better than a heap of volcanic ashes ; next, because
it is rather out of the way of shipping going from Suez to
Bombay ; thirdly, because the anchorage is none of the
best ; and lastly, because it is a little too close to the wilder
parts of Arabia. None of those objections apply to Berberah, which is the chief port of Somali Land, and which is
indeed the safest and best harbour on the western side of
the Indian Ocean.

It was therefore only natural that the Directors of the
East India Company should be anxious to know something
more of this strange country ; but they went to work with
that curious mixture of caution and generosity which was

wont to characterise all their dealings with those of their servants who stepped out of what Burton somewhere calls their "quarter-deck routine." When, in May, 1849, Sir Charles Malcolm, formerly Superintendent of the Indian Navy, in conjunction with Mr. William John Hamilton, the President of the Royal Geographical Society, asked for leave to investigate the Somali country, an answer was returned which deserves to be transcribed in full :—" If a fit and proper person volunteer to travel in the Somali country, he goes as a private traveller, the government giving no more protection to him than they would to an individual totally unconnected with the service. They will allow the officer who obtains permission to go, during his absence on the expedition, to retain all the pay and allowances he may be enjoying when leave was granted : they will supply him with all the instruments required, afford him a passage going and returning, and pay the actual expenses of the journey."

The projected expedition was kept in abeyance for a year, and was then offered by Sir Charles Malcolm to Dr. Carter of Bombay, who, however, was willing only to travel along the Somali coast in a cruiser, making occasional expeditions inland. Imperfect as it was, the plan was at first approved, but when Commodore Lushington, who was Dr. Carter's principal supporter, resigned his appointment the scheme was dropped, and then came Burton's opportunity. He purposed to start in the spring of 1854, and to penetrate by way of Harar and Gananah to Zanzibar. The matter was referred as usual to the Court of Directors, and in the meanwhile Burton obtained leave and a free passage for himself and his companion, Lieut. Herne, of the 1st Bombay (European) Fusileers. To the pair was added a third in the person of Lieut. Stroyan, I.N., and a fourth in that of Lieut. Speke of the 46th Bengal, N.I. The former had distinguished himself by his surveys on the coast of Western India, in Sind, and on the Panjab Rivers, and the latter was already well known as an amateur collector of the Fauna of Tibet and the Himalayas. It was not until October, 1854, that the sanction of the Court of Directors to the expedition was received at Aden.

Burton's first intention was to go with his three companions in a body, using Berberah as a base of operations, thence moving westwards to Harar, thence in a southeasterly direction towards Zanzibar. A glance at the map will show that this route would have been the best and quickest which could possibly have been adopted. Unfortunately other considerations intervened. Aden rejoiced in a Political Resident, Colonel—afterwards Sir James—Outram, and this functionary absolutely refused his consent to a plan which appeared to him and to the Adenese nothing short of a "tempting of Providence." Captain Playfair, his assistant, did all in his power to thwart Burton's views, and Dr. Buist, the Editor of the *Bombay Times* received a hint to "run down" the Somali Expedition—a task in which he was ably assisted by the Chaplain of Aden, whose unpopularity had gained for him a peculiarly abusive nickname which it is unnecessary to reproduce here. Subsequent events proved the opponents of the Expedition to be not far wrong, but the appearance of quailing before the Somali was not gratifying to the high-spirited men who were embarked upon it The Resident's will, however, was of necessity law, and as a consequence the whole scheme of the expedition was changed. Lieut. Herne was ordered to make his way, after the opening of the fair season, to Berberah, where no danger was apprehended, and where it was hoped that he might exercise a favourable influence in the Somal—which he certainly did. He went in October, and was joined by Lieut. Stroyan on the 1st of January, 1855, and together they 'inquired into the commerce, the caravan lines and the state of the slave trade, visited the maritime mountains, sketched all the places of interest, and made a variety of meteorological and other observations' as a prelude to more extensive research. Lieut. Speke was directed to land at Bunder Guray, a small harbour in the "Land of Safety," to trace the watershed of the Wady Nogál, buy horses and camels for the future use of the Expedition, and collect specimens of the reddish earth which, in the opinion of the earlier African travellers, denotes the presence of gold. He started on the 29th of October, 1854, but his expedition was a failure. He penetrated beyond the maritime chain of hills, but did but little good, and the observations in his journal, though not uninteresting in themselves, add very little to the sum of human knowledge.

Burton reserved for himself the post of danger. Once more he assumed the disguise of an Arab—this time dressing as a merchant, and not as a simple pilgrim—and prepared to visit the forbidden city of Harar. He left Aden on the 29th of October, 1854, arrived in Harar on the 3rd of January, 1855, and on the 9th of February following found himself at Aden once more to buy stores and provisions for a second and longer journey. Harar had never been visited ; it has a language of its own, and a history and traditions alike remarkable and interesting. Burton made the most of his brief stay, and of his journey afterwards through the Girhi mountains, the fruits of which may be seen, not merely in the text of 'First Footsteps in East Africa,' but in the Appendix, in which he has reduced this unwritten language to a regular grammar, with a vocabulary of some hundreds of words in which the etymology as well as the translation of each is given.

The journey was interesting, less, however, because of the incidents which marked it than from the use which it has proved to the Egyptians and the English who have occupied Harar successively. The people with whom our

Haji was thrown into contact were also a fine study of
savage anthropology. He sailed from Aden in a native
boat, manned by a crew of negroes, who had no sooner
got to sea than they threw off every trace of civilisation.
At Aden they had been decorous Arabs, shaven and
beturbaned ; at sea they threw off all pretence of decency,
doffing turbans and flowing robes, retaining only the loin
cloth, and anointing what Burton calls their "dark mo-
rocco " with an "unguent redolent of sheep's tail." The
description of the first night on board this ship shows
with what a savage race Burton had now to deal—a
savagery not mitigated by any of the traditions of El-
Islam, these wild Nomads being indeed but very indifferent
Moslems, and most of them living more or less by the slave
trade.   On the morning of the 31st of October, Burton's
boat entered the Zayla creek, and by noon was at the town.
As she threaded her way through the coral reefs of the
port he met another craft which brought bad news.
Burton's original intention had been to reach Harar by the
direct road through the Eesa country, which is marked
upon the map as practically a straight line. But the friendship between the Amir of Harar and the Governor of
Zayla had been broken through a quarrel amongst rival
clans about the profits of the slave trade. A large caravan
with nearly three hundred slaves had been attacked, the
wives and female slaves carried off and sold for ten dollars
a head, and a hundred wretched boys were savagely
mutilated. In revenge a peaceful traveller was at once
treacherously murdered, not because he had incurred the
hostility of his murderers by any overt act, but because his
Abbán or Protector, a functionary whom every traveller
in Somali Land is compelled to employ, was of the tribe
which had perpetrated the first outrage. " Truly African,"
is Burton's comment on the story. The result of this
condition of things was that the road was closed. It was,

too, said to be doubtful if Harar could be entered or left, the Amir having expelled all strangers, and the Gallas being in mortal terror of the smallpox.

Burton decided to land, however, and the ship after bumping on the coral once or twice, was anchored. 'My two companions, Somali policemen from Aden, caused me to dress,' he goes on, 'put me with my pipe and other necessaries into a cockboat and wading through the water, shoved it to shore. Lastly, at the Báb el-Sáhil, the seaward or northern gate, *they* proceeded to array themselves in the bravery of clean tobes and long daggers strapped round the waist ; each man also slung his targe to his left arm, and in his right hand grasped lance and javelin. At the gate we were received by a tall black spearman with a " Ho there ! to the Governor ! " and a crowd of idlers gathered to inspect the strangers. Marshalled by the warder, we traversed the dusty roads—streets they could not be called—of the old Arab town, ran the gauntlet of a gaping mob, and finally entering a mat door, found ourselves in the presence of the governor,' El-Hajj Sharmarkay, rather a remarkable personage. He claims to be the sixteenth in direct descent from the founder of the great Gerhajis and Awal tribes ; his enemies, however, say that his grandfather was an Abyssinian slave. Be this as it may, he has been raised chiefly by English influence to the chieftainship of his tribe. It may be said here that he has earned the favour with which he was treated, for, as early as May, 1825, he received from Captain Bagnold, our resident at Mocha, a testimonial and a reward for having saved the lives of the crew of a ship wrecked at Buhurra on the African coast. The testimonial ' strongly recommended him to the notice and good offices ' of the English, and when he went to Bombay shortly afterwards he found its value. In return he cherished the English connection even to his own detriment, and kept the French from obtaining a foot-

ing in Zayla. Burton had met Sharmarkay at Aden, where
he had been warmly commended to his good offices, but in
his character of Moslem merchant he had to be re-introduced
and to go through the usual lengthened formalities. That
done he was taken to one of the governor's houses where
he was installed as an honoured guest. So far did the
ceremony extend indeed, that the Haji insisted on sitting
on the floor while Burton occupied the divan. Then after
ushering in supper, the governor considerately remarked
that "travelling is fatiguing," and left Burton to his well-
earned repose. ' The well-known sounds of El-Islam
returned from memory. Again the melodious chant of the
Muezzin—no evening bell can compare with it for solemnity
and beauty—and in the neighbouring Mosque the loudly-
intoned Amíns and Allah Akbars, far superior to any organ,
rang in my ear. The evening gun of camp was represented
by the Nakkárah, or kettledrum, sounded about 7 P.M. at
the southern gate ; and at 10 a second drumming warned
the paterfamilias that it was time for home ; and thieves and
lovers, that it was the hour for danger of the bastinado.
Nightfall was ushered in by the song, the dance, and
the marriage festival—here no permission is required for
"native music in the lines"—and muffled figures flitted
mysteriously through the dark alleys. After a peep through
the open window I fell asleep, feeling once more at home.'

For twenty-six days Burton stayed on at Zayla tracing
out his intended route, interviewing guides, buying camels,
and sending for mules ; in fact, in all the multitudinous
and wearisome preparations for journeying in a country
where money is hardly known, and where, nevertheless,
everything has to be paid for pretty heavily. The life was
monotonous, but Burton is so much of an Arab himself
that he did not find it so, though most Englishmen would
probably weary of the routine in a day or two. The time
was spent somewhat as follows :—Rise with the earliest

dawn, escaping from close air and mosquitos ; then to the
terrace to perform one's devotions and make observation of
his neighbours ; breakfast at 6 A.M. off roast mutton and
sour grain cakes, which, as Burton remarks, is 'at this hour
a fine trial of health and cleanly living ;' after breakfast,
coffee, pipes, and a nap ; then 'provided with some
sanctified Arabic book,' prepare to receive visitors, who
come in by dozens, having apparently nothing to do, and
in particular, no business with the visitee ; at 11 A.M.,
when fresh water arrives from the wells, the governor
sends in dinner, boiled rice, mutton stews of exceeding
greasiness, maize cakes, sometimes fish, and generally
curds or milk ; more coffee and pipes ; for the natives a
nap, for the visitor his journal and studies ; at 2 P.M.
more visitors, who clamour at the door if delayed, and
angrily inquire if there is a Nazarene in the house ;
as the sun declines one escapes to the terrace to get
rid of the flies or dresses to walk, generally eastwards
to a point where there is a little mosque of wattle-work,
where Shantarah or Shakh (games resembling draughts
and backgammon respectively) may be played, or athletic
sports indulged in ; when tired of exercise comes a stroll
round to the southern gate, outside of which there is usually
a camp of Bedawin, who though wild people are not
usually ill-natured ;* before sunset it is necessary to be

* Burton's comment on these people is amusing—it should be
remembered, however, that it was written more than thirty years ago.
'The Bedawin, despite their fierce scowls, appear good-natured ; the
women flock out of their huts to stare and laugh, the men to look and
wonder. I happened once to remark, "Lo we come forth to look at
them and they look at us ; we gaze at their complexions and they
gaze at ours !" A Bedawin who understood Arabic translated this
speech to the others, and it excited great merriment. In the mining
counties of civilised England, where the genial brickbat is thrown at
the passing stranger, or in enlightened Scotland where hair a few
inches too long justifies " mobbing," it would have been impossible for
me to have mingled as I did with these wild people.'

within the gate once more, as at that time the gates are
locked and the keys carried to the Hajj ; the call to
evening prayer sounds from the Mosque but is not re-
sponded to with much enthusiasm by the Somalis, who
are not the most pious or reverent people in the world, and
who indeed have but little notion of a Supreme Being of
any kind ; then follows supper, the counterpart of the
mid-day dinner, after which all repair to the roof to enjoy
the prospect of the distant Tajurrah Hills and the moonbeams sleeping upon the nearer sea ; then two hours later
all spread their mats around the common room, pillow
their heads upon the wooden pillow of Somali Land—a
dwarf pedestal of carved wood, exactly such as may be
seen in Egyptian sepulchres, and address themselves to
slumber.

Such is the week-day routine. ' On Friday—our Sunday
—a drunken crier goes about the town threatening the
bastinado to all who neglect their prayers. At half-past
eleven a kettledrum sounds a summons to the Jámi or
cathedral. It is an old barn rudely plastered with whitewash ; posts or columns of artless masonry support the low
roof. . . . I enter with a servant carrying a prayer carpet,
encounter the stare of 300 pair of eyes belonging to parallel
rows of squatters, recite the customary two-bow prayer in
honour of the Mosque, placing a sword and rosary before
me, and then taking up a Koran read the Cow Chapter
(No. 18) loud and twangingly. At the Zohr, or mid-day
hour, the Muezzin inside the mosque repeats the call to
prayer, which the congregation, sitting upon their shins
and feet intone after him. This ended, all present stand
up and recite, each man for himself a two-bow prayer of
Sunnat, or custom, concluding with the Blessing on the
Apostle, and the Salam over each shoulder to all brother
believers. The Khatib then ascends his hole in the wall,
which serves for pulpit, and thence addresses us with, " The

peace be upon you, and the mercy of Allah and his benediction," to which we respond through the Muezzin, "And
upon you be peace and Allah's ruth." After sundry
other religious formulas, and their replies, concluding with
a second call to prayer, our preacher rises, and in the voice
with which Sir Hudibras was wont

> " To blaspheme custard through the nose,"

preaches El-Wa'az or the advice sermon. He sits down
for a few minutes, and then rising again recites El-
Na'at, or the Praise of the Prophet and his Companions.
These are the two heads into which the Moslem discourse
is divided ; unfortunately, however, there is no application.

During these twenty-six days of enforced delay Burton
made several excursions from Zayla, correcting in one
case the errors of Bruce, and resettling the site of the old
historic Zayla, the very ruins of which have now perished.
He succeeded besides in obtaining access to the historical
records of the town, out of which he compiled a brief local
history with which in this place we have, however, nothing
to do. He made various other excursions and entered upon
sundry other studies, but, in spite of all attempts at diver-
sion, the time hung heavily upon his hands. The delays
caused by African indolence, intrigue, and suspicion, were
well nigh interminable. Four months before leaving Aden,
Burton had taken the precaution of meeting the Governor
of the Somali country and of requesting him to select for
him an Abbán * and to provide camels and mules, while two

---

* " The Abbán acts at once as brother, escort, agent and interpreter,
and the institution may be considered the earliest form of transit dues.
In all sales he receives a certain percentage, his food and lodging are
provided at the expense of his employer, and he not unfrequently
exacts small presents for his kindred. In return he is bound to
arrange all differences and even to fight the battles of his client against
his fellow-countrymen. Should the Abbán be slain, his tribe is bound
to take up the cause and to make good the losses of their *protégé*."—
' First Footsteps in East Africa,' p. 89.

months before starting he had advanced all the necessary
funds. When he arrived at Zayla absolutely nothing had
been done. He impressed upon the Hajj Shermarkay the
necessity for speed ; he was promised that the messenger
for the cattle should be sent within an hour ; the messenger
received no order for ten days, and did not sail for a fortnight. At last, at the end of November, four camels were
procured, an Abbán was engaged, as were also two women
cooks and a fourth servant ; the luggage was repacked and
the endless preparations for the journey were completed.
It was not a particularly cheerful expedition on which the
party were to set out. The cold had driven the Bedawin
from the hills to the warm maritime plains, and, as one of
Burton's Arab companions explained, " Man eats you up,
the Desert does not." Man in Somali Land fully answers
this character. He is savage, treacherous, and ferocious in
no ordinary fashion ; there are constant blood feuds between
the tribes, and most of the tribesmen appear to be little
better than bloodthirsty brigands. Small wonder then if
the citizens of Zayla imagined Burton and his friends to be
" tired of their lives." Worn out with delays, and thoroughly
resolved to make the proposed journey, he gave the Abbán
peremptory orders to be in readiness to start on the 26th
of November, prepared to walk the whole distance to Harar
rather than be the victim of any further delay for cattle.
As the case had become hopeless, a vessel was descried
standing straight from Tajurrah—the chief market of beasts
of burden in that part of Africa—and suddenly as could
happen in the " Arabian Nights," four fine mules, saddled
and bridled after Abyssinian fashion appeared at the door.

Early in the morning, therefore, of the 27th of November,
1854, the mules and the paraphernalia of travel stood ready
for use. The camels were forced, with more or less
difficulty, to kneel and submit to their burdens, and at
3 P.M. the party sallied forth from the southern gate

already mentioned under the escort of a party of Arab matchlockmen. 'After half a mile's march we exchanged affectionate adieus, received much prudent advice about keeping watch and ward at night, recited the Fátihah with upraised palms, and with many promises to write frequently and to meet soon, shook hands and parted. The soldiers gave me a last volley, to which I replied with the " Father of Six "—*i.e.* a six-shot revolver.'

At this point it may be remarked that this was the most dangerous of all Burton's explorations, quite as difficult as Meccah ; and though it is not generally known, the only feat of exploration in history that comes up to it is Stanley's crossing Africa ; with this difference, that it was a comparatively short journey. Here is a sketch of the character which Burton had undertaken to assume on this perilous journey through the East African waste. To quote his own words :—'You will bear in mind, if you please, that I am a Moslem merchant, a character not to be confounded with the notable individuals seen on 'Change. Mercator in the East is a compound of trades-man, divine, and T. G. Usually of gentle birth, he is everywhere welcomed and respected ; and he bears in his mind and manner that, if Allah please, he may become Prime Minister a month after he has sold you a yard of cloth. Commerce appears to be an accident, not an essential, with him ; yet he is by no means deficient in acumen. He is a grave and reverend seignior, with rosary in hand and Koran on lip ; is generally a pilgrim ; talks at dreary length about Holy Places ; writes a pretty hand ; has read and can recite much poetry ; is master of his religion ; demeans himself with respectability ; is perfect in all points of ceremony and politeness, and feels equally at home whether Sultan or slave sit upon his counter. He has a wife and children in his own country, where he intends to spend the remnant of his days ; but " the world

is uncertain "—" Fate descends, and man's eyes seeth it not "
—" the earth is a charnel house : " briefly, his many wise
old saws give him a kind of theoretical conscientiousness
that his bones may moulder in other places but his
fatherland.'

The caravan with which this Moslem merchant had now
embarked was a somewhat singular one to European eyes,
the most singular point in connection with it being perhaps
the commanding place amongst the "working staff" which
was taken by the women who accompanied it. This is a
peculiarly African point of detail, and one by no means
peculiar to the remote corner of the "Dark Continent"
which Burton on this occasion set himself to explore.
Mr. Winwood Reade, in his book on the West Coast of
Africa which set all the Mrs. Grundys of the United
Kingdom wagging their heads and asking why this rude
and naughty person should be allowed to publish his
naked facts in prudish England, noticed and even dwelt
upon the curious interchange of duties and qualities between the sexes which Africa seems to engender. Burton
first brings it under notice in this book on the East Coast,
and his experience is certainly interesting from the ethnographical point of view, if from no other. In his caravan
he found two women, 'buxom dames about thirty years
old,' who looked like 'three average women rolled into
one,' and who emphatically belonged to 'that race for
which the article of attire called, I believe, a "bussle" would
be quite superfluous.' These women, during the long
march, carried pipe and tobacco, led the camels, adjusted
the burdens, and, at the halt, unloaded the cattle, disposed
the parcels in a semicircle, pitched over them the Gurgi, or
mat tent, cooked the food, made the tea or coffee, and
when all was done, bivouacked outside the tent—'modesty
not permitting the sexes to mingle.' The other animals in
the caravan consisted of the Abbán, a youth who was in

some sort a driver of the two women, three attendants
armed with bows, arrows, and lances, and five camels
laden with American sheeting, Cutch canvas, with indigo-
dyed calico sewn up in a case of matting to keep off the
wind and rain, and a load of bad Mocha dates for the
Somal, with a parcel of better for the travellers. The other
impedimenta comprise tobacco, beads, trinkets, mosaic-gold
earrings, necklaces, watches and other Brummagem goods ;
300 pounds of rice, a large pot full of " Kawurmeh " (sun-
dried meat boiled in large slices, broken to pieces, and
smothered in ghee or clarified butter), dates, salt, tea, coffee,
sugar, a box of biscuits in case of famine, " Halwá," or Arab
sweetmeats for use in bargaining, turmeric for seasoning, a
" simple *batterie de cuisine*"—by which we are to understand a few brass and iron pots—a few skins of drinkable
water, and a box of ammunition sufficient for a three
months' sporting tour. Last in the caravan comes a
Bedawi woman driving a donkey—' the proper "tail" in
these regions,' adds Burton, ' where camels start if followed
by a horse or mule.'

With this caravan Burton began his march down the
road which leads eastward from Zayla, often within sight
and sound of the sea, to Kuranyali, where he halted for a
day preparing water and milk for two long marches inland
over the waste lands towards the hills. That day was one
of misery. The heat was intense, and the little camp was
crowded with hungry visitors, importunate, like Burton's
own escort, for provisions of all kinds—their prejudices, and
not their religion, forbidding them to eat the fish with
which their coast abounds, the birds, hares, or antelopes,
which may be found in tolerable abundance on the borders
of the desert, and even the marrow and the flesh about the
sheep's thigh-bone. On the following day Burton was
anxious to get away, and the Bedawin as anxious to
detain him. He had sent instructions to his Abbán that

he wished to depart early in the afternoon : the Abbán promised compliance, and *more Africano* forthwith disappeared. About three in the afternoon the Bedawin arrived, and 'the speechifying presently commenced.' The wild men had an eye to the cloth and tobacco, and one of them was smitten by the 'bulky charms' of one of the feminine camel-drivers. The mules had been sent to the well, with orders to return before noon ; at 4 P.M. they were not visible. Burton sat on a cow's hide in the sun, ordered his men to begin loading the camels, despite the interference of the fifty Bedawin who had assembled. 'As we persisted,' he goes on, 'they waxed surlier, and declared all which was ours became theirs, to whom the land belonged. We did not deny the claim, but simply threatened sorcery-death by wild beasts and foraging parties to their "camels, children, and women." This brought them to their senses, the usual effect of such threats, and presently arose the senior, who had spat upon us for luck's sake. With his toothless jaws he mumbled a vehement speech, and warned the tribe that it was not good to detain such strangers ; they lent ready ear to the words of Nestor, saying, " Let us obey him, he is near his end ! " ' Then the mules arrived, but not the escort. Sundry paupers were willing enough to accompany the caravan, but their attentions were civilly declined, and the attendance of the Abbán and some of his kindred insisted upon. As the Bedawin were still troublesome, the services of Nestor were called for once more ; and when the aged champion had succeeded in silencing his kinsmen with " copious abuse "—for which he was rewarded with many thanks and many handfuls of tobacco—he blessed his visitors with fervour, and, what was more to the purpose, succeeded in procuring for them an exit from Kuranyali, attended by nothing worse than the escort of a gang of impudent boys, who seem, from Burton's humouristic account of them, to have been nothing better and nothing worse than their compeers of London or Paris.

From this point the caravan turned inland to the south-west, striking across the desert alluvial plain between the sea and the mountains. The Bedawin had delayed their start until six in the evening ; when they left they had to traverse a district honeycombed with the dwellings of field-rats, lizards, and ground-squirrels. After dark arose a cheerful moon, and with it came 'the howling of the hyenas, the barking of their attendant jackals, and the chattered oaths of the Hidinhilu bird.' * Still the caravan marched on, stopping only to raise the loads of the camels every quarter of an hour. Here Burton had an opportunity of seeing how really feeble a race were the Somal. He could carry his rifle ; they were unable to support the weight of their spears, and actually rode upon them. ' Briefly, an English boy of fourteen would have shown more bottom than the sturdiest.' (How thankful one is that the traveller did not say " public school boy " in this connection !)

At 11 P.M. the caravan halted for six hours, and rose under a cold moon to resume the journey. They marched forward until ten in the morning, through a country which, though barren, was not absolutely desert, and which had for tenants herds of innumerable gazelles and ostriches. The men slept through the middle of the day, waking only for the rice, which was boiled at noontide by the indefatigable women. In the evening the caravan came upon the trail of a large Habr Awal cavalcade. This sign of the immediate presence of their most intimate enemy appalled

* ' Of this bird,' says Burton, 'a red and long-legged plover, the Somal tell the following legend. Originally her diet was meat and her society birds of prey ; one night, however, her companions, having devoured all the provisions whilst she slept, she swore never to fly with friends, never to eat flesh, and never to rest during the hours of darkness. When she sees anything in the dark she repeats her oath, and according to the Somal keeps careful watch all night.'

Burton's companions, who dropped at once into silence and a panic of fear. But presently they reached the hills, where they were safe ; raiders will not risk their horses in these stony highlands. At 8 P.M., 'seeing the poor women lamed with thorns, and the camels casting themselves upon the ground,' Burton commanded a halt, and, despite all objections, a fire was lighted, the remainder of the store of bad milk was consumed, and the party—nine men and two women (the Bedawin ass-driver previously mentioned being apparently left out of account)—addressed themselves to sleep. Morning brought relief. The ride was resumed at 6 A.M., and in a short time an Eesa kraal was sighted, outside of which the camels were unloaded and the tents pitched. 'Presently,' says Burton, 'the elders appeared, bringing with soft speeches sweet water, new milk, fat sheep and goats, for which they demanded a Tobe, or six feet, of Cutch canvas. We passed with them a quiet luxurious day of coffee and pipes, fresh cream, and roasted mutton ; after the plain heats we enjoyed the cool breeze of the hills, the cloudy sky, and the verdure of the glades, made doubly green by comparison with the parched stubbles below.' On the following morning the kraal set out for the plains, and Burton had an opportunity of seeing two customs—the sick and decrepit were left behind for the lions and hyenas to devour, and before leaving the camp the migrators set fire to logs of wood and masses of sheep's earth, which even in rain will smoke and smoulder for weeks. The caravan went on its way in the opposite direction, ascending the Fiumara, or river-bed, and discovering the remains of a long gone by civilisation. The journey was hardly pleasant. The guides were pallid with cold, and at every turn expressed their dread of the rival tribes, which, in turn, were equally afraid of them. Ferocious though they are on occasion, they are essentially cowardly, and with their cowardice go two other qualities not unfrequently

associated amongst more civilised races—thievishness and
a love of gossip. The news of the whole Eastern world
flies through the country with almost incredible rapidity,
and Burton found that at this early date the Russian war
was a frequent topic of conversation, whilst at remote Harar
he heard of a storm which had damaged the shipping in the
harbour of Bombay only a few weeks before.

The cold on these "Ghauts" was troublesome, especially
in the early morning; the lions were a source of dread,
though not very dangerous save to sheep and cattle; the
insect life was multitudinous, especially in the form of ants
three-quarters of an inch long, armed with most villanous
stings; and the necessaries of life were scarce and dear, yet
the hills are in comparison with the plains below densely
populated, though by no means so thickly as in the early
days of El-Islam. When Burton's caravan crossed the ridge,
the fourth stage of the journey from Zayla to Harar, he had
spent ten days upon the journey, and the want of water
and forage had produced its customary effect upon the
cattle. 'The camels could scarcely walk, and my mule's
spine rose high beneath the Arab pad.' The temperature
could, however, scarcely have been really low, for although
at an altitude of 3350 feet, Burton found a buttercup, heard
a woodpecker, and arrived at the conclusion that the
climate resembled that of Southern Italy in winter. The
Bedawin, accustomed to the warmth of the plains, felt the
severity of the climate, and with teeth chattering with cold
stood about the fire 'closer than ever paterfamilias did in
England; they smoked their faces, toasted their hands,
broiled their backs with intense enjoyment, and waved their
legs to and fro through the flames to singe away the pile
which at this season grows long. The End of Time,* who

* " End of Time :"—A person who, from his smattering of learning
and prodigious rascality, is supposed to be typical of the prophesied
corruption of the Moslem priesthood in the last epoch of the world.

was surly, compared them with demons, and quoted the Arabs' saying :—"Allah never bless smooth man or hairy woman ! " '

Nearing Harar, on the morning of the 9th of December, Burton had another insight into the native character. His party reached a kraal about noon, and having announced their arrival by firing a pistol, waited the approach of the elders. In due course they came out and welcomed End of Time as a distinguished guest ; complimented one another gravely on their good intentions, and generally interchanged civilities. 'Presently,' says Burton, 'some warriors came out and inquired if we were of the caravan that was travelling last evening up a valley with laden camels. On our answering in the affirmative, they laughingly declared that a commando of twelve horsemen had followed us with the intention of a sham attack. This is a favourite sport with the Bedawin. When, however, the traveller shows fight the feint is apt to turn out a fact. On one occasion a party of Arab merchants not understanding " the fun of the thing," shot two Somal : the tribe had the justice to acquit the strangers, mulcting them, however, a few yards of cloth for the families of the deceased. In reply I fired a pistol unexpectedly over the heads of my new hosts, and improved the occasion of their terror by deprecating any practical facetiousness in future.' On the day following the caravan was halted, Burton having suffered from the bad water and the sudden changes of temperature. When the thermometer varies as much as 56° in twelve hours, the traveller must expect consequences.

Restored in part by a day's rest, Burton rode out to examine further the ruins of the ancient Moslem civilisation, returning to dismiss the men who had protected him on his journey from Zayla. Before they went there was an Homeric feast. A sheep was killed, disembowelled, dismembered, tossed into one of the huge cauldrons of the caravan and devoured within an hour, with draughts of milk as the accompaniment. Burton was, however, too ill to eat anything, and his companion, End of Time, finding him thus, insisted upon applying an Arab remedy by cauterizing him on the stomach in six places with fire produced by rubbing two pieces of dry wood together. Whether the remedy was effectual or not Burton has not told us, but he was well enough on the following day to give a lesson in single-stick to one of his Somal critics. After an afternoon spent in shooting, 'they boasted,' he says, 'of the skill with which they used the shield, and seemed not to understand the efficiency of a sword parry. To illustrate the novel idea, I gave a stick to the best man, provided myself in the same way, and allowed him to cut at me. After repeated failures, he received a sounding blow upon the least bony portion of his person : the crowd laughed long and loud, and the pretending " knight-at-arms " retired in confusion.'

On the following day they went elephant-hunting. Burton had been assured that elephants were as "thick as sand in the Harawwah "—the valley of Harar, in which he then was—but after a long ride they failed to find any. Day after day passed, during which the caravan was detained, and its leader was compelled to find similar matters of amusement and occupation. It was not until the 23rd of December that the caravan which Burton and his companions were destined to escort across the Marar Prairie was assembled, and in readiness to dare the brigands of the savage tribes of Somali Land. They had not much to lose it is true, but, in such a district, ' the smallest contributions are thankfully received by these plunderers.' They met none of them, but on the evening of the first day of the journey, a more dangerous guest appeared. ' Towards evening, as the setting sun sank slowly behind the distant western hills, the colour of the prairie changed from glaring

yellow to a golden hue, mantled with a purple flush inex-
pressibly lovely. The animals of the waste began to
appear. Shy lynxes and jackals, fattened by many sheep's
tails, warned my companions that fierce beasts were nigh,
ominous anecdotes were whispered, and I was told that a
caravan had lately lost nine asses by lions. As night came
on, the Bedawin Kafilah (caravan), being lightly loaded,
preceded us, and our tired camels lagged far behind. We
were riding in rear to prevent straggling, when suddenly
my mule, the hindermost, pricked his ears uneasily, and
attempted to turn his head. Looking backwards, I distinguished the form of a large animal following us with
quick and stealthy strides. My companions would not
fire, thinking it was a man : at last a rifle ball, singing
through the air—the moon was too young for correct
shooting—put to flight a huge lion. The terror excited
by this sort of an adventure was comical to look upon : the
valiant Beuh, who, according to himself, had made his
preuves in a score of foughten fields, threw his arms in the
air, shouting Libáh ! Libáh !!—the lion ! the lion !!—and
nothing else was talked of that evening.'

The rest of the journey seems to have been not a little
monotonous, consisting, as it did, in trumpery disputes
with successive chiefs and their tribes, and in mountain
travel at the rate of some five or six miles a day. Between
Zayla and Harar, by the somewhat roundabout route which
Burton was compelled by circumstances to take, the total
distance is 202 miles. He started with his caravan on
26th November, 1854, and did not arrive at his destination
until 4th January, 1855. It is true that he was more than
once detained by illness caused by the wretched food, the
bad water, the incessant exertion, and the want of rest.
One attack has already been mentioned ; another awaited
him on the last day of the year at a place called Sagharrah.
Here he found friends, and had an opportunity of testing

that genuine kindliness which underlies the external savagery of some of the African races. One sent to Harar for millet-beer; another went to the gardens in search of "kat," a medicinal herb of untold virtues; two sons of As Samattar insisted on firing the invalid with such ardour that no refusal could avail, and 'Khayrah, the wife, with her daughters, two tall, dark, smiling and well-favoured girls of thirteen and fifteen, sacrificed a sheep as my Fidá or expiatory offering. Even the Galla Christians who flocked to see the stranger, wept for the evil fate which had brought him so far from his fatherland to die under a tree. Nothing, indeed, would have been easier than such operation: all required was the turning face to the wall for four or five days. But to expire of an ignoble colic!—the thing was not to be thought of, and a firm resolution to live on, sometimes, methinks effects its object.' The vigorous resolution thus taken was effectual. On New Year's Day, 1855, Burton was better, and arose from his mat, dressed himself in his Arab best, and asked for a palaver with the Gerád (Chief). Together they retired to a safe place, where Burton read Sharmarkay's letter with much pomposity. The Gerád seemed gratified, and the twain went shooting. Suddenly there appeared to them five men, envoys of the Amir of Harar, who had come to settle the question of blood-money. After sitting for half-an-hour, during which they exchanged salutations with the Gerád, they took him aside privately, told him that the Arab (Burton) was not one of those who bought and sold, that he had no design but to spy out the wealth of the land, and the whole party must go as prisoners to Harar. The Gerád desired them to "throw far those words," but they were evidently unconvinced.

Being then in a "tight place" Burton determined to act with boldness. He wrote an English letter from the Political Resident at Aden to the Amir of Harar, proposing to deliver it in person and throw off his disguise. This he did mainly because his white face caused him to be suspected of being a Turk, but partly because boldness has ever succeeded best among the races in whose lands he had travelled. Another letter was written to Lieutenant Herne, with directions how to act in case of necessity, and this was left with End of Time. The luggage was divided, most of it being left at Sagharrah, and then at 10 A.M. on the 2nd of January, 'the villagers assembled, recited the Fatihah, consoling us with the information that we were all dead men.' The party—Burton and four Africans—moved forward through a lovely country, which, although his present anxieties must have been great indeed, 'reminded him of scenes whilome enjoyed in fair Touraine.' Presently they were stopped by certain Gallas, attendants upon the chief who owned the pass, or rather one of the two chiefs whose property it is, and who divide its profits year by year. It was with some difficulty that the little party escaped the attentions of these gentry, but at last it was done, and then, 'rounding Kondura's northern flank, we entered the Amir's territory : about thirty miles distant, and separated by a series of blue valleys, lay a dark speck upon a tawny sheet of stubble—Harar.'

After an hour's ride through thistles almost big enough to be called trees, they came upon an open rolling country, where was a village of Midgans, who collect the grain of the Gerád Adan—their protector for the time being. These good fellows were delighted to recognise " Mad Said," the new guide, and would have been as hospitable as they could, but for the whispered denunciations of two of the envoys who had seen Burton on the preceding day, and who threatened them with the vengeance of the Amir if they dared to feed " that Turk." In the morning Burton found that, in spite of their fair promises, these envoys had gone on to Harar, and accord-

CITY OF HARAR.

ingly, scenting danger, he left his journals, sketches, and other books, in charge of the village chief, and determined to carry nothing but his arms, and a few presents for the Amir. Then saddling up, the party rode forth, meeting on the way sundry parties of peasants returning from the market in Harar, and wondering aloud at "the Turk," concerning whom they had heard so many horrors. Then they came upon a Harar grandee mounted upon a handsome mule, and attended by seven servants, who carried gourds and skins of grain. Burton and the grandee exchanged courteous salutations, and the latter presented the adventurous traveller with a cup of water. An hour or so later the party halted in a narrow fenced lane. 'About two miles distant, on the crest of a hill, stood the city—the end of my present travel—a long sombre line, strikingly contrasting with the whitewashed towns of the East. The spectacle, materially speaking, was a disappointment : nothing conspicuous appeared but two grey minarets of rude shape ; many would have grudged exposing three lives to win so paltry a prize. But of all that have attempted, none have ever succeeded in entering that pile of stones : the thorough-bred traveller will understand my exultation, although my two companions exchanged glances of wonder.'

It was one thing to get to Harar ; it was quite another to obtain admission to the city. After a five hours' ride Burton reached the gate, and Mad Said accosting the warder, sent salams to the Amir, and requested the honour of audience. Whilst he was gone upon his errand, the little party sat upon a round bastion, and submitted to the scrutiny and the jesting of the idlers of the town, men, women, and children, and, amongst others, to the insolence of the two citizens who had been sent out to stop him. They were kept waiting for half-an-hour at the gate, and were then told by the returned warder to follow him. They

crossed the threshold—Burton, the first Englishman who
had ever been within the Secret City. They had an evil
quarter of an hour before they reached the palace, and
when they arrived found themselves in a place which was
infinitely more suggestive of a jail than of anything else.
On the left hand of the courtyard there was, indeed, ' a low
building of rough stone, which the clanking of frequent
fetters argued to be a state prison.' The palace is made of
rough stone and reddish clay, with no other insignia than a
thin coat of whitewash over the door. ' This,' says Burton,
' is the royal and vizierial distinction at Harar, where no
lesser man may stucco the walls of his house.' After a
further delay Burton was admitted to the presence of the
Amir, or as he styled himself, "the Sultan Ahmad bin
Sultan Abubakr," whom he found to be in appearance a
little Indian Rajah, etiolated of appearance, plain and
thin bearded, with a yellow complexion, wrinkled brows,
and protruding eyes. His throne was a common Indian
kursi, or raised cot, about five feet long, supported by a
dwarf railing. Round him, in double line, were ranged his
Court—his cousins and near relations, with their right arms
bared after the fashion of Abyssinia. Burton walked into
the vast hall, which is about 100 feet long, and saw two
long rows of Galla-spearsmen, between whose lines he had
to walk. They were large half-naked savages standing like
statues, with fierce moveable eyes, each holding with its
butt-end on the ground a huge spear with a head the size
of a shovel. He sauntered down them coolly, with his
eyes fixed upon their dangerous truculent-looking faces.
He had a six-shooter concealed in his waist-belt, and
determined at the first show of excitement to run up to
the Amir, and put it to his head, as the only means of
saving his life, but no such need occurred.

' I entered the avenue,' says Burton, ' with a loud " Peace
be upon you ! " to which H. H. replying graciously, and

extending a hand bony and yellow as a kite's claw, snapped his thumb and middle finger. Two chamberlains stepping forward, held my fore arms, and assisted me to bend low over the fingers, which, however, I did not kiss, being naturally averse to performing that operation upon any but a woman's hand. My two servants then took their turn : in this case after the back was saluted the palm was presented for a repetition. The preliminaries concluded, we were led to, and seated upon, a mat in front of the Amir, who directed towards us a frowning brow and an inquisitive eye. Some inquiries were made about the chief's health : he shook his head captiously, but inquired our errand. I drew from my pocket my own letter; it was carried by a chamberlain with hands veiled in his tobe to the great man, who, after a brief glance, laid it upon the couch and demanded further explanation. I then represented in Arabic that we had come from Aden, bearing the com · pliments of our Daulah or Governor, and that we had entered Harar to see the light of H. H.'s countenance : this information concluded with a little speech describing the changes of political agents in Arabia, and alluding to the friendship formerly existing between the English and the deceased chief Abubakr.'

The Amir smiled graciously, much to the relief of Burton, who knew not until that moment for what horrible fate he might not be reserved. He then made a sign to his treasurer—'a little ugly man, with a badly shaven head, coarse features, angry eyes and stubby beard'— directing the travellers to retire, and having allowed them once more to touch his hand, left them to be conducted to his second palace by the guard. The Bedawin could hardly believe that they had escaped alive, and grinned in the joy of their hearts—all the more when they found themselves provided at once with dinner from the chief's kitchen—'a dish of Shabta, holcus cakes soaked in sour milk, and thickly powdered with red pepper, the salt of this inland region.' When the party had eaten, the Treasurer again appeared, and led them to the house of the Wazir, the Gerád Mohammed, whom they found in a small room on the ground floor of his house hung round with varnished wooden bowls. The Minister received him courteously, inquired his will in good Arabic, to which Burton replied in .the terms he had used to the Amir, adding, however, some details concerning one Madar Fareh who had been sent by the Sultan Abubakr to the Governor of Aden with presents, and saying that it was the desire of our people to re-establish friendly relations and commercial intercourse with Harar. ' Khayr Inshallah! it is well if Allah please!'

Burton having taken leave returned to the house lent to him by the Amir, and having sent a six chambered revolver as a present to his host composed himself to rest, 'worn out by fatigue, and profoundly impressed with the *poésie* of our position. I was under the roof of a bigoted prince, whose least word was death ; amongst a people who detest foreigners ; the only European that had ever passed over their inhospitable threshold, and the fated instrument of their future downfall.'* He speedily found that the rumours of the severity of the Amir's rule were not unfounded, and that his people shared to the full his detestation of foreigners. The Amir himself is not especially ferocious, but the peculiar customs of the country would almost excuse him if he were. His great-grandfather died in prison ; his father narrowly escaped the same fate, and three of his cousins were, when Burton visited Harar, in confinement. These petty princes live in fact in an atmosphere of constant corruption, intrigue, jealousy, and

---

* Alluding to the old prediction that Harar would fall into the hands of the foreigner soon after the first " Nazarene " had found his way thither. It was curiously fulfilled.

suspicion, and it would be strange if it did not develop some of the worst qualities of human nature. His occupations, too, are hardly of an edifying character, consisting as they do either in spying his many stalwart cousins, indulging in vain fears of the Hajj Sharmarkay, and amassing treasure by commerce and escheats. His revenue is derived from an octroi, and from a tax on cultivation, which, being paid in kind, is naturally more productive than it is in name. He is said to have accumulated large hoards of silver, coffee, and ivory; and Burton relates that his own favourite attendant, "the Hammál," the Somali policeman from Aden, was once admitted to the inner palace where he saw 'huge boxes of ancient fashion supposed to contain dollars.' It is possible that the story may be true. Fines and confiscations are with the Amir, as with all Eastern potentates, the favourite punishment of offenders, and he is merciless in exacting them. 'I met at Wilensi,' says Burton, 'an old Harari whose gardens and property had all been escheated because his son fled from justice after slaying a man.' On the other hand, it must be remembered, that the general commerce of Harar is petty. The greatest merchant may bring to Harar £50 worth of goods, and he who has £20 of disposable capital is considered a wealthy man.

The travellers were allowed a few days' repose, during which they were called upon by the Arabs of Harar, whom Burton rightly describes as 'a strange mixture,' including as they did a Maghrabi from Fez, who was commander of the Amir's body-guard, a thorough-bred Persian, who seemed to know everybody, and was on terms of bosom friendship with half the world from Cairo to Calcutta, a boy from Meccah, a Muscat man, a native of Suez and a citizen of Damascus, the rest being Arabs from El-Yemen. After the Arabs came the Somal, amongst whom the Hammál found relatives, friends and acquaintances. On the day following

Burton and his companions were summoned to wait upon the Gerád Mohammed, the Wazir—or, as Englishmen following the spelling of Galland, whose version of the 'Arabian Nights' introduced Arabic literature to Europe in the last century, would probably spell it, the Vizier. Sword in hand, and followed by his two attendants, Burton walked to the palace, and found the Minister sitting with six of his brother councillors at the receipt of custom. Two were turbaned ; the rest sat in their bare and shaven heads, their Tobes * being, as is customary on ceremonial occasions, allowed to fall beneath their waists. The Grandees were eating Kát, or, as it is called in Harar, Ját—a plant which appears to fulfil to some extent the function of the Betel nut in India. 'It seems,' says Burton, 'to produce in them (the Arabs) a manner of dreamy enjoyment which, exaggerated by time and distance, may have given rise to that splendid myth the Lotos and the Lotophagi. It is held by the Ulema here, as in Arabia, "Akl el-Sálihin," or the Food of the Pious, and literati remark that it has the singular properties of enlivening the imagination, clearing the ideas, cheering the heart, diminishing sleep, and taking the place of food. The people of Harar eat it every day from 9 A.M. till near noon when they dine, and afterwards indulge in something stronger—millet-beer and mead.'

The Gerád was markedly courteous, and placed Burton

---

* The Tobe, it may be convenient to mention in this place, is the general garment of Africa from Zayla to Bornu. In the Somali country it is a cotton sheet eight cubits long, and two breadths sewn together. It is highly becoming as worn in Somali Land, and picturesque as the Roman toga, but in the case of women not perhaps the most decorous of dresses, for which reason women in the towns often prefer the Arab costume—a short-sleeved robe extending to the knee, and a futah, or loin cloth, *i.e.* a petticoat underneath. A cubit "according to the measure of a man" is eighteen inches—not 26½ as the school-books say—the length of a man's forearm from the elbow to the tip of the middle finger. The measure was invented by the sons of Noah—the children of Ham alone have retained it to this day.

at his right hand on the dais, where he sat and fingered his rosary, the Minister meanwhile transacting the business of the day. Then, as ever, with these singular people, religion came to the front. One of the elders took a large book from a little recess in the wall and began to recite a blessing on the Prophet and his Companions—a long litany which lasted half-an-hour. In the course of it Burton found an opportunity of making an impression on his hosts. 'The reader,' he says, 'misled by a marginal reference, happened to say "angels, men and genii." Opinions were divided as to the order of beings, when I explained that human nature, which, amongst Moslems, is not "a little lower than the angelic," ranked highest, because of it were created prophets, apostles and saints ; whereas, the other is but a " Wásitah," or connection between the Creator and his creatures. My theology won general approbation, and a few kinder glances from the elders.'

After prayers Burton and his attendants were admitted to a second audience with the Amir, who placed him on his right, side by side with the Gerád, the attendants occupying humbler mats opposite. The Amir inquired as to the changes which had taken place in Aden, and, having suddenly produced Burton's letter, called upon him in a suspicious fashion to explain its meaning. He was then asked by the Gerád if he came to buy or sell at Harar, to which he replied :—' We are no buyers or sellers : we have become your guests to pay our respects to the Amir— whom may Allah preserve !—and that the friendship between the two powers may endure.' The Amir, appearing satisfied, Burton pressed for a speedy answer, knowing the procrastinating habits of Africa, where two or three months sometimes pass before a definite answer to any communication is given. The only reply he could get came through the mouth of the Gerád,—" The reply will be vouchsafed," and with this Burton was obliged to be content.

Another personage now appeared upon the scene—one
Shaykh Jámi, one of the Ulema—a little black man with a
high reputation as an Alim or Savant, an ardent Moslem,
and an apostle of peace. This person had some authority
over the Amir, and had often been employed on political
missions amongst the different chiefs. Another important
personage, an aged eunuch, who having served five Amirs,
was allowed to remain in the palace, also befriended the
traveller. This latter, if not mad, looked as if he were, but
his conduct was sane. At dawn he sent in bad plantains,
wheaten crusts, and cups of unpalatable " coffee tea "—a
vile decoction, tasting like weak senna, and made by
infusing the toasted leaves of the coffee plant. Later on
came a second breakfast from the Amir—citrons, plantains, sugar-cane, limes, wheaten bread and stewed fowls.
After breakfast the palace became crowded with the
Harari, who, under the pretext of anxiety for the Sultan,
satisfied their curiosity with regard to the travellers.
Dinner—beef and bread, with red pepper—was sent from
the Amir's kitchen at noon. The travellers then had peace
for an hour or two, but in the afternoon the house filled
again with visitors—nobody ever seems to have had anything to do in Harar—and in the evenings the Galla tribesmen, reapers and threshers, who were gathering in the Amir's
harvest from a hill to the north of the city, were feasted in
Burton's quarters with flesh, beer and mead—greatly to
his discomfort. The tenor of these monotonous days
was varied only by perpetual reference to the rosary, con-
sulting soothsayers, and listening to reports and rumours
brought in, in such profusion by the Somal that the travellers
longed for their cessation. One of those rumours became
alarming. A youth arrived in Harar with a story that three
brothers—white men—had arrived in the Somali country,
who, though dressed as Moslems, were really Englishmen
in disguise, and in the employment of the Government.

At this crisis the Shaykh Jámi proved a most valuable ally. He had told Burton's follower, the Hammál, of an intended trip from Harar, and he in turn had suggested that the party might well escort him. The Shaykh at once offered to apply for leave from the Gerád Mohammed, and made an appointment for the morrow, at the time of Kát-eating. Accordingly, at 6 A.M. they were summoned, and received as usual with the greatest possible courtesy. By this time Burton had diagnosed the Gerád's malady —chronic asthma—and he promised to send from Aden the different remedies used by ourselves. The Gerád caught at the prospect of a release from his sufferings, and his courtiers urged him to lose no time. Presently the Minister was sent for by the Amir, and shortly afterwards Burton. The interview was entirely satisfactory. There was a long conversation about the state of Zayla, of Berbera, of Aden and of Stamboul ; the Amir put questions concerning the reason for the British occupation of Aden, and used some obliging expressions about desiring our friendship. He had, he said, a great respect for people who built large ships. On his part, Burton praised Harar cautiously, and expressed his regret that its coffee was not better known among the Franks. ' The small, wizen-faced man smiled as the Moslems say, "the smile of Omar" ; seeing his brow relax for the first time, I told him that being now restored to health we requested his commands for Aden. He signified consent with a nod, and the Gerád, with many compliments, gave me a letter addressed to the Political Resident, and requested me to take charge of a mule as a present. I then arose, recited a short prayer, the gist of which was that the Amir's days and reign might be long in the land, and that the faces of his foes might be blackened here and hereafter, bent over his hand and retired. Returning to the Gerád's levée hut, I saw by the countenances of my two Somali policemen that they were not a little anxious about the interview, and comforted them with the whispered word, " Achhá "—all right.'

Burton on these occasions is accustomed to bless his "lucky star." Those who have read the foregoing pages will probably think, however, that it was hardly luck which brought about his success in this dangerous adventure, but rather a combination of shrewdness, adaptability, common-sense, tact, and a marvellous knowledge of human nature, and especially of Arab human nature. To put the matter in another way : Burton, here, as on many other occasions of his adventurous life, illustrated the venerable motto of the Latin Delectus *Fortes fortuna juvat,* which may be glossed into " Fortune is kind to those who are able to command her," and that is what Burton proved himself to be whenever heroic work was to be done. In this instance he had hardly left the presence of the Amir, when a *contre-temps* arose which would have seriously discomposed a weaker man. The Gerád came, followed by two men bearing the arms of his servants, which had been taken from them on entering the city, and also the revolver which he had sent as a present to the Amir. The situation was embarrassing ; it was impossible to take back the present, and, on the other hand, Burton suspected some sort of finesse on the Amir's part to discover his feelings towards him. Without hesitation, Burton explained that the weapon was intended to defend the Amir's life, and for further effect snapped caps in rapid succession, to the dismay of the august company. ' The Minister returned to his master, and soon brought back the information that after a day or two another mule should be given to me. With suitable acknowledgments we arose, blessed the Gerád, bade adieu to the assembly, and departed joyful, the Hammál in his glee speaking broken English, even in the Amir's courtyard.'

On his return home, Burton found the Shaykh Jámi,

to whom he communicated the good news, and gave
thanks for his friendly aid. The twain had a long conversation, and our traveller succeeded in soothing the mind
of the worthy man as to a disputed point of Turkish
history, concerning which there had been a discussion.
Whilst they were conversing, Kabír Khalíl, one of the
principal Ulema, and one Haji Abdullah, a Shaykh of
distinguished fame, sent their salams. 'This,' says
Burton, 'is one of the many occasions in which, during a
long residence in the East, I have had reason to be
grateful to the learned, whose influence over the people,
when unbiassed by bigotry, is decidedly for good. That
evening there was great joy amongst the Somal, who had
been alarmed for the safety of my two companions ; they
brought them presents of Harari tobes and a feast of fowls,
limes, and wheaten bread for the stranger.' The day of
release came at last. These African cities, as Burton says
somewhere, 'are prisons on a large scale, into which you
enter by your own will, and, as the significant proverb says,
you leave by another's.' On the 11th of January the
second mule was sent, and, on the same day, Burton
inspected the library of the Shaykh Jámi—a collection of
books remarkable rather for their bindings than for their
literary merit—dined with him off the usual boiled beef
and bread, sprinkled with red pepper, and arranged to
meet at Wilensi. There was a parting visit to the Gerád,
remarkable only for his insistence in demanding remedies
for his asthma from Aden ; a delay of a day from bad
weather ; and finally, a joyful departure at dawn on
Saturday the 13th of January, 1855.

It is some evidence of the strain under which Burton had
been living during the previous fortnight, that he was
hardly in the saddle before the weakness and sickness
under which he had been labouring left him, and as he and
his companions passed the gate "a weight of care and

anxiety fell from him like a cloak of lead." The journey
was performed in safety as far as the place where the
property had been left. Entering the village, the travellers
discharged their fire-arms ; the women received them
with cries of joy, and, as they passed into the enclosure,
performed the "fola" by throwing over them some
handfuls of toasted grain.* "End of Time" came forward
to kiss Burton's hand, thankful for his return, as well he
might be, seeing that he had been half-starved, despite his
dignity as "Sharmarkay's Mercury." The Gerád Adan
and his sons were absent, but the good Khayrah and her
daughters did the duties of hospitality by cooking rice and
a couple of fowls. On the following morning the party
rode on to Wilensi, the people inquiring on the way if they
were the men "who had been put to death by the Amir
of Harar." At Wilensi the demonstrations of joy were
enthusiastic. The Kalendar was in a paroxysm of delight ;
both Schehrazade and Deenarzade—the women factotums
—were affected with giggling, and what might be blushing.
' We reviewed our property, and found that the One-Eyed
had been a faithful steward, so faithful indeed that he had
well-nigh starved the two women. Presently appeared the
Gerád and his sons, bringing with them my books ; the
former was at once invested with a gaudy Abyssinian tobe
of many colours, in which he sallied forth from the cottage
the admired of all admirers. The pretty wife Sudiyah
and the good Khayrah were made happy by sundry gifts
of huge Birmingham earrings, brooches and bracelets,
scissors, needles and thread. The evening as usual ended
in a feast.'

The party halted for a week at Wilensi, to repair
damages. A long desert march was before them, and

* Query—What relation has this custom to the idiotic one which
prevails in this country of throwing rice on a bride and bridegroom as
they depart for their honeymoon ?—Ed.

it was necessary to feed the men up to the necessary
condition before undertaking it. A Somali was sent into
Harar to buy provisions, and during the absence of this
man and the rest of the caravan, Burton busied himself
with collecting a vocabulary of the Harari tongue and
reducing it to a grammar. At the end of the week Shaykh
Jámi appeared, 'equipped as a traveller, with sword,
praying-skin, and water-bottle.' He was accompanied by
his brother, 'in no wise so prayerful a person,' and
by four burly, black-looking Widáds or disciples—youths
who were doubtless learned, pious and eloquent, but
whose aspect was not reassuring. Burton gave them a
supper of rice, ghee and dates, but evaded—though with
difficulty—under the pretext of ill-health, a proposal to
spend the night in pious exercises. The "trip" on which
the Shaykh was bound was to settle a claim of blood-
money amongst the Bedawin. The case was rich enough
in Somali manners to deserve to be transcribed here.
'One man gave medicine to another, who happened to die
about a month afterwards; the father of the deceased at
once charged the mediciner with poisoning, and demanded
the customary fine. On Sunday, the 21st of January, our
messenger returned from Harar, bringing with him supplies
for the road ; my vocabulary was finished, and, as nothing
detained us at Wilensi, I determined to set out the next
day. When the rumour went abroad, every inhabitant of
the village flocked to our hut with the view of seeing what
he could beg or borrow ; we were soon compelled to close
it, with peremptory orders that none should be admitted
but the Shaykh Jámi. The divine appeared in the
afternoon, accompanied by all the incurables of the
countryside ; after hearing the tale of the blood-money, I
determined that talismans were the best and safest of
medicines in those mountains. The Shaykh at first
doubted their efficacy ; but when my diploma, as a master

Sufi,* was exhibited, a new light broke upon him and his attendant Widáds. "Verily he hath declared himself this day," whispered each to his neighbour, still sorely mystified. Shaykh Jámi carefully inspected the document, raised it reverently to his forehead, and muttered some prayers ; he then in humble phrase begged a copy, and required from me " Ijázah," or permission to act as master. The former request was granted without hesitation, about the latter I preferred to temporise ; he then owned himself my pupil, and received as a well-merited acknowledgment of his services a pencil and a silk turban.'

The next day was fixed for departure, and then as usual in Africa everything had to be done. There was no coffee, no water-bags, and Deenarzade had gone to buy gourds in a distant village. No servants had been procured by the Gerád, although he had promised a hundred whenever they were required. And, at the last moment, one Abdo Aman, engaged in Harar as a guide to Berberah for the sum of ten dollars, incontinently demanded twenty. The occasion was one for a display of energy, and it was not wanting. Burton insisted on the huts being pulled down, and preparations for the start being made irrespective of the absence of the truants, and accordingly at 9 A.M. the cavalcade started. The journey across the prairie was anything but pleasant, threatened as Burton was on all hands with the consequences of the " blood feuds," of which there are so many amongst the African tribes, and worried as he was by the stupid and savage obstinacy of the people in his employment. To add to his troubles the camels had been half starved in the Girhi mountains, and a day's delay was necessary to recruit their strength. There was apparently an end to the expedition, and a weaker man might not unreasonably have turned his face to the wall. Just as things appeared at the worst, 'suddenly

---

* " Sufi-ism : the Eastern parent of Freemasonry."—BURTON.

appeared the valiant Beuh, sent to visit us by Dahobo, his gay sister.' He told Burton that a guide was in the neighbourhood, whereupon Burton proposed that Beuh should take charge of the caravan to Zayla, while he himself with three attendants took provisions for four days and pushed forward to Berberah on mule-back.

Then arose the usual demur and the usual bargaining, but at last all was arranged. Burton and his companions rose at dawn of the 26th of January, but they were unable to leave until 7 A.M., the whole of the party demanding individual palavers before allowing him to take his departure. One can well believe that it was 'not without apprehension' that he started. His total provision for a journey of at least four days consisted of 'five biscuits, a few limes and sundry lumps of sugar.' He knew that any delay or accident to the mules would bring the whole party to starvation ; that they were about to traverse a desert inhabited—so far as it was inhabited at all—by a tribe likely to be as pitiless to his followers as Nature herself; and he had besides the consolation of knowing that the whole party had only a single water-bottle. There was, however, nothing to be done but to put the best face on matters and take such goods as the gods might provide with a thankful heart, and so Burton with his three followers trotted off over the rugged ground which led into the Harawwah Valley. At Gudabirsi, a village of Somal, his companions halted to ask the news, and to distend themselves with milk, a process which was repeated a few miles further on. Burton's escort was now 'laying in a four days' stock.' At a kraal a little farther removed he picked up a guide with the euphonious name of "Dubayr"—the Donkey—who for five dollars and two cloths was willing to convoy them to Berberah. He knew the road, but he was the worst of guides, in that he could not ride, suffered horribly from thirst, and was only induced to refrain from

throwing himself on the ground and incontinently giving
up the ghost by promises of large additional presents and
by unlimited talk of food.   On the 26th, the party rode for
thirty-five miles, arriving at last at a large fold, where, by
removing the thorn fences, they found fresh grass for their
starving beasts.   The night was wet, but the drizzle though
it drenched their saddle cloths—their only bedding—did
not quench their thirst.   The morning of the 27th saw
them astir at dawn, and trotting eastwards in search of
a well.   The guide had promised one at every half mile :
now he owned with groans that they would not drink
before nightfall.   They rode on through a dreadful and
most uninteresting landscape tortured with thirst.   'For
twenty-four hours we did not taste water,' says Burton,
'the sun parched our brains, the mirage mocked us at
every turn, and the effect was a species of monomania.
As I jogged along with eyes closed against the fiery air,
no image unconnected with the want suggested itself.
Water ever lay before me—water lying deep in the shady
well—water in streams bubbling icy from the rock—water
in pellucid lakes inviting me to plunge and revel in their
treasures.   Now an Indian cloud was showering upon me
fluid more precious than molten pearl, then an invisible
hand offered a bowl for which the mortal part would have
gladly bartered years of life.   Then—drear contrast!—I
opened my eyes to a heat reeking plain, and a sky of that
eternal metallic blue so lovely to painter and poet, so blank
and deathlike to us whose καλòν was tempest, rainstorm,
and the huge purple nimbus.   I tried to talk—it was in
vain, to sing in vain, vainly to think, every idea was bound
up in one subject—water.'

   A few more hours and the little party would have been
food for the desert beasts.   Burton relates how his life was
saved by a bird.   When the caravan had been thirty-six
hours without water, could go no further, and were pre-

pared to die this worst of all deaths—the short twilight of the tropics was drawing in—Burton looked up and saw a Kattá or sand-grouse, with its pigeon-like flight, making for the nearer hills. These birds must drink at least once a day, and generally towards evening, when they are said to carry water in their bills to their young. He cried out, " See ! the Kattá ! the Kattá !!" All revived at once, took heart, and followed the bird, which suddenly plunged down about a hundred yards away, showing them a charming spring, a little shaft of water, about two feet in diameter, in a margin of green. They jumped from their saddles, and men and beasts plunged their heads into the water, and drank till they could drink no more. Burton has often said that he has never since shot a Kattá. At sunrise on the 28th they started once more, with gall-backed mules already becoming footsore. The party had consequently to struggle on at foot pace through dreary bush and desert plain. At night they began to ascend the lower slopes of a high range, and suddenly came upon a delicious well—water springing from the rock. The mules fell hungrily upon the succulent grass, and the travellers having quenched their thirst, prepared to pass the night as best they could, after a frugal supper—how frugal may be guessed from the list of the provisions in Burton's possession at the time of his separating from the caravan. The fear of lions drove them forward, however, and after a sufficient halt they remounted their mules, and began to ascend the stony face of the Eastern hill, through thick darkness deepening into mist. A heavy shower afforded a pretext for stopping at the bleak summit, and there they waited for day, having accomplished thirty-five miles of desert travel without seeing a human face.

The march was resumed on the 29th of January. At 10 A.M. a halt was called at a place where there was much grass, and where water was also to be found. Shortly after-

wards the march was again resumed—a toilsome journey
through rock and jungle thickly-interspersed with the
Arman Acacia. This shrub has a beautiful flower, with a
most pleasing fragrance, but even that beauty hardly
compensates for its thorns, two inches long, with points
like needles. At evening came a painful adventure. The
country was much disturbed, and the few men they met
prayed them to harry their neighbours' cattle. At last
they found a Bedawin, who promised after much persuasion
to take them to a village of the Ayyál Gedid-tribe. The
" Hammál," who had married a daughter of the tribe, and
had constituted his father-in-law Burton's protector at Berberah, promised all imaginable luxuries. " To-night we shall
sleep under cover and drink milk," quoth one hungry man,
who straightway was answered, " And we shall eat mutton."

Alas! for the vanity of human expectations! The
village turned out to be one belonging to the Ayyál
Shirdon—the bitterest foes of the Ayyál Gedid, and
nothing was to be obtained from it save threats and curses.
The same fate befel the party in the three villages of the
Ayyál Gedid, which they visited in succession, and the
Hammál was taunted accordingly. He explained their
inhospitality by saying that the men were all away, and
that the villages contained nothing but women, children,
servants and flocks. The guide reluctantly confessed that
no water was to be had nearer than Bulhár, whither accordingly they pushed on though well-nigh worn out with
fatigue. The guide could only plod on sadly in the rear,
and the animals, which were perpetually stopping as a hint
that they could go no further, were only kept in motion by
pricks of the spear. At midnight was heard the sound of
the distant sea : at three in the morning some holes were
found in a Fiumara full of bitter water rendered potable
by the recent rains, and ' truly delicious after fifteen hours
of thirst.' The mules were tethered and left to graze upon

the coarse stubbly grass, which saved them from starvation, and the weary travellers, regardless of the rain, coiled themselves in their saddle cloths, and slept like the dead.

At 6 in the morning of the 30th of January, the party started along the sea-coast for Berberah, travelling slowly and frequently halting. At noon they bathed in the sea, and afterwards while sitting upon the sands, his followers petitioned Burton to allow them to pass the kraals of their enemies, the Ahmed Ayyid by night. This request was granted—the more willingly, since rapid travelling was impossible. One mule was insensible even to spear pricks, and the Hammál was compelled to flog another wretched beast before him. At 3 P.M. they halted for a rest, and then having baited for a while, they finished their last mouthful of food and prepared for a long night march. It must have been a fearful time. They were in an enemy's country, their mules could scarcely walk, at every bow-shot they rolled on the ground and were only raised by the whip. A last halt was called within four miles of Berberah ; two of the men fall fast asleep on the stones ; one only, the Hammál, retained his strength and spirits and delighted his master with his " pluck." At last the journey was over. At 2 A.M. having marched at least forty miles the toil-worn little caravan entered Berberah, and halted at the place where Burton's comrades had already taken up their residence. ' A glad welcome, a dish of rice, and a glass of strong waters made amends for past privations and fatigue. The servants and the wretched mules were provided for, and I fell asleep conscious of having performed a feat which, like a certain ride to York, will live in local annals for many and many a year.'

Burton awoke soon after sunrise. The Berberah people had heard something of what he had done, and were utterly incredulous as to the possibility of his doing it. They could not believe that he had ridden from the Girhi Hills

in five days, still less that he had ever entered Harar.
Having satisfied them, as far as was possible, he first inspected his people, whom he found in excellent spirits and
temper, and his cattle, which were very much the reverse,
and then proceeded to examine the town, the appearance
of which aroused in his mind a renewal of the wonder that
any government could have selected Aden as a station,
when another and so fine a port was open to it. Aden, the
"Coal-hole of the East," is neither more nor less than a
volcanic cinder heap, with an atmosphere like the breath
of a furnace, and a wretched water supply. Berberah—the
Emporium of Eastern Africa—has a healthy climate, hot it
is true, but always open to the cooling and steady north
winds, a mild monsoon, an excellent harbour, a fine rolling
country, and a soil highly productive. It is the meeting
place of commerce ; has few rivals, and with half the sums
lavished in Arabia upon engineer follies of stone and lime,
the environs might at this time have been covered with
homes, gardens, and trees.

On the 5th of February, 1855, Burton took leave of his
comrades and went on board a native craft—*El-Kalam* or
The Reed; landed on the following day at Siyáro, nineteen
miles to the east of Berberah—inspected the walls and
gladdened with a few small presents the hearts of the
Bedawin who make a miserable living out of their ownership
of them—and continued his voyage at the exhilarating
rate of twenty miles in twenty-four hours. It seemed,
however, impossible to get the crew to face the perils of
the voyage to Aden, but after several days Burton
insisted on going on. He had been landed and had found
great difficulty in getting on board again. Once upon
the quarter deck :—

"Dawwir el-farmán"—shift the yard—I shouted with a
voice of thunder.

The answer was a general hubbub. "He surely will not

sail in a sea like this?" asked the trembling captain of my companions.

"He will!" sententiously quoth the Hammál with a Burleigh nod.

" It blows wind "—remonstrated the Rais.

" And if it blew fire?" asked the Hammál, with the *air goguenard,* meaning that from the calamity of Frankish obstinacy there was no refuge.

'A kind of death-wail arose during which, to hide untimely laughter, I retreated to a large drawer in the stern of the vessel called a cabin. There my ears could distinguish the loud entreaties of the crew, vainly urging my attendants to propose a day's delay. Then one of the garrison, accompanied by the captain who shook as with fever, resolved to act forlorn hope and bring a *feu d'enfer* of phrases to bear upon the Frank's hard brain. Scarcely however had the head of the sentence been delivered before he was playfully upraised by his bushy hair and a handle somewhat more substantial, carried out of the cabin and thrown like a bag of biscuit on the deck.'

After a scare of this kind resistance was of course useless. It came on to blow, and the night alternated between gusts of wind and gusts of prayer. Finally ' on the morning of Friday, the 9th of February, 1855, we hove in sight of Jebel Shamsán, the loftiest peak of the Aden Crater. And ere evening fell I had the pleasure of seeing the faces of friends and comrades once more.'

Burton's object in returning to Aden was to make preparations for a new Expedition Nilewards, *viâ* Harar, on a larger and more imposing scale. His arrangements were soon made, and on the 7th of April, 1855, he landed at Berberah at the head of a party of forty-two men. He had applied at Aden for some of the trained Somali police, but none could be spared, and he was, in consequence, compelled to take whatever recruits he could get—Egyptians, Arabs, Nubians and negroes. These men were armed with sabres and flint-muskets, and were commanded by one Mahmúd of the Mijjarthayn, better known at Aden as El-Bályuz, or the envoy. He had the reputation of being a shrewd manager, thoroughly well acquainted with the habits and customs as well as the geography of Somali Land. It had been proposed to establish an Agency, a short distance from, and opposite to, the town, and here the camp of the Expedition was pitched. The creek lay between the camp and the town, and the object of selecting this site was that the Expedition might have the protection of the gunboat which had brought it from Aden. Unfortunately, as will be seen, the commander of the schooner had orders to relieve the ship then employed in blockading the sea-coast of the Fazli chief, and so was unable to remain and superintend the departure of the Expedition as had been hoped.

All went well at first. The camp of Burton and his three lieutenants, Stroyan, Speke, and Herne, was regularly ordered, Stroyan's tent being on the extreme right, Speke's on the left, and the " Rowtie "—a sepoy's tent, pent-house shaped, supported by two uprights and a single traverse and open at one end, in which Burton and Herne slept— was in the middle. The camels were tethered in front on a sandy bed beneath the ridge, and in the rear stood the horses and mules. During the day-time all were on the alert : at night two sentries were posted, regularly relieved and visited by the Ras, El-Bályuz, and his English masters. Burton was well received in Berberah, and the chiefs listened with respectful attention to a letter from the Political Resident at Aden enjoining them to treat the Expedition with consideration and hospitality. There had been, of course, some little disputing with the towns-people and the elders of the great tribe of Eesa Musa touching the hire of camels and similar matters, but, as Burton says, 'such events are not worthy to excite attention in Africa.' The Shaykh Jámi of Harar, of whom mention has been made, soon put in an appearance, ate bread and salt with the travellers, recommended them to his countrymen, and availed himself of Burton's intervention to induce avaricious skippers to grant gratuitous passages to needy pilgrims to Meccah. The people generally, after a good deal of bragging and boasting became friendly, assisted in digging a well, and, in some cases, camped near the Expedition for protection. Everything in short promised fair, and there seemed to be no ground whatever for apprehension.

The whole of the camels necessary for the journey, fifty-six in number, had been purchased, and if the party had started at once there would probably have been no danger. They waited, however, for the mid-April mail, which was to bring instruments from England which they considered necessary, and also to see the close of the Berberah fair, which was in full swing when they landed. On the 9th of April, the monsoon began, with a violent storm. This was the signal for the Bedawin to migrate to the hills, they preferring to travel in the rainy season, on account of the abundance of water. Throughout the town the mats were stripped from the framework of stick and pole which was left to stand for use at the next fair season, and by the next day Berberah was almost deserted, save by a few pilgrims who wished to take ship and by merchants who were afraid of plundering parties. The roads out of Berberah were lined with travellers, amongst whom were the Shaykh Jámi and Burhále, the Abbáns or protectors of the party, who, having received permission to go with their families and flocks, left it in charge of their sons and relations.

On the 18th of April, a craft from Aden put into Berberah, with about a dozen Somal who were desirous of accompanying the caravan as far as Ogadayn, the southern

region. They would have sailed again the same evening,
but, fortunately for himself and his colleagues, Burton
ordered the commander and crew to be feasted with rice
and dates, and the vessel remained. That night the chapter
of disasters began.* Just at sunset there was a noise of
firing behind the tents. On going to ascertain the cause,
Burton found that the guard had fired over the heads of
three horsemen, supposing them to be scouts, the usual fore-
runners of a Somali raid. Burton rebuked them sharply,
telling them to reserve their fire for the future, but if they
were forced to shoot to do so at and not over the heads of
the foe. The strangers were then catechized and gave so
plausible an account of themselves that even the Ras
was deceived. The Bedawin had forged a report that Haj
Sharmárkay was lying in wait in the neighbouring port
of Siyáro with four ships, intending to bear down upon
Berberah when that town was deserted and re-erect his
forts there for the third time. They had been sent, they
said, to see if the vessel in the harbour were laden with
building materials, and they concluded their ingenious lie
by asking with a laugh if Burton and his companions
feared danger from the tribe of their own Abbáns.

---

* Speke's narrative of this affair which he published some years
later in 'Blackwood,' and afterwards reprinted in the pamphlet
" What led to the Discovery of the Sources of the Nile," differs
materially from Burton's, and also from the MS. report in his handwriting, which Burton has now in his possession. According to
Speke *he* was the head of the expedition ; *he* had given the order for
the night ; it was before *him* that the spies were brought ; *he* was the
first to turn out, and no one but *he* had the courage to defend himself.
The assumption of authority is somewhat ludicrous. Not merely is
all written and oral testimony against it, but it is obvious that such
an expedition could only be commanded by one who spoke Arabic
fluently, and of Arabic Speke was absolutely innocent. His share in
the affray really consisted in getting himself seriously wounded and
in rushing about dealing blows with the butt of an unloaded revolver.
—ED.

Believing their story, the usual two sentries were posted, and the camp settled down for the night in perfect confidence.

What followed must be told in Burton's own words :—

'Between 2 and 3 A.M., on the 19th of April, I was suddenly aroused by the Bályuz, who cried aloud that the enemy was upon us.* Hearing a rush of men like a stormy wind, I sprang up, called for my sabre, and sent Lieut. Herne to ascertain the force of the foray. Armed with a Colt he went to the rear and left of the camp, the direction of the danger, collected some of the guard— others having already disappeared—and fired two shots into the assailants. Then finding himself alone, he turned hastily towards the tent ; in so doing he was tripped up by the rope, and as he arose a Somali appeared in the act of striking at him with a club. Lieut. Herne fired, floored the man, and, rejoining me, declared that the enemy was in great force, and the guard nowhere. Meanwhile I had aroused Lieuts. Stroyan and Speke, who were sleeping in the extreme right and left tents. The former, it is pre-sumed, arose to defend himself, but, as the sequel shows, we never saw him alive.† Lieut. Speke, awakened by the report of firearms, but supposing it the normal false alarm —a warning to plunderers—he remained where he was ; presently, hearing clubs rattling upon his tent, and feet shuffling around, he ran to my Rowtie, which we prepared to defend as long as possible.

---

* The attacking party it appears was 350 strong : 12 of the Mikahil, 15 of the Habr Gerhajis, and the rest Eesa Musa. One As Ali wore, it is said, the ostrich feather for the murder of Lieutenant Stroyan.—ED.

† Mohammed, his Indian servant, stated that rising at my summons he had rushed to his tent, armed himself with a revolver, and fired six shots upon his assassins. Unhappily Mohammed did not see his master fall, and as he was foremost amongst the fugitives, scant importance attaches to his evidence.—BURTON.

'The enemy swarmed like hornets, with shouts and screams intended to terrify, and proving that over-whelming odds were against us. It was by no means easy to avoid in the shades of night the jobbing of javelins and the long heavy daggers thrown at our legs from under and through the opening of the tent. We three remained together. Lieut. Herne knelt by my right ; on my left was Lieut. Speke, guarding the entrance ; I stood in the centre, having nothing but a sabre. The revolvers were used by my companions with deadly effect ; unfortunately there was but one pair. When the fire was exhausted, Lieut. Herne went to search for his powder-horn, and, that failing, to find some spears usually tied to the tent-pole. Whilst thus engaged he saw a man breaking into the rear of our Rowtie-tent, and came back to inform me of the circumstance.

'At this time, about five minutes after the beginning of the affray, the tent had been almost beaten down—an Arab custom with which we were all familiar—and had we been entangled in its folds, we should have been speared with unpleasant facility. I gave the word to escape, and sallied out, closely followed by Lieut. Herne, with Lieut. Speke in the rear. The prospect was not agreeable. About twenty men were kneeling and crouching at the tent entrance whilst many dusk figures stood farther off or ran about shouting the war cry, or with shouts and blows drove away our camels. Among the enemy were many of our friends and attendants ; the coast being open to them they natu-rally ran away, firing a few useless shots, and receiving a modicum of flesh wounds.

'After sabre-ing through the mob at the tent entrance, imagining that I saw the form of Lieut. Stroyan lying upon the sand, I cut my way towards it amongst a dozen Somal, whose war-clubs worked without mercy, while the Bályuz, who was violently pushing me out of the fray, rendered the strokes of my sabre uncertain. This individual was cool and collected. Though incapacitated by a sore right thumb from using the spear he did not shun danger, and passed unhurt through the midst of the enemy ; his efforts, however, only illustrated the venerable adage : "Defend me from my friends." I turned to cut him down : he cried out in alarm ; the well-known voice caused an instant's hesitation : at that moment a spearman stepped forward, left his javelin in my mouth, and retired before he could be punished. Escaping, as by a miracle, I sought some support ; many of our Somal and servants lurking in the darkness offered to advance, but "tailed off" to a man as we approached the foe. Presently the Bályuz reappeared, and led me towards the place where he believed my three comrades had taken refuge. I followed him, sending the only man that showed presence of mind to bring back the Aynterad craft from the Spit into the centre of the harbour.* Again losing the Bályuz in the darkness I spent the interval before dawn wandering in search of my comrades, with my jaws and palate still spitted through by the spear, and lying down when overpowered with faintness and pain. As the day broke, with my remaining strength I reached the head of the creek, was carried into the vessel, and persuaded the crew to arm themselves and visit the scene of our disaster.'

Little more remains to be told. Lieut. Herne escaped uninjured, save for some stiff blows with the war-club. Lieut. Speke was less fortunate. His revolver failed him, and he was knocked down, searched and pinioned, but his captors were strangely merciful, one of them actually tying

---

* At this season native craft quitting Berberah make for the Spit late in the evening, cast anchor there and set sail with the land breeze before dawn. Our lives hung upon a thread Had the vessel departed as she intended the night before the attack, nothing could have saved us from destruction.—BURTON.

his hands in front at his request, and bringing water to
relieve the thirst caused by his first injury—a terrific blow
in the chest. Extricating his hands after a time he was
assailed by a murderous wretch, who made the most determined efforts to stab him, all unarmed as he was. How he
managed to escape the score of missiles hurled at him he
would probably have been puzzled to say, but he was
fortunate enough to get away in spite of eleven severe flesh
wounds, two of which completely pierced his thighs. He
not merely got away, but walked and ran a distance of
at least three miles. Fortunately he fell in with the
party sent in search of him, and was helped on board
by them. The corpse of Lieut. Stroyan, badly mutilated,
was brought on board, the survivors intending to carry it
to Aden. Decomposition set in so rapidly, however, that it
was committed to the sea on the 20th of April, Lieut.
Herne reading the funeral service. Two days later Burton
and his two surviving companions reached Aden, bringing
with them the shattered wrecks of the outfit with which
they had set out on the 7th.

The sequel to this remarkable Expedition was sufficiently
singular. Under the auspices of the Royal Geographical
Society, Burton went out in the autumn of 1856 on the
famous journey in which he took Speke as his second in
command, and which added in so remarkable a manner to
our geographical knowledge. On his way to Zanzibar from
Bombay he put into Aden, and discovered, to his surprise
and disgust, that the blockade of the Somali coast, consequent upon the destruction of his Expedition, had been
raised without any compensation for the losses which he
had sustained having been exacted. He accordingly
addressed a letter to the Secretary of the Royal Geographical Society, dated " H.E.I.C. sloop-of-war, *Elphinstone*,
15th of December, 1856," in which he pointed out that this
step was politically a mistake ; that in the case of the

Mary Ann brig, which was plundered near Berberah, in
1825, due compensation had been demanded and obtained,
and that the knowledge that such compensation would be
required in case of injury to a British subject was the only
protection strangers had. He was imprudent enough to
say a few plain truths in a plain way. He spoke, for
example, of the defenceless state of Berberah as inviting
the presence of the English, and of its eligibility for occupation, and the desirability of such occupation as a check
upon ambitious projects in the Red Sea. 'The Suez
Canal,' he said, 'may be said to have commenced. It
appears impossible that the work should pay in a commercial sense. Politically it may, if at least its object be,
as announced by the Count d'Escayrac de Lauture, at the
Société de Géographie, to throw open the road of India to
the Mediterranean and coasting trade, to democratize
commerce and navigation.' The first effect of the highway would be, as that learned traveller justly remarks, to
open a passage through Egypt to the speronari and
feluccas of the Levant, the light infantry of a more regular
force. Burton further went on to suggest the great desirability of strengthening the naval force at Aden for the
protection of British subjects in the neighbouring ports,
and in view of the importance of the Jeddah trade.
Referring to the reports of Captain Frushard, I.N., 'an
old and experienced officer . . . who had made himself
instrumental in quelling certain recent attempts upon
Turkish supremacy in Western Arabia,' he showed that
in the winter of 1856 thirty-five ships of English build,
nearly all carrying British colours, and supposed to be protected by a British register, had arrived and left Jeddah,
and that the imports to that place were valued at £160,000,
and the exports to £120,000, to which sums at least one-
third should be added ; 'as,' says Burton, 'speculation
abounds, and books are kept by triple entry in the Holy

Land.' He further remarked upon the importance of the trade of Hodaydah as calling for increased protection, and wound up his remonstrance concerning the shamefully reduced naval force in the Red Sea and the Indian Ocean, by pointing out the utter inadequacy of the two sailing-craft owned by the Bombay Government for the prevention of the slave-trade. He proposed, therefore, the addition of two screw-steamers small enough to enter every harbour and to work steadily amongst the banks on either shore, but large enough to be made useful in conveying English political officers of rank and Native princes when necessary. By means of these two steamers, and with an allowance for interpreters, and a slave approver in each harbour, Burton hoped that the trade in the Red Sea would soon receive its death-blow, and Eastern Africa its regeneration at our hands.

Burton's communication was forwarded in due course to the Bombay Government, and, on the 23rd of July, 1857, its answer was despatched :—

"Sir,—With reference to your letter, dated 15th December, 1856, to the address of the Secretary of the Royal Geographical Society of London, communicating your views on affairs in the Red Sea, and commenting on the political measures of the Government of India, I am directed by the Right Honourable the Governor in Council to state, your want of discretion and due respect for the authorities to whom you are subordinate, has been regarded with displeasure by the Government.

"I have the honour, &c.,

"H. L. ANDERSON, Secretary to Government."

This charming specimen of the snub-official was forwarded to Burton in due course, and reached him at Unyanyembe on the 6th of December, 1858. Burton, not unnaturally, felt the slight most keenly. 'I had,' he says, 'perhaps been Quixotic enough to attempt a suggestion that, though the Mediterranean is fast becoming a French lake,* by timely measures the Red Sea may be prevented from being con-verted into a Franco-Russo-Austrian lake. But an English-man in these days must be proud, very proud of his nation, and withal somewhat regretful that he was not born of some mighty mother of men—such as Russia and America —who has not become old and careless enough to leave her bairns unprotected, or cold and crusty enough to reward a little word of wisdom from her babes and sucklings with a scolding or a buffet.'

The " wigging " was not, however, without its alleviation, though Burton would have been thankful had it taken another form. With the despatch came a copy of a Bombay newspaper conveying intelligence of the massacre of nearly all the Christians at Jeddah, among the victims' being the British Consul, Mr. Page, and the French Consul and his wife. The news excited the greatest apprehension at Suez that the Arab population might attempt a repe-tition of the massacre, and on the application of the Vice-Consul 500 Turkish soldiers were landed to keep the peace.

Unjust and cruel though the rebuff was, Burton accepted it, and in a "service letter" expressed his regret that his communication should have contained any passages offen-sive to the powers that be. He also reminded the Secretary to the Government that he had received no reply to his letter sent from Zanzibar urging the claims of himself and his companions upon the Somal for the plunder of their property. The reply was a flat refusal. The late Governor-General had said, that, " Having regard to the conduct of the Expedition, his Lordship cannot think that the officers who composed it have any just claims on the Government

* This, it must be remembered, was written in 1855.

for their personal losses." This from Lord Dalhousie, the spoliator of Oude, is certainly rather—well courageous. The Expedition had failed, as has already been shown, because, for political reasons, it was found necessary to withdraw the gunboat as soon as Burton and his companions had landed. Once on the road there would have been comparatively little difficulty or danger, but a stay in the neighbourhood of Berberah during the time of the spring fair was exceedingly dangerous, though, no doubt, absolutely necessary, and the withdrawal of the gunboat multiplied the danger tenfold. It was, however, necessary to find a scapegoat, and Burton, being the most convenient, was chosen, instead of Colonel Coghlan, then Resident at Aden, and his Assistant, Captain (now Sir Lambert) Playfair.

CHAPTER V.

WITH BEATSON'S HORSE.

[FROM BURTON'S OWN MANUSCRIPTS.]

The Crimean War—Its causes—England and France—Burton in England—To Constantinople—Balaclava—Lord Raglan—Lord Cardigan and the charge of the Light Brigade—General Simpson —A welcome at Constantinople—Alison, Lord Strangford and General Mansfield—" The Great Eltchi "—General Beatson— The Bashi Buzouks—The staff of the Irregular Cavalry—Intrigues against Beatson—Mr. Vice-Consul Calvert—Furious dispatches —Spies in the camp— False reports — The operations before Sebastopol—An offer to relieve Kars—Why it was rejected, and why Lord Stratford was not impeached — Proposal to visit Schamyl—The Franco-Russian peace—Break up of the Irregular force—Beatson and Burton resign their commissions—The Sequel.

THE Crimean war is an affair of the last generation ; thirty years' distance has given it a certain perspective and assigned its proper rank and place in the panorama of the nineteenth century. Estimates of its importance of course vary ; while one man would vindicate its *péripeties* on the plea of being the first genuine attempt to develop the European concert, to create an international tribunal for the discouragement of the modern revival of *la force prime le droit*, and for the protection of the weak minority ; others, like myself, look upon it as an unmitigated evil to England. It showed up all her characteristic unreadiness, all her defects of organisation. It proved that she could not at that time produce a single great sailor or soldier. It washed her dirty linen in public to the disgust and contempt of Europe ; and, lastly, it taught her the wholly novel and unpleasant lesson of " playing second fiddle " (as the phrase is) to France. Considered with regard to her foreign affairs, this disastrous blunder lost us for ever the alliance of Russia, our oldest and often our only ally amongst the Continentals of Europe. It barred the inevitable growth of the "Northern Colossus" in a southern direction, and encouraged the mighty spread to the southeast, Indiawards, at the same time doubling her extent by the absorption of Turcomania.

The causes which led to the war are manifest enough. Some are trivial, like the indiscreet revelation of Czar Nicholas' private talk anent the "sick man," by the undiplomatic indiscretion of the diplomatist Sir Hamilton Seymour. Others are vital, especially the weariness caused by a long sleep of peace which made England, at once the most unmilitary and the most fighting of peoples, "spoil for a row." The belief in the wretched Turk's power of recuperation and even of progress had been diffused by such authorities as Lords Palmerston and Stratford de Redcliffe ; and *en route* to the campaign I often heard, to my disgust, British officers exclaim, "If there ever be a justifiable war (in support of the unspeakable Turk !) it is this !" Outside England the main moving cause was our acute ally, Louis Napoleon, whose ambition was to figure in the field arm-in-arm with the nation which annihilated his uncle. But he modestly proposed that France should supply the army, England the navy, an arrangement against which even now little could be said. Here, however, our jaunty statesman stepped in ; Cupidon (Lord Palmerston), the man with the straw in his mouth, the persistent "chaffer" of wiser men that appreciated the importance of the Fenian movement, the opposer of the Suez Canal,* the minister who died one

* Here, however, " Pam." was in the right. He foresaw that if the Canal was made, England would cling to Egypt and never again have a Crimean war. He also appreciated the vast injury which

day and was clean forgotten on the next, refused to
give up the wreath of glory ; and, upon the principle
that one Englishman can fight three Frenchmen, sent an
utterly inadequate force, and enabled the French to "revenge Waterloo." French diplomatists were heavily backed
against English ; a nervous desire to preserve the *entente
cordiale* made English generals and admirals (as at Alma
and the bombardment of Sebastopol) put up with the
jockeying and bullying measures of French officers. And
the alliance ended not an hour too soon. After French
successes and our failures, the *piou-piou* would cry aloud,
" Malakoff; yes, yes. Redan ; no, no ;" whereto Tommy
Atkins replied with a growl, "Waterloo ; you beggars ! "
And the English medal distributed to the *troupier* was
pleasantly known as the " Médaille de Sauvetage." At
the end of the disastrous year, 1855, England had come
up smiling after many a knock-down blow, and was ready
to go in and win. But Louis Napoleon had obtained all he
wanted; the war was becoming irksome to his fickle lieges;
so an untimely peace was patched up, and England was left
to pay the piper by the ever-increasing danger to India.

After the disastrous skirmish with the Somali at Berberah, it is no wonder if I returned to England on sick
certificate, wounded and sorely discomfited. The Crimean
War seemed to me some opportunity of recovering my
spirits, and as soon as health permitted I applied myself to
the ungrateful task of volunteering. London was then
in the liveliest state of excitement about the Crimean

would accrue to our Eastern monopoly. But he never could do
anything *sérieusement*, and he would humbug his countrymen with
such phrases as a "ditch in the sand." He knew as well as any man
that the project was feasible, and yet he persuaded Admiral Spratt
and poor Robert Stephenson to join in his little dodge. I lost his
favour for ever by advocating the Canal, and by proposing to assist
the Fenians to emigrate at the expense of that fatal humbug, the
" coffin squadron," on the West Coast of Africa.

X 2

bungles, and the ladies pitilessly cut every officer who shirked his duty. So I read my paper about Harar before the Royal Geographical Society, and had the pleasure of being assured by an ancient gentlemen, who had never smelt Africa, that when approaching the town I had crossed a large and rapid river. It was vain for me to reject this information ; every one seemed to think that he must be in the right.

Having obtained a few letters of introduction, and remembering that I had served under General James Simpson at Sakhar in Sind, I farewelled my friends, and my next step was to hurry through France and to embark at Marseille on board one of the Messageries Impériales bound for Constantinople. Very imperial was the demeanour of her officers ; they took command of the passengers in most absolute style ; and severely wigged an English colonel for opening a port and shipping a sea. I was ashamed of my countryman's tameness, and yet I knew him to be a brave man. The ship's surgeon was Dr. Nicóra, who afterwards became a friend of ours at Damascus, where he died attached to the French Sanitary establishment. He talked much, and could not control his Anglophobia and hatred of the English. The only pleasant Frenchman on board was General MacMahon, then fresh from his Algerian Campaign, and newly transferred to the Crimea, where his fortunes began.

It was a spring voyage over summer seas, and in due time we stared at the Golden Horn, and lodged ourselves at Missiri's hotel. The owner, who had been a dragoman to Eöthen, presumed upon his reputation, and made his house unpleasant : his wine, called " Tenedos," was atrocious ; his cooking third-rate, and his prices first-rate. He sternly forbade "gambling," as he called card- playing, in his rooms, private as well as public ; and we had periodically to kick downstairs his impudent dragomans who brought us his insolent messages. However, he had some excuse. Society at Missiri's was decidedly mixed : "baháduring" was the rule, and the extra military swagger of the juveniles, assistant-surgeons, commissariats, and such genus, booted to the crupper, was a caution to veterans.

At Stamboul I met Fred. Wingfield, who was bound to Balaclava, as assistant under unfortunate Mr. Commissary-General Filder, and had to congratulate myself upon my good fortune. We steamed together over the unhospitable Euxine, which showed me the reason for its sombre name : the waters are in parts abnormally sweet, and they appeared veiled in a dark vapour, utterly unknown the blues, amethyst and turquoise, of that sea of beauty, the Mediterranean ; the same is the case with the smaller Palus Mæotis—Azoff. After the normal three days we sighted the Tauric Chersonese, the land of the Cimmerians and Scythians, the colony of the Greeks, the conquest of Janghiz and the Khans of Turkey, and finally annexed by Russia after the wars in which Charles XII. had taught the Slav to fight. We then made Balaclava (Balik-liva, Fish town) ; with its dwarf Fjord dug out of dove-coloured limestones, and forming a little port stuffed to repletion with every manner of craft. But it had greatly improved since October 17, 1854, when we first occupied it and formally opened the absurdly so-called siege, in which we were as often the besieged as the besiegers. Under a prodigiously fierce-looking provost-marshal, whose every look meant "cat," some cleanliness and discipline had been introduced amongst the suttlers and scoundrels who populated the townlet. Store ships no longer crept in, reported cargoes which were worth their weight of gold to miserables living

"On coffee raw and potted cat,"

and crept out again without breaking bulk. A decent

road had been run through Kadikeui (Cazi's village) to camp and to the front, and men no longer sank ankle deep in dust, or calf deep in mud. In fact, England was, in the parlance of the ring, getting her second wind, and was settling down to her work.

The unfortunate Lord Raglan, with his *courage antique*, his old-fashioned excess of courtesy, and his nervous dread of prejudicing the *entente cordiale* between England and France, had lately died. He was in one point exactly the man *not* wanted. At his age, and with one arm and many infirmities, he could not come up to the idea of Sir Charles Napier's model officer under similar circumstances— "eternally on horseback, with a sword in his hand, eating, drinking, and sleeping in the saddle." But with more energy and fitness for command, he might have deputed others to take his place. A good ordinary man, placed by the folly of his aristocratic friends in extraordinary circumstances, he was fated temporarily to ruin the prestige of England. He began by allowing himself to be ignobly tricked by that shallow intriguer Maréchal de Saint Arnaud, *alias* Leroy. At Alma he was persuaded to take the worst and the most perilous position ; his delicacy in not disturbing the last hours of his fellow Commander-in-Chief prevented his capturing the northern forts of Sebastopol, which Todleben openly declared were to be stormed by a *coup de main ;* and he allowed Louis Napoleon in the *Moniteur* to blame only England for the laches of the French. After the "last of European battles fought on the old lines," at Inkerman, where the Guards defended themselves like prehistoric men, with stones, Lord Raglan suffered his whole army to be surprised by the Russians, and to be saved by General Bosquet, with a host of Zouaves, Chasseurs, and Algerian Rifles. No wonder that a Russian General declared, "the French saved the English at Inkerman as the Prussians did at Waterloo, and Europe believed that France would conquer both Russia and England, the first by arms and the second by contrast." The "thin red line" of Balaclava allowed some national Chauvinism, but that was all to be said in its favour, except that the gallantry of the men was to be equalled only by the incompetency of their chiefs.

I passed a week with Wingfield and other friends in and about Balaclava, paying frequent visits to the front and camp. A favourite excursion from the latter was to the monastery of St. George, classic ground, where Iphigenia was saved from sacrifice. There was a noble view from this place, a foreground of goodly garden, a deep ravine clad with glorious trees, a system of cliffs and needles studding a sunny beach, and a lively stretch of sparkling sea. No wonder that it had been chosen by a hermit, whose little hut of unhewn rocks lay hard by : he was a man upwards of sixty, apparently unknown to any one, and was fed by the black-robed monks· At Kadikeui also I made acquaintance with good Mrs. Seacole, who did so much for the comfort of the invalids, and whom we afterwards met with lively pleasure at Panama.

The British cavalry officers in the Crimea were still violently excited by reports that Lord Cardigan was about returning to command. And after a long experience of different opinions on the spot, I came to the following conclusion. The unhappy charge of the "Six Hundred" was directly caused by my old acquaintance Captain Nolan, of the 15th Hussars. An admirable officer and swordsman, bred in the gallant Austrian cavalry of that day, he held and advocated through life the theory that mounted troops were an over-match for infantry, and wanted only good leading to break squares, and so forth. He was burning also to see the Lights outrival the Heavies, who, under General Scarlett had charged down upon Russians said to be four times their number. Lord Lucan received an order to take, from General Liprandi, a Russian 12-gun battery on the Cause-way Heights, and he sent a *verbal* message by Nolan, then General Airey's aide-de-camp, to his brother-in-law Lord Cardigan, there being bad blood between the two. Nolan, who was no friend to the Hero of the Black Bottle, delivered this order disagreeably, and when Lord Cardigan showed some hesitation, roughly cut short the colloquy with "You have your commands, my Lord!" and pre-pared, as is the custom, to join in the charge. Hardly had it begun than he was struck by a shot in the breast ; and as he did not fall at once, some one asked Lord Cardigan where he was, and the reply came, "I saw him go off howling to the rear!" During the fatal charge Lord Cardigan lost his head, and had that *moment de peur* to which the best soldiers are at times subject : he had been a fire-eater with the saw-handles, and his world expected too much of him. Again, a man of ordinary pluck, he was placed in extraordinary circumstances ; and how few there are who are born physically fearless : I can count those known to me on the fingers of my right hand. Believing that his force was literally mown down, he forgot his duty as a commanding officer, and, instead of rallying the fugitives, he thought only of a *sauve qui peut*. Galloping wildly to the rear, he rushed up to many a spectator ; amongst others to my old Commander General Beatson, nervously exclaiming, "You saw me at the guns?" and almost without awaiting a reply, rode on. Presently returning to England, he had not the sound sense and good taste to keep himself in the background, but received a kind of "ovation," as they call it, the ladies trying to pluck hairs from his charger's tail by way of keepsakes. Of course he never showed face again in the Crimea. The tale of this ill-fated and unprofessional charge has now changed complexion. It is held up as a *beau fait d'armes*, despite the best bit of military criticism that ever fell from soldier's lips : " *C'est beau, mais ce n'est pas la guerre*," the words of General Bosquet, who saved the poor remnants of the Lights.

At head-quarters I called upon the Commander-in-Chief, General Simpson, whom years before I had found in charge of Sakhar, Upper Sind, held by all as well-nigh superannuated. He was supposed to be one of Lever's heroes, the gigantic Englishman who during the occupation of Paris broke the jaw of the duelling French officer and spat down his throat. But age had told upon him mentally as well as bodily, and he became a mere plaything in the hands of the French, especially of General Pélissier, the typical Algerian officer, who well knew when to browbeat and when to cajole. " Jimmy Simpson," as the poor old incapable was called, would do nothing for me, so I wrote officially at once to General Beatson, whom I had met at Boulogne, volunteering for the irregular cavalry, then known as " Beatson's Horse ; " and I was delighted when my name appeared in orders.

Returning to Constantinople, I called upon the Embassy then in summer quarters at Therapia, where they had spent an anxious time. The gallant Vukatos, Russianised in Boutakoff, a Greek, who in the nineteenth century belonged to the heroic days of Thermopylæ and Marathon, and who was actually cheered by his enemies, with the little merchant brig the *Vladimir*, alias Arciduca Giovanni, had shown himself a master-breaker of blockades, and might readily have taken into his head to pay the Ambassador a visit. I looked forward to a welcome, and found one. A man who had married my aunt, Robert Bagshaw, of Dovercourt, M.P., and quondam Calcutta merchant, had saved from impending bankruptcy the house of Alexander and Co., to which Lady Stratford belonged.

Nothing quainter than the contrast between that highly respectable middle-class British peer and the extreme wildness of his surroundings. There were but two exceptions to the general rule of eccentricity ; one Lord Napier and Ettrick, with his charming wife, and the other Odo (popularly called O'don't !) Russell, who died as Lord Ampthill, Ambassador to Berlin. It was by-the-bye no bad idea to appoint this high-bred and average-talented English gentleman to the Court of Prince Bismarck, who disliked and despised nothing more thoroughly than the pert little political, the " Foreign Office pet" of modern days. Foremost on the roll stood Alison, who died Minister at Teheran. He was in character much more a Greek than an Englishman, with a peculiar *finesse*, not to put too fine a point upon it, which made him highly qualified to deal with a certain type of Orientals. He knew Romaic perfectly, Turkish well, Persian a little, and a smattering of Arabic ; so that most unlike the average order of ignorant secretaries and unalphabetic attachés, he was able to do good work. He seemed to affect eccentricity, went out walking in a rough coat, with a stick torn from a tree, whence his cognomen the " Bear with the ragged staff" ; and at his breakfasts visitors were unpleasantly astonished by a weight suddenly mounting their shoulders in the shape of a bear-cub with white teeth and ugly claws. Alison managed to hold his own with his testy and rageous old chief, and the following legend was told of him : "Damn your eyes, Mr. Alison, why was not that despatch sent ? " " Damn your Excellency's eyes, it went this morning." Miladi also seemed to regard his comical figure with much favour. At Teheran he did little good, having become unhappily addicted to "tossing the elbow," which in an evil hour was reported home by my late friend Edward Eastwick ; and he married a wealthy Levantine widow, who pre-deceased him : on this occasion he behaved uncommonly well by returning her large fortune to her family. Next to him in office, and far higher in public esteem, ranked Percy Smythe, who succeeded his brother as Lord Strangford. Always of the weakest possible constitution, and so purblind, that when reading he drew the paper across his nose, he fulfilled my idea of the typical linguist in the highest sense of the word ; in fact, I never saw his equal, except perhaps Professor Palmer, who was murdered by Arábi's orders almost within sight of Suez. He seemed to take in a language through every pore, and to have time for all its niceties and eccentricities : for instance, he could speak Persian like a Shirází, and also with the hideous drawl of a Hindostani. Yet his health sent him to bed every night immediately after dinner. He dressed in the " seediest " of black frock-coats, and was once mightily offended by a Turkish officer, who, over-hearing us talking in Persian about " Tasáwwuf " (Sufyism), joined in the conversation. He treated me with regard because I was in uniform, but looked upon Smythe with such contempt that the latter exclaimed, " Hang the fellow ! can't he see that I'm a gentleman ? " Some years afterwards, when he came to the title, he married Emily Beaufort, whose acquaintance he made through reviewing her book, ' Syrian Shrines,' &c., and who was like him in body and mind. When she was a little tot of twelve, I saw her at the head of her father's, the Hydrographer's, table, laying down the law on professional matters to grey-headed admirals. The last of the staff was General Mansfield, who held General Beatson in especial dislike, for " prostitution of military rank." I have the most unpleasant remembrance of him ; he afterwards became Commander-in-Chief of the army in India.

The Ambassador, whose name was at that time in every mouth, was as remarkable in appearance as in character and career. When near sixty years of age he had still the clear-cut features and handsome face of his cousin, whom he loved to call the "great Canning," and under whom he, like Lord Palmerston, had begun official life as private secretary. One of the cleanest and smoothest shaven of old men, he had a complexion white and red, and his silver locks gave him a venerable and pleasing appearance, whilst his chin, that most characteristic feature, showed in repose manliness, and his "Kaiser-blue" eye was that of the traditional Madonna. Only at excited moments the former tilted up with an expression of reckless obstinacy, and the latter flashed fire like an enraged feline's. The everyday look of the face was diplomatic, an icy impassibility (evidently put on and made natural by long habit); but it changed to the scowl of a Medusa in fits of rage ; and in joyous hours, such as sitting at dinner near the beautiful Lady George Paget—whose like I never saw—it was harmonious and genial as a day in spring. Such was the personal appearance of the man who, together with the Emperor Nicholas, one equally if not more remarkable both in body and in mind, set the whole western world in a blaze. I heard the origin of the blood-feud minutely told by the late Lord Clanricarde, one of the most charming *raconteurs* and original conversationalists ever met at a London dinner-table. Mr. Stratford Canning became in early manhood Chargé d'Affaires at Constantinople, and took a prominent part in the Treaty of Bucharest, which the Czar found, to speak mildly, unpalatable. Hence, some years after, when the Embassy at St. Petersburg fell vacant, the Emperor refused to receive this *persona ingrata*, and aroused susceptibilities, which engendered a life-long hatred and a lust for revenge. Lastly, after the affair of 1848, the "Eltchi" persuaded his unhappy tool, the feeble-minded sultan, Abd-el-Majid, whom he scolded and abused like a naughty schoolboy, now by threats, then by promises, to refuse giving up the far-famed Hungarian refugees. This again became well known to all the world, and thus a private and personal pique between two elderly gentlemen of high degree involved half Europe in a hideous war, and was one of the worst disasters ever known to English history, by showing the world how England could truckle to France, and allow her to play the leading part.

Lord Stratford had, as often happens to shrewder men, completely mistaken his vocation. He told me more than once that his inclinations were wholly to the life of a *littérateur*, and he showed himself unfit for taking any save the humblest *rôle* among the third-rates. He had lived his life in the East, without learning a word of Turkish, Persian, or Arabic. He wrote "poetry," and, amid the jeers of his staff, he affixed to a rustic seat near Therapia, where Lady Stratford had once sat, a copy of verses beginning—

"A wife, a mother to her children dear,"

with rhyme "rested here" and reason to match. After his final return home, he printed a little volume of antiquated "verse or worse" with all the mediocrity which the gods and the columns disallow, and which would hardly have found admittance to the Poet's corner of a country paper. His last performance in this line was a booklet entitled, "Why I am a Christian?" (he, of all men!) which produced a shout of laughter amongst his friends. They vowed that he was mentally, a fair modern Achilles

"Impiger, iracundus, inexorabilis, acer;"

but of his "Christianity," the popular saying was "he is a Christian and he never forgives." His characteristic was vindictiveness: he could not forget (and here he was right), but also he could not forgive (and here he was wrong). One instance, he tried to hunt out of the service, Grenville Murray whose 'Roving Englishman' probably owed much

of its charm to Dickens' staff on 'Household Words.'
Yet Murray, despite all his faults, was a capable man, and
a government more elastic and far-seeing, and less "respectable" than that of England, would have greatly profited
by his services. Lord Stratford could not endure badinage,
he had no sense of humour; witness the scene between
him and Louis Napoleon's ambassador, General Baraguay
d'Hilliers, recorded by Mr. Consul Skene in his 'Personal
Reminiscences.' He abhorred difference of opinion, and
was furious with me for assuring him that "Habash" and
"Abyssinia" are by no means equivalent and synonymous
terms; he had been enlightening the Porte with information that Turkey had never held a foot of ground in
Habash where the Turk, as my visit to Harar showed,
had been an occupant, well hated as he was well known.
And when in a rage, he was not pleasant; his eyes
flashed fury, his venerable locks seemed to rise like the
quills of a fretful porcupine, he would rush round the
room like a lean maniac, using frightful language, in fact
"landgwidge" as the sailor hath it, with his old dressing-
gown working hard to keep pace with him; and when
the fit was at its worst he would shake his fist in the
offender's face.

The famous Ambassador struck me as a weak stiff-
necked, and violent old man, whose strength physically
was in his obstinate chin, together with a "pursed up
mouth and beak in a pet;" and morally in an exaggerated
"respectability," iron-bound prejudices and profound self-
esteem. He had also a firm respect for rank, and the
divine right of kings, as witness his rage when the young
Naval Lieutenant, Prince of Leiningen was ordered by a
superior officer to "swab decks." He lived long enough to
repent the last step of his official life. After peace was
concluded a visit to the Crimea greatly disgusted him.
With a kind of bastard repentance, he quoted John Bright

WITH BEATSON'S HORSE.   319

and the Peace Party, in his sorrow at having brought about
a campaign, whose horrors contrasted so miserably with its
promised advantages. In the next Russo-Turkish war, he
remembered that some 10,000 English lives, and £80,000,000
had been sacrificed to humble Russia, whose genius and
heroism had raised her so high in the opinion of Europe,
only to serve the selfish ends of Louis Napoleon, to set up
Turkey, and the Sultan (Humpty-Dumpty who refused
to be set up), and to humour the grudges of two rancorous old men.   So he carefully preached non-inter-
vention to England.   He took his seat in the House
of Lords, but spoke little, and when he spoke mostly
broke down.   Of his literary failures I have already
spoken, yet this was the "Great Eltchi" of Eöthen, a
man who gained a prodigious name in Europe, chiefly
by living out of it.

After seeing all that was to be seen at Therapia
and Constantinople, I embarked on an Austrian Lloyd
steamer and ran down to the Dardanelles, then the head-
quarters of the Bashi-Buzouks. The little town shared in
the factitious importance of Gallipoli and other places
more or less useful during the war. It had two Pashas,
civil and military, with a large body of Nizám, or Regulars ;
whilst the hillsides to the north were dotted with the white
tents of the Irregulars. General Beatson had secured fair
quarters near the old windmills, and there had established
himself with his wife and daughters. I at once recognized
my old Boulogne friend, although slightly disguised by
uniform. He looked like a man of fifty-five, with bluff
face and burly figure, and probably grey hair became him
better than black. He always rode English chargers of
good blood, and altogether his presence was highly effective. There had been much silly laughing at Constantinople, especially amongst the grinning-idiot tribe, about his
gold coat, which was said to stand upright by force of

embroidery. But here he was perfectly right and his
critics perfectly wrong. He had learnt, by many years'
service, to recognize the importance of show and splendour
when dealing with Easterns ; and no one had criticised the
splendid Skinner or General Jacob, of the Sind Horse, for
wearing a silver helmet and diamond-studded sabre-tasche.
General Beatson had served thirty-five years in the Bengal
Army, and was one of the few amongst his contemporaries
who had campaigned in Europe during the long peace
which followed the long war. In his subaltern days he had
volunteered into the Spanish Legion under the command
of General Sir de Lacy Evans; and after some hard
fighting there he had returned to India, and had seen not
a few adventures. When the Crimean War broke out he
went to headquarters at once, and for the mere fun of the
thing joined in the Heavy Cavalry charge. In October,
1854, the Duke of Newcastle, then Minister of War, addressed him officially, directing him to organise a corps of
Bashi-Buzouks, not exceeding in number 4000, who were
to be independent of the Turkish Contingent, consisting of
25,000 regulars under General Vivian. So, unfortunately
for himself, he had made the Dardanelles his head-
quarters, and there he seemed to be settled with his
wife and family. Mrs. Beatson was a quiet-looking little
woman, who was reputed to rule her spouse with a rod of
iron in a velvet case, and the two daughters were charming
girls, who seemed to have been born on horseback, and
who delighted in setting their terriers at timid aides-de-
camp and teaching their skittish Turkish nags to lash out
at them when within kicking distance.

General Beatson at once introduced me to his staff and
officers, amongst whom I found some most companionable
comrades. There were two ex-Guardsmen, poor Charlie
Wemyss, who died in London years after, chronically impecunious, and Major Lennox Berkeley, who is still living.

Of the Home Army were Lieut.-Colonel Morgan, ex-
cavalry man, and Major Synge, and India had contributed
Brigadier-General De Renzie Brett, Hayman, Money,
Grierson and others. Sankey, whom I had known in
Egypt, and whose family I had met at Malta, had been
gazetted as Lieut.-Colonel. There was also poor Blakeley,
of the gun, who afterwards died so unhappily of yellow
fever at Chorillos, in Peru.

But there were unfortunately black sheep among the
number. Lieut.-Colonel Fardella had only the disadvantage of being a Sicilian, but Lieut.-Colonel Giraud, the
head interpreter, was a Smyrniote and a Levantine of the
very worst description ; and worse still, there was a Lieut.-
Colonel O'Reilly, whose antecedents and subsequents were
equally bad. He had begun as a lance-corporal in one of
Her Majesty's Regiments, which he had left under dis-
creditable circumstances. In the Bashi-Buzouks he joined
a faction against General Beatson, and when the war was
over he openly became a Mussulman, and entered the
Turkish service. He left the worst of reputations between
Constantinople and Marocco, and Englishmen had the best
reason to be ashamed of him. In subsequent years to
the Massacre of Damascus, the English Government had
chosen out Fuad Pasha, a witty, unscrupulous, and over-
clever Turk, and proposed him as permanent Governor-
General of the Holy Land, to govern in a semi-inde-
pendent position, like that of the Khedive of Egypt. No
choice could be worse, except that of the French, who
favoured, with even more ineptitude, by way of a rival
candidate, their Algerian Captive, the Emir Abd el Kadir,
one of the most high-minded, religious, and honourable of
men, who was utterly unfit to cope with Turkish roguery
and Syrian rascaldom. The project fell through, but till his
last day Fuad Pasha never lost sight of it, and kept up
putting in an appearance by causing perpetual troubles

amongst the Bedawin and the Druses. This man O'Reilly was one of his many tools, and, at last, when he had brought about, against the Turkish Government, an absurd revolt of naked Arabs upon the borders of the Hamáh Desert, he was taken prisoner and carried before Rashid Pasha, then the Governor-General, and in his supplications for pardon he had the meanness to kneel down and kiss the Turk's boot.

But worse still was the position of the affairs which met my eyes at Dardanelles. Everything had combined to crush our force of Irregulars. First there was the Greek faction, who, naturally hating the English and adoring the Russians, directed all their national genius to making the foreigners fail. Their example was followed by the Jews, many of them wealthy merchants at the Dardanelles, who in those days, before the Jüdenhetze, loved and believed in Russia, and had scanty confidence in England. The two Turkish Pashas were exceedingly displeased to see an *Imperium in imperio*, and did their best to breed disturbance between their Regulars and the English Irregulars. They were stirred up by the German engineers who were employed upon the fortifications of the Dardanelles, and these men strongly inoculated them with the idea that France and England aimed at nothing less than annexation ; hence the Pashas not only fomented every disturbance, but they even supplied our deserters with passports and safe conducts. The French played the usual friendly-foelike part. The envy, jealousy and malice of the *Gr-r-rande Nation* had been stirred to the very depths by the failure of their Algerian Général Yousouf in organising a corps of Irregulars, and they saw with displeasure and disgust that an Englishman was going to succeed. Accordingly, M. Battus, the wretched little French Consul for the Dardanelles, was directed to pack the local press at Constantinople (which was almost wholly in Gallic interests) with the falsest and foulest scandals. He had secured the services of the 'Journal de Constantinople,' which General Beatson had, with characteristic carelessness, neglected to square, and his cunningly concocted scandals found their way not only into the Parisian but even into the London Press.

But our deadliest enemies were of course those nearest home. Mr. Calvert was at that time Vice-Consul for the Dardanelles, and he openly boasted of its having been made by himself so good a thing that he would not exchange it for a Consulate-General. I need not enter into the subsequent course of this man, who, shortly after the Crimean War, found his way into a felon's jail at Malta for insuring a non-existing ship. He had proposed to General Beatson a contract in the name of a creature of his own who was a mere man of straw, and it was at once refused, because although Mr. Vice-Consul Calvert might have gained largely thereby, Her Majesty's Government would have lost in proportion. This was enough to make a bitter enemy of him and he was a manner of Levantine, virulent and unscrupulous as he was sharp-witted. He also had another grievance : in his consulate he kept a certain Lieutenant Ogilvy, who years afterwards fought most gallantly in the Franco-German war, and was looked upon after he was killed as a sort of small national hero. He and his agents were buying up cattle for the public use and it was a facetious saying amongst the " Buzoukers," as the Bashi-Buzouk officers were called, that they had not left a single three-legged animal in the land. It is no wonder that the reports of these men had a considerable effect upon Lord Stratford, who already was profoundly impressed with the opinions of unhappy Lord Raglan, the commander who by weak truckling to the French, a nettle fit only to be grasped, had more than once placed us in an unworthy position. He was angrily opposed to the whole scheme ; it was contrary to precedent ; Irregulars were unheard of at Waterloo and the idea was offensive because unknown to the good old stock-and-pipeclay school. But for a campaign these men are invaluable to act as eyes and feelers for a regular force. The English soldier unless he be a poacher—by the bye one of the best—cannot see by night ; his utter want of practice gives him a kind of noctilypia, and he suffers much from want of sleep. His Excellency already had his own grievance against General Beatson, being enormously scandalized by a letter from the Irregular officer casually proposing to hang the military Pasha of the Dardanelles if he continued to interfere and report falsely concerning his force. And I must confess the tone of my general's letters was peculiar, showing that he was better known to " Captain Sword " than to " Captain Pen." When he put me in orders as Chief of Staff, I overhauled his books and stood aghast to see the style of his official despatches. He was presently persuaded with some difficulty to let me mitigate their candour under the plea of copying, but on one occasion after the copy was ready, I happened to look into the envelope and I found :

" P.S.—This is official ; but I would have your lordship to know that I also wear a black coat."

Fancy the effect of a formal challenge to mortal combat, " pistols for two and coffee for one," upon the rancorous old man of Constantinople, whose anger burnt like a red-hot fire, and whose revenge was always at a white heat. I took it out, but my general did not thank me for it. The result of these scandalous rumours was that Lord Stratford deemed fit to send down the Dardanelles (for the purpose of reporting the facts of the case) a certain Mr. Skene.

I have no intention of entering into the conduct of this official, who had been an officer in the English army, and · who proposed to make himself comfortable in the Consulate of Aleppo. He has paid the debt of Nature, and I will not injure his memory. Suffice it to say that he was known on the spot to be taking notes, that every malignant won his ear, and that he did not cease to gratify the Ambassador's prejudices by reporting the worst.

General Beatson was peppery, like most old Indians, and instead of keeping diplomatically on terms with Mr. Skene he chose to have a violent personal quarrel with him. Consequently Mr. Skene returned to Constantinople, and his place was presently taken by Brigadier T. G. Neil, who appeared in the same capacity—note-taker. His offensive presence and bullying manner immediately brought on another quarrel, especially when he loudly declared that "he represented Royalty"; and he became a universal unfavourite with Beatson's Horse. He afterwards served in the Indian Mutiny, and there he ended well. He made an enormous reputation at home by recklessly daring to arrest a railway clerk, and he was shot before his incapacity could be discovered.

I was also struck with consternation at the state and condition of Beatson's Horse, better known on the spot as the "Báshi Buzouks," the correct term in Turkish is Básh Buzuk, equivalent to "Tête-pourrie," and it succeeded the ancient Dillis, or madmen, who in the good old days represented the Osmanli irregular cavalry. It was the habit of these men in early spring, when the fighting season opened, to engage themselves for a term to plunder and loot all they could (and at this process they were first-rate hands), and to return home when winter set in. General Beatson wisely determined that his 4000 sabres should be wholly unconnected with the 25,000 men of the Turkish contingent. He wished to raise them in Syria, Asia Minor, Bulgaria, and Albania, to regiment them according to their nationalities, and to officer them like sepoy regiments with Englishmen and subalterns of their own races. The idea was excellent ; but it was badly carried out, mainly by default of the War Office, who had overmuch to do, and would not be at the trouble of sending out officers. So the men, whose camps looked soldier-like enough, were left lying on the hill-sides, and Satan found a very fair amount of work for them. This was, however, chiefly confined to duelling and other such pastimes. The Arnauts or Albanians, who generally fought when they were drunk, had a peculiar style of monomachy. The principals, attended by their seconds and by all their friends, stood close opposite, each holding a cocked pistol in his right and a glass of raki or spirits of wine in his left hand. The first who drained his draught had the right to fire, and generally blazed away with fatal effect. It would have been useless to discourage their practice; but I insisted upon fair play. Although endless outrages were reported at Constantinople very few really took place; only one woman was insulted, and robbery, especially with violence, was exceptionally rare. In fact, the "Tête pourrie" contrasted most favourably with the unruly French detachments at Gallipoli and with the turbulent *infirmiers* of the Nagara Hospital. With the English invalids at the Abydos establishment no dispute ever arose.

The exaggerated mutinies were mere sky-larking. After a few days' grumbling, a knot of "rotten heads" would mount their nags with immense noise and clatter; and, loudly proclaiming that they could stand the dulness of life no longer, would ride away, hoping only to be soon caught. But the worst was that I could see no business doing; there were no morning roll-calls or evening parades, no drilling or disciplining of the men, and the General contented himself with riding twice a day through the camp and listening to many grievances. However, as soon as I was made Chief of the Staff, I persuaded him that this was not the thing, and induced him to establish all three, and to add thereto a riding school for sundry officers of infantry who were not over-firm in the saddle, and also to open a school of arms for the benefit of all—the last thing a British officer learns is to use his "silly" sword—and the consequence was that we soon had a fine body of well-trained sabres ready to do anything or to go anywhere. The *maître d'armes* was an Italian from Constantinople; he began characteristically by proposing to call out the little consul, M. Battus, whilst another proposed making love to Madame. Alas! it was too late.

On September the 12th, a gunboat dressed in all her colours steamed at full speed down the Dardanelles, and caused immense excitement in camp. The news flew like wildfire that Sebastopol had been captured : it proved, to say the least, premature, and the details filled every Englishman with disgust. I need not describe the grand storming of the Malakoff, which gave Pélissier his bâton de Maréchal, or the gallant carrying of the Little Redan by Bourbaki. But our failure at the Great Redan was simply an abomination. Poor old Jemmy Simpson was persuaded by Pélissier to play this second part, and to attack from the very same trench that sent forth the unsuccessful assault of June the 18th. About half the force required was dispatched, and these were mostly regiments which had before suffered severely ; and the bravest of them could only stand up to be shot down, instead of sneaking, as not a few did, in the trenches. Lastly, instead of leading them himself, the Commander-in-Chief sent General Wyndham, whose gasconnade about putting on his gloves under fire seems to be the only item of this disgraceful affair which appears known to and remembered by the British public. The result of our attack was simply a *sauve qui peut*, and *proh pudor!* the Piedmontese General Cialdini was obliged to order up one of his brigades to save the British. Continentals attributed this systematic paucity of our troops in the most urgent emergencies, either to inconsiderate

national parsimony or to overweening contempt for the
enemy. It was nothing of the kind ; it resulted from the
normal appointment of thoroughly incapable commanders.
The private soldier was perfectly right who volunteered
(before Lord Raglan) that he and his comrades were
ready to take Sebastopol by storm, under the command
of their own officers, if not interfered with by the Generals.

I now thought that I saw my way to a grand success,
and my failure was proportionately absurd. This was
nothing less than the relief of Kars, which was doomed
to fall by famine to the Russians. Pélissier and the Frenchmen were long-sighted enough to know the culminating
importance of this stronghold as a *pierre d'achoppement* in
the way of Russia, and possibly, or rather probably, they
had orders from home. However, they managed to keep
Omar Pasha and his Turkish troops in the Crimea, where
the large force was compelled to lie idle, instead of being
sent to attack the Trans-Caucasian provinces, in which
they might have done rare good service. So, when Omar
Pasha, on the 29th September, gloriously defeated the
Russians before the walls of Kars, his victory was useless,
and he was compelled to retire. Had the affair been
managed in another way, England might have struck a
vital blow at Russia, by driving her once more behind
the Caucasus, and by putting off for many a year the
threatened advance upon India, which is now one of our
cauchemars.

Meanwhile the reports concerning the siege of Kars,
whose gallant garrison was allowed to succumb to hunger,
cholera, and the enemy, was becoming a scandal. It was
reported that General Williams, who, with the Hungarian
General Kmety, was taking a prominent part in the
defence, addressed upwards of eighty officials to Lord
Stratford without receiving a single reply : in fact, Mr.
Skene's book shows that the great man only turned them

into ridicule. However, the "Eltchi" feared ultimate consequences, and wrote to Lieutenant-General (afterwards
Sir Robert J. Hussey) Vivian, to consult him concerning
despatching on such errand the Turkish contingent, consisting, as it may be remembered, of 25,000 Nizam or
regulars, commanded by a sufficiency of British officers.
The answer was that no carriage could be procured.
Lieutenant-General Vivian had seen some active service in
his youth, but he was best known as an Adjutant-General
of the Madras army—a man redolent of pipe-clay and
red tape, and servilely subject to the Ambassador. So
I felt that the game was in my hands, and proceeded in
glorious elation of spirits to submit my project for the
relief of Kars to His Excellency. We had 2640 sabres in
perfect readiness to march, and I could have procured
any quantity of carriage. The scene which resulted passes
description. It ended, however, with "Of course, you'll
dine with us to-day."

*　　　*　　　*　　　*

It was not until some months afterwards that I learnt
what my unhappy plan proposed to do. Kars was doomed
to fall, as a make-weight for the capture of half of Sebastopol, and a captain of Bashi Buzouks had madly attempted
to arrest the course of *la haute politique.*

The tale of the fall of Kars is pathetic enough. While
the British officers dined with General Mouravieff, the
gallant Turkish soldiers, when ordered to pile arms and
march off under escort, dashed their muskets to the ground,
and cried, "Perish our wretched Viziers, who have shamed
us with this shame." And the disastrous and dishonourable
result brought about by our political ineptitude has never
ceased to weaken our prestige in Central Asia. Civilised
Turks simply declared that an officer of artillery sent out
as Commissioner by England, had unwarrantably interfered with the legitimate command of Kars, where Turkey

had a powerful army, and an important position ; and that by keeping the soldiers behind walls when all knew the city could not be saved, he had lost both army and city. The criticism was fair and sound.

General, afterwards Sir W. F., Williams, of Kars, was at first in huge indignation, and declared that he would persuade the Government to impeach Lord Stratford. But on the way he was met by an offer of the command at Woolwich, which apparently made him hold his peace. He was somewhat an exceptional man. For years an instructor of the Turkish artillery, then English member of the Mixed Commission for the Topography of the Turco-Persian frontier, and finally Queen's Commissioner with the Turkish army at Kars, he had never learnt a word of Turkish. Of course he was hustled into the House of Commons—whenever a man makes himself known in England that is apparently his ultimate fate. But he fell flatly, even as Kars did, before the sharp tongue of Bernal Osborne. During some debate on the Chinese Question he had assured the House that he was an expert, because he had had much experience of Turkish matters, " Oh ! the fall of Kars," cried the wit, and the ex-Commissioner was extinguished for ever.

Lord Stratford, I suppose, by way of consoling me, made an indirect offer through Lord Napier and Ettrick about commissioning me to pay an official visit to Schamyl, whom some call " the Patriot," and others "the Bandit" of the Caucasus. The idea was excellent but somewhat surprised me. Schamyl had lately been accused, amongst other atrocious actions, of flogging Russian ladies whom he had taken prisoner, and I could not understand how Lord Stratford, who had an unmitigated horror of all Russian cruelties, and who always expressed it in the baldest terms, could ally himself with such a ruffian. Possibly the political advantages in his opinion counterbalanced the demerits ;

for had Schamyl been fairly supported, the Russian conquest of the Great Mountain might have been retarded for years. I consulted on the subject Alison and Percy Smythe, and both were of the same opinion, namely, that although there were difficulties and dangers, involving a long ride through Russian territory, the task might have been accomplished. They relied greatly upon the ardent patriotism of the Circassian women who then filled the great harems of Constantinople. I should not have seen a single face, except perhaps that of a slave girl, but I should have been warmly assisted with all the interest the fair patriots could make. So I began seriously to think of the matter; but the first visit to Lord Stratford put it entirely out of my head. I asked his Excellency what my reply was to be should Schamyl ask me upon what mission I had come. "Oh! say that you are sent to report to *me.*" "But, my Lord, Schamyl will expect money, arms, and possibly troops; and what am I to reply if he asks me about it? Otherwise he will infallibly set me down for a spy, and my chance of returning to Constantinople will be uncommonly small."

However, the "Eltchi" could not see it in that light, and the project fell through.

Here also, although somewhat out of place, I may relate my last chance of carrying out a project upon which I was very warm, namely, to assist Circassia and to attack Georgia.

On returning to London I received a hint that Lord Palmerston had still some project of the kind, and was willing that I should be employed on it. So I wrote a number of letters which I was allowed to publish in the *Times* upon the subject of levying a large force of Kurdish Irregular Cavalry; and these, being borrowed from the excellent work of Sir Henry Rawlinson, found favour with the public. But presently came the Franco-Russian peace of 1856. France, who had won all the credit of the mismanaged campaign because she washed her dirty linen at home and who had left all the discredit to England, whose practice was the opposite, lost all interest in the war. Louis Napoleon was thoroughly satisfied with what he had done, and Russia, after a most gallant and heroic defence of her territory, wanted time to heal her wounds. Accordingly the Treaty of Paris was signed, the result being that fifteen years afterwards, when France was in her sorest straits, Russia, with the consent of England, tore up that instrument and threw it in our face.

After this fruitless visit to Constantinople I returned post haste to the Dardanelles, where I found the Bashi Buzouks, like the unfortunate Turks at Kars, in a state of strait siege. On the morning of the 26th of September we were astounded to see the Turkish Regulars drawn out in array against us; infantry supported by the guns which were pointed at our camp, and patrols of cavalry occupying the rear. Three war steamers commanded the main entrance of the town, and the enemy's outposts were established within 300 yards of the First Regiment of Beatson's Horse, evidently for the purpose of ensuring a sanguinary affray. The inhabitants had closed their shops, and the British Consulate was deserted. The steamer *Redpole* was sent off in hottest haste to Constantinople with a report that a trifling squabble between the French *infirmiers* and the Bashi Buzouks had ended in deadly battle, and that most terrible consequences were likely to ensue.

General Beatson at once issued an order to his men, who were furious at this fresh insult, and requested permission to punish the aggressors by taking their guns; and by means of his officers he restrained the natural anger of his much-suffering soldiers. The result was a triumph of discipline, and not a shot was fired that day. About 4 P.M. the military Pasha, ashamed of his attitude, marched the Regulars back to their barracks, but he did not fail to complain to Constantinople of General Beatson's order keeping his men in camp "till the Turkish authorities should have recovered from their panic, and housed their guns." Meanwhile the *Redpole* had also carried from the English and the French Consuls an exaggerated account of the state of affairs and earnestly requesting reinforcements. The reply was an order from Lieut.-General Vivian removing General Beatson from command, and directing him to make it over to Major-General Richard Smith, who appeared at the Dardanelles on the 28th of September, supported by a fresh body of Nizam ; and, lest any insult might be omitted, 300 French soldiers had been landed at the Nagara Hospital to attack us in rear.

General Beatson was at the time suffering from an accident, and he was utterly unfitted for business. So Major Berkeley and I collected as many of the officers as we could at head-quarters, and proposed to go in a body to General Smith and lay the case before him. We assured him that all the reports were false, and proposed to show him the condition and the discipline of the Bashi Buzouks. We also suggested that Brigadier-General Brett might be directed to assume temporary command of the force until fresh instructions should be received from General Vivian. Of course General Smith could not comply with our request, so we both declared that we would send in our resignations : after an insult of the kind we felt that we could no longer serve with self-respect. It was this proceeding, I suppose, which afterwards gave rise to a report that I had done my best to cause a mutiny.

On the last day of September, General Beatson with his Chief of Staff and Military Secretary left the Dardanelles for ever. Arrived at Buyukdere a report was sent to Lieut.-General Vivian, and he presently came on board, when a lengthened communication passed between the generals. Rumours of a Russian attack had induced a most conciliatory tone. General Vivian appeared satisfied with the explanation and listened favourably to General Beatson's urgent request for permission to return at once to the Dardanelles. He asked expressly if the "Buzouker" could keep his men in order. The answer was a decided affirmative, which appeared to have considerable weight with him, and he expressed great regret for having, under a false impression, written an unfavourable letter to Lord Panmure—the tone of whose correspondence had been most offensive. He stated, however, that nothing could be done without the order of Her Majesty's Ambassador; and, promising to call upon him for instructions, he left the steamer about mid-day, declaring that he would return in the course of the afternoon. After a few hours, appeared, instead of General Vivian, a stiff official letter directed to General Beatson. The interview with Lord Stratford had completely altered the tenour of his official conduct.

On the 12th of September, General Beatson had reported officially to Lords Panmure and Stratford the efficient state of his force, concerning which General Smith had written most favourably. An equally favourable view was expressed in the public press by that prince of war correspondents, William Henry Russell, whose name in those days was quoted by every Englishman. General Beatson begged to be sent on service, offering upon his own responsibility to take up transports, and to embark his men for Eupatoria, Yenikali, Batoum, Balaclava, or —— that unhappy Kars. To this no reply was returned.

Nothing now remained to be done, and on the 18th of October we left Therapia *en route* to England. I now determined to follow none but the career of an explorer, a pathfinder; and in 1856 much remained to be done, especially in Central Africa. But every year the area of discovery shrinks ; and soon, very soon, only those places will be left unvisited which are either too fatal for common-sense to attempt, or too expensive for individuals to under-take. The reader must not confound the explorer, pure and simple, with the minors of the same profession. First we have the tourist, the globe-trotter, who runs about the earth either singly or in pairs or in packs, under Messrs. Cook, Gaze, and others. Secondly, there is Master Shoetie, the traveller proper, who mostly wanders the world with an especial object of his own ; and thirdly, the Discoverer who stands many degrees above the heads of his wandering fellows. The latter should be to the manner born and bred ; but I spare the reader a list of his requisites.

The sequel to this affair was sufficiently remarkable. General Beatson came home and attempted to take civil proceedings against his enemies. Chief amongst them was Mr. Skene—one of the Consuls already referred to—who from the inception of General Beatson's scheme had shown himself most bitterly opposed to it, and who had used all his influence to make General Beatson's position untenable. Mr. Skene had even said that, " when General Smith arrived at the Dardanelles, General Beatson assembled the commanding officers of the regiments and actually endeavoured to persuade them to make a mutiny in the regiments against General Smith, that two of these commanding officers then left the room, saying they were soldiers, and they could not listen to language which they thought most improper and mutinous, that these two were Lieut.-Colonels O'Reilly and Shirley, that General Beatson subsequently had a sort of Round Robin prepared by the chief interpreter, and sent round to the different officers in the hope that they would sign it, refusing to serve under any other general than himself, that both of these mutinous attempts are said to have originated from Mr. (*sic*) Burton, who it also appears kept the order from Lord Panmure, placing the Irregular Horse under Lieut.-General Vivian for three whole weeks, unknown to any one but General Beatson, and that the order was not promulgated until after General Smith had arrived." General Beatson went into the witness-box and categorically denied the charges made against him. Burton followed and gave evidence to the same effect, as did also General Watt ; but there was a great difficulty in proving the publication of the libel, the War Office, then represented by Mr. Sidney Herbert, refusing to produce certain letters. Mr. Skene was very ably defended by Mr. Bovill (afterwards Lord Chief Justice), Mr. Lush (afterwards a Judge), and Mr. Garth, and he brought forward a considerable number of witnesses including General Vivian himself. Their evidence, however, tended rather to establish the case against him, so that he was compelled to plead that his libel was a privileged communication. Mr. Baron Bramwell confined himself in his summing-up strictly to the legal aspects of the case, but he allowed his view of Mr. Skene's conduct to be very distinctly understood. The jury, a special one, after half an hour's deliberation, returned a verdict for the defendant on technical grounds, but added a rider to their verdict, expressive of their disgust at Mr. Skene's having refrained from retracting his charges against General Beatson, when he found how utterly without foundation they were. The verdict of the jury was confirmed on appeal, but it was generally felt that General Beatson had fully vindicated his character, and had very successfully exposed the conspiracy against the Irregulars, which had ended so disastrously for him and for his officers. The characters of the plaintiff and the defendant respectively may be estimated from one small circumstance. Beatson began his action just as the Indian Mutiny broke out, and being reasonably enough refused an extension of leave for the purpose of prosecuting it, went out to India. When the Mutiny was suppressed he obtained six months leave without pay, for the purpose of prosecuting his case. Mr. Skene had obtained the appointment cf Consul at Aleppo, and could have reached England in a fortnight, but he chose to remain at his Consulate, though there would have been no difficulty in obtaining leave of absence on full pay. Under such circumstances it was perhaps hardly worth while for his counsel to dwell upon the cruelty of pushing on this case in his absence—a complaint, for which the presiding judge somewhat emphatically declared, that there was not the smallest foundation.—ED.

CHAPTER VI.

ZANZIBAR—A TRIAL TRIP.

From Bombay to Zanzibar—The Tumbutus—Death of Sayyid Said—
State affairs—The Consular service—Native insolence—Hatred of
missionaries and German traders—Preparations for departure—
Said bin Salim—An Arab ship—Oriental delays—Pemba Island—
A change of weather—The Mombas Mission—M. Rebmann—A
complication—M. Rebmann does not go—Native quarrels—The
Coast tribes—Mombasah to Wazin—Pangna-ni—A native concert—
Ways and means—A jungle stream—A hospitable reception—The
jungle by night—Chogwe—A fresh start—An inland march—"An
original"—An imperfect equipment—Lost !—" Sultan Crocodile"
—Incidents of travel—Gossip—A thunderstorm in the tropics—A
mutiny—Use of the Beloch—Fugá—The Travellers' Bungalow—
The Sultan—The Elixir of life—The rains set in—Descent to the
Lowlands — A dreary day — Chogwe once more—A Behemoth
battue—Results of the trial trip—African fevers—Miserable nights
—The Batela at last—Preparations for the approaching journey—
An official plot.

IT need scarcely be said that Burton returned from his
abortive attempt at active service in the Crimea disgusted
with the present and hopeless as to his prospects of promotion. Under the circumstances it is not surprising that
his eyes turned longingly once more to Africa, where at
least he might hope for fewer jealousies and less red-tape.
He accordingly placed himself in communication with the
Royal Geographical Society, which at that time contemplated an expedition to the interior of Africa with the
object of discovering the sources of the grand old Nile,
and of opening up as fully as possible the resources of the
mighty continent, the heart of which no Englishman had

ever penetrated. His views were after due consideration
adopted, and in the autumn of 1856 he set out upon the
longest, the greatest, and, as the event proved, the most
disastrous of his journeys, one from which he reaped
naught save the disgust natural to a man who sees the
credit of his greatest achievement snatched from him
by a false friend. Another generation will do Burton
justice : up to the present time he has certainly failed
to obtain it. How the injustice was done will be told in
its proper place, and even at the risk of laying myself
open to the charge of speaking harshly of a dead man,
and raking up a long-forgotten scandal, I shall place
before the world, with all the perspicacity at my command,
the truth about the Burton and Speke controversy. In
the meanwhile, I have to tell the story, first of the trial
trip to the Zanzibar coast towns, with an excursion to the
mountain range, which lies some eighty miles inland, and
which in the course of another century or so will be the
sanatorium of Eastern Africa. Then will follow the expedition to Lake Tanganyika, which properly begins with
Burton's departure from England in September, 1856, and
ends with his landing at Southampton on his return on the
20th of May, 1859—two years and a half of such hardship,
toil, and suffering as have fallen to the lot of few.

The expedition originated in a proposal by M. Erhardt,
an energetic member of the unfortunate Mombas Mission, to
explore a vast inland sea, of which he had heard from the
natives as existing in the centre of Africa. M. Erhardt proposed to make the attempt with a modest outfit to cost
£300 ; but his information was so obviously untrustworthy,
and his qualifications were so very doubtful, that the Royal
Geographical Society declined to entertain the proposal.
Burton's scheme was a very different one. He desired to
organize " an expedition primarily for the purpose of
ascertaining the limits of the ' Sea of Ujiji or Unyamwezi

ZANZIBAR (FROM THE SEA), 1856.

Lake,' and secondarily to determine the exportable produce of the interior and the ethnography of its tribes "—
not so ambitious a scheme as those of his predecessors, but
one which was perhaps more likely to be crowned with
success. The Society approved the proposal, and made
application to the Foreign Office for a grant. Lord
Clarendon—perhaps the most enlightened member of his
party—was then, fortunately, Foreign Secretary, and he
agreed to a grant of £1000, which unfortunately proved
totally inadequate for the purposes of the expedition ; and
the Court of Directors of the East India Company, though
they could not be persuaded to contribute to the expenses,
gave Burton two years' leave of absence from regimental
duty to enable him to take command. He was further
directed to report himself to Lord Elphinstone at Bombay,
and to Lieut-Colonel Hamerton, H.B.M.'s Consul and
Political Agent at Zanzibar.

On the 2nd of December, 1856, therefore, Burton having
returned to Bombay for a short time after his unhappy
experiences with Beatson's Horse in the camp on the Bos-
phorus, and having obtained official permission for Lieut.
Speke to accompany him, sailed in the H. E. I. C.'s sloop
of war *Elphinstone*, Capt. Frushard, R.N., on a journey to
Zanzibar. The voyage was neither smooth nor eventful.
There was a stiff breeze followed by a high combing sea
and an occasional squall, but the wind was a 'soldiers'
wind from first to last, and the good old ship (she was in
her thirty-third year), making runs of from 150 to 200
knots a day, accomplished the 2500 miles between Bombay
and Zanzibar in eighteen days. On the afternoon of the
18th of December, she hove in sight of Pemba, or Jezirat
el-Khazrá, "the Emerald Isle," and on the same night
anchored off Tambutu, one of the long narrow coralline reefs
which fringe the East African coast. The people of this
region appeared to Burton to be a somewhat degraded race

of serviles who have preserved a great variety of heathen abominations. Thus for example they beat and insult the dead in every conceivable way, much after the fashion of the Arawak Indians of Guinea ; taunt the corpse with its forlorn state as compared with that of yesterday, and visit a kind of Trophonius' cave for purposes of divination. To make up for the vileness of man, nature seems to be exceptionally bountiful ; the breezes are as spice-laden as those of Ceylon, though, by the way, Europeans are very careful to exclude the perfume which the night breeze wafts from the island.

The travellers found that they had landed at an unfortunate moment. On arriving at Zanzibar the whole place was apparently in mourning. There were no Friday flags flying, and as they passed the guard ship *Shah Allum*, an old 50-gun ship, of Bombay build, no colours were hoisted, and the sailors shouted some information which none on board the *Elphinstone* could understand. When at last she had anchored in Front Bay, had fired her salute of 21 guns, and had been duly answered, it was time to land and to obtain an explanation of the mystery. The first visit paid was, of course, to H. B. M.'s Consul, Colonel Hamerton, who explained that H. H. Sultan Sayyid Said of Mascat had died on his way from Arabia to Zanzibar. 'State affairs,' adds Burton, 'had not been settled between the rival brothers, Sayyid Suwayni the eldest, and successor to whom Oman had been left and Sayyid Majid installed by his father Viceroy of the African possessions.' Majid had moreover had a severe attack of small-pox, and hesitated to show himself to the people, and the British resident being himself in ill-health, the island was in a state of confusion and anarchy, while the people of the Zanzibar mainland were suffering in addition from drought and famine. When to these facts are added the highly " Conservative " character of the European and

American merchants, the more than doubtful disposition of some of the missionaries, the natural suspiciousness of a people who find Europeans anxious to settle on their seaboard, and the interested jealousies of the Arabs who saw their craft in danger, no one will be surprised to discover that Burton found himself in a very awkward and difficult position. Had it not been for the support of Colonel Hamerton it would indeed have been almost impossible to move. This indefatigable officer, to whose commanding merits no sort of justice has been done, had succeeded in vindicating the British name and honour in Zanzibar. When first appointed Consul and Resident, both offices were at their lowest point of reputation. The white man was treated as an object of contempt. One American trader-Consul had been solemnly horsed upon a slave's back and "bakured" (whipped) in his own consular house, and under his own consular flag. A Sawáhíli would at any time enter a merchant's office, put his feet upon the table, call for the brandy and draw his knife if refused. Negro fishermen would anchor their craft close to a European window and climb the mast to enjoy the spectacle of the "Kafirs" feeding. Arabs jostled strangers in the streets, drove them from the centre and forced them to pass on the left hand. At night no one dared to carry a lantern, and a promenade in the dark drew down insults upon the unfortunate pedestrian, who was esteemed fortunate if he escaped grievous violence. Even the "mild Hindú" was insolent to a degree almost beyond precedent, and had it not been for the goodwill of the Sayyid Said, and the steady and courageous perseverance of Colonel Hamerton, life would soon have been altogether unbearable for white men in Zanzibar. The victory was not won without loss. When Burton reached the place on this occasion, at the end of 1856, he found Colonel Hamerton, at the age of fifty, with the constitution and appearance of a man of something over seventy, completely overwhelmed by his labours and the climate, to which he succumbed shortly afterwards.

In view of the projected exploration of the interior, on which Burton and his employers were bent, Colonel Hamerton had not the smallest hesitation in pledging his word, and even in swearing by the "Kalmat Ullah" (Koran) that the Expedition was wholly composed of British officers, that neither "Dutchmen," as the German traders are called, nor missionaries had anything to do with it, and that its objects, whatever else they might have been, had certainly nothing to do with trade, missionary enterprise or treason to the State.   Had the Consul hesitated all would have been lost.   Fortunately he was prompt and decisive, and he not merely gave his own recommendations to Burton, but enlisted in his favour an Omani nobleman, the Sayyid Sulayman bin Hamid bin Said, "the noble Omani never neglects the name of his grandsire," who had governed Zanzibar during the minority of Sayyid Khalid and whose influence was strong upon the sea-board.   The aged chief provided plenty of recommendations ; the Banian Collector of Customs supplied Burton with orders for money upon the Hindu coast merchants, and a guide to the interior was soon found in the person of a half-caste Arab, one Said bin Salim el-Lamki, an ugly, timid, nervous-valorous sort of personage who could not bear hunger or thirst, fatigue or want of sleep, and who, until fate threw him in Burton's way, had not walked a single consecutive mile. The sketch which is given of him in ' Zanzibar ' is too long for transcription, but it has many features of no little humour.   In truth this Mr. Forcible-Feeble must have been an interesting study.   He was a Mahometan of the Khariji schism, the faith by the way appears to have broken up in the course of time into as many sects as . Wesleyanism itself, and he was as particular concerning Arabic ritual as a "hardshell-baptist" concerning the dogmas of his particular creed. His philosophy was summed up in an Arab verse which he would "croon" for hours and which Burton thus translates:

> ' The knowledge of this nether world,
>   Say, friend, what is it, false or true?
> The false what mortal cares to know?
>   The true, what mortal ever knew?'

Burton's reasons for taking this unsatisfactory specimen of humanity were simple enough. In the first place his presence in the Expedition was a pledge of its respectability; in the second he was known (after a fashion) to be a Court spy, and so could report favourably of its members, and in the third he had a great knowledge of local details, and was well acquainted with the coast. ' During the first trip,' says Burton, ' I found him full of excellent gifts. Courteous, thoroughly good-tempered, and apparently truthful, honest and honourable—a bright exception to the rule of his unconscientious race.' But he did not "wear well." The varnish disappeared, and in a short time he proved himself as great a liar and as inveterate a thief as any of his compeers. Besides Said bin Salim Burton engaged also two Portuguese "boys" from Goa who turned out faithful and honest.

On the evening of Sunday, Jan. 4, 1857, Burton bade farewell to his host, Colonel Hamerton, and went on board the wretched old Arab craft which had been hired for him, expecting to sail at once. He ought, however, to have known what African promises really mean, and should not in reason have been surprised to find that he was after all detained for two days and a half before he could effect a start. It was, indeed, 7 o'clock in the morning of the 8th of January when his ramshackle craft made Kokoto-ni the usual point of departure from Zanzibar Island—18·30 geographical miles from, and north with three miles east of Zanzibar city. Here a brief halt was made for Burton to examine the country and buy provisions. Sail was set amidst stormy weather; the crew grew terrified, and insisted on "downing" the sail, and contenting themselves with progress at the rate of one knot per hour. The consequence was that it was the morning of the 10th before Pemba Island was sighted, and the evening of the same day before the travellers were permitted to anchor. On the day following Burton landed to find himself in an atmosphere of most admired humidity, excellent doubtless for vegetable growth, but almost fatal to human beings. His first visit was of course to the Wali. This Governor, however, was absent at Zanzibar, and was consequently represented by his brother, who lay upon his bed shaking with fever. The party next waited upon the Collector of Customs, by whom they were received in the most friendly and hospitable manner—an earnest of the treatment they were to receive all along the coast. This good fellow sent for the water-casks of Burton's craft, and had them filled with fresh pure water from the streamlet which runs behind the fort—very different stuff, Burton tells us, from the water of the wells near the anchorage-ground of Zanzibar. Finally, he accompanied the travellers, in company with the chief notables to their landing-place, and sent them off in his own boat laden with rice and provisions.

On leaving Pemba some very "dirty weather" was encountered, and for a while Burton debated within himself whether it would not be almost advisable to "get out and walk." Happily the scene changed on the 16th of January, and the worn-out old tub in which he was embarked was able to make Mombasah, a miserable settlement, once the capital of the King of the Zinj, concerning whom Arab travellers and geographers have written a variety of marvels. No sooner had Burton anchored than Said bin Salim went ashore, and speedily returned, accompanied by the Banian Collector of Customs, who was the bearer of a civil message from the Jemadar, or Fort Commandant. Two of the people of the place came with him, and in a short time the whole party were clambering up a dwarf tunnel which led from the beach to the town—a confused heap of brown thatched huts clustering round a few one-storied flat-roofed boxes of glaring lime and coral rag.

On the following morning, Burton not having gained much by his intercourse, such as it had been, with the authorities, girded up his loins to pay a visit to M. Rebmann, of the Mombas Mission at Kisulodi-ni, his station. The journey was through one of those mangrove swamps which are so familiar to every African traveller, and lasted for seven hours, during which time, however, no more than ten miles were traversed. A walk of five miles further brought them to the Mission House of Rabai-Mpia, where Burton and his following were hospitably entertained. The object of his visit was to present a certain letter from the Secretaries of the Church Missionary Society in London, authorizing M. Rebmann to accompany the East African Expedition if he chose to do so, at the charges of the Society. M. Rebmann seemed at first very willing to go, but on cooler reflection he changed his mind. He had seen enough of the interior; he was not in very good health; he was inclined to think that Burton relied too much on the arm of flesh, and above all things he had to remember his instructions from home :—" The Committee have only to remark that they entirely confide in you as one of their missionaries, that wherever you go you will maintain all the Christian principles by which you are guided ; that should you see fit to go with the Expedition, your experience and knowledge of the language may prove very valuable, while you may also obtain access to regions and tribes where missionary enterprise may hereafter be carried on with renewed vigour." As, however, Burton had been pledged by Colonel Hamerton at Zanzibar to avoid

"Dutchmen" and proselytizing, no arrangement could be come to, and the parties to the proposed treaty parted with expressions of esteem and goodwill, the sincerity of which, on Burton's side at all events, was proved by his reproduction of them ten years later in the curious two volumes in which he describes his first visit to Zanzibar. Happily Burton was able to repay some of the kindnesses he had received. In the course of his stay in and near Mombasah, he had heard that the Mombas Mission House had been plundered by the Wamasái. Hastening to the spot he found the rumour untrue, but it was "a shadow forethrown by coming events"—in other words, if it were not true to-day, it was exceedingly possible that it might come truth to-morrow. Burton insisted, therefore, on Madame Rebmann, an English woman, being sent down to Mombasah, and before he left he had the satisfaction of seeing her boxes packed and despatched. Only a few weeks after he met the unfortunate M. Rebmann in Zanzibar, whither he had been driven by a raid of the plundering Wamasái.

Burton and his party left Kisulodi-ni on 22nd January, 1857. A few nights afterwards fires were observed upon the neighbouring hills, and the Wanyika scouts came in with the report that the Wamasái were advancing in force. The news was but too true. The plundering hill-men, some 800 spears in number, fell fiercely upon the scattered villages of the lowlands, killing the people and driving off their cattle. They rushed down to the shore, and were met by a body of 148 matchlock-men—Arabs and Beloch, Wasawáhíli and slaves—before whom the bandits fled in-continently. Instead, however, of following up their victory, the soldiers at once dispersed to secure the plundered cattle ; the Wamasái rallied, drove off their conquerors, of whom they killed twenty-five, and then retired to the hills, where they amused themselves with exterminating as many

Wanyika as they could catch, and with eating their fill of stolen beef.

On the whole Burton was not very favourably impressed with the coast tribes. He found them insolent, cowardly and bigoted, thieves and liars of the first water, and ready to cheat and swindle on the smallest possible provocation. One elderly worthy, the Jemadár Tangái, courteously insisted on supplying the explorers with an escort, his object being to exchange his worthless swords for English guns and revolvers. His son sent goats and fruits, for which he received the normal return gifts : unsatisfied, he demanded clothes, gunpowder, and——a gold chronometer ! The very Hindus required a lesson in civility. The only person with whom Burton could be on friendly terms was the Wali, or Governor Khalfán bin Ali el-Bu Saidi, an Arab gentleman of the best type, who was on board when Sayyid Said died, and gave the particulars of that event to Burton. The *animus* of the rest of the Mombasah people was, however, such as made residence amongst them anything but pleasant, whilst the utter absence of all notions of decency and morality is simply hateful.

The party remained, nevertheless, at Mombasah, pursuing its geographical and ethnographical inquiries until the 24th of January, 1857, when it once more took ship, and in the course of eight hours brought up in Gazi Bay—a mere roadstead, protected from the swell of the Indian Ocean by nothing save a few "washes" and a coralline islet. At some distance inland lies the settlement, surrounded by plantations, and inhabited by Arabs, who live in comfort unmolested by the Wadigo savages to whom the land belongs. In accordance with his usual custom, Burton visited the place, where he was courteously and even hospitably received. At dawn, on the following day, he again made sail, landing in the course of the day at Wasin, a filthy hole, inhabited by a race of savages, who received

him with churlish discourtesy, and upon whom he took a
characteristic revenge. 'After fighting through the jungle,
we came upon two pits sunk in the soft rock: Said bin
Salim was bitterly derided whilst he sounded the depth—
40 feet—and by way of revenge I dropped a hint about
buried gold, which has doubtless been the cause of aching
arms and hearts to the churls of Wasin.' In this way the
journey along the coast continued, a halt being made at
every convenient point and information being sought as to
routes to the interior, and as to the various races. Cor-
rections of some of the marvellous mis-statements in
Mr. Cooley's book were also noted—a labour which probably accounts for the extreme acerbity with which at a
later date that gentleman threw himself into the Nile
controversy. Six days were thus passed at Tanga, one of
the most important of these coast settlements, the days
being spent in shooting-excursions to the interior, and the
evenings in the collection of information.

At last, sail was hoisted on the 5th of February, at 5 A.M.,
and early in the day the port of Pangna-ni was made. 'It
was necessary,' says Burton, 'to land with some ceremony
at a place which I determined to make our starting-point
into the interior. Presently, after arrival, I sent Said bin
Salim, in all his bravery, to deliver the Sayyid of Zanzibar's
circular letters addressed to the Wali, or Governor, to the
Jemadar, to the Collector of Customs, and to the several
Diwans. All this preparation for a trifle of 80 miles ! But
we are in Africa, and even in Europe such a raid through an
enemy's country is not always easy. My companion (Speke)
and I landed in the cool of the evening with our Portuguese
servants and our luggage. We were received with all the
honours of noise and crowding. The orchestra consisted of
three monstrous drums (Ngoma Khu), caissons of cocoa-
trunk covered at both ends with goat-leather and pounded
like the pulpit with fist ; and of Siwa or bassoons of hard

black wood, at least five feet long. These were enlivened by a pair of Zumári, or flageolets, whose vile squeaking set the teeth on edge, by the Zeza or guitar, the Kinánda or banjo, by the Barghumi or Kudu horn, and by that instrument of dignity, the Upatu, a brass pan, the primitive cymbal, whose bottom is performed upon by little sticks like cabbage-stalks. The Jemadar Asad Ullah, came *en grand' tenue*. The Diwans capered and pyrrhic'd before us with the pomp and circumstance of drawn swords, whilst the prettiest of the slave-girls, bareheaded, and with hair *à la Brutus*, sang and flapped their skirts on the ground, performing a *pavane* with a very modest and downcast demeanour as if treading upon a too hot floor. . . . After half an hour's endurance of this purgatory we were led to our sleeping-places, the upper rooms, or rather room of the Wali, or Governor's house—its owner was one Meriko, a burly black freeman of the late Sayyid Said—and there the evening was spent by us over consideration of ways and means.'

This last was a very serious matter. Money is the sinews of war everywhere, and especially in Eastern Africa, and Burton was so ill-provided on this, his trial trip, that he was compelled to content himself with a walking excursion to Fuga. The question of bakhshish next came to the front. Muigni Khatib, son and heir to Sultan Kimero, and a black of most unprepossessing appearance, sent to demand a present in the name of his father, then on his way to Zanzibar to explain certain derelictions of duty. Needless to say he was refused, and that in his own tone of studied insolence. The same fate befel the Diwans who claimed a present for their saltatory performances of the night before. At last, weary of importunity Burton completed his preparations, paid off the craft Riámi, rejected the Diwans, who wished to accompany the Expedition as spies, left Said bin Salim and Gaetano, one of the Goanese lads,

in the house of the Wali Meriko, and under pretext of a
shooting excursion hired a long canoe and four men, loaded
it with the luggage required for a fortnight, and started
with the tide at 11 A.M., on the 6th of February, 1858.
The journey up the stream was through a new and strange
country. The water swarmed with wild creatures, hippopotamus and crocodile ; myriads of monkeys gambolled
through the trees of the forest, while on the river 'their
elder brethren,' the jungle men and women, 'planted
their shoulder cloths, their rude crates, and their coarse
weirs upon the muddy inlets where fish abounded.' The
vegetable world around was equally strange. The brab, or
wild date, much used for mats, contrasted with the devil's
date, which, 'eccentric in form and frondage, curved arms
sometimes 30 and even 35 feet long, over the dancing wave ;
this dwarf giant of the palms has no trunk to speak of, but
each midrib is thick as a man's thigh, and the vegetable
kingdom cannot show such a length of foliage. Opposed
to this tree, which appears to be all foliage and no trunk,
were others all trunk and no branches, crowned simply by
a few leaves and flowers. On the watery margin were
thousands of snowy lilies, some closed by day, others
basking in light and air against the black green growth
and bituminous brown of the back water. 'In scattered
spots were inhuman traces of human presence ; tall arecas
and cocoas, waving over a now impenetrable jungle ;
whilst plantains, sugar canes, limes and bitter oranges,
choked with wild verdure, still lingered about the broken
homestead and around the falling walls blackened by the
murderers' fire. And above all,' adds Burton, 'reigned the
peculiar African and tropical stillness of noontide, deep
and imposing, broken only by the curlew's scream or by
the tepid breeze rustling the tree-tops in fitful gusts,
whispering among the matted foliage, and swooning away
upon the warm bosom of the wave.'

Through scenes like those the canoe was paddled and poled throughout the livelong day, until, at evening, the tide running like a mill race compelled the crew to pole up a little inlet to Pombui or Kipombui, a stockaded village on the left bank of the river. Here Burton and Speke met a far more hospitable reception than they had reason to anticipate. The villagers flocked out to welcome their visitors ; laid down a bridge of cocoa-ribs, brought chairs, and offered a dish of small green mangoes—here a great luxury. They sat until midnight enjoying the extraordinary beauty of the scene, the sight of the glowing stars, the myriads of fire-flies, and the soft sound of the evening breeze, broken only by the crash and splash of leviathan and behemoth, as they forced their way through the jungle, or plunged into the stream. At midnight, when the tide flowed strong, the way was resumed. The crocodiles and hippopotami were numerous and noisy, and the boatmen entreated Burton to frighten a certain pernicious "rogue," whose villanies had gained for him the royal title of Sultan Mamba, or King Crocodile. They heard the grunts and splashings with which the huge beasts made their way up the slippery banks to fields and plantations, then all was silent as the grave. Suddenly out of the gloom 'the near voice of a man startled us as though it had been some ghostly sound. At 2 A.M., reaching a cleared tract on the river side, the "ghaut," or landing place, of Chogwe, we made fast the canoe, looked to our weapons, and covering our faces against the clammy dew, we lay down to snatch an hour's sleep.' It is significant of the slow rate of African travel, that although Burton had started at 11 A.M., though his men had been rowing and poling almost continuously until sunset, and from midnight until two in the morning, the distance traversed was no more than 13½ miles.

Chogwe is a not very inviting outpost of Zanzibar, and is

occupied by a Jemadar and 25 Beloch—a circumstance
which is mainly due to the publication in the *Church
Missionary Intelligencer,* in 1850, of what it called the
"fact," that "the Imam of Zanzibar had not one inch of
ground between the island of Wazin and the Panga-ni
River." The "fact" was brought to the notice of the
Sultan Sayyid, who promptly answered it by garrisoning
Chogwe and Tongwe. For strategical and political reasons
this step may have been eminently desirable, but for any
others it was as eminently the reverse. The situation of the
place is simply detestable. Water is distant, the rugged
soil produces nothing but stunted manioc, and when the
periodical inundation subsides the miasma prostrates the
garrison with fever and diarrhœa. The men abhor the
place, but find some small consolation in the fact that
Chogwe, being on the main road to Usumbárá, affords
opportunity for "an occasional something in the looting
line." In this delightful spot Burton made, as may be
imagined, no long stay, but confiding his project to the
Jemadar obtained from him a promise of assistance,
moyennant $10, of which he probably retained one-half for
his own uses. For this he supplied four matchlock men,
who were to act as guard, and four slave-boys to act as
porters. He was to have provided two guides as well, but
they dwindled down to one, and he a slave. One night
was spent in the Maychán, or raised platform, where wind,
dust and ants combined to make the travellers miserable.
Next morning preparations were made for the start. The
kit was cut down to those matters which were absolutely
necessary—'surveying instruments, weapons, waterproof
blankets, tea, sugar and tobacco for ten days, a bag of dates,
and three bags of rice. About noon, issuing from our shed,
we placed the baggage in the sun ; thus mutely appealing
to the "sharm "—shame or sense of honour—possessed by
our Beloch *employés.'* The start did not, however, take

place until 5 P.M., when Burton had his first experience of
a scene which, in the course of the next few years, became
only too familiar. The slaves rushed at the loads, each
trying to secure the lightest, and bolting forward to avoid
the heavier burdens, regardless of what was left behind.
Past experience had, however, taught him what to do on
such occasions, and 'the nuisance endured till abated by
an outward application easily divined.' At last, some
approach to peace and order was obtained ; the company
set forth in straggling Indian file, escorted by the con-
sumptive Jemadar—consumption, and lung and bronchial
diseases are terribly common in these miasmatic countries
—and most of his party, and the road to Tongwe was
finally taken.

The track led over stony ridges, then into a dense
thorny thicket wholly impassable during the rains. Two
hours of marching through a country abounding with
game, which could be heard but not seen, carried the travellers over some six miles of ground, as shown by the
pedometer, to a partially cleared ring in the thorny jungle,
where was water and also—'the Formican fiend, the bull
dog ant,' an insect half an inch long, whose sting is like
that of a red hot needle, and which will allow itself to be
cut in two rather than release its hold. As the people
stooped to drink, they were seized by these dreadful creatures, 'when suddenly all began to dance and shout like
madmen, pulling off their clothes, and frantically snatching
at their lower limbs.' In spite of the ants, however, the
evening was passed in revelry. 'It was a savage opera
scene. One recited his Koran, another prayed, a third
told funny stories, while a fourth trolled out in minor key
lays of love and war made familiar to my ear upon the
rugged Sindian hills. This was varied by slapping away
the lank mosquitoes that flocked to the gleaming camp
fires, by rising occasionally to rid ourselves of the ants,

and by challenging the small parties of savages who, armed
with bows and arrows, passed amongst us carrying grain to
Pangna-ni.' Of course a watch was set : equally of course it
was absolutely useless. The camp held high revel during
the earlier hours of the night when there was no danger,
but slept like the dead through the "small hours," which
African freebooters and indeed the dishonest of all races
chose for their ignoble exploits.

When at daybreak on the following morning the expedition again set forward it was with greatly diminished
numbers, the Jemadar crippled by the moonlight and the
heavy dews returned with his following to Chogwe, while
Burton and his party continued their march to Tongwe.
After five or six bad miles, they found themselves ' between
winter and summer.' The little ridge which they reached
at 8 A.M. enjoyed a delicious summer from the sea and was
scourged with the blasts of winter from the deep and
forested valley to landward. From this point half an hour's
walking brought the travellers to the " Fort "—a crenellated,
flat-roofed, and whitewashed room, 14 feet square, and
sheltering two Beloch ' who figure on the muster roll as
20 men '—wretched creatures who are the slaves of super-
stitious terrors, and who are very scantily fed and provided
for. It is hardly surprising to find that the Jemadar's orders
to supply an escort to Burton were treated as though they
had never been written. With much difficulty he at last
succeeded in getting together a small party, amongst whom
was a certain " Bombay," alias Sidi Mubárak, the best of all
the hard bargains whom Burton and Speke managed to pick
up for the great journey which they had in contemplation.
This man was something of an original and in his way
passing honest. He worked well ; not because he cared for
his work or for his masters, but—because as he ingenuously .
explained—"his duty towards his belly made him work." He
began by escorting the party to Fugá, as head gun-carrier ;

on the march to the Lakes, he was Speke's confidential
servant, and was literally, from his master's ignorance of the
native tongues, the only person besides Burton with whom
he could communicate. On the second expedition (Speke
and Grant's) he was made commander of the Wasawáhíli
—almost the only instance of one of this race not proving
"a failure in the end." There were, as was but natural,
endless difficulties in getting away with a "scratch team"
like this. One man would not go because the "Rider
King" kept the gunpowder ; another started for home
because he was refused some dates, and on the night before
the start it required all the efforts of Burton's gun-carrier,
Sidi Mubárak Bombay,* to prevent a general break up.

After a night of tropical silence the start was made on the
morning of the 10th of February. The luggage was again
reduced to the smallest possible compass—only those
things being taken without which it was impossible to move
—sextant and horizon, compasses and stand, common and
boiling point thermometer, water proof bag, with materials
for journalizing and sketching, arms and ammunition, presents for the Sultan Kimwere, provisions and a bottle of
cognac for use in case of need, bedding, lights, and cooking
apparatus. What were really wanted were water-skins,
beads, and "domestics" (*i.e.* calico), as Burton presently
found to his cost. The start was made at 6 A.M., and for
three hours the party had to literally cut their way through
rushes and tiger grass. They struck the Pangna-ni road
at last, and finding some water, rested by it, bad though it
was. The want of gourds and water-skins began to make
itself felt ; the party divided in search of water ; the guides

---

* Sidi Mubárak Bombay, whose name will be frequently met with
in the next chapter, proved himself fully worthy of the confidence
which Burton reposed in him, and when Stanley went upon his
memorable and successful journey in search of Livingstone in 1871,
he was appointed chief of the caravan.

turned out to be almost absolutely useless, and at last it was found necessary to halt by the side of the first stream they could discover. They had travelled "three leagues, and a bittock," but the way had been so rough that they fancied the distance at least double—a misery which was not decreased by the fact of Burton and his immediate companions having to go supperless to rest. The truants were found in the morning; peace was made, and a morning of rest and *Kayf* indulged in. A fresh start was made in the afternoon, and after walking for three hours and covering ten miles—wonderfully rapid travelling for Africa—they found themselves "opposite Kohode," the village of a friendly Mzegura chief. "Sultan Mamba," having recognized the Beloch, forthwith donned his scarlet cloak, superintended the launching of the village canoe from its cajan house; stood surrounded by the elders watching their transit, and as the party landed wrung their hands with rollicking greetings, and with three immoderate explosive cachinnations, which render the African family to all appearance so "jolly" a race.

Unfortunately "Sultan Mamba" (the Crocodile), was about as disreputable a scoundrel as even Africa has produced—which is saying a good deal. Burton describes him as a ' stout, jolly, beardless young black, with the laugh of a boatswain, and the voice of one calling in the wilderness.' He went once to Zanzibar, where his eyes were opened to the truths of Islam by a venerable Msawáhíli D.D., who enrolled him amongst the Faithful, and conferred his own name upon him, making him his son by adoption. But when Mamba returned to his native hills, his newly acquired religion fell from him like a cloak; he turned away from prayer and ablution and grace generally, and inclined himself to the more congenial practices of highway robbery and hard drinking. He sat with the travellers during half the next day, begging for everything he saw, from a barrel of gunpowder or a Colt's revolver down to a bottle of brandy. All these things were refused in turn, and the Sultan was constrained to content himself with two caps, a pair of muslins, and a cotton shawl. He was very anxious to do a little trade in black ivory. His people, he said, had but three wants, powder, ball, and brandy, and in return they would supply men, women, and children. 'Our parting,' adds Burton, 'was truly pathetic. He swore he loved us, and promised us on the down march the use of his canoe. But when we appeared with empty hands and neither caps nor muslins remained, Sultan Mamba scarcely deigned to notice us, and the river became a succession of falls and rapids.'

The journey was resumed at seven the next morning—far too late for comfort, since by that hour the sun had attained considerable power, and those who had been in the shade up to that time felt it with double intensity. After crossing an alluvial plain, singularly fertile and in-tersected by a river which needed only the absence of crocodiles to be perfectly beautiful in every sense, they halted from 10 A.M. to 4 P.M. under the shade of a spread-ing tamarind tree, where the villagers came out to gaze upon them for hours together. They were, however, timid rather than dangerous, though their Sultan strode about spear in hand highly indignant that Burton would not enter his hut and drop some cloth. Extra porters were wanted here, but unfortunately Burton had neither beads nor Merkáni (American domestics), and not a porter was to be had. Resuming the march in the afternoon, by five o'clock the village of Msiki-Mguru was reached. This place was about twelve miles from the starting point in the morning. The travellers were received with sufficient hospitality, but the night was spent, not in sleep, but in battling with in-sect plagues of every kind. The people were friendly, and very anxious to do a little traffic in slaves, but they were preoccupied with the dread of the hostile Wamasái—a dread which was but too well founded. Scarcely had Burton and his companions left the country, when a band of wild spearmen attacked two neighbouring villages, slaughtered the headmen and the peaceable cultivators, and drove off the cattle in triumph. The country around was found to be a veritable realisation of Douglas Jerrold's saying—"tickle the earth with a hoe, and it smiles with a golden harvest." The people seemed peaceable and contented ; none fled at the sight of a white face ; none refused to salute the strangers, and at times the cry of "Yámbo : " (the state ; *i.e.* of health) would be heard from a dozen different quarters. One difficulty only beset the caravan. In skirting a village they were peremptorily called upon to halt, not so much for the sake of taking toll, as from the desire of the headman to hear all the news of the day. These people, strange as it may seem, are the most inveterate gossips in the world, and anything, lie or truth, in the way of novelty, is acceptable. On this occasion, however, the dread of an approaching rain-storm had sharpened the tempers of all the travellers, and they broke loose from their persecutors with sarcastic advice to them to stop them if they could.

The day did not end altogether prosperously. About 4 P.M. a tremendous storm of thunder and lightning, rain and a raw southwest wind drove the entire party into the palaver-house of a village—a wretched shed consisting of a few posts supporting a thatched roof, with a mud floor and some stones for seats. Here fires were lighted to keep off fevers, and after the usual quarrel amongst the Beloch on the question of rations, preparations were made for a most comfortless night. By 11 in the morning, the rain partially cleared off, and a start was made. The chilliness of the last eighteen hours, was replaced by that "reeking, fetid, sepulchral heat which travellers in the tropics have learned to fear," but it gave way after an ascent of some hours to a sweet and rarefied air which all sat down to enjoy. Their comfort was, however, of short duration. The man Wazíra who had been prating all the morning about the serious nature of the undertaking on which they had embarked, had succeeded in corrupting three fresh porters who had been hired on the preceding day. These men threw down their loads and positively refused to go on unless a certain number of cloths were sent forward to propitiate the magnates of Fugá. The use of the Beloch then became apparent. With a grin of contempt they pulled the porters up from the ground, loaded them in spite of their remonstrances and forced them to go on their way. The journey then lay up the rough bed of a mountain torrent, which brought the caravan to the summit of the pass, from which another walk of some three miles on the flank of the domed hills led to the objective point of the journey—Fugá.

Fugá being one of the cities which the stranger is forbidden to enter, our wayfarers were led to a cluster of four tattered huts, standing some 300 feet below the settlement, and serving all the purposes of the "Travellers' Bungalow" in India. The cold rain and the sharp rarefied air made any shelter acceptable. No time was, therefore, lost in clearing out the sheep and goats from the huts, in housing the valuables, and in sending the faithful Sidi Bombay with an appropriate and respectful message to the Sultan, craving the honour of an interview. Before dark appeared three bareheaded Mdoe or Ministers, with the announcement that the Council must sit upon two questions, (1) Why the travellers had come through the hostile Wazegura country and (2) when would the Sultan's Mganga, or Magician, find an hour propitious for the ceremony. To this the quick-witted Hamdan at once replied that Burton and his companions were also Mganga, able to measure the moon and the stars, and to control the wind and the rain. The bold assertion had its effect. At 6 P.M. the three ministers, out of breath with running, reappeared with an immediate summons to the Palace. Three Beloch were allowed as escort, but their arms were taken from them, and the swords of Burton and his companion were demanded. These, however, they insisted upon retaining, and with them they were accordingly ushered into the presence of the Sultan.

Him they found to be an old, old man, emaciated, beardless, toothless, wrinkled, with shaven head and hands and feet stained with leprous spots. His subjects declared him a centenarian, and he was to Burton's eyes obviously dying of old age and decay. His dress was a Surat cap greatly the worse for wear, and a loin-cloth as tattered. He lay upon a couch of bamboo and cowskin, covered with an ancient Persian rug, and he was wrapped in a doubled cotton cloth of the kind called in India do-pattá. The " palace " was a filthy hut, crowded with functionaries as dirty as their master, but all tolerably civil. "After com'lements " Burton and his companion were motioned to seat themselves on low stools in front of the Sultan, and were welcomed to Fugá. No one being present, who could read the introductory letter from the Sayyid of Zanzibar, Burton was compelled to do so himself. The Sultan having heard that his visitors could read stones and herbs, as well as the stars, concluded that they must be European medicine men, and commanded them to prepare at once a draught which should restore him to health and strength. They were compelled to excuse themselves on the plea of having left all their drugs at Pangna-ni. The Sultan was not altogether satisfied with the excuse but he accepted it, gave the travellers leave to wander about the hills at their pleasure, and after keeping them in talk for half-an-hour, renewed his welcome to them and dismissed them. On their return to the Travellers' Bungalow, they sent off their present to the Sultan with all due ceremony ; receiving in return a fine bullock, a basket full of sima—young Indian corn, pounded and boiled to a thick hard paste—and balls of unripe bananas peeled and mashed up with sour milk. The Beloch addressed themselves to the manufacture of beef, and devoured their steaks with all the energy of savage natures. 'That day' adds Burton, 'we had covered ten miles, equal perhaps to thirty on a decent road in a temperate clime. The angry blast, the dashing rain, and the groaning trees formed a concert which heard from within a warm hut, affected us pleasurably : I would not have exchanged it for the music of Verdi. We slept sweetly as only travellers can sleep.'

When Burton and his companions arose up early in the morning they found that the rainy season at Fugá had set in, though the half of February had not yet passed. Heavy clouds rolled up from the south-west, and for the next forty-eight hours came a succession of "drip, drizzle, and deluge." The sky was so utterly clouded that not a star was to be seen, and consequently no observation could be made. It was dangerous to linger in Usumbárá. The inevitable "seasoning fever" was threatening the entire Expedition ; the men were by no means clad to resist the cold, and in a very short time the rains would turn the lowlands into a hotbed of disease and death. On Monday, the 16th of February therefore, Burton, and his companion Speke, formally took leave of the Sultan Kimwere. The monarch was grievously displeased that they had not been able to discover in their wanderings over his hills the true elixir of life. 'I felt sad,' Burton says, 'to see the fretful lingering look with which he accompanied his Kua-heri —farewell (à tout jamais !), but his case was far beyond my skill.' The departure, next day, was anything but pleasant. The three porters who had been engaged had run away, "characteristically futile," without even claiming their hire, and it was impossible to replace them. The

Beloch had gorged themselves faint with beef, and had overloaded the slaves with the hide, the horns, and huge collops of raw meat. In a few hours they had exchanged the elevation of 4000 feet for one of 1000, and at once felt shorn of half their strength. On the third night they slept at Kohode, where the graceless Sultan Mamba, the King Crocodile, allowed them to be ferried over upon a bundle of cocoa fronds. From this point the expedition determined to follow the river course downwards, with the view of ascertaining whether there were so many falls and rapids as had been described to them. The native attendants and the Beloch grumbled at the severity of the journey ; but tact and management soon induced them to face its perils, though the slaves whimpered under the splashing rain, and the numbing, gusty wind. The way was enough to make more valiant men quail. Rain, wind, a track slippery with ooze and mire, and crossed at every few yards with troublesome thorn trees—the reader will remember the thorns of a few pages back, two inches long and with points like needles—overgrown with sedgy spear and tiger grass, and constantly interrupted with half-exposed roots, which many a time and oft gave the unwary traveller a troublesome fall. Above all the air was damp, and oppressive, thick with steamy moisture, and saturated with a feverish fetor from the decaying vegetation.

The day was long and dark, and dreary enough to satisfy even an American poet, nor was the evening much more cheerful. At sunset tall cocoas were seen, and presently crossing a long wooden bridge, made rickety for easier defence, the party entered Kizungu, an island settlement of Wazegúra. The head men received them with some cere-mony, cleared a hut of its inmates, placed cartels upon the ground outside, and seated Burton and his friends in a ring for a noisy palaver. The talk was good enough, but it led to little. Kizungu (which by the way the omniscient

Mr. Cooley twice mis-spells) was distracted with wars and rumours of wars ; the Beloch suggested treachery ; the travellers fired their revolvers into tree trunks, and reloaded for the public benefit, but, alas ! though solid dollars were offered for rice and ghi (clarified butter), provisions were unobtainable. The escort went to bed supperless, and in a corresponding temper, and the chiefs would have fared badly had not one of the elders brought an elderly hen and a handful of red rice, which were soon dispatched. The night was stormy, yet despite smoke, wet beds, chirping crickets, and other plagues, the blustering wind, and the continuous pattering of rain, the travellers slept. By 7 A.M. they were "on the tramp" again, and by nine o'clock they stood upon an eminence to view the falls of Pangna-ni, not yet swollen to their fullest bulk, but still imposing and interesting.

The heat grew intense as the day went on, and at 10 A.M. the Beloch, worn out with famine and fatigue, threw themselves on the ground, and swore they could go no further. Half-an-hour's rest, a cocoa-nut each, and above all a pipe, restored something of vigour to the party. The march was resumed over a rolling waste of thin grass ; villages became numerous as the party advanced, and at 3 P.M., after a weary stage of fourteen miles, they found themselves once more within the shelter of "friendly Chogwe." The garrison turned out with all the honours, marvelling much to see the party returned so soon from Fugá, where, as at Harar, a visitor can never reckon upon prompt dismissal. A few days were devoted to rest, and "kitchen physic." The feet, which had been cut by hard boots and shoes, often wetted, and often dried, were beneficently attended to ; the chafings caused by heat and constant perspiration were treated with flour and white of egg, and then within a very brief space Burton and Speke moved down upon Pangna-ni. Said bin

Salim received them with joyous demonstrations ; the Portuguese lad, who had gone with Burton, had escaped with nothing worse than a few sick headaches, whilst his confrère Valentino had been wholly free from the African fever. After a day or two Burton returned to Chogwe, paid his bills—not exorbitant under the circumstances— and then started in search of hippopotamus, the ferocious-looking and simple-minded ruminant of whom African travellers tell such marvels, and who is such a very common-place creature after all. Not, indeed, that he is altogether harmless. Captain Owen's officers, when ascending these streams, had their boats torn by Behemoth's hard teeth ; in the Pangna-ni River one of the breed delighted to upset boats in his rude waggishness, and once broke a negro's leg. In Burton's own expedition one canoe was smashed by a blow from Kiboko's forehead, and the corvette's gig suddenly uplifted on Behemoth's tusk points showed a pair of corresponding holes in her bottom.

The fighting, it must be confessed, does not impress the stay-at-home traveller with much enthusiasm. The first shot at the hippopotamus scatters, and the poor brute ' slips down like a seal.' The second brings better fortune. ' As the smooth water undulates, swells and breaks a way for the large square head eight ounces of lead fly in the right direction. There is a splash, a struggle ; the surface foams, and Behemoth with open mouth, like a butcher's stall, and bleeding like a gutter-spout, plunges above the surface. Wounded in the cerebellum he cannot swim straight, he cannot defend himself. . . . Returning to Kiboko, the Beloch are excited, and as the game rises again, matchlocks bang dangerously as popguns. Presently the Jemadar, having expended three bullets—a serious matter with your Oriental pot-hunter—retires from the contest, as we knew he would, recommending the beasts to us. Bombay punches on the boatmen, who complain that a dollar a day does not justify their facing death. At last a *coup de grâce* speeding through the ear finds out the small brain ; the brute sinks, fresh gore purples the surface, and bright bubbles seethe up from the bottom. Hippo has departed this life : we wait patiently for his re-appearance, but he re-appears not. At length Bombay's sharp eye detects a dark object some hundred yards down stream : we make for it, and find our "bag" brought up in a shallow by a spit of sand, and already in process of being ogled by a large fish-hawk. The fish-hawk pays the penalty of impudence. We tow the big defunct to the bank, and deliver it to a little knot of savages, who have flocked down to the stream with mouths watering at the prospect of creek-bullock beef. . . . The insufferable toughness and coarseness, to say nothing of the musky bouquet, do not recommend it to Europeans. The Washenzi, or pagans, how-ever, will feast royally, grease themselves with the dripping, and at sundown bring us, according to agreement, the tusks, teeth and skull picked clean as a whistle is said to be.'

The details of the battue seem hardly worth recalling after so long an interval. Let it suffice to say that by 10 A.M. six of the mighty beasts had fallen, and many more had been wounded, but then there was little more that was new and less that was interesting to tell. Burton even ' found the massacre monotonous, and such cynegetics little more exciting than pheasant shooting.' There was small prospect of other game ; Chogwe offered but few attrac-tions, and so, on the 26th, the party left the Bazaar, Speke walking to Pangna-ni and making a route survey by the way, while the Jemadar and his tail escorted Burton in the large canoe. So far the trial trip had been successful ; 150 miles had been covered in eleven days, and a fair amount of experience had been acquired. M. Erhardt's somewhat romantic maps had been corrected, and a valuable stock of experience as to the estimation and

measuring of distances had been acquired. When the
party returned to Pangna-ni, however, it seemed probable
that all the toil would be thrown away. Speke spent an
hour in company with his sextant, amidst the dews of the
second night. On the day following, Burton and he walked
out under a glowing sun, to examine a limestone cavern,
concerning which the natives had told the most exaggerated stories. When they returned they found the
Portuguese Gaetano ill with all the symptoms which
presage a severe and even malignant bilious fever. A few
hours afterwards Speke was down, and on the following day Burton followed suit. It is a remarkable illustration of the fact, that natives enjoy no immunity from
these diseases, that Sidi Bombay had a severe attack in the
following June. The time of illness was by no means one
of unmitigated enjoyment. The Jemadar seeing that he
could do nothing committed the patients to Allah and to
Said bin Salim and departed; the Banians, by way of
making themselves agreeable, sat by the bedsides of the
sick men for hours asking the silliest of questions, and
driving away all repose; gnats and flies added to the
horrors of fever during the day; mosquitoes stang and
sang songs of triumph over their heads at night, and rats
nibbled their feet, while torturing thirst made the terrible
sleeplessness still more terrible. The batela which Colonel
Hamerton had promised to send for the travellers was due
on the 1st of March, the rogues who navigated it had turned
out of their way to visit their homes at Tumbátu, and it was
not until the 5th of March that she made the harbour.
Said bin Salim got the luggage on board at once; and at
dawn the next day sail was made, and the same afternoon saw Burton once more within the pale of Eastern
civilisation. Colonel Hamerton at once sent his guests
to bed where they stayed a full week, but they did not
recover their normal health for at least a month.

The illness was got rid of for the time, but its seeds were left in Burton's system for many years to come, and when he embarked on the great journey, which will be described in the succeeding chapter, it constantly broke out afresh both in him and in Captain Speke. The latter suffered from partial blindness and from deafness of a peculiarly painful kind during the most important part of his journey, while Burton himself was liable to constant attacks of this fever, which had become an intermittent, during the whole of the long journey to and from Lake Tanganyika.

For some time Burton was engaged in preparations for his approaching Expedition. He made an excursion to the Copal Region, in deference to the views of the Geographical Society from which he was able to bring back little in the way of novel information. In the midst of many troubles he found that his report to the Secretary of the Royal Geographical Society had not been forwarded. No one knew where it was or what had become of it, and it was not for ten years that anything was heard of it. Then and only then it turned up quite promiscuously, as Mrs. Gamp would say, in a strong box at Bombay. The sketches and field books over which it might reasonably have been supposed that some little care would have been expended were found in an equally miscellaneous fashion. They had been left in a drawer somewhere or other, and no man regarded them. One portion was discovered in a very singular manner. It was stolen at Fernando Po. Colonel Maude, the Queen's equerry, was attracted by the label on a Letts' Diary, outside an old book shop, " Captain Burton's Travels in Africa: Original MS." He bought it, and called on Lord Derby—left it in the hall—his Lordship coming down, saw the book, recognised Burton's handwriting, and wrote to Colonel Maude for permission to restore the diary to its rightful owner.

CHAPTER VII.

TO LAKE TANGANYIKA.

A long journey in prospect—M. Erhardt's proposal—M. Rebmann—
A "Jackass frigate"—Landing from Zanzibar—African delays—
Speke, a "novice lunarian"—The rascal Ramji—A dismal start—
The "second departure"—Desertions—Start from Bomani—The
monotony of East African travel—An African day—Halting—A
traveller's evening—African music—A region of graves—Speke's
illness—Death of Colonel Hamerton—Burton down with fever—
Murder of M. Maizan—A jungle march—The African ass—Cares
of the journey—A malarious region—At the head of the river valley
—A hot-bed of pestilence—A bibulous prince—"The Delectable
Mountains and the Slough of Despond"—Small pox—A turning-
point — African ingratitude — The Beloch—A "Commando"—A
"Tirekeza" or afternoon march—The sufferings of explorers—The
air of the mountains — The "half-way house" — Black-mail—
"Knowledge"—Signor Magombo — A down caravan — Burton's
difficulties—"Prince Shortshanks"—More delay—A heavy toll—
The "Fiery Field"—Its people—Kazeh—A friendly reception—
The hospitable Arab—Snay bin Amir the generous—An Arab
market—The usual difficulties—Illness amongst the Expedition—
Danger of death.

AT noon on the 16th of June, 1857, the *Artemise*, one of
the old "jackass frigates" of the Indian Navy, sailed out of
the harbour of Zanzibar with the Expedition on board,
and at 6 P.M. on the following day anchored off Wále
Point, a long low bush-grown landspit, about eighty-four
miles distant from the little town of Bágámoyo, where it
anchored for ten days before the caravan could depart for
the interior. The difficulties in the way of the Expedition
appeared almost insuperable. The Sultan of Zanzibar,

who seems to have behaved with a kindness and courtesy
which would have been an honour to the most civilised
of European princes, had sent forward the half-caste Arab,
Said bin Salim, with orders to act as Ras Káfilah, or
Caravan Guide, and to obtain porters. Said did not like
the duties imposed upon him, and dreaded the hatred
which he might incur from his fellows to such an extent,
that, although he had accepted $300 from the public funds
advanced by Colonel Hamerton, and had been promised
an ample reward in hard coin contingent on his good
behaviour, he did his work as ill as he could. Accompanied by a Banian of Zanzibar, called Ramji, who had
been sent forward to engage men to go up the country,
he found the work was so ill-performed that out of the 170
men required, only 36 were available when Burton landed.
The remainder, hearing that their employer was a white man
(Muzungu), had retired—forgetting, however, to return the
advances they had received. This was a serious blow to the
Expedition at the outset. Its means, as has been shown
above, were not illimitable : £1000 does not go very far
when it has to be divided amongst a couple of hundred
greedy savages in the course of two years and a half ; and
since in Central Africa money did not exist in 1858, any
more than in 1887, it was necessary to carry the materials
of barter—cotton-cloth, brass wire, and beads. Burton's
other equipage was also far from light. Under the impression that "vert and venison" abounded in the interior,
he had stocked himself with ammunition—1600 pounds of
ball, grape, and shot, six fire-proof magazines, and two small
kegs of fine powder and four ten-pound kegs of a coarser
sort for the use of the escort. The Said bin Salim's
neglect of duty entailed endless trouble, and seriously
injured the Expedition. The greater part of the ammunition,
and a small portable iron boat, which had already been found
exceedingly useful, were perforce left behind, together with

certain Hindus who had been hired to forward them, and
—unfortunate mistake—paid in advance. These goods
were to have been despatched in ten days : it was actually
eleven months before they appeared.

The difficulties of the Expedition were, however, only
beginning. During the brief detention off Wále Point the
latitude and longitude of the estuary of the Kingáni, the
main artery of these regions, was settled by Speke who—
strange qualification for an African explorer—was a
" novice lunarian " and was compelled to seek for aid from
one Mohammed bin Khamis, ' who had read his " Norie "
in England.' Then followed sundry other failures, and
an enforced residence of some time in Kaole—short for
Kaole-Urembo—one of the typical African settlements,
and the enlistment of a number of half-bred Beloch and
" Wámrima "—rogues and thieves—who were, unfortunately,
about the only people who could be enlisted in Kaole for
the purposes of the Expedition. The escort had been,
unwisely as it turned out, allowed to leave the Artémise,
and their comrades in arms had talked them half crazy with
fear. One of the Beloch declared that nothing less than
100 guards and 150 guns and several cannon would ensure
a safe passage into the interior ; another told wonderful
tales of the risks they ran amongst the savages who would
shoot arrows high into the air from points of vantage in the
trees ; others talked of officials on the coast who had sent
letters to the interior forbidding white men to enter the
jungles. The number of fables told on this occasion was
like to the number of fools—infinite. Suffice it to say that
Burton's unwilling followers were assured that the Khar-
gadan, or rhinoceros, is a match for 200 men ; that armies
of elephants attack the camps by night, and that the
" craven hyæna " does more damage than the Bengal tiger. ·

The meaning of the delay crept out after a time. It was
neither more nor less than a " plant," to use a somewhat

vulgar expression, to force Burton to engage for six months
a host of lazy black fellows at a price, payable in advance,
be it remarked, for which the same men might have been
bought as slaves in the open market. Then came a
difficulty about asses. " The rascal Ramji " demanded and
obtained for the hire of certain of these animals to the
Lake about twice their intrinsic value. Lastly, Colonel
Hamerton's health—not improved by a diet of morphia,
sugar, and cocoanut milk, for a confirmed liver complaint—
gave out, and he was compelled to return to Zanzibar,
though with a courage which Burton justly describes as
"sublime," he declared himself, in spite of Burton's entreaties, determined to remain near the coast until he heard
of the safe transit of the caravan through the lands of the
dreaded Wazarámo. This farewell over, Burton left the
Artémise and landed definitely at Kaole. The success of
the journey was assumed by his native servants and by
the half-caste Portuguese to be doubtful from the first,
so that his first evening ' in the solitude and the silence
of the dark Gurayza ' was anything but cheerful. Nor
indeed was there much to inspire cheerfulness. His friend,
Dr. Steinhäuser—' a sound scholar, a good naturalist, a
skilful practitioner,' whose presence would have been invaluable in a land where a " medicine man " is a man of
power and authority—was unable to accompany him
through ill health, and the Persian war had prevented the
fitting out of a surveying vessel, in consequence of which
he had no assistant competent to conduct the astronomical
and meteorological observations.* Sayyid Said, Sultan of
Zanzibar and sincere friend of the English, had died a
fortnight before the Expedition arrived there ; Lieut.-

---

* Speke asserts that he did all the astronomical work, and taught
Burton the geography of the country through which they travelled—
a statement which means no more than that he had a happy knack of
making field surveys.

Colonel Hamerton was found to be in rapidly failing
health, and compelled to lead a recluse life which prevented
him from attending to really essential business, and finally,
the Expedition was starting at the fatal season when the
shrinkage of the waters after a wet monsoon would render
the unknown land a very hotbed of pestilential fever.

Under such conditions it is hardly a matter for surprise that Burton started in anything but hopeful spirits.
Nor were the circumstances of the first start calculated to
improve them. The first stage of the journey was to
Kuingáni—"the cocoa-plantation near the sea"—a little
place an hour and a half's march inland. Thither the main
body under Speke preceded him, leaving him to follow,
accompanied by Said bin Salim, his Goanese servant
Valentine, three Beloch and two slaves, with the rear of the
baggage on three Unyamwezi asses, wild kicking and
plunging brutes which rushed at one another, bolted, shied
and played pranks, in a fashion which caused Valentine to
exclaim piteously, "Un-ká nám gadhá—their name *is*
jackass." At last, near sunset, 'one of these half wild
brutes sank suddenly girth deep, in a patch of boggy mire,
and the three Beloch, my companions, at once ran away,
leaving us to extricate it as best we could. This little
event,' adds Burton, 'had a peculiar significance to one
about to command a party composed principally of asses
and Beloch.'

A short halt was necessary at Kuingáni—not that anybody would of his own free will stay in so insect-ridden
a place—and at last, at four in the afternoon, all accounts
having been settled, and final farewells said, a short march
of an hour and a half brought the caravan to the next
village. This was the "second departure." In Eastern
countries two are usually sufficient ; in Africa three are the
rule, "the little start, the great start, and the final start."
Accordingly, on the 30th of June there was another forced

halt, and here, says Burton, he ' tasted all the bitterness that can fall to the lot of those who explore regions unvisited by their own colour.' The air of Bománi is stagnant, the sun fiery, and clouds of mosquitoes make the night miserable. Then there were the men to deal with, and if Nature were harsh, man was a thousand times more so. Some clamoured for tobacco and got it ; some asked for guitar strings and were silenced with beads, and all 'born donkey-drivers complained loudly of the hardship and the indignity of having to load and lead an ass.' The guide, after drawing twenty dollars on account, refused to conduct the caravan, and the European members of the Expedition were openly charged with being infidels who were unfit to carry the Moslem flag. It was only by a threat of the strongest measures that this nuisance was stopped. Worst of all, perhaps, were the rumours of impending danger to the Expedition from native jealousy and dread of intrusion. It was not so much that there was any real danger as that these rumours completely demoralized the men and caused them on the march to turn out with tremulous alacrity on the very slightest alarm. The reports had a third ill-effect, inasmuch as they induced the slaves and servants to desert. 'The reader,' says Burton, 'may realize the extent of this African traveller's bane by the fact that, during my journey to Ujiji, from Said bin Salim, the Arab leader of the caravan, to the veriest pauper there was not one that did not, or did not attempt to, desert.'

The start from Bománi was effected on the 1st of July, after preparations which lasted from 6 A.M. to 3 P.M. Strict orders were issued. Two Beloch were told off to each donkey, one to lead the other to drive. In case of attack, those nearest the head of the file were to leave their asses and hurry to the front, while the rest were to rally round Burton's flag in the rear, thus protecting the beasts and the baggage. The only result of these elaborate preparations was that after a two-mile tramp through an umbrageous forest, and then down an easy descent across fertile fields into a broken valley, the caravan had degenerated into a mere mob of soldiers, slaves, and asses. They camped for the night at the little village of " Mkwáju lá Mvuáni—the Tamarind in Ruins," and after losing three of

THE WAZARAMO TRIBE.

Said bin Salim's slaves, prepared in the early morning for the third and final departure. So much greater promptitude was exhibited on this occasion that by 7.30 A.M. the caravan was once more on its " dew dripping way."

In camp that afternoon Burton was advised to halt on the morrow, and send forward a message to the next chief—a step which he peremptorily refused to take, knowing that it implied the loss of at least three days. During the debate on the subject one of the Beloch from Zanzibar drew his sword upon an old woman who would not part with a basket of grain. The consequence was, of course, that the difficulty of the negotiation was considerably increased. A liberal present smoothed matters over, and at four o'clock the women of the village performed a dance for the edification of the travellers. The night was an uncomfortable one. The Beloch were terrified by the sound of distant drums, which sounded like the firing of guns, and might mean either fighting or feasting ; and the wild men, amongst whom they were, kept up a continuous shouting to drive away the hippopotami from the Kaigáni River—a stream about fifty yards wide, too deep to be fordable, and swarming with crocodiles, hippopotami, and a peculiar dark green and scaleless fish, which tastes, says Burton, 'like liquid mud.'

The direful monotony of East African travel precludes all attempt to describe Burton's adventurous journey from day to day. I must content myself therefore with extracting his account of the proceedings of a single day, premising that it answers pretty accurately for every day spent in actual travelling.

' At 3 A.M. all is silent as the tomb, even the Mnyámwezi watchman nods over his fire. About an hour later the red-faced apoplectic chanticleer—there are sometimes halfa-dozen of them—the alarum of the caravan, and a prime favourite with the slaves and porters, who carry him on their banghy-poles by turns, and who drench him with water when his beak opens under the sun, flaps his wings and crows a loud salutation in the dawn ; he is answered by every cock and cockerel within ear-shot. I have been lying awake for some time, longing for the light, and when in health, for an early breakfast. At the first paling of the east, the torpid Goanese are called up to build a fire, they tremble with the cold (thermometrically averaging 60° F.) and they hurry to bring food. Appetite, somewhat difficult at this hour, demands a frequent change of diet ; we drink sweet warm water when procurable, all our tea and coffee having been damaged ; or we eat rice-milk and cakes raised with whey, or a porridge not unlike water-gruel. Whilst we are so engaged, the Beloch chanting the spiritual songs which follow prayers, squat round a cauldron placed upon a roaring fire, and fortify the inner man with boiled meat and grain, with roasted pulse and tobacco.

'About such time, 5 A.M., the camp is fairly roused, and a little low chatting becomes audible. This is a critical moment. The porters have promised overnight to start early, and to make a long wholesome march. But, 'uncertain, coy, and hard to please,' they change their minds like the fair sex ; the cold morning makes them unlike the men of the warm evening and perhaps one of them has fever. Moreover, in every caravan there is some lazy, loud-lunged, contradictory and unmanageable fellow, whose sole delight is to give trouble. If no march be in prospect, they sit obstinately before the fire warming their hands and feet, inhaling the smoke with averted heads, and casting quizzical looks at their fuming and fidgety employer. If all be unanimous, it is vain to attempt them ; even soft solder is but "throwing comfits to cows." We return to our tent. If, however, there be a division, a little active stimulating will cause a march. Then a louder conversa-tion leads to cries of " Kwecha ! Kwecha ! Pakia ! Pakia ! Hopa ! Hopa ! Collect ! pack ! set out ! Safári ! Safári leo !" —A journey, a journey to day ! and some peculiarly African boasts :—P'hunda ! Ngami ! I am an ass ! a camel !—accompanied by a roar of bawling voices, drumming, whistling, piping, and the braying of barghúmi, or horns. The " sons of Ramji," or personal slaves hired to us by that worthy, come in a body to throw our tents, and to receive small burdens, which, if possible, they shirk ; sometimes the head-man Kidogo does me the honour to inquire the programme of the day. The porters, however, hug the fire till driven from it, when they unstack the loads piled before our tents and pour out of the camp or village. My companions and I, when well enough to ride, mount our asses, led by the gun-bearers, who carry all necessaries for offence and defence ; when unfit for exercise, we are borne in hammocks, slung to long poles, and carried by two men at a time. The Beloch tending their slaves hasten off in a straggling body, thinking only of escaping an hour's sun. The Jemadar, however, is ordered to bring up the rear with Said bin Salim, who is cold and surly, abusive, and ready with his rattan. Four or five packs have been left upon the ground by deserters, or shirkers, who have started empty-handed ; consequently our Arab either double loads more willing men, or persuades the "sons of Ramji" to carry a small parcel each, or that failing, he hires from some near village a few porters by the day. This, however, is not easy, the beads have been carried off, and the most tempting promises without pre-payment, have no effect upon the African mind.

'When all is ready, the Kirangozi or Unyámwezi guide, rises and shoulders his load, which is ever one of the lightest. He deliberately raises his furled flag, a plain blood red, the sign of a caravan from Zanzibar, much tattered by the thorns, and he is followed by a privileged Pagázi, or porter, tom-toming upon a kettle-drum, much resembling a European hour-glass. The dignitary is robed in the splendour of scarlet broad cloth, a narrow piece about six feet long, with a central aperture, like a Poncho, for the neck, and with streamers dangling before and behind ; he also wears some wonderful head-dress, the spoils of a white

and black "tippet-monkey," or the barred skin of a wild cat,
crowning the head, bound round the throat, hanging over
the shoulders, and capped with a tall cup-shaped bunch of
owls' feathers, or the gorgeous plumes of the crested crane.
His insignia of office are the kipungo, or fly-flapper, the
tail of some beast which he affixes to his person as if it
were a natural growth, the konce, or hooked iron spit,
decorated with a central sausage of parti-coloured beads,
and a variety of oily little gourds containing snuff, simples
and "medicine," for the road, strapped round his waist.
He leads the caravan, and the better to secure the
obedience of his followers, he has paid them in a sheep
or a goat, the value of which he will recover by fees
and superiority of rations—the head of every animal
slaughtered in camp, and the presents at the end of the
journey are exclusively his. A man guilty of preceding
the Kirangozi is liable to fine, and an arrow is extracted
from his quiver to substantiate his identity at the end of
the march. Pouring out of the kraal in a disorderly mob,
the porters stack their goods at some tree distant but a
few hundred yards, and allow the late, the lazy, and the
invalids to join the main body. Generally at this con-
juncture the huts are fired by neglect or mischievousness.
The khambi, or encampment, especially in winter, burns
like tinder, and the next caravan will find a heap of hot
ashes and a few charred sticks still standing. Yet, by way
of contrast, the Pagazi will often take the trouble to denote
by the usual signposts to those following them that water
is at hand. Here and there a little facetiousness appears in
these erections, a mouth is cut in the tree-trunk to admit
a bit of wood simulating a pipe, with other representations
still more waggish.

‘ After the preliminary halt the caravan forming into
the order of march, winds, like a monstrous land-serpent,
over hill, dale and plain. The Kirangozi is followed by an

Indian file ; those nearest to him, the grandees of the gang, are heavily laden with ivories : when the weight of the tusk is inordinate, it is tied to a pole and is carried palanquin-fashion by two men. A large cow-bell, whose music rarely ceases on the march, is attached to the point which is to the fore ; to the bamboo behind is lashed the porter's private baggage,—his earthen cooking-pot, his water-gourd, his sleeping mat, and his other necessaries. The ivory carriers are succeeded by the bearers of cloth and beads, each man, poising upon either shoulder, and some-times raising upon the head for rest, packs that resemble huge bolsters, six feet long by two in diameter, cradled in sticks, which generally have a forked projection for facility of stacking and re-shouldering the load. The sturdiest fellows are usually the lightest loaded ; in Eastern Africa, as elsewhere, the weakest go to the wall. The maximum of burden may be two farsilah ("frails"), or seventy pounds avoirdupois. Behind the cloth bearers straggles a long line of porters and slaves, laden with the lighter stuff, rhinoceros teeth, hides, salt-cones, tobacco, brass wire, iron hoes, boxes and bags, beds and tents, pots and water-gourds, mats and private stores. With the Pagazi, but in separate parties, march the armed slaves, who are never seen to quit their muskets, the women and the little toddling children, who rarely fail to carry something, be it only of a pound weight, and the asses neatly laden with saddle-bags of giraffe or buffalo-hide. A "Mganga" almost universally accompanies the caravan, not disdaining to act as a common porter. The "parson" not only claims, in virtue of his sacred calling, the lightest load ; he is also a stout, smooth, and sleek-headed man, because, as usual with his class, he eats much and works little. The rear is brought up by the master or masters of the caravan, who often remain far behind for the convenience of walking and to prevent desertion.

'All the caravan is habited in its worst attire, the East African derides those who wear upon a journey the cloth which should be reserved for display at home. If rain fall they will doff the single goat's-skin hung round their sooty limbs, and, folding it up, place it between the shoulder and the load. When grain is served out for some days' march, each porter bears his posho or rations fastened like a large "bussle" to the small of his back. Upon this again, he sometimes binds, with its legs projecting outwards, the three-legged stool, which he deems necessary to preserve him from the danger of sitting upon the damp ground. As may be imagined, the barbarians have more ornament than dress. Some wear the ugala, a strip of zebra's mane, bound round the head with the bristly parti-coloured hair standing out like a saint's "gloria:" others prefer a long bit of stiffened ox-tail, rising like a unicorn's horn, at least a foot above the forehead. Other ornaments are the skins of monkeys and ocelots, rouleaus and fillets of white, blue or scarlet cloth, and huge bunches of ostrich, crane, and jays' feathers crowning the head, like the tufts of certain fowls. Their arms are decorated with massive ivory bracelets, heavy bangles of brass or copper, and thin circlets of the same metal ; beads in strings and bands, adorn their necks, and small iron bells, a "knobby" decoration, whose incessant tinkling harmonises, in African ears with the regular chime-like "Ti-ti! Ti-ti! tang!" of the tusk-bells, and the loud broken "Wa-ta-taa!" of the horns, are strapped below the knee or round the ankle by the more aristocratic. All carry some weapon ; the heaviest armed have a bow and a bark quiver full of arrows, two or three long spears and assegais, a little battle-axe borne on the shoulder, and the sime or dudgeon.

'The normal recreations of a march are, whistling, singing, shoutihg, hooting, horning, drumming, imitating the cries of birds and beasts, repeating words which are never used except on journeys—a "chough's language, gabble enough and good enough"—and abundant squabbling; in fact perpetual noise which the ear however soon learns to distinguish from the hubbub of a halt. The uproar redoubles near a village, where the flag is unfurled and where the line lags to display itself. All give vent to ,loud shouts, "Hopa! hopa!—go on! go on! Mgogolo! —a stoppage! Food! food! Don't be tired! The kraal is near—home is near! Hasten, Kirangozi—Oh! We see our mothers! We go to eat!" On the road it is considered prudent as well as pleasurable to be as loud as possible, in order to impress upon plunderers an exaggerated idea of the caravan's strength; for equally good reasons silence is recommended in the kraal. When threatened with attack and no ready escape suggests itself, the porters ground their loads and prepare for action. It is only self-interest that makes them brave. I have seen a small cow, trotting up with tail erect, break a line of 150 men carrying goods not their own. If a hapless hare or antelope cross the path, every man casts his pack, brandishes his spear, and starts in pursuit; the animal never running straight is soon killed, and torn limb from limb, each negroid helluo devouring his morsel raw. Sometimes a sturdy fellow "renowns it" by carrying his huge burden round and round, like a horse being ringed, and starts off at full speed. When two bodies meet, that commanded by an Arab claims the road. If both are Wanyámwezi, violent quarrels ensue, but fatal weapons, which are too ready at hand, are turned to more harmless purposes, the bow and spear being used as whip and cudgel. These affrays are not rancorous till blood is shed. Few tribesmen are less friendly for so trifling an affair as a broken head; even a slight cut or a shallow stab is little thought of; but, if returned with interest, great loss of life may arise from the slenderest cause. When friendly caravans meet, Kiran-

gozis sidle up with a stage pace, a stride, a stand, and with
sidelong looks prance till arrived within distance; then
suddenly and simultaneously "ducking," like boys "giving
a back," they come to logger-heads and exchange a butt
violently as fighting rams. Their example is followed by
all with a rush and a crush, which might be mistaken
for the beginning of a faction fight, but it ends, if there be
no bad blood, in shouts of laughter. The weaker body
however must yield precedence, and offer a small present
as blackmail.

'About 8 A.M., when the fiery sun has topped the trees,
and a pool of water, or a shady place, appears, the planting
of the red flag, the braying of a barghumi, or koodoo's
horn, which, heard at a distance in the deep forests, has
something of the charm which endears the *Cor de Chasse*
to every woodman's ear, and sometimes a musket-shot or
two announces a short halt. The porters stack their loads,
and lie or loiter about for a few minutes, chatting, drinking,
and smoking tobacco and bhang, with the usual whooping,
screaming cough, and disputing eagerly about the resting-
place for the day. On long marches we then take the
opportunity of stopping to discuss the contents of two
baskets which are carried by a slave under the eye of the
Goanese.

'If the stage be prolonged towards noon, the caravan
lags, straggles, and suffers sorely. The heat of the ground,
against which the horniest sole never becomes proof, tries
the feet like polished-leather boots on a quarter-deck in
the dog-days near the Line; and some tribulation is caused
by the cry, "M'iba hapa!—thorns here!" The Arabs and
the Beloch must often halt to rest. The slaves ensconce
themselves in snug places; the porters, propping their
burdens against the trees, curl up, dog-like, under the
shade; some malinger; and this, the opportunity preferred
for desertion, is an anxious hour to the proprietor, who, if

he would do his work " deedily," must be the last in the kraal. Still the men rarely break down as in Indian marching; the African caravan chooses to end the day, rather than to begin it, with a difficulty—the ascent of a hill, or the fording of a stream. They prefer the strip of jungle at the farther end of a district or a plantation, for safety as well as for the comfort of shade. They avoid the vicinity of rocks ; and on desert plains they occupy some slightly rising ground, where the night cold is less severe than in the lower levels.

'At length an increased hubbub of voices, blended with bells, drums, fifes and horns, and sometimes a few musket-shots, announce that the van is lodged, and the hubbub of the halt confirms the pleasing intelligence that the journey is shortened by a stage. Each selfish body then hurries forward to secure the best bothy in the kraal, or the most comfortable hut in the village, and quarrels seem serious. Again, however, the knife returns home guiltless of gore, and the spear is used only as an instrument for sound belabouring. The more energetic at once apply themselves to "making all snug" for the long hot afternoon and the nipping night ; some hew down young trees, others collect heaps of leafy boughs ; one acts architect, and many bring in huge loads of firewood. The East African is so much accustomed to house-life, that the bivouac in the open appears to him a hardship ; he prefers even to cut out the interior of a bush and to squat in it, the portrait of a comfortable cynocephalus. We usually spread our donkey-saddles and carpets in some shade, awaiting the arrival of our tents, and its erection by the grumbling "sons of Ramji." If we want a hut, we draw out the man in possession like a badger—he will never have the decency to offer it. As a rule, the villagers are more willing to receive the upward-bound caravans than those who, return-ing, carry wealth out of, instead of into, the country.

Merchants, on account of their valuable outfits, affect, except in the safest localities, the khambi rather than the village ; the latter, however, in miasmatic lands, is not only healthier, despite its uncleanliness, but it is also more comfortable, plenty and variety of provisions being more readily procured inside than outside. The Arab's khaymah is a thin pole or ridge-tent, of flimsy domestics, admitting sun and rain, and, like an Irish cabin, permitting at night the occupant to tell time by the stars ; yet he prefers it, probably, for dignity to the bothy, which, in this land of verdure and cool winds, is a far more comfortable lodging.'

The halts are managed in different ways, according to the different tribes. One will willingly admit strangers into their villages, another will refuse the privilege altogether. In a third case caravans seize the best lodgings by force ; while, in a fourth, strangers have to pitch their tents in the clear open spaces in the midst of the villages. In Ugogo strangers rarely enter the hamlets, the huts being foul, and the people dangerous ; but throughout Eastern and Central Unyámwezi caravans defile into the villages without hesitation, while in Western Unyamwezi the doors are often closed against strangers. Each tribe has, in short, its own customs, but it may be taken as an axiom that nothing— not even the permission to camp out—can be had for nothing in Eastern or Central Africa. When a kraal has to be built a hedge of thorns, flimsy, but impassable to naked legs and feet, is set up round the caravan, and rough wattled huts, with a covering of grain, cane or grass are built within. Rations are not served out until this work is done ; then, when the cattle have been "off-packed," and water has been brought in from the pit or stream, fires are lighted, and all apply themselves to the pleasant business of refection. Burton found the negro races very like froward and ill-conditioned children, especially in this

matter of food. At home, when they eat their own provisions, they content themselves with a single meal of flour
and water once a day. When they eat the food provided
for them by others they eat greedily, and complain that
they are starved. If eight days' rations are served out at
once they will devour the whole in three, and clamour for
more, which the Arabs do not, as a rule, give them, treating them, as the savage delights to be treated, with alternate gorging and starvation. Between their dozen meals
of porridge—'stick-jaw dough and pearly holcus, like
small shot, rat-stews and boiled weeds—which they devour
till their bulge appears like the crop of a stuffed turkey,
they puff clouds of pungent tobacco, cough and scream
over the jungle bhang, and chew ashes, quids, and pinches
of red earth—probably the graves of white ants.'

Burton's own day, when not actually travelling, was
sufficiently wearisome, passed chiefly under a spreading tree
or under a bower of leafy branches, and very seldom in the
flimsy tent. Its occupations were the diary and sketch-
book, with a little business—doling out cloth, persuading
the porters to scour the country for provisions, attending
at the killing of the bullocks, when such a luxury could be
obtained. 'Dinner at 4 P.M. breaks the neck of the day.
Provisions of some kind are mostly procurable; our diet,
however, varies from such common doings as the hard
holcus-stone, the tasteless bean-broth, and the leathery
goat steak, to fixings of delicate venison, fatted capon, and
young guinea-fowl or partridge, with "bread sauce," composed of bruised rice and milk. At first the Goanese
declined to cook "pretty food," as pasties and rissoles, on
the plea that such things were impossible on the march;
they changed their minds when warned that persistence in
such theory might lead to a ceremonious fustigation.'
Burton also succeeded in inducing them to refrain from
serving Speke and himself with the worst part of the food

they cooked, and keeping the best for their own consumption, but he failed to get them to prepare tea or
coffee in a civilised fashion.

Night was ushered in with tethering the asses and

LADIES' SMOKING PARTY, UNYÁMWEZI.

penning and pounding the cattle, in spite of which much
time was lost by the carelessness of the blackfellows, who
do their work in such a way that some or all of the *bétail.*
are lost every second day. The loads are collected and
counted, and that done, if provisions have been plentiful,

and if there is a bright moonshine, the evening is given up to merriment—dancing, which is a very vigorous exercise indeed, and singing. The hierophant of the Metropolitan Tabernacle will perhaps be glad to know that his dictum as to dancing is strictly observed in Eastern and Central Africa. The men dance by themselves, and ' when the fun threatens to become too fast and furious the song dies and the performers, with loud shouts of laughter, throw themselves on the ground to recover strength and breath. Then comes the turn of the ladies, who " prefer," ' says Burton, 'to perform by themselves, and perhaps in the East ours would do the same, if a literal translation of the remarks to which a ball always gives rise amongst Orientals, happened by misfortune to reach their refined ears.' After the dancing would come music, with the accompaniment of chatting, squabbling, and talking around the fires. Burton gives the following as a specimen of the songs, premising that " wicked " must be taken to mean simply the man who is fully alive to the wickedness of other people. ' Moreover,' he says, ' despite my " wickedness," they used invariably to come to me for justice and redress, especially when proximity to the coast encouraged the guide and guards to bully them.' Here followeth the anthem :—

" Muzungu Mbaya " (the wicked white man) goes from the shore,
    Puti! Puti! (I can only translate it by " Grub! grub!")
We will follow " Muzungu Mbaya,"
    Puti! Puti!
As long as he gives us good food!
    Puti! Puti!
We will traverse the hill and the stream,
    Puti! Puti!
With the caravan of this great mundewa (merchant).
    Puti! Puti! &c., &c.

About 8 P.M.—they keep early hours in Central Africa— the cry of " Lala! lala! "—sleep—resounds, and is willingly obeyed by all except the women, who will sometimes awake to gossip even at midnight. One by one the camp sink into slumber as the great stars come out. 'At this time especially, when in the jungle bivouac, the scene often becomes truly impressive. The dull red fires flickering and forming a circle of ruddy light in the depths of the black forest, flaming against the tall trunks and defining the foliage of the near trees, illuminate lurid groups of savage men in every variety of shape and posture. Above, the dark purple sky studded with golden points domes the earth with bounds narrowed by the gloom of night. And behold in the Western horizon a splendid crescent with a dim, ash-coloured globe in its arms, and crowned by Hesperus sparkling like a diamond, sinks through the vast of space, in all the glory and gorgeousness of Eternal Nature's sublimest works. From such a night, methinks, the Byzantine man took his device, the Crescent, and the Star.'

Such a caravan as Burton's, and indeed as that found necessary by all African travellers, could advance only very slowly. At the start in the early morning, perhaps four statute miles per hour might be covered, but after the enthusiasm of the start had evaporated, the four miles per hour soon dwindled down into about 2·25 or 1·75 geographical miles measured by compass from point to point. In clear country an allowance of 20 per cent. must be made for winding roads : in closer country from 40 to 50 per cent., and the traveller must use his discretion between these two extremes. The net result is that an ordinary journey through the wilds seldom exceeds six geographical miles projected in a straight line, and never exceeds ten, which last distance can be accomplished only under special pressure. Burton has given a great number of corroborative facts to this conclusion with which it is unnecessary to trouble the reader. The point remains that progress in East Africa is exceedingly slow, and that the consequences of such tardiness in malarious regions were, if not disastrous, at least terribly painful to the white members of the Expedition.

Under these conditions the long, tedious, and dangerous journey to Lake Tanganyika began. The incidents were few, but their significance was great. First of all the caravan passed through a region so thickly peopled with graves as to ' make the blackness of my companions pale,' says Burton. Then came in the same day a difficulty about toll, which was not settled until the matchlock men (the Beloch) had prepared to open fire. Then, later on, came a dispute between the two parties of Beloch—those sent by the Prince as a permanent guard, and those enlisted at Kaole—which ended in thirteen men of the latter class starting up and setting forth on their way home without a word of explanation. Had this been allowed to pass without notice, a further desertion would have followed, which would have ended in the party losing about two-thirds of its strength. Burton was equal to the occasion. He sent for the Jemadars, and in their presence wrote a letter to the dreaded "Balyuz" strongly denouncing their conduct. The Consul was supposed to be still on board the *Artémise* at anchor off Kaole, and the letter produced its anticipated effect. Seeing the bastinado in the near future, if the men were not promptly recovered, one of the Jemadar slung his shield over his arm, and soon found means to bring back the runaways to their camp and to common-sense. The squabbling did not, however, cease, and within four-and-twenty hours one of the Beloch drew his dagger upon one of Said ben Salim's " children," who, in turn, pointed his Tower musket at him. There was a furious hubbub, but Said, after screaming " shrilly as a woman" at the combatants, succeded in restoring peace.

To add to the miseries of the situation, Speke began to fall ill at this point. The damp, heat, and the reeking miasma told upon his constitution, and the fatal African fever laid its grasp upon him. In a day or two more he was prostrate ; the caravan was of necessity halted, and Burton had to go out with his gun to seek for meat, the supply having fallen short. When the march was resumed through the malarious plain of the Kingani River—which the Arabs call Wady el-Maut and Dar el-Jua, "the Valley of Death, and the Home of Hunger"—Speke was compelled by sickness to ride, and thus the asses' backs, sore and weakened with fatigue, were saddled with a double burden. To add to these troubles, news arrived of the death of the English Consul at Zanzibar, who had been a warm friend of the Expedition and of Burton personally. The Arabs knew of the event before Burton, but kept their knowledge to themselves. When at last he discovered it, it served only to stimulate their already ardent desire to return to Zanzibar. Burton was, however, firm and pressed on, amidst almost overwhelming difficulties. Thus, on the 8th of July, his camping ground was a ragged kraal on the tree-lined bank of a half-dry Fiumara, a tributary of the neighbouring river. ' The water was bad, and a mortal smell of decay was emitted by the dark, dank ground. It was a mild day. From the black brumal clouds, driven before furious blasts pattered rain drops like musket bullets, splashing the already saturated earth. The tall stiff trees bent before the gusts ; the birds screamed as they were driven from their perching places ; the asses stood with heads depressed, ears hung down, and shrinking tails turned towards the weather, and even the beasts of the wild seemed to have taken refuge in their dens.' Provisions were not to be had, wherefore the men ate double quantities of the rations they carried with them, and then came to beg for their dismissal on the plea of hunger.

It is hardly a matter for wonder that under these circumstances the health of the party generally broke down. At Tunda, "the Fruit "—so called because no fruit grows there—Burton arose after a night passed within the depressing influence of the river with 'aching head, burning eyes, and throbbing extremities.' Speke, whom, it may be mentioned here, Burton never speaks of by name, was recovering, but Said bin Salim had been attacked during the rainy night by a severe Mkunguru, or seasoning fever, and begged for a halt, even if it were for only an hour. Even this had to be refused. Said was put upon an ass, and the weary march was resumed, the guides seizing the occasion to lead the caravan astray. A halt was called perforce, and on the following day the journey was continued through a population not precisely hostile, but timid and suspicious, and terribly frightened of the arms carried by the party. The greatest caution and circumspection were necessary, especially as Speke was no linguist, and could communicate with the caravan only through the Beloch, who spoke a bastard kind of Hindustani. Burton, on whom all the real work of the expedition fell, was, on the eleventh day after leaving Kaole, in such a state of weakness and prostration as to be hardly able to stand, and was compelled, in consequence, to ride, though he could hardly sit upright. Still, however, he persevered, and had, on the 14th of July, the consolation of knowing that he had passed through the most perilous part of his journey, in which was included the scene of the treacherous murder of M. Maizan, the French explorer, without any accident, save the loss of a double-barreled elephant-gun. In eighteen days, from the 27th of June to the 14th of July, despite the sickness of Speke, of his Arab "manager," and of himself, he had accomplished a march of 118 indirect statute miles, and had entered K'hutu, the safe rendezvous of foreign merchants.

The march was resumed on the following day, through a thick and tangled jungle, swarming with animal life, from the gigantic Gnu, which the porters declared to be capable of charging a caravan, to the land crab and the ant. At Kiruru, the village which was reached on this day, after a march of six hours, Burton found a cottage, where he 'enjoyed for the first time an atmosphere of sweet, warm smoke.' Speke, more fastidious, preferred the recking miry tents, and so laid the foundation of that fever which a few months afterwards threatened his life. Then came another bad time. The torrents of rain, and the depth of mud, rendered a two days' halt necessary, despite the danger to an ass caravan from hyænas, leopards and crocodiles, and when the march was resumed, it was through a tract of country where the thick grass drips with dew until mid-day, and the black ground is greasy and slippery. The road soon became even worse—jungle, forest, barrens of the low mimosa and dreary savannahs, intersected by deep nullahs. In three places the caravan crossed bogs of from one hundred yards to a mile in width, knee deep in mud. The porters plunged through them "like laden animals," and it was found necessary to hold Burton upon his ass. These troubles over, Burton forged somewhat ahead, and arrived at Dut'humi, the settlement of an Arab slave trader—Sayf bin Salim—of no very good character. Presently Speke staggered in, 'too ill too speak,' and then 'by slow degrees, and hardly able to walk, the Arab, the Beloch, the slaves, and the asses, each and every one having been bogged in turn.' At this point the caravan was detained for nearly a week. This day's journey through a hideously malarious country had brought on attacks of marsh fever, which, in Burton's case, lasted for twenty days. These attacks thoroughly prostrated him, though they were not quite so severe as in Sind. Speke was worse. He had a fainting fit which strongly resembled a sunstroke, and which seemed permanently to affect his brain. The two Goanese

yielded to maladies which in their case were brought on
wholly by over-eating, and if they had not been forced to
move they would probably never have risen again.

There were other troubles of the journey hardly less severe.
The riding asses having been given up for loads, those who
should have ridden were often compelled to walk, even when
the premonitory symptoms peremptorily suggested rest.
Riding was, however, by no means an unmitigated joy·
The ass of Africa requires something more than the bridle
which Solomon thought the only thing necessary. He is
stubborn and vicious ; he shies and stumbles ; he rears and
he runs away ; he hogs and he bucks ; he prefers holes
and hollows ; he insists on being led, and if any pace
beyond two miles an hour is required of him he requires a
second man to follow and thwack him during the whole
march ; he has round flanks, a short back, no particular
shoulder, and his pasterns are so straight and stiff that his
gait is a wearisome, tripping hobble. The laden asses gave
as much trouble as those used for riding. With proper care
there would have been less difficulty, but care in an African
is as rare as humour in a Scot. The result was that the
burdens were put on without the smallest attention to
girthing and balancing, so that at every broken ground the
parcels were thrown down and the whole labour of the
morning had to be repeated. During the illness of Burton
and his companion the animals were never pounded for the
night ; the ropes and cords intended to secure the herd
were regularly stolen, and many beasts having thus been
lost the Expedition was near being brought to a premature
close. 'Every morning,' says Burton, 'dawned upon me
with a fresh load of cares and troubles, and every evening
reminded me as it closed in, that another and a miserable
morrow was to dawn. But " in despair," as the Arabs say,
" are many hopes ; " though sorrow endured for the night,
and many were " white " with anxiety, we never relinquished

the determination to risk everything, ourselves included, rather than to return unsuccessful.'

Dut'humi, where Burton was thus detained, is, in spite of its climate, a favourite resort of the Arab slave-traders, who sometimes reside there for months at a time for the purpose of buying slaves cheaply and of recruiting their broken fortunes for a trip into the interior. The effect of all this is to keep up a constant feud amongst the chiefs, so that scarcely a month passes without fields being laid waste, villages burnt down, and the unhappy peasantry carried off to be sold. One such raid took place while Burton was in Dut'humi, and it was not for an English officer and gentleman to stand by and see this iniquity done without a vigorous protest. He accordingly headed a small expedition against the chief who had been guilty of it, rescued the five unhappy wretches who had been kidnapped, and restored them to their homes. This—which Burton lightly calls 'an easy good deed'—being done, he indited with swimming head a report to the Royal Geographical Society, and an urgent request for medical comforts, especially quinine and narcotics, to the British Consul at Zanzibar, which he entrusted to the care of one of his men, together with a recommendation for his promotion. The hired escort from Kaole was dismissed for the simple reason that Burton could not afford to keep it. Said bin Salim, to whom the charge of the money of the country —the 'white and blue cottons, some handsome articles of dress, 20,000 strings of white and black, pink, blue and green, red and brown porcelain beads, needles, and other articles of hardware'—had been entrusted, had been too lavish, and during his illness his " children " had looted the stores. Three months' supplies had disappeared in as many weeks ; the thirteen men composing the permanent guard had increased the number of their laden asses from two to five, and for a considerable time afterwards the " sons of

Ramji" could afford to expend four to five cloths upon a goat.

On resuming his journey, Burton found himself in an equally wretched country with that which he had left. The start was made on the 24th of July, and after leaving the cultivated region, the travellers were once more in a malarious district—'a jungle where the European traveller realises every preconceived idea of Africa's aspect, at once hideous and grotesque. . . . The black greasy ground veiled with thick shrubbery supports in the more open spaces screens of tiger and spear grass, twelve and thirteen feet high, with every blade a finger's breadth, and the towering trees are often clothed from root to twig with huge epiphytes, forming heavy columns of densest verdure and clustering upon the tops in the semblance of enormous birds' nests. The footpaths, in places "dead"—as the natives say—with encroaching bush are crossed by llianas, creepers, and climbers, thick as coir cables, some connecting the trees in a curved line, others stretched straight down the trunks, others winding in all directions round their supports, frequently crossing one another like network, and stunting the growth of even the vivacious calabash, by coils like rope tightly encircling its neck. The earth, ever rain-drenched, emits the odour of sulphuretted hydrogen, and in some parts the traveller might fancy a corpse to be hidden behind every bush.' The atmosphere matches the landscape—a wild sky with frequent and drenching rain, squalls, and chilling winds, or a heavy pall of dull dark-grey cloud, always, whether hot or cold, saturated with damp. 'That no feature of miasma might be wanting to complete the picture, filthy heaps of the rudest hovels, built in holes in the jungle, sheltered their few miserable inhabitants, whose frames are lean with constant intoxication and whose limbs distorted by ulcerous sores attest the hostility of nature to mankind.' And this dreary country extends from Central K'hutu to the base of the Usagara mountains.

After a journey of a month—a fortnight being the time usually spent upon it—Burton and his following came upon the outskirts of the Zungomero districts, where he found the thirty-six Wanyámwezi who had been sent on in advance. This district is the head of the great river valley, a plain of black earth and sand, prodigiously fertile and hideously unwholesome. The sun draws up poison from the putrid earth, and the heavy dews are dreaded even by the natives. A prolonged halt causes terrible sickness amongst the porters and slaves of a caravan, and the excessive humidity of the atmosphere causes an amount of inconvenience and annoyance which it is difficult to overestimate. The springs of powder flasks snap like toasted quills; the best percussion-caps, though labelled "waterproof," will not detonate unless carefully stowed away in waxed cloths and tinned boxes, and gunpowder, if not kept from the air, refuses to ignite—in those days, it should be noted, "drawn cartridges" and breechloading guns had not come into use; 'metals are ever rusty, paper loses its substance, clothes have a perpetual feeling of damp about them, while matches, whether German phosphorus or English wax, turn to paste.' In spite of this drawback Zungomero is the great centre of East African trade, especially in the matter of slaves, and it has a more or less settled population, who appear, in default of meat and poultry, to live chiefly on pombé, or native beer, and some one or other of the numerous preparations of the *Cannabis Indica*—the Indian bhang. The country is, or was when Burton made his journey, in a shocking state, being overrun by an army of touters, who amuse themselves whilst waiting for the ivory traders with ravaging the villages and carrying off the people into slavery. As this is done in the name of His Highness the Sultan and

the chief nobles of Zanzibar, and as the Wakhútu are a
timid race, there would seem to be no hope but in sub-
mission. The worst of the matter is that there is really no
alternative. Among the free and independent tribes of
Southern Africa the English traveller finds the work of
exploration comparatively easy. In Eastern and Central
Africa every man's hand is against the hand of every other.
The slave-trade practically annihilates the better feelings
of humanity. 'Though the state of the Wakhútu appears
pitiable,' says Burton, 'the traveller cannot practise pity:
he is ever in the dilemma of maltreating or being mal-
treated. Were he to deal civilly and liberally with this
people he would starve : it is vain to offer a price for even
the necessaries of life ; it would certainly be refused,
because more is wanted, and so on beyond the bounds of
possibility. Thus, if the touter did not seize a house, he
would never be allowed to take shelter in it from the
storm ; if he did not enforce a "corvée," he must labour
beyond his strength with his own hands ; and if he did not
fire a village and sell the villagers, he might die of hunger
in the midst of plenty. Such in this province are the
action and reaction of the evil.'

Here in this hotbed of pestilence, Zungomero, Burton
and Speke had to wait for a fortnight for the twenty-two
promised porters. It was hardly a pleasant time. Burton's
only lodging was under the closed eaves of a hut built
in the African fashion, one abode within another ; and the
only shelter from the tropical rain was a roof which was
about as effective against it as a sieve. By way of making
things pleasant, the Beloch, who had expected everything
to be done for them, lay out in the rain for a week rather
than take the trouble of building a shed for themselves,
and made themselves utterly obnoxious to the villagers by
their pertinacious habits of thievery, in which they were
rivalled by Said bin Salim, the Arab slave-trader of

Dut'humi, already mentioned. This worthy had offered
the services of his gang to carry the baggage half way over
the mountains to Ugogo for sixty dollars. Thinking his
terms exorbitant, Burton declined the proposal, whereupon
the man, who had begged unscrupulously for 'drugs, tea,
coffee, spices, everything,' all the way from Dut'humi,
levanted after having caused the desertion of nine porters
whom Burton had hired at his headquarters, and carrying
with him a quantity of cloth and Muinyi Wariza's sword.
Three armed men were sent to compel the return of the
stolen goods, by force if necessary, but they succeeded in
bringing back only the sword and an impudent letter.
Burton made formal complaint to the Sayyid Majid, 'but
the arm of Zanzibar has not yet reached K'hutu.' It is,
however, worth while to note that this man was the sole
base exception to the hospitality and courtesy of the
Omani Arabs with whom Burton came in contact.

The Muinyi Wariza mentioned above was a somewhat
remarkable personage. He spoke five African dialects,
and when sober would do the work of three ordinary men.
But, alas! he seldom *was* sober, entertaining an undying
fondness for pombé, or holcus beer, and alternating between
the states of maudlin apathy and violent pugnacity. For
the rest he was not in any sense trustworthy. 'Linguists
are a dangerous class,' says Burton, oblivious of the famous
dilemma about the Cretans, ' as the annals of old India
prove : I doubt a bi-lingual Eastern man, and if he can
speak three languages I do not doubt him at all.' Wariza
justified the opinion which his master had formed of him.
True to his exceedingly mixed blood—his father was a
half-caste Masawáhíli, and his mother a Mzaramo slave—he
began well and finished badly, and neither he nor his five
messmates saw the sea of Ujiji in Burton's company.

The Expedition left Zungomero on the 7th of August,
1857, fairly martyrised by miasma, and Burton and his

companion both so feeble that they could hardly sit their
asses, and almost wholly deaf. For some time their way lay
up the rising ground, and by the evening they had arrived at
Mzizi Mdogo, or the " Little Tamarind." The effect of the
change from the frowsy miasmatic air of the plains to the
dryer and colder air of the mountains was magical ; health
and strength returned, and even the Goanese shook off the
remittent fever which had tortured them in the Zungomero. The air was clear and cool, the sun was bright and
large—' nowhere have I seen,' says Burton, ' the rulers of
night and day so large ; ' the jungle with its dismal
exuberance, and the plains of monotonous grass, gave way
to tall solitary trees, amongst which the lofty tamarind-
rose was conspicuously graceful, and the open plain intersected with streams, nullahs, and stagnant pools gave way
to dry healthy slopes, with steep pitches and gently-
shelving hills. It was indeed the " Delectable Mountains
after the Slough of Despond." All was not, however, bliss,
even in this temporal paradise. On the day following
many skeletons were passed—skeletons of porters and
others, who had been stricken down by small-pox and left
by their companions to perish. One caravan had been
met which had lost fifty of its number by the fell malady,
and the spectacle had been only too frequent of men
staggering on blinded by disease, and of mothers carrying
on their backs infants as loathsome as themselves. Several
of Burton's own men must have been infected. They
lagged behind, and probably threw themselves into the
jungle, for when the path was revisited on the return of the
party, no sign of them was discovered.

The day's march was a long and tedious one through a
country alternately hilly and jungly, but ending at a kraal
in a delightful spot equal to Mzizi Mdogo in purity of air,
and having a fair prospect of the Highlands of Dut'humi.
There was a forced halt. The asses were giving out, and

the Beloch were suffering from colic ; the Wanyámwezi were incapacitated by the premonitory symptoms of small-pox from carrying their packs, and the symptoms of ague were making their appearance. When the start was made at last over a wild country intersected with nullahs, or rather dry ditches, and down through a Fiumara, dry during the hot season, and altogether and at every season, horrible, it was made under circumstances of the most depressing kind, and the sight of numerous corpses of travellers who had preceded the caravan and fallen by the way, did not tend to reassure the already half de-spairing travellers. 'Our Moslems passed them with averted faces, and a low "la haul!" of disgust, and a decrepid old Wanyámwezi porter gazed at them and wept for himself.' To add to Burton's worries, his instruments had been so carelessly treated that he was in the matter of gauging heights by the well-known process of "boiling the thermometer" reduced to a couple of bath thermo-meters, which, in spite of all his precautions, and of the after-thought of boiling the same instruments for cor-rective purposes at Bombay, deprived many of his obser-vations of that scientific accuracy which the explorer most eminently desiderates.

Zenhwe was the turning point of the Expedition's diffi-culties. The asses had died off until only twenty-three were left ; the Beloch had doubled their requirements, and the caravan troubles generally had multiplied. A grand *tamashá* followed. Burton wished the porters to carry the property of his Belochs, the Belochs refused to give it up, argument was found to be impossible with unreason-able men, an exuberant "row" began in the camp, "that man's life" was openly threatened, and finally there was a strike. Said bin Salim came to say that his men wanted a sheep a day—men who, when in Zanzibar, probably saw meat once a year—and that being refused, demanded three cloths daily instead of one. Burton offered two—they straightway demanded four, and being refused, marched away in a body with noisy protestations of their intention to return to Zanzibar—which would not have been difficult, seeing that they had contrived on the way to steal quite enough to pay all the expenses of their return journey, and leave them a handsome surplus on arrival. The case was the usual one in dealing with the savage races. Honesty and gratitude are words which have no meaning for them. These men had been treated with exceptional kindness. One of them, who suffered from dysentery, had been regularly supplied with food prepared by Burton's own cook and allowed to ride on an ass when his masters trudged on foot, all feeble and fevered as they were. Yet he was amongst the ringleaders of this servile revolt, and would apparently have felt no compunction in taking "that man's" life. Eventually the storm blew over with, as the Spanish proverb has it, "more noise than nuts." The start was ordered for the next day—August 17th—and the ringleaders of the revolt came to kiss their master's hand, and assure him that it was not they who had intended to desert him, but he who had intended the same scurvy trick by them. 'As this required no reply,' says Burton, 'I mounted and rode on.' The deserters came in on that day, shouldering their luggage as the asses had been taken from them, and professing abundant penitence. Next morning the Beloch were assembled and harangued— *Anglicé* roundly scolded—for their misdeeds. They were wondrous penitent—they had taken opium, they had been seduced by the Wiswas, tempted of the Devil, and they would do so no more. They were, of course, forgiven, and they kept their promises until Ugogo was reached, when they once more showed themselves in their true character.

It may at this point be advisable to recall what manner

of men these Beloch really were. Soldiers in the service of the Sultan of Zanzibar, they had been lent by him to Burton to accompany him in his journey to "create an impression," and to make the "blameless Æthiopians" afraid. They detested the service for which they had been detailed ; held themselves to be servants, not of Burton, but of their Prince, and on the journey proved that their constitutions, capped by a long course of East African vices, had not the smallest real stamina. Under the slightest attack of fever they threw themselves on the ground, and for anything like actual soldierly duty they proved themselves utterly incompetent. They were insolent, intrusive, vain and braggart. 'Gratitude they ignored ; with them a favour granted was but an earnest of favours to come, and one refusal obliterated the trace of a hundred largesses. Their objects in life seemed to be eating and buying slaves ; their pleasures drinking and intrigue. Insatiable beggars were they ; noisy, boisterous, foul-mouthed knaves, swearers "with voices like cannons," rude and forward in manner, low and abusive in language, so slanderous that for want of other subjects they would calumniate one another, and requiring a periodical check to their presumption. I might have spent,' Burton goes on to say, 'the whole of my day in superintending the food of these thirteen "great eaters and little runners." Repeatedly warned by myself and by my companion, that their insubordination would prevent our recommending them for recompense at the end of the journey, they could not check repeated ebullitions of temper. Before arrival at the coast they seemed to have made up their minds that they had not fulfilled the conditions of reward. After my departure from Zanzibar, however, they persuaded Lieut.-Col. Hamerton's successor to report officially to the Government of Bombay · "the claims of those men, the hardships they endured, and the fidelity and perseverance they showed." '

Fever and small-pox, the deaths of three asses, one from fatigue, one from having been torn by a hyæna, a third from weakness, coupled with the necessity for leaving behind another that had been stung by bees, reduced the carrying capacity of the caravan to very small proportions. Supplies were terribly scarce, and it was only after a long delay that the Expedition could move on. The monotony of the journey was, of course, varied by sundry incidents. Thus, on the 23rd of August, the travellers had a very practical experience of what the African slave trade really means. After falling into a network of paths, the road was lost. Presently the caravan found itself amidst the *débris* of a once flourishing village. The huts were torn and half-burnt, the ground strewed with nets and drums, pestles and mortars, cots, and fragments of rough furniture. There were no traces of blood, but it was obvious that a " commando" had taken place. Two of the wretched villagers were lurking in the jungle, afraid to return to their homes; for the rest, all was desolation and despair. Burton's caravan, however, spent the night in this deserted village, drumming, singing and gleaning all that the slave-hunting gang had left. On the next day three other plagues of Central Africa were encountered, a small red ant with a cruel sting ; an ant with "a bull-dog head and powerful mandibles," which wages war upon rats, mice, lizards and snakes, and, when occasion serves, upon man also; and, lastly, the "tzetze," that horrible fly which Lord Sherbrooke, when he was simple Mr. Lowe, thought to be the most potent argument against that expedition to Abyssinia which gave a title to Lord Napier of Magdala. Later on, the caravan came upon another plague, the white ants, the *Chunga Mchwa*, a dismal insect which abounds in these regions in sweet red clay soil, and cool, damp places. Its powers are astonishing. 'A hard clay bench has been drilled and pierced like a sieve by these insects in a single night, and bundles of reeds, placed under bedding, have, in a few hours, been converted into a mass of mud; straps were consumed, cloths and umbrellas were reduced to rags, and the mats used for covering the servants' sleeping car were in the shortest possible time so tattered as to be unserviceable.' Man has his revenge, however. The termite eats his property; he eats the termite, which, though he is not a particularly savoury morsel, helps to satisfy the passionate craving for animal food which this part of the tropics produces.

The toil of travel made itself especially felt here. Long distances had to be traversed, and for many miles together water is hardly to be obtained. Caravans have, therefore, to resort to what is technically called a "Tirikeza," or afternoon march, one of the severest trials which the explorer in Central Africa has to undergo. At eleven in the morning the whole camp is thrown into confusion, although a start will not be made until two or three o'clock in the afternoon. 'Having drunk for the last time, and filled their gourds for the night, the wayfarers set out when the mid-day ends. The sun is far more severely felt after the sudden change from shade than during the morning marches, when its increase of heat is slow and gradual. They trudge under the fireball in the firmament, over ground seething with glow and reek, through an air which seems to parch the eyeballs, and they endure this affliction till their shadows lengthen out upon the ground. The "tirikeza" is almost invariably a lengthy stage, as the porters wish to abridge the next morning's march, which leads to water. It is often bright moonlight before they arrive at the ground, with faces torn by the thorns projecting across the jungly path, with feet lacerated by stone and stub, and occasionally a leg lamed by stumbling into deep and narrow holes, the work of

field rats and various insects.' Such a march was that of
the 3rd of September, which began at 1 P.M. and ended
at six, when the caravan camped for the night in a cleared
space in the thick thorn jungle, where the near presence of
the hyæna and the alarm of the asses made sleep a matter
of no small difficulty.

The next day found the caravan in the depth of winter.
' Under the burning, glaring sun, the grass becomes white
as the ground, the field stubbles stiff as harrows, stained
only by the shadows of passing clouds ; the trees, except
upon the nullah banks, are gaunt and bare ; the animals
are walking skeletons ; and nothing seems to flourish but flies
and white ants, caltrops and grapple plants.' The caravan
certainly did not flourish. Speke was again ill with a
bilious fever ; Valentine and Gaetano, the Goanese, were
groaning with "ang dukhta"—body pains ; three of the
Wanyámwezi were unable to walk ; an ass had been lost ;
and Burton's own beast, having broken a tooth in fighting,
had incapacitated itself for food or drink, so that he had to
transfer himself to the last of the Zanzibar donkeys, which
was sore-backed and painfully feeble. Happily, the cloud
had its silver lining. As soon as the camp was formed,
the villagers flocked down from the hillsides to barter
their animals and grain, milk, honey, and clarified butter
—a delightful change to men who had been living for
weeks upon holcus and bajri, with an occasional treat of
" kennel-food," broth and beans. Next morning witnessed
the arrival of a caravan of Wanyámwezi porters, 400
strong, marching to the coast with ivory. Civilities were
interchanged. The Arabs wanted cloth to feed their
slaves and porters ; Burton and Speke were glad to supply
them in exchange for fine white rice, salt and a goat.
Better still, the Arabs were induced to part with two asses,
one of which carried Burton to the Central Lake, and
afterwards back to Unyányembe ; the other, a one-eyed

brute, which was so incurably vicious that the Beloch nicknamed him " Shaytan yek-chashm " (the one-eyed fiend),
and after a few days turned him loose in the wilderness.
Before the two caravans separated, maps and a report of
progress were drawn up to be forwarded to the secretary
of the Royal Geographical Society, and Burton indented
once more upon the Consul, and the Collector of Customs
at Zanzibar, for drugs, medical comforts, and an extra
supply of cloth and beads.

What followed must be given in Burton's own words.
' Trembling with ague, with swimming heads, ears deafened
by weakness, and limbs that would hardly support us, we
contemplated with a dogged despair the apparently perpendicular path that ignored a zigzag, and the ladders of
root and boulder hemmed in with tangled vegetation, up
which we and our starving, drooping asses were about to
toil. On the 10th of September we hardened our hearts,
and began to breast the Pass Terrible. My companion
was so weak that he required the aid of two or three
supporters; I, much less unnerved, managed with one.
After rounding, in two places, wall-like sheets of rock—at
their bases green grass and fresh water were standing
close to camp, and yet no one had driven the donkeys to
feed—and crossing a bushy jungly step, we faced a long
steep of loose white soil, and rolling stones, up which we
could see the Wanyámwezi porters swarming, more like
baboons scaling a precipice than human beings, and the
asses falling after every few yards. As we moved slowly
and painfully forwards, compelled to lie down by cough,
thirst, and fatigue, the " sayhah," or war-cry, rang loud from
hill to hill, and Indian files of archers and spearmen
streamed like black ants in all directions down the path.
The predatory Wahumba, awaiting the caravan's departure,
had seized the opportunity of driving the cattle and
plundering the villages of Inenge. Two passing parties of

men, armed to the teeth, gave us this information ; whereupon the negro 'Jelai' proposed, fear-maddened, a *sauve
qui peût*, leaving to their fate his employers, who, bearing
the mark of Abel in this land of Cain, were ever held to
be the head and front of all offence. Khudabakhsh, the
brave of braves, being attacked by a slight fever, lay
down, declaring himself unable to proceed, moaned like a
bereaved mother, and cried for drink like a sick girl. The
rest of the Beloch, headed by the Jemadar, were in the

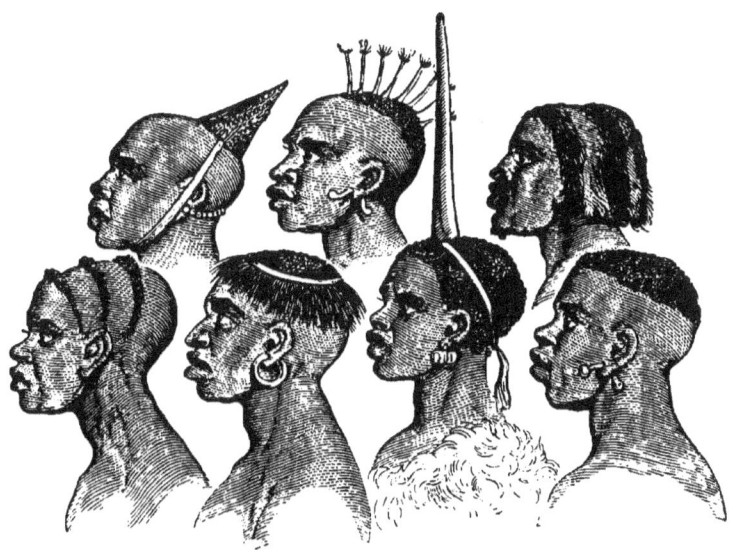

HEAD-DRESSES OF THE WANYÁMWEZI.

rear ; they had levelled their matchlocks at one of the
armed parties as it approached them, and but for the
interference of Kidogo blood would have been shed.

'By resting after every few yards, and by clinging to our
supporters, we reached, after about six hours, the summit
of the Pass Terrible, and there we sat down amongst the
aromatic flowers and bright shrubs—the gift of mountain
dews—to recover strength and breath. My companion
could hardly return an answer—he had advanced mechanic-

ally, and almost in a state of coma. . . . Somewhat revived
by the *tramontana* which rolled like an ice-brook down the
pass, we advanced over an easy steep of rolling ground,
decked with cactus and the flat-topped mimosa, with green
grass and bright shrubs, to a small and dirty khambi in a
hollow flanked by heights, upon which several settlements
appeared. At this place, called the "Great 'Rubeho," in
distinction from its western neighbour, I was compelled to
halt. My invalid sub. had been seized with a fever fit that
induced a dangerous delirium during two successive nights ;
he became so violent that it was necessary to remove his
weapons, and, to judge from certain symptoms, the attack
had a permanent cerebral effect. Death appeared stamped
upon his features, yet the Beloch and the "sons of Ramji"
clamoured to advance, declaring that the cold disagreed
with them. On the 12th September, the invalid, who,
restored by a cool night, at first proposed to advance, and
then doubted his ability to do so, was yet hesitating, when
the drum signal sounded without my order. The Wanyámwezi porters instantly set out. I sent to recall them,
but they replied that it was the custom of their race never
to return ; a well-sounding principle, against which they
never offended except to serve their own ends. At length
a hammock was rigged up for my companion, and the
whole caravan broke ground.' *

The air of the hills restored the travellers—not before it
was time. When Burton came to examine the loads
carried by his porters, he found to his dismay that the
outfit, which had been intended to last a year, had been
half exhausted in three months. Said bin Salim, when
interrogated on the subject, was perfectly cool. They had

---

* This hammock, by the way, was one of four which Burton had
brought from Zanzibar. Slung to poles they form the conveyance
which is called by Indians, the Manchil ; by the Portuguese, Manchila,
and in West Africa, " Tipoia."

enough to reach Unyányembe, where certainly they would
be joined by the escort of twenty-two porters. "But how
do you know that?" inquired Burton. "Allah is all-
knowing," replied Said, "but the caravan will come!"
'Such fatalism,' says Burton, 'is infectious. I ceased to
think upon the subject.' It was as well that he should
clear his mind of all anxieties. He was on the verge of
Ugogo—a region 'stern and wild, the rough nurse of
rugged men.' His Beloch were as cross as naughty
children, 'ever their case when cold and hungry'; the
"sons of Ramji" had combined with the porters in refusing
to carry Speke ; the asses, frightened by the wild beasts,
broke loose at night ; Said bin Salim, selfish and surly,
left to Burton the task of bringing up the rear ; and the
Beloch—degenerate offspring of a hybrid race—'wept at
the necessity of carrying their gourds and skins.' The
journey lay down the western slopes of this Via Mala—a
road composed of boulders and water-worn stones reposing
in a sandy bed, and with branches of thorny trees occasionally overarching it. For eight mortal hours the caravan
descended ; then came night and camp, but the Beloch did
not arrive until 10 P.M. Four hours more on the following
day placed the caravan on the plains of Ugogo. In the
course of the hurried, scrambling down-hill journey, sundry
goods—all-important to the explorers—were left behind.
It is characteristic of the African, whatever his tribe may
be, that the party sent back to recover them returned
empty-handed, with terrible tales of the hardships and
perils they had gone through, and that some months afterwards an up caravan found the articles in the spot where
they had been left and, for a consideration, gave them up
to their owners at Unyányembe. The explanation is, of
course, that the party Burton sent back preferred a day
under the shade of the trees to a rather troublesome journey
across a difficult country.

At Ugogo—the half-way house between the coast and Unyányembe—a halt of three days was found necessary to recruit the party, and to lay in provisions for four desert marches. The place, which stands 2760 feet above the sea level, proved a fair sanitarium. Speke, recovered from his fever, was able to go out with his gun, and to bring home abundant partridge and guinea-fowl; the Beloch and the " sons of Ramji " and the porters began to throw off their complaints : the only obstinate invalids were the two Goanese. The number of asses had diminished to nine, but Burton was able to secure the services of fifteen Wanyámwezi porters, who were perhaps more useful and less troublesome. The march began on the 22nd September—a dreary and thirsty journey, diversified only by a hurried dislodgment at the instance of a swarm of wild bees, and by the desertion of one of the new porters, to whom had been committed the charge of a portmanteau containing the Nautical Almanac for 1858, the surveying books, and the greater part of the paper, pens and ink. Burton sent men back in search of the missing goods, but it would seem that they, like their predecessors, preferred sauntering and idling to the simple work of doing their duty. An afternoon's march followed, during which the supplies of liquid ran low, the Wanyámwezi porters preferring to carry the liquor, of which they were the bearers inside instead of outside their ebony skins. At the camping ground, however, a journey of four miles out procured for the caravan a supply of the elixir of life, and harmony was once more restored.

On the 26th, the jungle-kraal was left, and the Ziwa reached—a place 3100 feet above the sea level, and the deepest of the many inundated grounds on the western side of the Marenga Mk'hali. Here the travellers found the system of blackmail, so much dreaded by travellers, in fullest force Up to this point the chiefs had been con-

tented with moderate presents : here in Ugogo they take
" tribute," by force if necessary. None can evade payment,
nor is any tariff in existence. The sum exacted is fixed
by the traveller's dignity and outfit, which by means of his
slaves are as well known to every Sultan as to himself.
On this account there was abundant trouble at the Ziwa.
One Marena, for example, the Sultan of a new settlement,
came in to demand toll. Remonstrance—to the effect that
the caravan was not about to pass through his territory—
was unavailing. When, however, he found that the white
man was determined, and that in proof of his determination
he ordered out his asses and had them saddled and loaded,
he changed his tone, and from a bully became a beggar.
Kidogo, head man of the " sons of Ramji," relenting, gave
him two cloths and a few strings of beads, wisely preferring this small expenditure to the chance of a fight of
arrows during the night. Very soon the country people
came flocking in ' with bullocks, sheep, goats and poultry,   ،
water-melons and pumpkins, honey, butter-milk, whey
and curdled milk, and abundance of holcus and calabash
flour.'

Four days were spent—wasted, Burton would probably
say—at the Ziwa, and on the last of them—September 30th
—appeared a large caravan, headed by ' Said bin Mohammed, of Mbuamaji, with Khalfan bin Khamis,' and several
other Arabs of the coast, bringing with them news from
the seaboard, and, better still, the missing portmanteau,
which was ransomed for a couple of cloths. On the
following day the two caravans, travelling together, left
Ziwa late in the morning, and after crossing the lower
levels, debouched upon the table-land of Ugogo. The
people were curious, but not uncivil, and Burton remarks
that ' such inquisitiveness is amongst barbarians generally
a proof of improvability—of power to progress.' For all
that, the curiosity of the people was somewhat tiresome,

and their habit of following and keeping up with the
caravan on its march "truly unseemly." Part of the
difficulty arose, no doubt, from the evil reports of two half-
caste Arabs, who, in preceding Burton and his followers,
had spread the most ridiculous reports about them.
'They had one eye each, and four arms ; they were full
of "knowledge," which in those lands means magic ; they
caused rain to fall in advance, and left droughts in their
rear ; they cooked water-melons, and threw away the
seeds, thereby generating small-pox ; they heated and
hardened milk, thus breeding a murrain amongst cattle ;
and their wire, cloth and beads caused a variety of mis-
fortunes ; they were kings of the sea, and therefore white-
skinned and straight-haired—a standing mystery to these
curly-pated people—as are all men who live in salt waters,
and next year they would return and seize the country.'
Otherwise the journey through the Ugogo country was—
like the annals of a happy and well-governed nation—
devoid of exciting events. The only matter deserving in
the smallest degree such an epithet was the visit of one
Magomba, the most powerful of the Wagogo chiefs, who
came to levy blackmail. The description of this person
deserves transcription. 'Magomba was a black and
wrinkled elder, drivelling and decrepid, with a half-
bald head, from whose back and sides depended a few
straggling corkscrews of iron-gray ; he wore a coat of
castor-oil and a "Barsati" loin-cloth, which grease and
use had changed from blue to black. A few bead-strings
decorated his neck; large flexible anklets of brass wire
adorned his legs, solid brass rings, single and in coils,
which had distended his earlobes almost to splitting, were
tied by a string over his cranium, and his horny soles
were defended by single-soled sandals, old, dirty, and
tattered. He chewed his quid, and he expectorated without mercy ; he asked many a silly question, yet he had

ever an eye to the main chance. He demanded and received five " cloths with names," which I was again compelled to purchase at an exorbitant price from the Beloch and slaves, one coil of brass wire, four blue cottons, and ten "domestics;" the total amounted to fifty shukkahs, here worth at least fifty dollars, and exhausting nearly two-thirds of a porter's load. His return present was the leanest of calves; when it was driven into camp with much parade, his son, who had long been looking out for a fit opportunity, put in a claim for three cottons.'

The old chief was not satisfied with enforcing tribute. Before the caravan was allowed to depart he exacted an oath from Kidogo that his Wazungu—("white men")— would not smite the land with drought or fatal disease, declaring that all we had was in his hands. This was true enough, and it is an evidence of what the African explorer has to risk. Had this chief chosen to turn "rusty," there was absolutely nothing to protect Burton and his companion Speke. All those who accompanied them would, in the event of a surprise or attack, have taken care of themselves, and the white men *must* have perished. Burton's reflections on this state of things are worth noting. 'We should have been as safe,' he says, 'with six as with sixty guns; but I would by no means apply to these regions Mr. Galton's opinion, "that the last fatal expedition of Mungo Park is full of warning to travellers who propose exploring with a large body of men." For though sixty guns do not suffice to prevent attack in Ugogo, 600 stout fellows armed with the "hot-mouthed weapon" might march through the length and breadth of Central Africa.'

Another down caravan—from the interior to the coast, that is to say—appeared on the 8th of October, and once more Burton sent down reports and letters, life certificates and indents upon Zanzibar for drugs, medical comforts, cloths and beads. On the 10th came an "ugly march,"

when the porters deserted by wholesale; Said bin Salim
and the Jemadar hurried forward, and Burton was left to
manage the start for the Tirikeza, or afternoon march,
absolutely without assistance. Speke was helpless. 'My
companion,' says Burton—and it is curious to note how
chivalrously he refrains from mentioning Speke's name—
'lay under a calabash, almost unable to move.' The ·
Kidogo, with the cowardly courage of his race, had appro-
priated his stalwart Mnyamwezi ass, and left in its place
a wretched animal, incapable of bearing the lightest load.
The Beloch Belok refused to carry the only gourd of
water, and when the rear of the caravan was about to
march, Kidogo, the only man who knew the way, hastened
on so fast that Burton, and those who were with him, were
left to do the best they could in the midst of a labyrinth of
elephants' tracks, hedged in by thorns and brambles, which
tore skin and clothes with an edifying impartiality. Difficulties of this kind were what Burton had to contend with
throughout the entire thirty months of his journey. The
people he had to encounter were savages, and savages,
moreover, of the kind who appear to be incapable of civilisation. They have neither heart nor conscience, neither
gratitude nor sense of duty, neither honour nor honesty.
To use a homely phrase of Ben Jonson, they have "their
brains in their bellies and their guts in their heads;" and
so when, a day or two after this trick had been played off
upon him, the Beloch refused their escort to the baggage,
Burton ordered a goat to be killed, and having served out
rations to the "sons of Ramji" and the porters, gave these
fellows none. The consequences threatened to be serious.
There was endless grumbling in the four dialects of the
Beloch, and noisy threatening to desert, but the night
brought counsel, and in the morning the demeanour of the
men was as cringing as ever, and they were quite ready to
escort the caravan through the territories of the most

powerful of the Wagogo chiefs, M'ana Miaha, surnamed
Maguru Mafupi, or " Shortshanks," who drinks pombé, or
native beer, with clockwork regularity every day until he
has attained the height of an African's bliss, *i.e.*, until he is
dead drunk.

This amiable potentate is in the habit of detaining the
Wanyámwezi caravans to hoe his cornfields and sometimes
in the spring will insist on imposing a *corvée* of six
days upon these unfortunates before he will consent
to receive their presents. Burton and his party were a
little more fortunate, but even they had to wait for five
days. On the afternoon after their arrival it would have
been "indecent" to disturb his Highness ; on the first
morning he was was "sitting upon pombé," in other words
getting drunk as fast as he could ; on the second day he
received a deputation from Burton somewhat scurvily
and demanded that the two caravans which had now
amalgamated should pay toll separately, declaring that he
would in Burton's case be satisfied with nothing less than
six porters' loads. About one twelfth of that quantity was
offered him, upon which he became furious and drove the
embassy from his presence. On the following day the
coast Arabs took their turn with "his Highness" and were
equally ill received, her Highness the spouse of " Shortshanks" being so justly indignant with the flimsiness of a
piece of chintz which was offered to her that she took up a
wooden ladle and drove the offenders out of doors. On
the fifth day, however, the crisis came. The timid Said
made way for the fiery Kidogo and his Highness was
informed that whether he accepted the gifts or rejected
them the caravan would move on the following afternoon.
The toll received by this unconscionable extortioner
amounted to one coil of brass wire, four " cloths with names,"
eight domestics, eight blue cottons and thirty strings of
coral beads. He asked for much more, but Burton

compromised the matter with a couple of yards of crimson broad-cloth.

The Coast Arabs left 'with rage in their hearts and curses under their tongues,' but they were compelled to dissemble that ill feeling by the knowledge that the merest pretext—touching a woman, offending a boy or taking the name of the Sultan in vain—is sufficient in Ugogo to afford an excuse for further mulcts of cloth. It was pleasant for all to escape from the crowded strip of foul jungle where the last five days had been spent amidst insect plagues—tsetze and ants of a peculiarly poisonous type which stung the asses to madness and rendered valuable articles valueless night by night. The day had its drawbacks, however, for fifteen of the porters deserted in the night and the last survivor of the thirty asses brought from Zanzibar was torn by a hyæna and had to be left behind to die. Speke rode forward on the ass which had been given by Abdullah bin Nasib, but Burton, who, as commander of the Expedition, naturally brought up the rear, was compelled, though tottering with fatigue and weakness, to walk, his own ass being required to carry two bags of clothes and shoes. The Beloch and the rest behaved with their customary egregious egotism. The water gourds were drained almost as soon as the caravan had started and the sons of Ramji, who, after reaching the resting place, had returned with abundant supplies for their comrades, hid their vessels on Burton's approach. Surmulla, a donkey driver of the worst type of surly negro, flatly refused a draught of water to his suffering master, and some of the Beloch seized upon a porter belonging to a caravan that had passed Burton and his companions on the march and were found attempting half by promises and half by threats to make them carry their sleeping mats and empty gourds. Help came towards the end of the long march. Sidi Bombay, Speke's gun carrier, and the most good-natured man of the whole party, having reached the halting place, had returned in hot haste with an impromptu refection of scones and hard boiled eggs and, what was even more important to the weary traveller, with an ass which carried him into the camp.

This camp was pitched under the shade of a huge calabash tree and was well supplied with water. A halt of two days was of necessity made in it for the purpose first of collecting a week's provisions and next of settling the toll or blackmail to be paid to the chief. This was arranged with perhaps a little less difficulty than usual and the journey over the desert tract between Ugogo and Unyámwezi—the "Fiery Field"—began, on the 20th of October. The march was through a narrow and winding path in the thorny jungle with thin, hard grass straw growing on a glaring white and rolling ground. Happily water was found at the mid-day halt and at sunset the camp was pitched in a place where the pure element was found in abundance in holes some five feet deep. On the second day the start was made at dawn: the leaders of the Expedition did not arrive at the halting place until noon, and their people, who contrived to lose on the way three boxes of ammunition and all the bullet moulds, straggled in about sunset. It was hopeless to attempt to recover these things and they were perforce abandoned. By the 22nd of October Speke was once more incapacitated for walking, an ass was unloaded ; its burden was distributed amongst the sons of Ramji, and Speke was mounted. The day was long, the journey seemed interminable and, in the afternoon the ass in question frightened, no doubt by some invisible wild animal whom it had detected by scent, threw its invalid rider heavily to earth, breaking its girth in the effort.

That night the camp was at Jiwe la Mkoa, where as Burton puts it 'the neck of the desert is broken,' but where provisions were piteously scarce. One goat skin of grain and a few fowls were all that could be obtained, and with these things the voyagers were fain to be content. Next day came a long Tirikeza—afternoon march—through a region not absolutely desert ; wild but fairly well watered, and showing signs of elephant and rhinoceros, giraffe, and antelope. The usual incidents of African travel followed, and by the end of October the caravan reached the un-savoury Wakimbu village of Tula or Tura—a place inha-bited by 'a timid and ignoble race—dripping with castor or sesamum oil, and scantily attired in shreds of unclean cotton or greasy goat skins.' Here the last of the asses bought at Zanzibar gave up the ghost, and it became necessary in consequence to hire fresh porters. The march was resumed. Day after day passed by with the usual incidents repeated and re-repeated with the most ex-asperating monotony. One day the " Sons of Ramji " grow restive under their light loads, and fling down their packs only to take them up again after stern remonstrance—a performance which they repeat at intervals during the rest of the journey. On another day Said bin Salim asks the Commander of the Expedition if he thinks himself strong enough to dare the—generally imaginary—dangers of the road between Unyámwezi Land and Ujiji—a question which he repeats at intervals until Ujiji is in sight. Then comes an adventure with a small Sultan—an elderly gentleman who has seen the world, but who appears with ' an old Barsati round the loins, and a grimy Subai loosely thrown over the shoulders—redolent of boiled frankin-cense.' He is eminently polite and gracious ; presents the caravan with a bullock, and succeeds in obtaining not much more than twice its value in cloth. His village is distinguished amongst the villages of Central Africa by the appearance of crosses and serpent-like ornamentation in white ashes on the walls of the houses—a fact which will interest all who have read Mr. Ferguson's elaborate work on 'Tree and Serpent Worship.' Another Sultan—these titles are really almost as amusing as the assumptions of "his Excellency the Governor-General of all the Indies" whom Burton met at Goa—presents the caravan with a fine fat bull, so wild that no one dares approach him, and it is found necessary to bring his existence to a premature close with a couple of rifle bullets. There were, of course, the usual difficulties about the baggage. A porter imprudently lagged behind in the forest of Kigora, and was robbed of his burden of clothes, umbrellas, books, ink, journals and botanical collections. The clothes were recovered at the cost of 'a scarlet waistcoat and four domestics' (cloths), but the other contents of the portmanteau were irrecoverably lost. Burton's journey was really unfortunate in this respect. There is always a great deal of risk in African travel, but he had to contend with something worse than negro greed and negro recklessness. 'My field and sketch-books,' he says, 'were entrusted to an Arab merchant, who preceded me to Zanzibar; they ran no other danger, except from the carelessness of the Consul, who unfortunately for me succeeded Lieut.-Colonel Hamerton.'

On the 7th of November, 1857, the 134th day after leaving the coast, the caravan having marched at least 600 miles prepared to enter Kazeh, the principal "Bandari," or station, of Eastern Unyámwezi, and the capital village of the Omani merchants. There has been talk of another afternoon march, but the firmament seemed on fire, the porters were fagged, and the whites felt feverish. A compromise was therefore entered into. The "Tirikeza" was given up, and five rounds of blank cartridges were served out to each of the sons of Ramji to be blazed away on entering the Arab headquarters. 'All, of course,' says Burton, 'had that private store which the Arabs call "El-Akibah"—the ending; it is generally stolen from the master

and concealed for emergencies with cunning care. They
had declared their horns' to be empty, and said Kidoko,
" Every pedlar fires guns here—shall a great man creep into
his Tembe (lodging) without a soul knowing it ?"' The
entry into Kazeh was imposing. Hanga was left at dawn ;
the Beloch put on that one fine suit without which the
Eastern man rarely travels ; at 8 A.M. a halt was called to
enable the stragglers to come up, and then 'when the line
of porters becoming compact began to wriggle, snake-like,
its long length over the plain, with floating flags, booming
horns, muskets firing like saluting mortars, and an uproar
of voice which nearly drowned the other noises, we
made a truly splendid and majestic first appearance. The
road was lined with people who attempted to vie with us
in volume and variety of sound : all had donned their best
attire, and with such luxury my eyes had been long unfamiliar.' The Arabs gave Burton the most courteous and
cordial reception, treating him practically as one of themselves. He and Speke were taken to the house of Musa
Mzuri—handsome Moses—an Indian merchant, to whom
Burton bore a letter of introduction from the Sayyid Majid
of Zanzibar, and as Musa was absent on a trading expedition, the honours were done by his agent, who established
him in the vacant house of Abayd bin Sulayman, who had
lately returned to Zanzibar.

After their usual gracious custom the Arabs left Burton
to himself for a day to rest and dismiss his porters. Then
followed the first ceremonious call. All the Arab merchants
in the place, in number about a dozen, visited the travellers,
and to them was submitted the official circular of the Sultan
of Zanzibar to his subjects in African territory recommending Burton and his companions to their care. Nothing
could have been more gratifying than their reception.
'Striking, indeed,' says Burton, 'was the contrast between
the open-handed hospitality and the hearty good will of

this truly noble race, and the niggardness of the savage
and selfish African—it was heart of flesh after heart of
stone. A goat and a load of the fine white rice grown in
the country were the normal prelude to a visit, and to
offers of service which proved something more than a *vox
et præterea nihil.* Whatever I alluded to, onions, plantains,
limes, vegetables, tamarind-cakes, coffee from Karágwah,
and similar articles only to be found amongst the Arabs
were sent at once, and the very name of payment would
have been an insult.' Snay bin Amir, Musa's agent, who
sixteen years before had been a confectioner in Muscat,
and who was now one of the richest dealers in ivory—
black and white—in Eastern Africa, was determined that
none should outdo him in generosity, and accordingly
sent two goats to Burton and Speke, and two bullocks to
the Beloch and the sons of Ramji. More than this, he
'enlisted porters for the caravan to Ujiji, he warehoused
my goods, he disposed of my extra stores, and finally
he superintended my preparations for the down march.
During two long halts at Kazeh he never failed, except
through sickness, to pass the evening with me, and from
his instructive and varied conversation was derived not a
little of the information contained in the second volume
of the original edition of " The Lake Regions of Central
Africa." ' Snay bin Amir, slave-dealer though he was,
seems to have been a singularly favourable specimen of
his race. He had, in the fifteen years before Burton met
him, travelled much, visiting the coast and navigating the
great Lake Tanganyika, he was as familiar with the
languages, the religion, the manners and the ethnology of
the African as with those of his natal Oman. He had read
much, seriously and not merely for amusement, he had a
wonderful memory, fine perceptions, and a wonderful power
of language : he was brave, prudent and yet punctilious on
all questions of honour ; and finally, as is not always the

case in the East, he was as honest as he was honourable. He was, in a word, to quote the saying of Burton, 'the stuff of which friends are made,' and a true and constant friend Burton found him during his stay in Kazeh and afterwards.

The travellers were detained at Kazeh from the 8th of November to the 14th of December, 1857. The place is like Zungomero in K'hutu, the great meeting-place of merchants, and the point whence caravans radiate into the interior of Central Intertropical Africa. 'Here the Arab merchant from Zanzibar meets his compatriots returning from the Tanganyika Lake and from Uruwwa. North-wards, well-travelled lines diverge to Nyánza Lake, and the powerful kingdoms of Karágwah, Uganda and Unyoro ; from the South Urori and Ubena, Usanga and Usenga send their ivory and slaves, and from the south-west the Rukwa Water, Khokoro, Ufipa and Murungu must barter their valuables for cottons, wires and beads.' Detention is thus a matter of course. The porters, whether engaged at the coast or at the Tanganyika Lake, here disperse, and a fresh gang must be collected—not always an easy matter, especially when the season for sowing the grain is drawing nigh. In Burton's case the difficulties were unusually great and had he not learned the lesson of firmness and govern-ment he might have fared badly. First came the Beloch, headed by their Jemadar, to demand a reward for safe conduct. This Burton promised should be given to them when they reached the end of the up-march. Derwaysh, the pragmatical, declared that " without bakhshish there would be no up-march." Speke was called in to see the words taken down in writing, whereupon the Beloch changed their tone, and from threatening became humble and begged for salt and spices. Having received of these matters pro-bably more than they had ever possessed at one time in their lives before they withdrew, complaining to Said bin

Salim of the parsimony of their master. They sent for tobacco, a goat, gunpowder and bullets ; they obtained four cloths for tinning their solitary copper-pot, and for repairing a couple of old matchlocks ; they sold a keg of gunpowder committed to their charge ; they were treated with extreme kindness ; they were well lodged, and so well paid that they could daily indulge in such luxuries as sheep, goats and fowls, 'yet,' says Burton, ' they did not fail with their foul tongues ever ready as the Persians say for " spitting at Heaven," to charge their kind hosts with the worst crime that the Arab knows—niggardliness.'

The usual difficulties followed. There was haggling and counter-haggling. The porters wanted leave of absence and their chief wanted better terms for them. Snay bin Amir did his best, but he could only get in some ten men ; the peasants came, looked at the packs, chaffered about hire, and promised to return *mañana*—to-morrow, never. The rains came, pleasant enough with the contrast between the freshness of the air and the verdure of the scenery, after the dust, heat and desolation that preceded the first showers, but anything but pleasant from another point of view. Strangers always suffer severely from the sudden changes of temperature, and Unyámwezi speedily became a hot-bed of ague. Speke was comparatively strong, but the Goanese suffered terribly from a bilious remittent fever ; Bombay, the good-natured, was laid up with a shaking ague, and the Beloch and the sons of Ramji had to pay the penalty of their excesses on the march. Burton himself followed the example of the party. Snay bin Amir, the wise Arab, tried his remedies, including the actual cautery and a poultice of powdered ginger, upon him without effect, and then insisted upon his seeing a witch who was celebrated for her cures throughout the country-side to visit him. The Mganga—a wrinkled old beldame, with greasy skin, hair set off by a mass of time-coloured pigtails, arms adorned with copper bangles, and carrying a girdle of small gourds dyed black with oil and use—presented herself. She examined the patient's mouth, enquired anxiously about poison, drew from her gourd a greenish powder which she mixed with water and administered to the patient. The powder caused abundant and even super-abundant sneezing, which the Mganga hailed with trans-ports of joy. A powder of another kind was applied to the head and the witch withdrew, declaring that the sleep which was sure to come would effect a cure, and that she would call on the morrow. The morrow came. Sleep had not visited the sufferer's eyelids, nor did the witch return. The fever with its usual accompaniments of 'distressing weakness, hepatic derangements, burning palms, and ting-ling soles, aching eyes, and alternate thrills of heat and cold,' lasted for a month. Madame Mganga meanwhile absconded to indulge in unlimited pombé for a week.

Other troubles arose. The Beloch grew " uncomfort-able," and while professing the utmost desire to depart, revelled in such pleasures as Kazeh could afford. Said bin Salim showed the evil strain in his blood—his mother was a Malagash slave—and presumed upon his usefulness and became first sulky and then "contrarious rude " to Speke, disrespectful to Burton, and finally dishonest, with the result of bringing about a violent quarrel between his master and himself which did not end until their final parting on the coast. Everything would have been lost in fact but for the excellent behaviour of the good Snay bin Amir. His slaves strung in proper lengths upon palm-fibre the beads sent up loose from Zanzibar, he distributed the bales in due proportions for carriage, he made candles of mingled wax and tallow for the Expedition, and he had Valentine—Burton's Goanese servant—taught some of the refinements of cookery; he sent into the country for plantains and tamarinds, then unprocurable at Kazeh ; he brewed a quantity of beer and mawa, or plantain wine ; he bullied the Beloch and the Sons of Ramji ; he gave the most valuable information in sketching the outlines of the Kinyámwezi or languages of Unyámwezi, and by his distances and directions Burton was enabled to lay down the southern limits and general shape of the Nyánza, or Northern Lake, as correctly as they were afterwards determined by Captain Speke.* More than all, Snay bin Amir took charge of letters and papers intended for home, undertook to forward the lagging gang expected from the coast, and, in a word, did everything that kindness and human brotherliness could suggest to alleviate Burton's trouble.

At last it became evident that a movement must be made. Porters were not to be had, and so the march was determined upon with or without their assistance. 'After much murmuring,' Speke went on ; three days later Burton followed—'in truth more dead than alive—the wing of Azrael seemed waving over my head,' he says, 'even the movement of the Manchila was almost unendurable.' There were the usual delays. Speke had to go back to Kazeh for reinforcements ; Burton went forward to collect a gang for the journey westward. He had to halt for two days at Yombo ; a filthy little place where provisions were procurable only in the most homœopathic quantities, but redeemed from its dulness by the beauty of its women, three of whom, Burton says, 'would be deemed beautiful in any part of the world. Their faces were purely Grecian ; they had laughing eyes, their figures were models for an artist with

"Turgide, brune e ritondette mamme,"

like the "bending statue that delights the world " cast in bronze. The dress, a short kilt of calabash fibre, rather set off than concealed their charms, and though destitute of

---

* The maps of the Royal Geographical Society establish this fact.

petticoat or crinoline they were wholly unconscious of indecorum.'

The caravan went on. Twenty porters had been hired, fifteen of whom appeared at the moment of the departure, while the number of the Beloch was reduced to eleven. On the 22nd of December, Speke rejoined his companion, bringing with him four loads of cloth, three of beads, and seven of brass wire ; but, unfortunately, the Hindús at Zanzibar had behaved with what Burton very leniently calls 'culpable neglect.' Lieut.-Colonel Hamerton being dead, they seem to have thought that they were at liberty to do as they pleased, and they accordingly executed the commission with which they had been entrusted in a fashion only to be described as scandalous. The cloth was of the worst and flimsiest description, the beads were the cheap white and the useless black—the latter had to be thrown away as not worth the carriage—and the whole had been entrusted to two men who knew that they might plunder at will and who did so. No letters had been forwarded and no attention whatever had been paid to Burton's repeated entreaties for drugs and other stores. The fault, of course, lay with the Consul, who had, as Burton says, 'unhappily' succeeded Lieut.-Colonel Hamerton, and who does not seem to have had much sympathy with schemes of Central African exploration. The men Speke had brought in proved not much better than their supplies. They would not halt for a day, professing the utmost impatience to reach Msene, and it was found necessary to humour them. They went their own way ; marched double marches and arrived at their destination one day before Burton and his party, who had travelled leisurely and had used the longer and more cultivated route.

Burton's own time was not superabundantly agreeable. The African fever held him in its iron grip, and it was necessary if he were to travel at all that he should be carried in a manchil. On the 23rd of December, the last of the six Hammáls who had been hired to carry the hammocks disappeared. They had been an unsatisfactory race from the first, incapable of carrying a palanquin properly, disorderly, turbulent, and unamenable to discipline. By way of stimulating them *not* to do their duty, Said bin Salem, the Jemadar, and the Beloch, had impressed upon them that Burton's days were numbered, and that it was useless to take any thought for him. On Christmas Day, therefore, Burton again mounted his ass and trudged manfully on through the western third of the Wilyankuru district, where he was well received by a wealthy proprietor, Salim bin Said, a worthy and kind-hearted Arab who was only too eager to display the great virtue of the East—hospitality. 'He led me,' says Burton, 'to a comfortable lodging, placed a new cartel in the coolest room, supplied meal, milk and honey, and spent the evening in conversation with me. He was a large middle-aged man, with simple, kindly manners, and an honesty of look and words which rendered his presence exceedingly prepossessing.'

On the 30th of December, without other incidents to diversify the march than those of every-day life, Burton had reached the district of Msene, where the dense wild growth lately traversed suddenly opens out and discloses to the west the prospect of a most fertile country. The caravan was as usual halted and formed up, and entered the settlement with the usual pomp and circumstance. Msene is a curious place, neither town nor country, consisting, in fact, of a knot of scattered hamlets, and surrounded by high hills, which attract the rain and make the district one of the most unhealthy in Africa. It is fertile and productive ; provisions of all kinds are freely exported : it is also a place of gross and systematic debauchery—' all, from Sultan, to slave, are intoxicated whenever the material is forthcoming, and the relations between the sexes are of the

loosest description. The drum is never silent, and the
dance fills up the spare intervals of carouse till exhausted
nature can no more.' In this den of iniquity Burton was
delayed for ten days—not very agreeably spent, since the
weather was most ungodly and the view from the windows
simply one of black and dirty puddles. For the rest, ' the
temptations of the town rendered it almost impossible to
keep a servant or a slave within doors ; the sons of Ramji
vigorously engaged themselves in trading, and Muinyi
Wazira in a debauch which ended in his dismissal. Gaetano
had repeated epileptic fits, and Valentine rushed into the
room half crying, to show a white animalcule—in this
country called Funza—which had lately issued from his
" buff." * . . . I received several visits from the Sultan
Maranza. His first greeting was, " White man, what pretty
thing hast thou brought up from the shore for me ? " He
presented a bullock, and received in return several cloths
and strings of beads ; and he introduced to us a variety of
princesses, who returned the salutes of the Beloch and
others with a wild effusion. As Christmas Day had been
spent in marching, I hailed the opportunity of celebrating
the advent of the New Year. Said bin Salim, the Jemadar,
and several of the guard, were invited to an English dinner
on a fair sirloin of beef and a curious succedaneum for a
plum-pudding, where neither flour nor currants were to be
found. A characteristic trait manifested itself on this
occasion. Amongst Arabs, the remnants of a feast must
always be distributed to the servants and slaves of the
guests ;—a " brass knocker " would lose a man's reputation.
Knowing this, I had ordered the Goanese to do in Rome
as the Romans do ; and, being acquainted with their
peculiarities, I paid them an unexpected visit, when they
were found so absorbed in the task of hiding under pots
and pans, every better morsel from a crowd of hungry

* Apparently the grub of the Tzetze-fly.

peerers, that the interruption of a stick was deemed necessary.'

With great difficulty Burton contrived to leave Msene on the 10th of January, 1858—the journey westward was so greatly dreaded. And no wonder; the climate is horrible, damp and cold, with superabundant vegetation and its consequences; the rain is all but incessant, and the paths are mere lines pitted with deep holes and worn by cattle through the jungle. For three days the party marched onwards through this jungly and fetid desert, parts of which are believed to be the most unwholesome spots in Africa. On the 13th, it was found necessary to take a strong step. Kidogo and his men had become insufferable, wherefore in spite of the protestations of Said bin Salim and the Jemadar, Burton dismissed them, fearing that if they were retained they would compromise the success of the Expedition. That such a thing was by no means improbable, may be judged by the fact that the men had openly boasted of their intention to prevent the Expedition from embarking on the sea of Ujiji. They were accordingly sent back, in spite of their protestations and promises of amendment; and three days afterwards the caravan entered Kajjanjeri, a hateful place, with a still more hateful climate. Here Burton was again seized with fever, complicated with the partial paralysis produced by malaria. The attack was frightfully severe, and for a time Burton thought that there was nothing for it but to lay him down and die. How bad it was may be judged from the muscular contractions above and below the knees, lasting for nearly a year, whilst the numbness of the hands and feet disappeared even more slowly. Ill though he was, Burton felt that it was useless to remain in this hotbed of pestilence, and so, in spite of incalculable difficulties in procuring porters, he succeeded in getting himself carried to Usagozi, and on the tenth day from his first attack he was once more able to mount his ass.

Another difficulty assailed him. Speke, whose blood was greatly impoverished by fever and unsuitable food, fell ill again, and came near losing his sight; the Goanese, Valentine, was affected in a somewhat similar way, and Burton only warded off an attack of inflammatory ophthalmia by a free use of what he calls "camel medicine." After three days the caravan was, however, able to go on until it reached Wanyika, on the last day of January. Here they were delayed for a day by the all-absorbing question of blackmail to the ruling chief, which was at last settled by the payment of ' forty cloths, white and blue, six Kilindi, or coil bracelets, and two Fundo (or 100 necklaces) of coral beads.' The toll was equivalent to £50 English.

FALCON AND GAZELLE.

(*Drawn by Wolf.*)

LONDON: PRINTED BY WILLIAM CLOWES AND SONS, LIMITED,
STAMFORD STREET AND CHARING CROSS.